The Boy
Next Door

The Boy Next Door

MEGGIN CABOT

AVON BOOKS

An Imprint of HarperCollins*Publishers*

Designed by Nicola Ferguson

ISBN 0-7394-2822-5

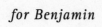

for Benjamin

Acknowledgments

Many thanks to
Beth Ader, Jennifer Brown,
Laura Langlie, and David Walton.

The Boy
Next Door

To: Mel Fuller <melissa.fuller@thenyjournal.com>
From: Human Resources <human.resources@thenyjournal.com>
Subject: Tardiness

Dear <u>Melissa Fuller</u>,

This is an automated message from the Human Resources Division of the *New York Journal*, New York City's leading photo-newspaper. Please be aware that according to your supervisor, <u>**managing editor George Sanchez**</u>, your workday here at the *Journal* begins promptly at <u>**9 AM**</u>, making you <u>**68**</u> minutes tardy today. This is your <u>**37th**</u> tardy exceeding twenty minutes so far this year, <u>**Melissa Fuller**</u>.

We in the Human Resources Division are not "out to get" tardy employees, as was mentioned in last week's unfairly worded employee newsletter. Tardiness is a serious and expensive issue facing employers all over America. Employees often make light of tardiness, but routine lateness can often be a symptom of a more serious issue, such as

- alcoholism
- drug addiction
- gambling addiction
- abusive domestic partner
- sleep disorders
- clinical depression

and any number of other conditions. If you are suffering from any of the above, please do not hesitate to contact your Human Resources Representative, <u>Amy Jenkins</u>. Your Human Resources Representative will be only too happy to enroll you in the *New York Journal*'s Staff Assistance Program, where you will be paired with a mental health professional who will work to help you achieve your full potential.

<u>Melissa Fuller</u>, we here at the *New York Journal* are a team. We win as a team, and we lose as one, as well. <u>Melissa Fuller</u>, don't you want to be on a winning team? So please do your part to see that you arrive at work on time from now on!

Sincerely,
Human Resources Division
New York Journal

Please note that any future tardies may result in suspension or dismissal.

To: Mel Fuller <melissa.fuller@thenyjournal.com>
From: Nadine Wilcock <nadine.wilcock@thenyjournal.com>
Subject: You are in trouble

Mel, where were you? I saw that Amy Jenkins from Human Resources skulking around your cubicle. I think you're in for another one of those tardy notices. What is this, your fiftieth?

You better have a good excuse this time, because George was saying a little while ago that gossip columnists are a dime a dozen, and that he could get Liz Smith over here in a second to replace you if he wanted to. I think he was joking. It was hard to tell because the Coke machine is broken, and he hadn't had his morning Mountain Dew yet.

By the way, did something happen last night between you and Aaron? He's been playing Wagner in his cubicle again. You know how this bugs George. Did you two have another fight?

Are we doing lunch later or what?

Nad :-)

To: Mel Fuller <melissa.fuller@thenyjournal.com>
From: Aaron Spender <aaron.spender@thenyjournal.com>
Subject: Last night

Where are you, Mel? Are you going to be completely childish about this and not come into the office until you're sure I've left for the day? Is that it?

Can't we sit down and discuss this like adults?

Aaron Spender
Senior Correspondent
New York Journal

To: Mel Fuller <melissa.fuller@thenyjournal.com>
From: Dolly Vargas <dolly.vargas@thenyjournal.com>
Subject: Aaron Spender

Melissa—
Don't get the wrong idea, darling, I WASN'T spying on you, but a girl would have to be BLIND not to have noticed how you brained Aaron Spender with your bag last night at Pastis. You probably didn't even notice me; I was at the bar, and I looked around

because I thought I heard your name, of all things—weren't you supposed to be covering the Prada show?—and then BOOM! Altoids and Maybelline all over the place.

Darling, it was precious.

You really have excellent aim, you know. But I highly doubt Kate Spade meant that adorable little clutch to be used as a projectile. I'm sure she'd have made the clasp stronger if she'd only known women were going to be backhanding the thing around like a tennis ball.

Seriously, darling, I just need to know: Is it all over between you and Aaron? Because I never thought you were right for each other. I mean, the man was in the running for a Pulitzer, for God's sake! Although if you ask me, anyone could have written that story about that little Ethiopian boy. I found it perfectly maudlin. That part about his sister selling her body to provide him with rice . . . please. Too Dickensian.

So you aren't going to be difficult about this, are you? Because I've got an invite to Steven's place in the Hamptons, and I was thinking of inviting Aaron to mix Cosmos for me. But I won't if you're going to go Joan Collins on me.

P.S.: You really should have called if you weren't going to come in today, darling. I think you're in trouble. I saw that little troll-like person (Amy something?) from Human Resources sniffing around your desk earlier.

XXXOOO

Dolly

To: Mel Fuller <melissa.fuller@thenyjournal.com>
From: George Sanchez <george.sanchez@thenyjournal.com>
Subject: Where the hell are you?

Where the hell are you? You appear to be under the mistaken impression that comp days don't have to be prearranged with your employer.

This is not exactly convincing me that you are columnist material. More like copyedit material, Fuller.

George

To: Mel Fuller <melissa.fuller@thenyjournal.com>
From: Aaron Spender<aaron.spender@thenyjournal.com>
Subject: Last night

This is really beneath you, Melissa. I mean, for God's sake, Barbara and I were in a *war zone* together. Anti-aircraft fire was exploding all around us. We thought we'd be captured by rebel forces at any moment. Can't you understand that?

It meant nothing to me, Melissa, I swear it.

My God, I should never have told you. I thought you were more mature. But to pull a disappearing act like this . . .

Well, I'd never have expected it from a woman like you, that's all I have to say.

Aaron Spender
Senior Correspondent
New York Journal

To: Mel Fuller <melissa.fuller@thenyjournal.com>
From: Nadine Wilcock <nadine.wilcock@thenyjournal.com>
Subject: This isn't funny

Girl, where are you? I'm really starting to get worried. Why haven't you called me, at the very least? I hope you didn't get hit by a bus or something. But I suppose if you did, they'd call us. Assuming you had your press pass with you, that is.

All right, I'm not really worried that you're dead. I'm really worried you're going to get fired, and I'm going to have to eat lunch with Dolly again. I was forced to order in with her since you're MIA, and it nearly killed me. The woman had a salad with no dressing. Do you get where I'm coming from here? NO DRESSING.

And then she felt compelled to comment on every single thing I put in my mouth. "Do you know how many grams of fat are in that fry?" "A good substitute for mayonnaise, you know, Nadine, is low-fat yogurt."

I'd like to tell her what she can do with her low-fat yogurt.

By the way, I think you should know that Spender's going around saying you're doing this because of whatever went down between the two of you last night.

If that doesn't get you in here, and pronto, I don't know what will.

Nad :-)

To: George Sanchez <george.sanchez@thenyjournal.com>
From: Mel Fuller <melissa.fuller@thenyjournal.com>
Subject: Where the hell I was

Since it is apparently so important to you and Amy Jenkins that your employees account fully for every moment they spend away from the office, I will provide you with a detailed summary of my whereabouts while I was unavoidably detained.

Ready? Got your Mountain Dew? I hear the machine down in the art department is fully operational.

Mel's Morning:
7:15— Alarm rings. Hit snooze button.
7:20— Alarm rings. Hit snooze button.
7:25— Alarm rings. Hit snooze button.
7:26— Wake to sound of neighbor's dog barking. Turn off alarm.
7:27— Stagger to bathroom. Perform morning ablutions.
7:55— Stagger to kitchen. Ingest nourishment in form of Nutri-grain bar and Tuesday night's take-out kung pao.
7:56— Neighbor's dog still barking.
7:57— Blow dry hair.
8:10— Check Channel One for weather.
8:11— Neighbor's dog still barking.
8:12— Attempt to find something to wear from assorted clothes crammed into studio apartment's single, refrigerator-sized closet.
8:30— Give up. Pull on black rayon skirt, black rayon shirt, black sling-back flats.
8:35— Grab black bag. Look for keys.
8:40— Find keys in bag. Leave apartment.
8:41— Notice that Mrs. Friedlander's copy of the *New York Chronicle* (yes, George, my next-door neighbor subscribes to our biggest rival; don't you agree with me now

that we really ought to do something to draw more senior readers?) is still lying on the floor in front of her
apartment door. She is normally up at six to walk her
dog, and takes her paper in then.

8:42– Notice that Mrs. Friedlander's dog is still barking. Knock
on door to make sure everything is all right. (Some of us
New Yorkers actually care about our neighbors, George.
You wouldn't know that, of course, since stories about
people who actually care for others in their community
don't make for very good copy. Stories in the *Journal*,
I've noticed, tend to gravitate toward neighbors who
shoot at, not borrow cups of sugar from, one another.)

8:45– After repeated knocks, Mrs. Friedlander still does not
come to door. Paco, her Great Dane, however, barks with
renewed vigor.

8:46– Try handle to Mrs. Friedlander's apartment door. It is,
oddly enough, unlocked. Let myself inside.

8:47– Am greeted by Great Dane and two Siamese cats. No sign
of Mrs. Friedlander.

8:48– Find Mrs. Friedlander facedown on living room carpet.

Okay, George? Get it, George? The woman was facedown on her
living room carpet! What was I supposed to do, George? Huh? Call
Amy Jenkins down in Human Resources?

No, George. That lifesaving class you made us all take paid off,
see? I was able to tell that not only did Mrs. Friedlander have a
pulse, she was also breathing. So I called 911 and waited with her
until the ambulance came.

With the ambulance, George, came some cops. And guess what
the cops said, George? They said it looked to them as if Mrs. Friedlander had been struck. From behind, George. Some creep whacked
that old lady on the back of the head!

Can you believe it? Who would do that to an eighty-year-old
woman?

I don't know what this city is coming to, George, when little old ladies aren't even safe in their apartments. But I'm telling you, there's a story here—and I think I should be the one the write it.

Whadduya say, George?

Mel

To: Mel Fuller <melissa.fuller@thenyjournal.com>
From: George Sanchez <george.sanchez@thenyjournal.com>
Subject: There's a story here

The only story here is the one I haven't heard. And that would be the story of why, just because your neighbor got whacked on the head, you couldn't come into the office, or even call anyone to let him know where you were.

Now that is a story I'd really enjoy hearing.

George

To: George Sanchez <george.sanchez@thenyjournal.com>
From: Mel Fuller <melissa.fuller@thenyjournal.com>
Subject: Where I was

George, you are so coldhearted. I found my neighbor facedown in her living room, the victim of a brutal attack, and you think all I should have been concerned about was calling my employer to explain why I was going to be late?

Well, I'm sorry, George, but the thought never even crossed my mind. I mean, Mrs. Friedlander is my friend! I wanted to go with her in the ambulance, but there was the little problem of Paco.

Or should I say the big problem of Paco. Paco is Mrs. Friedlander's Great Dane, George. He weighs a hundred and twenty-nine pounds, George, which is more than I weigh.

And he needed to go out. Badly.

So after I took him out, I fed him and watered him and did the same to Tweedledum and Mr. Peepers, her Siamese cats (Tweedledee, sadly, expired last year). While I was doing this, the cops were checking her door for signs of forced entry. But there was none, George.

Do you know what this means? It means she probably knew her attacker, George. She probably let him in of her own volition!

Even more bizarrely, there was $276 in cash in her purse that had been left untouched. Ditto her jewelry, George. This was no robbery.

George, why don't you believe there's a story here? Something is wrong. Very wrong.

When I finally did get to the hospital, I was informed that Mrs. Friedlander was in surgery. Doctors were frantically trying to relieve the pressure on her brain from a giant blood clot that had formed beneath her skull! What was I supposed to do, George? Leave? The cops couldn't get in touch with anybody from her family. I'm all she has, George.

Twelve hours. Twelve hours it took them. I had to go to her apartment to walk Paco twice before the surgery was even finished. And when it was, the doctors came out and told me it had only been partially successful. Mrs. Friedlander is in a coma, George! She may never come out of it.

And until she does, guess who's stuck taking care of Paco, Tweedledum, and Mr. Peepers?

Go on. Guess, George.

I'm not trying to get sympathy here. I know. I should have called. But work was not necessarily foremost in my mind at the time, George.

But, listen, now that I'm finally here what would you think

about letting me write up a little something about what happened? You know, we could hit it from the be-careful-who-you-let-into-your-apartment angle. The cops are still looking for Mrs. Friedlander's closest relative—her nephew, I think—but when they find him, I could interview him. You know, the woman really was a wonder. At eighty, she still goes to the gym three times a week, and last month she flew to Helsinki for a performance of the *Rings*. Seriously. Her husband was Henry Friedlander, of the Friedlander twistie fortune. You know, those twist-ties that go on garbage bags? She's worth six or seven million at least.

Come on, George. Let me give it a try. You can't keep me doing gossip for Page Ten forever.

Mel

To: Mel Fuller <melissa.fuller@thenyjournal.com>
From: George Sanchez <george.sanchez@thenyjournal.com>
Subject: You can't keep me doing gossip for Page Ten forever

Yes, I can.

And do you know why? Because I am the managing editor of this newspaper, and I can do whatever I want.

Besides, Fuller, we need you on Page Ten.

Would you like to know why we need you on Page Ten? Because the fact is, Fuller, you care. You care about Winona Ryder's legal battles. You care that Harrison Ford's had a chemical peel. You care about Courtney Love's breasts, and whether or not they are silicone.

Admit it, Fuller. You care.

The other thing ain't a story, Fuller. Old ladies get bonked on the head for their Social Security checks every day.

It's called a telephone. Next time, call.
Capisce?
Now get me the copy on the Prada opening.

George

To: George Sanchez <george.sanchez@thenyjournal.com>
From: Mel Fuller <melissa.fuller@thenyjournal.com>
Subject: I do not care about Courtney Love's breasts. . . .

. . . and you'll be sorry for not letting me run with the Fried-lander story, George. I'm telling you, there's something there. I can smell it.

And by the way, Harrison would NEVER get a chemical peel.

Mel

P.S.: And who doesn't care about Winona Ryder? Look how cute she is. Don't you want her free, George?

To: Human Resources <human.resources@thenyjournal.com>
From: Mel Fuller <melissa.fuller@thenyjournal.com>
Subject: My Tardiness

Dear Human Resources,
What can I say? You caught me. I guess my

- alcoholism
- drug addiction
- gambling addiction
- abusive domestic partner
- sleep disorders
- clinical depression

and any number of other conditions have finally caused me to hit bottom. Please enroll me in the Staff Assistance Program right away! If you could hook me up with a shrink who looks like Brendan Fraser, and preferably conducts his therapy sessions with his shirt off, I'd appreciate it.

Because the primary condition from which I am suffering is that I'm a twenty-seven-year-old woman living in New York City, and I cannot find a decent guy. Just one guy who won't cheat on me, doesn't live with his mother, and isn't turning to the Arts section of the *Chronicle* first thing Sunday morning, if you know what I mean. Is that asking so much???

See if your Staff Assistance Program can handle that.

Mel Fuller
Page Ten Columnist
New York Journal

To: Aaron Spender <aaron.spender@thenyjournal.com>
From: Mel Fuller <melissa.fuller@thenyjournal.com>
Subject: Can't we sit down and discuss this like adults?

There's nothing to discuss. Really, Aaron, I'm sorry for throwing my bag at you. It was a childish outburst that I deeply regret.

And I don't want you to think that the reason we're breaking up has anything to do with Barbara. Really, Aaron, we were over a long time before you ever told me about Barbara. Let's face it, Aaron, we're just too different: You like Stephen Hawking. I like Stephen King.

You know it would never have worked.

Mel

To: Dolly Vargas <dolly.vargas@thenyjournal.com>
From: Mel Fuller <melissa.fuller@thenyjournal.com>
Subject: Aaron Spender

I did not throw my bag. It slipped out of my hand when I was reaching for my drink, and accidentally flew through the air and hit Aaron in the eye.

And if you want him, Dolly, you can have him.

Mel

To: Nadine Wilcock <nadine.wilcock@thenyjournal.com>
From: Mel Fuller <melissa.fuller@thenyjournal.com>
Subject: Where I was

Okay, okay, I should have called. The whole thing was just a nightmare. But get this. This, you're never going to believe:

Aaron cheated on me in Kabul.

That's right. And you'll never guess with whom. Seriously. Try to guess. You never will.

All right, I'll tell you: Barbara Bellerieve.

Uh-huh. You read that correctly: Barbara Bellerieve, respected senior ABC news correspondent, most recently host of the television news magazine *TwentyFourSeven*, and voted one of *People* magazine's fifty most beautiful people last month.

Can you believe she slept with AARON??? I mean, she could have George Clooney, for God's sake. What would she want with AARON???

Not that I didn't suspect. I always thought those stories he kept e-mailing in during that month he was on assignment were way too smug.

You know how I found out? Do you? He TOLD me. He felt he was "ready to reach the next level of intimacy" with me (three guesses as to what level THAT is), and that in order to do so he felt he had to "make a clean breast" of it. He says ever since it happened he's been "wracked with guilt" and that "none of it meant anything."

God, what a putz. I can't believe I wasted three months of my life on him.

Are there no decent men out there? I mean, besides Tony. I swear, Nadine, your boyfriend is the last good man on earth. The last one! You hang on to him, and don't let go, because I'm telling you, it's a jungle out there.

Mel

P.S.: Can't go to lunch today, I have to go home and walk my neighbor's dog.
P.P.S.: Don't ask; it's a long story.

To: Mel Fuller <melissa.fuller@thenyjournal.com>
From: Nadine Wilcock <nadine.wilcock@thenyjournal.com>
Subject: That jerk

Look, the guy did you a favor. Be honest, Mel. Did you really picture a future for the two of you? I mean, he smokes a PIPE, for crying out loud. And what's with all that classical music? Who does he think he is, anyway? Harold Bloom?

No. He's a reporter, just like the rest of us. He's not out there writing fine literature. So what's with that bust of William Shakespeare he keeps on top of his monitor?

The man is a big phony, and you know it, Mel. That's why, in spite of the fact you two went out for three months, you never slept with him.

Remember?

Nad ;-)

To: Nadine Wilcock <nadine.wilcock@thenyjournal.com>
From: Mel Fuller <melissa.fuller@thenyjournal.com>
Subject: That jerk

I never slept with him because of that goatee. How was I supposed to sleep with someone who looks like Robin Hood?

He didn't want me enough even to shave.

What's wrong with me, Nad? Am I really not worth shaving for?

Mel

To: Mel Fuller <melissa.fuller@thenyjournal.com>
From: Nadine Wilcock <nadine.wilcock@thenyjournal.com>
Subject: That jerk

Give up the pity quest, Mel. You know you're gorgeous. The man is obviously suffering from a psychiatric disorder. We should sic Amy Jenkins on him.

Why can't you go to lunch today? And don't worry, I don't mean Burger Heaven. If I don't get down to a size 12 in two months, the wedding's off. Every girl in my family has worn my mother's dress to her wedding. I am not going to be the first Wilcock to schlep out to Klinefeld's.

Nad :-)

To: Nadine Wilcock <nadine.wilcock@thenyjournal.com>
From: Mel Fuller <melissa.fuller@thenyjournal.com>
Subject: Lunch

Can't do lunch. I have to go home and walk Mrs. Friedlander's dog.

Did you hear the latest? Chris Noth and Winona.

I'm not kidding. They were seen kissing in front of Crunch Fitness Center on Lafayette Street.

How could she be so blind? Can't she see he isn't any good for her? I mean, look what he did to poor Sarah Jessica Parker in *Sex and the City*.

Mel

To: Mel Fuller <melissa.fuller@thenyjournal.com>
From: Nadine Wilcock <nadine.wilcock@thenyjournal.com>
Subject: Reality check

Mel, I hate to break this to you, but *Sex and the City* is a fictional program. You might have heard already that there are these things called TV shows? Yeah, they are fictional. What happens on them in no way reflects real life. For instance, in real life, Sarah Jessica Parker is married to Matthew Broderick, and so whatever Chris Noth's character did to her character on her show, it didn't actually happen.

In other words, I think you should be less concerned for Winona, and more worried about yourself.

That's just my opinion, of course.

Nad

To: Mel Fuller <melissa.fuller@thenyjournal.com>
cc: Nadine Wilcock <nadine.wilcock@thenyjournal.com>
From: Tim Grabowski <timothy.grabowski@thenyjournal.com>
Subject: CONFIDENTIAL

All right, girls, hold on to your hats. I got the information you requested, the salary increases for next year. It wasn't easy.

If you tell anybody where you got this information, I will accuse you both of having gambling addictions, and you'll be yanked into the Staff Assistance Program before either of you can whistle "Dixie."

Here goes:

Name:	Position:	Salary:
Peter Hargrave	Editor in Chief	$120,000
George Sanchez	Managing Editor	$85,000
Dolly Vargas	Style Editor	$75,000
Aaron Spender	Chief Correspondent	$75,000
Nadine Wilcock	Food Critic	$45,000
Melissa Fuller	Page Ten Columnist	$45,000
Amy Jenkins	Human Resources Administrator	$45,000

Read it and weep, girls.

Timothy Grabowski
Computer Programmer
New York Journal

To: Mel Fuller <melissa.fuller@thenyjournal.com>
From: Nadine Wilcock <nadine.wilcock@thenyjournal.com>
Subject: CONFIDENTIAL

I can't believe Amy Jenkins makes as much as we do. What does SHE do? Sits around and listens to people whine all day about their dental plan.

　　Please.

I'm surprised about Dolly. I'd have thought she made more. I mean, how does she keep herself in Hermès scarves on a mere $75,000 a year?

Nad ;-)

To: Nadine Wilcock <nadine.wilcock@thenyjournal.com>
From: Mel Fuller <melissa.fuller@thenyjournal.com>
Subject: CONFIDENTIAL

Are you kidding? Dolly comes from money. Haven't you ever heard her talk about how she used to summer in Newport?

I was going to ask Aaron out for an I-forgive-you drink after work—NOT to get back together with him, just so he'll stop with the Wagner already—but now that I see how much more he makes than I do, I can't even bear to look at him. I KNOW I'm a better writer than he is. So what's he getting $75,000 per year, while I'm stuck at $45,000, doing fashion shows and movie premieres?

Mel

To: Mel Fuller <melissa.fuller@thenyjournal.com>
From: Nadine Wilcock <nadine.wilcock@thenyjournal.com>
Subject: CONFIDENTIAL

Um, because you're good at them? Fashion shows and movie premieres, I mean.

Nad ;-)

P.S.: I have to do that new Peking duck place on Mott. Come with me.

To: Nadine Wilcock <nadine.wilcock@thenyjournal.com>
From: Mel Fuller <melissa.fuller@thenyjournal.com>
Subject: Lunch

I can't. You know I can't. I've got to walk Paco.

Mel

To: Mel Fuller <melissa.fuller@thenyjournal.com>
From: Nadine Wilcock <nadine.wilcock@thenyjournal.com>
Subject: Lunch and that dog

Okay, how long is this going to go on? You and that dog, I mean?
I can't be going out to eat by myself every day. Who's going to
keep me from ordering the double-patty cheddar melt?
    I am serious. This dog thing is not working for me.

Nad

To: Nadine Wilcock <nadine.wilcock@thenyjournal.com>
From: Mel Fuller <melissa.fuller@thenyjournal.com>
Subject: Lunch and that dog

What am I supposed to do, Nadine? Let the poor thing sit in the apartment all day until he bursts? I know you aren't a dog person, but have
some compassion. It's only until Mrs. Friedlander gets better.

Mel

P.S.: This just in: Harrison Ford and his wife? On again. I swear it. His publicist just called.

I'm just glad for the kids, you know? Because that's what it's all about.

To: Mel Fuller <melissa.fuller@thenyjournal.com>
From: Nadine Wilcock <nadine.wilcock@thenyjournal.com>
Subject: It's only until Mrs. Friedlander gets better

And when is THAT going to be? Earth to Mel. Come in, Mel. The woman is in a COMA. Okay? She is COMATOSE. I think some alternative arrangements for the woman's pets need to be made. You are a DOORMAT. A COMATOSE woman is using you as a DOORMAT.

   The woman has to have some relatives, Mel. FIND THEM.

   Besides, people shouldn't keep Great Danes in the city. It's cruel.

Nad :-(

P.S.: You are the only person I know who still cares about Harrison and his wife patching things up. Give it up, girl.

To: Mel Fuller <melissa.fuller@thenyjournal.com>
From: Don and Beverly Fuller <DonBev@dnr.com>
Subject: Debbie Phillips

Melissa, honey, it's Mom. Look, your father and I got e-mail! Isn't it great? Now I can write to you, and maybe you'll answer for a change!

Just kidding, sweetheart.

Anyway, Daddy and I thought you'd want to know that little Debbie Phillips—you remember Debbie, don't you? Dr. Phillips's little girl? He was your dentist. And wasn't Debbie Homecoming Queen your senior year in high school? Anyway, Debbie's just got married! Yes! The announcement was in the paper.

And do you know what, Melissa? The *Duane County Register* is on the line now. . . . Oh, Daddy says it's ON-LINE, not on the line. Well, whatever. I get so confused.

Anyway, Debbie's announcement is ON-LINE, so I am sending it to you, as what they call an attachment. I hope you enjoy it, dear. She's marrying a doctor from Westchester! Well, we always knew she'd do well for herself. All that lovely blonde hair. And look, she graduated summa cum laude from Princeton! Then she went to law school. So impressive.

Not that there's anything wrong with being a reporter. Reporters are just as important as lawyers! And Lord knows we all need to read some nice gossip now and then. Why, did you hear about Ted Turner and Martha Stewart? You could have knocked me over with a feather.

Well, enjoy! And you make sure you lock your door at night. Daddy and I worry about you, living there in that big city all alone.

Bye for now,

Mommy

Attachment: ✉ (Glam photo of wedding couple)

Deborah Marie Phillips, the daughter of Dr. and Mrs. Reed Andrew Phillips of Lansing, was married last week to Michael Bourke, the son of Dr. and Mrs. Reginald Bourke of Chapaqua, New York. The Rev. James Smith performed the ceremony at the Roman Catholic Church of Saint Anthony in Lansing.

Ms. Phillips, 26, is an associate at Schuler, Higgins, and Brandt, the international law firm based in New York. She received a bachelor's degree from Princeton, from which she graduated summa cum laude, and a law degree from Harvard. Her father is a dentist and oral surgeon in Lansing, operating the Phillips Dental Practice.

Mr. Bourke, 31, received a bachelor's degree from Yale and an MBA from Columbia University. He is an associate at the investment banking group of Lehman Brothers. His father, now retired, was the president of Bourke & Associates, a private investment firm.

After a honeymoon trip to Thailand, the couple will reside in Chapaqua.

To: Mel Fuller <melissa.fuller@thenyjournal.com>
From: Dolly Vargas <dolly.vargas@thenyjournal.com>
Subject: Mothers

Darling, when I heard all that anguished shrieking from your cubicle just now I thought at the very least Tom Cruise had finally come out of the closet. But Nadine tells me it's just because you received an e-mail from your mother.

How well I understand. And I am so glad my mother is far too drunk ever to learn to operate a keyboard. I highly suggest you send your doting parents a case of Campari and have done with it. Trust me, it's the only way to shut them up on the dreaded subject of "M." As in, "Why aren't you M yet? All your friends are M. You aren't even trying to get M. Don't you want me to see my grandchildren before I die?"

As if I would EVER give birth. I suppose a well-mannered little six-year-old would be all right, but they simply don't COME that way. You have to TRAIN them.

Too tiresome. I can understand your anguish.

XXXOOO

Dolly

P.S.: Did you notice Aaron shaved? It's a pity. I never realized what a weak chin he has.

To: Mel Fuller <melissa.fuller@thenyjournal.com>
From: Amy Jenkins <amy.jenkins@thenyjournal.com>
Subject: Staff Assistance Program

Dear Ms. Fuller,
You might think it amusing to make light of the Human Resources Department's Staff Assistance Program, but I can assure you that we have helped many of your coworkers through dark and difficult times. Through counseling and therapy, they have all gone on to lead meaningful, profitable lives. I find it disheartening that you would belittle a program that has done so much for so many.

Please note that a copy of your latest e-mail has been placed in your personnel file, and will be available to your supervisor during your next performance review.

Amy Jenkins
Human Resources Administrator
New York Journal

To: Amy Jenkins<amy.jenkins@thenyjournal.com>
From: Mel Fuller <melissa.fuller@thenyjournal.com>
Subject: Staff Assistance Program

Dear Ms. Jenkins,

What I find disheartening is the fact that I reached out to you and all the other Human Resource Administrators, and instead of being given the aid I so desperately need, I was brutally rebuffed. Are you saying that my chronic status as a single woman is not worthy of assistance? Do I have to tell you how demoralizing it is to buy Lean Cuisines Fiesta Meals for One every night at the Food Emporium? What about having to order my pizza by the slice? Do you think that isn't whittling away at my self-esteem, slice by disheartening slice?

And what about salad? Do you have any idea how many pounds of lettuce I have ingested in an effort to maintain my size 6 figure, so that I might entice a man? Even though it goes against every fiber of my feminist being to cater to the misogynistic mores that exists in Western culture that insist that attractiveness is equal to one's waist size?

If you are trying to say that being a single woman in New York City is not a disability, then I respectfully submit that you visit a Manhattan deli on a Saturday night. Who do you see crowded around the salad bar?

That's right. The single girls.

Face reality, Amy. It's a jungle out there. It's kill or be killed. I am merely suggesting that you, as a mental health expert, accept that truth, and move on.

Melissa Fuller
Page Ten Columnist
New York Journal

To: Mel Fuller <melissa.fuller@thenyjournal.com>
From: George Sanchez <george.sanchez@thenyjournal.com>
Subject: Cut it out

Stop teasing Amy Jenkins down in Human Resources. You know she doesn't have a sense of humor.

If you have so much free time, come to me. I'll give you plenty to do. The obit guy just quit.

George

To: Mel Fuller <melissa.fuller@thenyjournal.com>
From: Aaron Spender <aaron.spender@thenyjournal.com>
Subject: Forgive me

I don't know where to begin. First of all, I can't stand this. You ask what "this" is.

I'll tell you: "This" is sitting here all day, seeing you there in your cubicle, knowing that you said you never want to speak to me again.

"This" is watching you walk toward me, thinking you might have changed your mind, only to have you pass by without so much as even glancing in my direction.

"This" is knowing that you'll walk out of here at the end of the day, that I will have no idea where you will be, what you will do, and that an abyss of time will elapse before you walk back in here the next day.

"This" is—or should I say, "these are"?—the countless hours during which my mind leaves me, and pursues you out the door, following you in a journey that leads nowhere, right back where I started, sitting here thinking about "this."

Aaron Spender
Senior Correspondent
New York Journal

To: Aaron Spender <aaron.spender@thenyjournal.com>
From: Mel Fuller <melissa.fuller@thenyjournal.com>
Subject: "This"

That was really moving, Aaron. Have you ever considered writing fiction for a living?
    Seriously. I think you've got real talent.

Mel

To: Nadine Wilcock <nadine.wilcock@thenyjournal.com
From: Tony Salerno <foodie@fresche.com>
Subject: We got e-mail

Nad!!! Look!!! We got e-mail!!!
    Isn't it righteous? You can write to me at foodie@fresche.com. Get it? I'm foodie because I'm the chef!!!
    Anyway, just thought I'd say hi. Now we can e-mail each other all day long!
    What are you wearing? How come you never wear to work that bustier I got you?
    Do you want to know tonight's specials?

- Asparagus tips wrapped in salmon
- Soft-shell crab
- Lobster bisque
- Pasta puttanesca
- Red snapper in an orrechiette sauce
- Filet mignon
- Crème brûlée

I'll save you some bisque.

Hey, by the way, my uncle Giovanni's throwing us an engagement party next weekend. Nothing fancy, just out by the pool at his house in Long Island. So keep Saturday free!

Love you,
Tony

To: Mel Fuller <melissa.fuller@thenyjournal.com>
From: Nadine Wilcock <nadine.wilcock@thenyjournal.com>
Subject: Another one

Look, Tony's uncle Gio is throwing us an engagement party (yes, another one) and I'm telling you right now, YOU HAVE GOT TO COME. Seriously, Mel, I don't think I can handle another round of Salernos without you. You know what they're like.

And this one has a pool. You know they're going to throw me in. You just know it.

Say you'll come and keep me from being humiliated. PLEASE.

Nad :-O

P.S.: And don't you be giving me that damned DOG excuse again.

To: Nadine Wilcock <nadine.wilcock@thenyjournal.com>
From: Mel Fuller <melissa.fuller@thenyjournal.com>
Subject: I can't

You know I can't go. How am I supposed to go all the way out to
Long Island when I have Paco to think of? You know he has to go
out every four to five hours. I am wearing out my Steve Maddens
as it is, running back and forth between the office and my apartment building, trying to get there in time to take him out. There's
no way I can go all the way out to Long Island. The poor thing
might explode.

Mel

P.S.: Vivica—you know, the supermodel, and Donald Trump's latest
arm candy—has dumped him! Seriously! She's dumped the Donald!
He is said to be devastated, and she's gone into hiding.
    Poor things. I really thought that one was going to work out.

To: Mel Fuller <melissa.fuller@thenyjournal.com>
From: Nadine Wilcock <nadine.wilcock@thenyjournal.com>
Subject: Paco

Okay, this is ridiculous. Mel, you cannot put your life on hold just
because your next-door neighbor happens to be in a coma. Seriously. There must be someone in the woman's family who can look
after that stupid dog. Why do YOU have to do it?
    You've done enough, for God's sake. I mean, you probably
saved her life. Let someone else handle Paco and his digestive
schedule.

I mean it. I am not getting into that pool on my own. If you don't find this woman's next of kin, I will.

Nad :-(

P.S.: Excuse me, I understand your concern for Winona, but the Donald? And Vivica, the Victoria's Secret Wonder Bra girl? They'll be fine. Trust me.

To: Nadine Wilcock <nadine.wilcock@thenyjournal.com>
From: Mel Fuller <melissa.fuller@thenyjournal.com>
Subject: Paco

It's easy for you to say let someone else handle Paco. My question would be: WHO?

Mrs. Friedlander's only living relative is her nephew, Max, and not even the cops have been able to find him to tell him what happened to her. I know he lives somewhere in the city, but his phone number's unlisted. Apparently, he's some up-and-coming photographer with pictures in the Whitney, or something. At least, according to his aunt. And quite popular with the ladies . . . ergo, the unlisted number, I assume so the ladies' husbands can't track him down.

And of course his aunt doesn't have his number written down anywhere because she undoubtedly had it memorized.

In any case, what can I do? I can't put the poor thing in a kennel. He's already freaked out enough about his owner being . . . well, you know. How can I leave him locked up in some cage somewhere? Seriously, Nadine, if you saw his eyes, you wouldn't be able to do it, either. He is the sweetest thing I've ever seen, and that includes nephews.

If only he were a man. I'd marry him. I swear it.

Mel

To: Nadine Wilcock <nadine.wilcock@thenyjournal.com>
From: Tony Salerno <foodie@fresche.com>
Subject: What do you mean you're not going?

Nadine, you HAVE to go. The party is for YOU. Well, you and me.
You can't not go.

And don't give me any of that bull about how you don't want
anybody in my family to see you in a swimsuit. How many times
do I have to tell you that you are the hottest girl in the world? Do
you think I care what size you wear? You have it going on, girl.

Only you should wear those thongs I bought you more often.

I don't understand what difference it makes whether or not Mel
goes. Why do women always have to do things together? It doesn't
make any sense.

Besides, if you feel that strongly about it, just tell them you
have an ear infection and can't get in the water.

Jeez. I don't get you dames. I really don't.

Tony

To: Mel Fuller <melissa.fuller@thenyjournal.com>
cc: Nadine Wilcock <nadine.wilcock@thenyjournal.com>
From: Dolly Vargas <dolly.vargas@thenyjournal.com>
Subject: Your little problem

Darlings:
I couldn't help but overhear your little tête-à-tête in the ladies' just
now. I was otherwise occupied, or I would have joined in (we really
ought to talk to someone about how narrow those stalls are). Fortunately, Jimmy—you know, the new fax boy—is quite surprisingly
flexible, or we never would have managed. ;-)

First of all, Mel, sweetheart, Max Friedlander did not have just any old picture in the Whitney—which you would know, if you ever ventured out of Blockbuster long enough to take in some real culture. He had a stunning self-portrait on display there for the Biennial, in which he was sans apparel. If you ask me, the man's a photographic genius.

Though that may not be where his true talent lies, judging by that photo . . . if you get my drift.

And I'm sure you do.

Anyway, he has, for reasons unfathomable to me, chosen to cheapen his gift by prostituting himself out for photo shoots, such as, just as an example, last winter's *Sports Illustrated* swimsuit issue. And he just finished up the Victoria's Secret Christmas catalog, I believe.

All you have to do, children, is contact those so-called publications, and I'm sure they'll know how to get a message to him.

Well, ta for now.

XXXOOO

Dolly

P.S.: Oh, Mel, about Aaron. Look, can't you throw him a bone? He's no good to me like this. And all that Wagner is giving me a migraine.

To: Nadine Wilcock <nadine.wilcock@thenyjournal.com>
From: Mel Fuller <melissa.fuller@thenyjournal.com>
Subject: Max Friedlander

Listen, thanks to Dolly, I think I've finally managed to track down Max Friedlander!

At least, no one seems to have his number, but I've got an

e-mail address. Help me draft a note to him. You know I don't do well with groveling.

Mel

To: Max Friedlander <photoguy@stopthepresses.com>
From: Mel Fuller <melissa.fuller@thenyjournal.com>
Subject: Your aunt

Dear Mr. Friedlander,
I hope you get this. You are probably not aware that the police have been trying to reach you for several days now. I am sorry to inform you that your aunt, Helen Friedlander, has been seriously injured. She has been the victim of an assault in her apartment.

She is currently listed in critical condition at Beth Israel Hospital here in New York. Unfortunately, she is in a coma, and the doctors have no way of knowing if she will ever come out of it.

Please, Mr. Friedlander, if you get this message, call me as soon as possible on my cell phone, 917-555-2123, or if you prefer, please feel free to e-mail me. We need to discuss how you think your aunt would best like her pets cared for while she is in the hospital.

I know this is the last thing you need to be worried about right now, considering how grave your aunt's condition is, but I can't imagine that, being the great animal lover she is, your aunt didn't have some sort of proviso arranged for just this sort of circumstance. I am her next-door neighbor (in apartment 15B), and I have been walking Paco and taking care of your aunt's cats, but I'm afraid that my schedule does not allow for full-time pet care. Taking care of Paco is beginning to affect my job performance.

Please contact me as soon as you can.

Melissa Fuller

To: Mel Fuller <melissa.fuller@thenyjournal.com>
From: Nadine Wilcock <nadine.wilcock@thenyjournal.com>
Subject: The letter

I like it. Short but sweet. And it gets the point across.

Nad :)

P.S.: I think it's good you left out the part about all your tardies. No one in the real world cares about tardies. Just at OUR $@%#ing workplace does anyone keep track of how late we are.

To: Nadine Wilcock <nadine.wilcock@thenyjournal.com>
From: Mel Fuller <melissa.fuller@thenyjournal.com>
Subject: The letter

Yeah, but do you think he'll even get it? From what I can tell based on the people I've talked to so far, this Max Friedlander seems to be taking the role of playboy artiste to brand new heights. In fact, I can't believe he's never hit Page Ten before!

Plus, it seems like he's always on the road. The guy was in Thailand on a shoot last month, Hawaii last week, and this week, who knows? Nobody seems to have any idea where he is.

Oh, and it's no good trying his cell phone: According to *Sports Illustrated*, he lost it scuba diving in Belize.

If he even gets this message, does he sound to you like the kind of guy who'll even do anything about it?

I'm a little worried.

And it's okay, I guess. I mean, I'm bonding with the cats (well, Mr. Peepers won't come out from under the bed), and Paco's like my best friend now.

But I've gotten five more of those tardy warnings from Human Resources. They are seriously going to put me on probation! But what can I do? Paco NEEDS a good hour-long walk in the morning.

Still, if I have to ditch out of one more society function because I have to get home to walk that dog, I'm pretty sure I'm going to get fired. I completely missed the Sarah Jessica Parker thing the other night because Paco wouldn't go. I had to walk him for like *an hour.*

George was furious, because the *Chronicle* got the scoop on us.

Though what the *Chronicle* is doing, reporting on celeb gossip, I can't imagine. I always thought they were too highbrow for that!

Mel

To: Tom Barrett <concierge@paradiseinn.com>
From: Max Friedlander <photoguy@stopthepresses.com>
Subject: Message

To whom it may concern:
Please deliver the following message to Vivica Chandler, who is staying in the Sopradilla Cottage.

Viv—
Do not—I repeat, DO NOT—accept any messages, telephone calls, faxes, e-mails, etc., for me from a woman named Melissa Fuller.

No, don't worry, she's not one of my exes. She's my aunt's next-door neighbor. Apparently, Helen took a tumble, and this Fuller woman is trying to get in touch with me about the stupid dog.

But we aren't going to let her ruin our little getaway together, are we?

So, don't even answer the door until I get there. I'm just finishing up the Neve Campbell shoot, and then I'll be taking the red-eye out from LAX, so I ought to be there in time to watch the sunset with you, baby. Keep the champagne chilled for me.

Love ya,
Max

To: Max Friedlander <photoguy@stopthepresses.com>
From: Tom Barrett <concierge@paradiseinn.com>
Subject: Message

Dear Mr. Friedlander,
It is my pleasure to inform you that your message for Miss Chandler has been delivered.

If there is anything else we here at the Paradise Inn can do to make your stay an enjoyable one, please do not hesitate to let us know.

We look forward to your joining us tomorrow.

Sincerely,
Tom Barrett
Concierge
Paradise Inn
Key West, Florida

To: Mel Fuller <melissa.fuller@thenyjournal.com>
From: Max Friedlander <photoguy@stopthepresses.com>
Subject: My aunt

Dear Ms. Fuller,
I am shocked. Deeply shocked and appalled to hear what has happened to my aunt Helen. She is, as I'm sure you know, my only living relative. I cannot thank you enough for the efforts you've gone
to in order to contact me and let me know about this tragedy.

Although I am currently on assignment in Africa—perhaps
you've heard of the drought here in Ethiopia? I am doing a photo
shoot for the Save the Children fund—I will begin making prepara-
tions to return to New York at once. If my aunt should wake before
I get there, please assure her that I am on my way.

And thank you again, Ms. Fuller. Everything they say about
cold and unfeeling New Yorkers is obviously untrue in your case.
God bless you.

Sincerely,
Maxwell Friedlander

To: John Trent <john.trent@thenychronicle.com>
From: Max Friedlander <photoguy@stopthepresses.com>
Subject: S.O.S.

Dude.
I'm in trouble.
    You've got to help me out.
    I'm serious. You don't know what's at stake here: I have a
chance for an extended vacation with Vivica.

Yeah, you read that right. Vivica. The supermodel. The one who just dumped Trump. The one in those ads for that new bra with the water pump. The one on the *Sports Illustrated* cover.

Yeah. THAT one.

But it's not going to work out, buddy, if you don't do me a little favor. Just one little favor. That's all I'm asking.

And I know I don't have to remind you about that time I saved your you-know-what in Vegas. Remember? Spring break, our senior year? I've never seen anybody drink as many pitchers of margaritas as you did that night. I'm telling you, man, you'd be paying alimony right now if it weren't for me. I SAVED you. And you swore to me the next day (by the pool, remember?) that if there was ever anything you could do for me, you'd do it.

Well, today's the day. I'm calling it in. The favor.

Crap, they're making me put away my electronic devices for takeoff. Write back, man.

Max

To: Jason Trent <jason.trent@trentcapital.com>
From: John Trent <john.trent@thenychronicle.com>
Subject: Max Friedlander

I knew it was coming. I knew it was coming, and just now it arrived: A dispatch from Max Friedlander, demanding payback for a favor he did me our senior year in college.

My God, that was ten years ago. The man has a mind like a sieve. He can't remember his own Social Security number, but this "favor" I owe him he remembers. What did I ever do to deserve this?

You remember Max, don't you, Jase? He was my roommate

senior year, the one I got my first apartment with when I moved to the city after college. That dive in Hell's Kitchen, where the guy got stabbed in the back the first night we were there—remember? It was in the papers the next day . . . I think that's what led to my deciding to become a crime reporter, as a matter of fact.

Remember how Mim offered to get me out of the lease so I could move in with her and live, to quote Mim, "like a human being"? God, after two months of living with Max, I almost took her up on it. It's like the guy still thought we were in college—half of Manhattan used to show up in our living room for Monday night football every week.

No hard feelings when I moved out, though. He still calls me every few months to catch up.

And now this.

God only knows what Max wants me to do for him. Rescue a raftful of refugee Cuban ballerinas, I suppose. Or house the Australian rugby team. Or loan him the $50,000 he owes to the Russian mob.

I am seriously considering leaving the country, Jase. Do you think Mim would let me have the Lear for the weekend?

John

To: John Trent <john.trent@thenychronicle.com>
From: Jason Trent <jason.trent@trentcapital.com>
Subject: Max Friedlander

I hesitate to ask, of course, but as your big brother I feel I have a right to know:

What, precisely, did Max Friedlander do for you that left you owing him this enormous debt?

Jason

P.S. Stacy says when are you coming to visit? The kids have been asking about you. Brittany's riding post, and Haley won best jumper at last week's exhibit.

P.P.S. No go on the Lear. Julia's using it.

To: Jason Trent <jason.trent@trentcapital.com>
From: John Trent <john.trent@thenychronicle.com>
Subject: Max Friedlander

Her name was Heidi. She was a showgirl. She had feathers in her hair, and a dress cut down there.

Okay, not really. But her name was Heidi, and she was a showgirl. And apparently I was determined to make her the first Mrs. John Trent.

You wouldn't understand, of course, having never done anything even slightly disreputable in all of your thirty-five years, but try, Jason, to put yourself in my shoes:

It was spring break. I was twenty-two. I was in love.

I'd had way too many margaritas.

Max dragged me out of the wedding chapel, sent Heidi home, took away my keys so I couldn't follow her, sobered me up, and put me to bed.

I still think of her sometimes. She had red hair, and was slightly bucktoothed. She was adorable.

But not worth THIS.

John

P.S.: Congratulate Haley and Brittany for me. Are you going out to the Vineyard this weekend? I could meet you all there.

Depending on whatever this favor of Max's turns out to be.

To: John Trent <john.trent@thenychronicle.com>
From: Jason Trent <jason.trent@trentcapital.com>
Subject: Max Friedlander

Ah. It is all become clear now. I know how you are when it comes to redheads.

So just what IS the favor he wants you to do him in return?

Jason

P.S.: No, we're going to the place in the Hamptons. You're welcome to join us.

To: Max Friedlander <photoguy@stopthepresses.com>
From: John Trent <john.trent@thenychronicle.com>
Subject: S.O.S.

I don't even want to ask. What is it that you want me to do for you, Max?

And please, I'm begging you, nothing illegal in New York, or any other state.

John

To: John Trent <john.trent@thenychronicle.com>
From: Max Friedlander <photoguy@stopthepresses.com>
Subject: S.O.S.

Look, it'll be a piece of cake: All I want you to do is be me. Just for a week or two.

Well, okay, maybe a month.

Simple, right? Here's the 411:

My aunt—you know, the filthy stinking rich one who always kind of reminded me of your grandma, Mimi, or whatever the hell her name is. The one who was so mean about our apartment? The neighborhood wasn't *that* bad.

Anyway, my aunt apparently suffered a senior moment and let a psychopath into her place, who conked her on the head and fled, and now she's in the vegetable crisper at Beth Israel.

There is a chance—albeit a small one—according to her doctors, that she might come out of it.

So you understand that it simply won't do to have her waking up and finding out that her beloved Maxie didn't fly to her side as soon as he heard about her accident. Auntie Helen's will is arranged 80/20—80 percent of the $12 million my aunt is worth goes to me upon her demise, and 20 percent goes to various charitable organizations she sponsors. We wouldn't want there to be any sort of untimely shift in those percentiles, now would we, on account of Maxie turning out to have been playing house with a supermodel during this alarming tragedy?

Of course we wouldn't. Which is where you, my friend, come in:

You're going to tell this neighbor of hers that you're me.

That's it. Just be me, so Ms. Melissa Fuller reports back to Auntie Helen—if she ever comes around, which is extremely doubtful—that, yes, her beloved nephew, Maxie, did show up as soon as he heard about her little accident.

Oh, yeah, and you might have to walk the dog a few times. Just to shut the neighbor up.

And, of course, if the old biddy shows the slightest sign of rejoining the conscious, you call me. Got it? And I'll rush right back.

But since I figure the chance of an eighty-year-old woman springing back from this kind of thing is pretty much nil, I won't be expecting to hear from you.

You know I wouldn't ask you to do this if we weren't talking

Vivica here. Okay? VIVICA. The girl is supposedly very well versed in yoga.

YOGA, Trent.

You do this for me, and your slate's clean, dude. Whadduya say?

Max

To: Max Friedlander <photoguy@stopthepresses.com>
From: John Trent <john.trent@thenychronicle.com>
Subject: S.O.S.

Let me see if I've got this straight:

Your aunt was the victim of a brutal assault, and you don't even care enough to postpone your vacation?

That is cold, Friedlander. Really cold.

Essentially, what you want me to do is impersonate you. Is that it?

I think I'd rather be married to the showgirl.

John

To: John Trent <john.trent@thenychronicle.com>
From: Max Friedlander <photoguy@stopthepresses.com>
Subject: S.O.S.

You crime reporters are all alike.

Why do you have to make it sound so underhanded? I told

you, Helen's in a coma. She's never even going to know about it. If she croaks, you tell me, I come back to arrange the funeral. If she comes out of it, you tell me, I come back to help her convalesce.

But as long as she's unconscious, she's never going to know the difference. So why postpone anything?

Besides, we're talking Vivica here.

You see how easy things can be if you don't overanalyze them? You were always like this. I remember those multiple-choice tests we'd get in Bio, you were always, "It can't be A—that's too obvious. They must be trying to trick us," and so you'd choose D, when the answer was CLEARLY A.

As long as Auntie Helen—and her lawyers—doesn't know any better, why not let me enjoy my well-earned little vacation? Placate this neighbor of hers. That's all I'm asking. Just take over the dog-walking duties.

I think it's a very small price to pay, considering that I kept you from making the worst mistake of your entire life. You think old Mimsy would still be inviting you up to those soirees on the Vineyard if you had a Vegas showgirl for a wife?

I think not.

I think you owe your buddy Maxie, but good.

Max

To: Jason Trent <jason.trent@trentcapital.com>
From: John Trent <john.trent@thenychronicle.com>
Subject: Max Friedlander

He wants me to pretend to be him and walk his comatose aunt's dog while he's off partying with a supermodel.

I guess it could be worse. A lot worse.
So why do I have such a bad feeling about it?

John

To: John Trent <john.trent@thenychronicle.com>
From: Jason Trent <jason.trent@trentcapital.com>
Subject: Max Friedlander

You're right. It could be worse. Are you going to do it?

Jason

P.S.: Stacy says to tell you she's got the perfect girl for you: Haley's dressage instructor. Twenty-nine, size 4, blond, blue-eyed, the works. What do you say?

To: Jason Trent <jason.trent@trentcapital.com>
From: John Trent <john.trent@thenychronicle.com>
Subject: Max Friedlander

Why not?
I mean, walking an old lady's dog . . . how bad can that be?

John

P.S.: You know I can't stand dressage. There's something unnatural about making a horse dance.

To: John Trent <john.trent@thenychronicle.com>
From: Jason Trent <jason.trent@trentcapital.com>
Subject: Max Friedlander

The horses don't dance in dressage, you moron. They step.

And have you ever considered that you and Heidi might have been perfectly suited for one another? I mean, with the kind of luck you've been having with women lately, Heidi could very well have been your last chance at real happiness.

Just think, if you'd followed your heart, instead of Max Friedlander's head, you could be the one providing Mim with a grandkid in December, instead of me.

Jason

To: Jason Trent <jason.trent@trentcapital.com>
From: John Trent <john.trent@thenychronicle.com>
Subject: Max Friedlander

Have I mentioned lately how much I hate you?

John

To: Max Friedlander <photoguy@stopthepresses.com>
From: John Trent <john.trent@thenychronicle.com>
Subject: S.O.S.

Okay, I'll do it.

John

To: John Trent <john.trent@thenychronicle.com>
From: Max Friedlander <photoguy@stopthepresses.com>
Subject: Operation Paco

All right. I'll let the neighbor know to expect you (I mean, me) tonight for the big key pickup. She's got my aunt's spare. It has not apparently occurred to her to wonder why Aunt Helen never gave me a key to her place. (That fire in her last apartment was not my fault. There was something wrong with the wiring.)

Remember, you're supposed to be me, so try to act like you care about the old lady's hematoma, or whatever it is.

And listen, as long as you're being me, could you try to dress with a little . . . what's the word I'm looking for here? Oh, I know. STYLE. I know for guys like you who are born into money, the instinct is to downplay the trillions you're worth.

And that's cool with me. I mean, I can understand this whole thing you're doing, getting a real job instead of the cushy family one your big brother offered.

And I'm totally fine with it. If you want to pretend like you're only making forty-five grand a year, that's just great.

But while you're being me, could you PLEASE not dress like a grad student? I am begging you: No Grateful Dead T-shirts. And those deck shoes you always wear? Would something in a tassel kill you?

And for the love of God, invest in a leather jacket. Please. I know it will mean touching some of those precious millions in that trust fund your grandfather left you, but, really, something NOT from the Gap would be good.

That's all. That's all I ask. Just try to look good when you're imitating me. I have a reputation to uphold, you know.

Max

P.S.: The neighbor left a number, but I lost it. Her e-mail's melissa.fuller@thenyjournal.

To: Max Friedlander <photoguy@stopthepresses.com>
From: John Trent <john.trent@thenychronicle.com>
Subject: S.O.S.

Christ, Friedlander, she works for the *New York JOURNAL*???

You didn't say that. You didn't say anything about your aunt's neighbor working for the *New York Journal*.

Don't you get it, Max? She might KNOW me. I'm a journalist. Yeah, we work for rival papers, but for God's sake, the field's pretty small. What if she opens the door and it turns out we've been to the same conferences—or crime scenes?

Your cover will be blown.

Or do you not care?

John

P.S.: And how am I supposed to e-mail her? She's going to know I'm not you when she reads my address.

To: John Trent <john.trent@thenychronicle.com>
From: Max Friedlander <photoguy@stopthepresses.com>
Subject: Operation Paco

Of course I care. And don't worry, I already checked her out. She does the gossip page.

I doubt you've been running into any gossip columnists at the crime scenes you've been covering lately.

Max

P.S.: Apply for a second e-mail account.
P.P.S.: Quit bugging me. Vivica and I are trying to watch the sunset.

To: Max Friedlander <photoguy@stopthepresses.com>
From: John Trent <john.trent@thenychronicle.com>
Subject: I'm not happy

Gossip? She's a gossip columnist, Max? She's going to know I'm not you for SURE.

John

To: Max Friedlander <photoguy@stopthepresses.com>
From: John Trent <john.trent@thenychronicle.com>
Subject: I'm not happy

Max? MAX??? WHERE ARE YOU?

To: Nadine Wilcock <nadine.wilcock@thenyjournal.com>
From: Mel Fuller <melissa.fuller@thenyjournal.com>
Subject: Max Friedlander

Oh, my God, Nadine! I heard from him!

He's on assignment in Ethiopia, photographing little starving kids for the Save the Children fund! And I've just asked him to leave to come home and take care of his aunt's dog!

What kind of a horrible bitch must I seem to him? Oh, God, I knew I shouldn't have tried to contact him.

Mel

To: Mel Fuller <melissa.fuller@thenyjournal.com>
From: Nadine Wilcock <nadine.wilcock@thenyjournal.com>
Subject: Max Friedlander

What's more important to him, a bunch of starving kids he doesn't know or his aunt's dog?

I don't mean to sound cold, but starving children or not, the man has to take some responsibility.

Besides, his aunt is in a coma, Mel. I mean, if your only living relative is in a coma, you come home, for God's sake, starving kids or no.

When's he getting here, anyway? Are you going to be able to make the pool party? Because Tony's threatening to break off the engagement if I don't go.

Nad :-/

To: Mel Fuller <melissa.fuller@thenyjournal.com>
From: Dolly Vargas <dolly.vargas@thenyjournal.com>
Subject: Max Friedlander

Darling, I could hear you shrieking all the way in the art department. I thought at the very least the cast of *Friends* was breaking up.

But now I find out it's only because Max Friedlander e-mailed you.

But what's this I hear about him doing it from in Ethiopia? Max Friedlander would NEVER go to Ethiopia. My God, it's so . . . dusty there.

You must be confusing him with someone else.

Now, listen, about Aaron: I am bound and determined to make him into something I wouldn't be ashamed to introduce to Stephen. So do you think he'll resist strongly to my steering him over toward Barney's? He's simply got to have some linen pants, don't you think? He'll look so devastatingly F. Scott Fitzgerald in linen.

Can you say something, darling, next time you pass him on your way to the copier? Something completely cutting, like "nice khakis," ought to put him exactly where I want him.

XXXOOO

Dolly

To: Don and Beverly Fuller <DonBev@dnr.com>
From: Mel Fuller <melissa.fuller@thenyjournal.com>
Subject: Debbie Phillips

Hi, Mom. Sorry it took me so long to get back to you. Things here have been pretty busy, like I mentioned to you over the phone. I'm still walking Mrs. Friedlander's dog, but tonight her nephew is supposed to come by, and hopefully we'll work something out.

Which is good because I've been getting into trouble at work for being late every day. I don't know why people in Human Resources have such an axe to grind against us everyday working stiffs. It's like they think they're special or something, because they control what goes into our performance files.

Anyway, other than the stuff with Mrs. Friedlander (don't worry, Mom, this building is very safe. Besides, you know my apartment is rent-controlled—it's not like I can just move. And I always lock my door, and I never open it to strangers—besides, Ralph, the doorman, would never let a stranger up without buzzing me first), things have been going okay. I'm still stuck on Page Ten—I can't convince Mr. Sanchez, my boss, that I really could do hard reporting, if he'd let me.

Let's see, what else? Oh, I broke up with that guy I told you about. It wasn't going anywhere. Well, at least, I didn't see it going where he saw it going. Besides, it turns out he was cheating on me with Barbara Bellerieve. Well, I guess he wasn't really cheating since he and I never really did anything anyway—don't let Daddy read this, all right?

Oh, there's the buzzer. Mrs. Friedlander's nephew is here. I have to go.

Love,

Mel

To: Mel Fuller <melissa.fuller@thenyjournal.com>
From: Don and Beverly Fuller <DonBev@dnr.com>
Subject: Strange men

Melissa! You call me as soon as that man is gone! How could you let a man you've never met before into your apartment? He could be that serial killer I saw on the *Inside Edition*! The one who puts on his victims' clothes and strolls around in them after he's done hacking their bodies into pieces!

If you don't call Daddy and me within one hour, I'm telephoning the police. I mean it, Melissa.

Mommy

To: Mel Fuller <melissa.fuller@thenyjournal.com>
From: Nadine Wilcock <nadine.wilcock@thenyjournal.com>
Subject: Max Friedlander

So??? What was he like???

Nad

To: Mel Fuller <melissa.fuller@thenyjournal.com>
From: Tony Salerno <foodie@fresche.com>
Subject: Well???

DON'T TELL NADINE I WROTE THIS.

But listen, Mel, you have GOT to get this guy to take over the dog-walking thing for you. Because if you don't, and you can't come to this engagement party at my uncle Giovanni's, Nadine's going to have a nervous breakdown. I swear to God. Don't ask me why, but she's got this thing with her weight, and she needs, like, your moral support or something every time she has to get into a bathing suit.

As her maid of honor, it is your duty to appear with her at this party on Saturday. So get this dude to walk the dog that day, okay?

If he gives you a hard time, let me know. I'll take care of him. People think guys who cook can't be tough, but that's not true. I'll do to the guy's face what I did to tonight's special, which happened to be veal piccata—pounded flat and swimming in the lightest white wine sauce you ever tried. I'll give you the recipe if you want later.

NOW, DON'T FORGET!!!

Tony

To: John Trent <john.trent@thenychronicle.com>
From: Max Friedlander <photoguy@stopthepresses.com>
Subject: Operation Paco

You wore tassels, right? On your shoes? When you went to see her tonight?

Just tell me you wore tassels.

Max

To: John Trent <john.trent@thenychronicle.com>
From: Jason Trent <jason.trent@trentcapital.com>
Subject: How'd it go?

Just wondering how your little performance went this evening.

And Stacy wants to know if you're still coming for dinner on Sunday like we planned.

Jason

To: John Trent <john.trent@thenychronicle.com>
From: Max Friedlander <photoguy@stopthepresses.com>
Subject: HI!!!

HI!!! THIS IS VIVICA, MAX'S FRIEND, WRITING TO YOU ON E-MAIL! MAX IS IN THE HOT TUB BUT HE ASKED ME TO ASK YOU HOW IT WENT WITH THAT WEIRD LADY WHO HAS THE DOG PROBLEM. DID SHE BELIEVE THAT YOU ARE MAX???

IT IS WEIRD TO BE WRITING TO YOU SEEING AS HOW I DON'T EVEN KNOW YOU. WHAT IS THE WEATHER LIKE IN NEW YORK? HERE IT IS EIGHTY AND BEAUTIFUL.

WE SAW SOME PERFORMING CATS TODAY. IT WAS CRAZY!!! WHO KNEW CATS COULD DO THAT???

OH, MAX SAYS TO ASK YOU TO CALL HIM HERE AT THE HOTEL AS SOON AS YOU GET THIS MESSAGE. THE NUMBER IS 305-555-6576. ASK FOR THE SOPRADILLA COTTAGE. SOPRADILLA IS A FLOWER. IT GROWS ALL OVER KEY WEST. KEY WEST IS ONLY NINETY MILES FROM CUBA, WHERE I ONCE DID A SWIMSUIT SHOOT.

UH-OH, I HAVE TO GO, MAX IS HERE.

VIVICA

To: Nadine Wilcock <nadine.wilcock@thenyjournal.com>
From: Mel Fuller <melissa.fuller@thenyjournal.com>
Subject: What was he's like?

Okay, the stats:

I would say six foot one or two. Big shoulders. I mean really big. Dark hair, but not too dark. Hazel eyes. You know the kind.

Sometimes green. Sometimes brown. Sometimes searing into my soul. . . .

Just kidding.

As for the rest:

I don't know. It's kind of hard to explain. He wasn't what I was expecting, that's for sure. I mean, from what I'd heard, about the modeling shoots and everything, I was expecting a real smooth operator, you know?

But what kind of smooth operator goes around in a Grateful Dead T-shirt? And he had on jeans. And deck shoes with no socks.

I expected Gucci loafers at least.

And he was so modest—I mean, for a guy who entered a nude picture of himself into the Biennial. I think Dolly must be exaggerating about that. Maybe he wasn't really nude. Maybe he was wearing one of those flesh-colored body stockings they wear, you know, in the movies.

And he didn't want to talk about his trip to Ethiopia at all! When I mentioned the work he was doing for the Save the Children fund, he actually seemed embarrassed and tried to change the subject.

I tell you, Nadine, he doesn't seem at all the way Dolly described him.

Even Mrs. Friedlander didn't do him justice. She's always talked about him as if she thought he was a little irresponsible, but I'm telling you, Nadine, he didn't seem that way to me. He asked all sorts of things about what happened—I mean about the break-in, and all. Although I guess it wasn't really a break-in, since the door wasn't even locked. . . .

Anyway, it was really touching how much he seemed to care about his aunt. He asked me to show him where I found her, and how she was lying, and if anything was missing. . . .

It was almost as if he'd had some experience dealing with violent crime. . . . I don't know. Maybe there were some catfights at the Victoria's Secret shoot???!

Another odd thing: He seemed kind of surprised at how big Paco is. I mean, considering that I know Mrs. Friedlander had Max over for dinner at least a few months ago, and Paco's five years old, so it's not like he could have grown any. When I mentioned how last week Paco practically wrenched my shoulder out of its socket, Max said he didn't see how a frail old lady could walk such a big dog on a regular basis.

Isn't that funny? I guess only a nephew would think of Mrs. Friedlander as frail. She's always seemed like a tough old bird to me. I mean, considering that last year she hiked all over Yosemite. . . .

Anyway, Nadine, I'm so glad you made me get in touch with him! Because he said he didn't feel right about me walking Paco with my hurt shoulder and all, and that he was going to move in next door, to take care of the animals and sort of keep an eye on things.

Can you believe that? A man who actually takes care of his responsibilities? I am still in shock.

I have to go—someone's at the door. Oh, God, it's the cops!

Gotta go—

Mel

To: Nadine Wilcock <nadine.wilcock@thenyjournal.com>
From: Mel Fuller <melissa.fuller@thenyjournal.com>
Subject: What was he like?

Okay, the cops are gone. I explained about my mother and her obsession with the transvestite killer. They didn't even get that mad.

Anyway, Nadine, do you want to know something else? About Max Friedlander, I mean. If you can stand it. . . .

From where I'm sitting, at my desk at home, I can see into his apartment—I mean, Mrs. Friedlander's apartment. Right into the spare bedroom. Mrs. Friedlander always kept the mini-blinds in that room down, but Max opened them right up (to look at the city lights, I guess—we do have that nice view here on the fifteenth floor) and I can see him lying on the bed, typing something on his laptop. Tweedledum is on the bed beside him, as is Paco, of course (no sign of Mr. Peepers, but then, he's shy).

I know it's wrong to look, but, Nadine, they look so nice and happy in there!

And I guess it doesn't hurt that Max really has very nice forearms. . . .

Oh, God. I had better go to bed. I think I'm getting slaphappy.

Love,
Mel

To: Jason Trent <jason.trent@trentcapital.com>
From: John Trent <john.trent@thenychronicle.com>
Subject: How'd it go?

She's a redhead.
    Help.

John

To: Mel Fuller <melissa.fuller@thenyjournal.com>
From: Dolly Vargas <dolly.vargas@thenyjournal.com>
Subject: Max Friedlander

Darling, did I overhear you correctly when I ran into you and Nadine at Starbucks this morning? Did you say Max Friedlander actually *moved in next door* to you?

And that you were actually *spying* on him?

And that you saw him *naked*???

I seem to have gotten some water in my ears last weekend at Stephen's, so I just want to make sure I heard you right before I call every single person I know and tell them.

XXXOOO

Dolly

To: Mel Fuller <melissa.fuller@thenyjournal.com>
From: Nadine Wilcock <nadine.wilcock@thenyjournal.com>
Subject: Dolly

Mel—
Would you stop obsessing? Who is she going to tell? Dolly doesn't know that many people here at the office.

And the ones she does know all hate her and wouldn't believe her anyway.

Trust me.

Nad

To: Mel Fuller <melissa.fuller@thenyjournal.com>
From: Aaron Spender <aaron.spender@thenyjournal.com>
Subject: You

Mel, did I hear this from Dolly correctly? Did a naked man move in next door to you? What happened to the old lady? Did she end up dying? I hadn't heard. I'm very sorry for your loss, if that's the case. I know the two of you were fairly close, for Manhattan neighbors.

But I don't think it's appropriate for a man to parade around nude in front of his neighbors. You really ought to complain to the co-op board about this, Melissa. I know you are only renting, and that you don't like to make waves because you have such a good deal on the place, but this kind of thing could be perceived as a sexual assault. Really, it could.

Melissa, I was wondering if you'd given any thought to what I said in the elevator the other day. I really meant it. I think it's time.

I remember that day when we went walking through Central Park during your lunch hour. It seems so long ago, but it was only last spring. You purchased a hot dog from an outdoor vendor, and I urged you not to, because of that story I did on carcinogens in street-cart food.

I'll never forget the way your blue eyes flashed at me as you said, "Aaron, in order to die, you have to live a little first."

Melissa, I've decided: I want to live. And the person I want to live with, more than anyone else in the world, is you. I believe I am ready to make a commitment.

Oh, Melissa, please won't you let that commitment be with you?
Aaron

Aaron Spender
Senior Correspondent
New York Journal

To: Mel Fuller <melissa.fuller@thenyjournal.com>
From: George Sanchez <george.sanchez@thenyjournal.com>
Subject: Tardiness

So, Dolly tells me you finally got in touch with the dog guy. That would explain why you were on time this morning for the first time in twenty-seven days.

Congratulations, kid. I'm proud of you.

Now if you'd just start handing in your copy on time I won't have to fire you. But I guess I shouldn't count on that happening, since I hear this new neighbor of yours looks pretty good in the buff.

George

To: Dolly Vargas <dolly.vargas@thenyjournal.com>
From: Mel Fuller <melissa.fuller@thenyjournal.com>
Subject: Max Friedlander

Dolly, I swear to God, if you tell one more person that I saw Max Friedlander naked I will personally come over there and put a stake through your heart, which I hear is the only way to stop someone like you.

He was not NAKED, okay? He was fully clothed. FULLY CLOTHED AT ALL TIMES.

Well, except for his forearms. But that's all I saw, I swear it.

So, stop telling people otherwise!!!

Mel

To: Mel Fuller <melissa.fuller@thenyjournal.com>
From: Dolly Vargas <dolly.vargas@thenyjournal.com>
Subject: Max Friedlander

Darling, have I struck a nerve or something? I've never seen you use all caps quite so strenuously. Max must have really made an impression on you for you to be so heated up.

But then, he has that effect on women. He can't help it. Pheromones, you know. The man is lousy with them.

Well, must go. Peter Hargrave is taking me to lunch. Yes, that's right: Peter Hargrave, the editor in chief. Who knows, when I get back from lunch, I just might have a nice fat promotion.

But don't worry, I won't forget the little people.

XXXOOO

Dolly

P.S.: What do you think of Aaron's new pants? Aren't they just the thing? Hugo Boss.

I know, I know. But it's a start.

To: Tony Salerno <foodie@fresche.com>
From: Mel Fuller <melissa.fuller@thenyjournal.com>
Subject: Saturday

Hi! Just a quick note to tell you not to worry—I'll be there Saturday.

Yes, the dog guy actually showed up!
See you then.
Proud to be your future wife's maid of honor,

Mel

To: John Trent <john.trent@thenychronicle.com>
From: Jason Trent <jason.trent@trentcapital.com>
Subject: How'd it go?

She's a redhead? That's IT? You're just going to leave me hanging here?
    WHAT HAPPENED???

Jason

P.S.: Stacy wants to know, too.

To: Jason Trent <jason.trent@trentcapital.com>
From: John Trent <john.trent@thenychronicle.com>
Subject: How it went

Sorry. I got hung up on a story, and then I had to go back to Fried-lander's aunt's place to walk the dog. Max failed to mention that the misleadingly named Paco is a GREAT DANE. The dog weighs more than Mim.

So what do you want to know?

Did she believe I was Max Friedlander? I am sorry to say that she did.

Did I play the part of Max Friedlander to perfection? I guess I must have, or she wouldn't have believed I was he.

Do I feel like a grade-A heel for doing it? Yes. Self-flagellation for me.

The worst part is . . . well, I already told you the worst part. *She thinks I'm Max Friedlander.* Max Friedlander, the ingrate who doesn't even seem to care that someone coldcocked his eighty-year-old aunt.

Melissa cares, though.

That's her name. The redhead. Melissa. People call her Mel. That's what she told me. "People call me Mel." She moved to the city right after college, which makes her about twenty-seven years old, since she's lived here for five years. Originally, she's from Lansing, Illinois. Have you ever heard of Lansing, Illinois? I've heard of Lansing, Michigan, but not Lansing, Illinois. She says it's a small town where you can walk down Main Street and everyone goes, "Oh, hi, Mel."

Just like that. "Oh, hi, Mel."

On her bookshelves are, among a great many other books, copies of every single thing ever written by Stephen King. Melissa has a theory that for every century there's a writer who sums up the popular culture of the time, and for the nineteenth century it was Dickens, and for the twentieth it was Stephen King.

She says it has yet to be determined who is going to be the voice of the twenty-first century.

You know what my ex, Heather (you remember Heather, don't you, Jason? The one you and Stacy referred to as the mouth breather?), had on her bookshelves, Jason?

The complete works of Kierkegaard. She'd never read Kierkegaard, of course, but the book covers matched the color of her sofa cushions.

That's what she saw me as. Heather, I mean. A six-foot-two checkbook that could pay off her decorating bill.

Remind me again why Mim was so upset when Heather and I broke it off?

Oh, and when I got there, she offered me beer. Melissa, not Heather.

Not seltzer. Not wine. Not Glenfiddich on the rocks, or a Cosmo. Beer. She said she had two kinds: Light and root. I had root. So did she.

She showed me where Max's aunt keeps the dog and cat food. She told me where to buy more, in case I ran out. She told me what Paco's favorite walks were. She showed me how to lure a cat named, and I kid you not, Mr. Peepers, out from underneath the bed.

She asked me about my work for the Save the Children fund. She asked me about my trip to Ethiopia. She asked me if I'd been to visit my aunt in the hospital, and if it had upset me very much, seeing her with all those tubes coming out of her. She patted me on the arm and told me not to worry, that if anyone could come out of a coma, it was my aunt Helen.

And I stood there and grinned like an idiot and pretended I was Max Friedlander.

Anyway, I'm moving in. To Helen Friedlander's apartment. So, if you need to call me, the number's 212-555-8972. Only don't call. Loud ringing noises, I've discovered, upset Mr. Peepers.

Gotta go.

John

To: John Trent <john.trent@thenychronicle.com>
From: Jason Trent <jason.trent@trentcapital.com>
Subject: Who are you?

And what have you done with my brother?

He used to be a rational human being until he started pretending to be Max Friedlander and met this Melissa person.

ARE YOU INSANE??? You can't move into that woman's apartment. What is wrong with you? GET OUT NOW WHILE YOU STILL CAN.

Jason

To: John Trent <john.trent@thenychronicle.com>
From: Jason Trent <jason.trent@trentcapital.com>
Subject: I think it's sweet

Hi, John. It's Stacy. Jason let me read your last e-mail. I hope you don't mind.

I also hope you don't listen to him. I think what you are doing is very sweet, helping out that poor girl next door with the old lady's pets. Jason is trying to tell me that you aren't doing it to be nice, and something about red hair, but I am not listening to him. He has a very sick mind. He told me just the other day that the music on my pregnancy exercise video sounds like the music from a porno!

When has he ever watched porn, is what I would like to know.

Anyway, I'm just saying, don't you feel bad about pretending to be this Max person. It's for a greater good. And why don't you ask the little redhead over for dinner on Sunday night? I'll make sure I tell the girls to call you Max. They'll think it's fun, I'm sure. Like a game!

Well, that's all for now. Hope to see you soon.
Your loving sister-in-law,

Stacy

To: Michael Everett <michael.everett@thenychronicle.com>
From: John Trent <john.trent@thenychronicle.com>
Subject: Contact

Please note that for the next several weeks, I will be available only
by cell phone. Do not leave messages for me on my home phone. I
can always be reached by e-mail, either at this address or my new
one, jerrylives@freemail.com.
    Thanks.

John Trent
Senior Crime Correspondent
New York Chronicle

To: Jason Trent <jason.trent@trentcapital.com>
From: jerrylives@freemail.com>
Subject: For Stacy

Dear Stacy,
I'd just like to thank you for being so understanding about my cur-
rent situation. You see, my brother, your husband, has a tendency
to take a very cynical view of everything.
    Don't ask me how he got this way, since Jason has always been
the lucky one: He's the one who got the head for business, while all
I got was, if you'll excuse the cliché, the bod for sin.

He was also lucky enough to get you, Stacy. I guess it's easy for a guy who's got such a gem for a wife to sit back and criticize the rest of us poor slobs, who can't even find a geode out there, let alone a jewel. I guess Jason doesn't remember how hard it was for him to meet a girl who was actually attracted to him, and not the Trent family fortune.

Apparently, Jason doesn't remember Michelle. Be sure to ask him about Michelle, Stacy. Or Fiona, for that matter. Or Monica, Karen, Louise, Cathy, or Alyson.

Go on, ask him. I'd be curious to see what he has to say about any of them.

What Jason doesn't seem to realize is that he has already found the best girl in the world. He forgets that some of us losers are still out there looking.

So tell your husband to cut me a little slack, will you, Stacy?

And thanks for the invitation, but if it's all right with you I'll skip dinner this Sunday.

Love,
John

P.S.: Write back to me at my new address, listed above. I'm not sure whether it works yet.

To: jerrylives@freemail.com
From: Jason Trent <jason.trent@trentcapital.com>
Subject: Your new email address

John:
Jerry lives? Are you insane? Have you lost your mind? THAT's the address you chose as your "redhead safe" account?

You might be surprised to know that most girls don't like Jerry

Garcia, John. They like Mariah Carey. I know this from watching VH1.

And stop writing to my wife. All I've heard from her all day is Who's Alyson? Who's Michelle?

Next time I see you, Jerry, you are a dead man.

Jason

To: Jason Trent <jason.trent@trentcapital.com>
From: <jerrylives@freemail.com>
Subject: Jerry

You're wrong. Most girls prefer Jerry Garcia to Mariah Carey. I just took an office poll, and Jerry won over Mariah by a margin of nearly five to one—although the girl from the mailroom doesn't like either of them, so her vote doesn't count.

Besides, I looked at Melissa's CDs when she was in the kitchen getting the root beer, and I didn't see a single thing by Mariah Carey.

You know nothing about women.

John

To: jerrylives@freemail.com
From: Jason Trent <jason.trent@trentcapital.com>
Subject: You know nothing about women

And you do???

Jason

To: Sergeant Paul Reese <preese@eightyninthprecinct.nyc.org>
From: John Trent <john.trent@thenychronicle.com>
Subject: Helen Friedlander

Reese—
I was wondering if you could do me a favor. I need a look at anything you've got on Helen Friedlander, 12-17 West 82nd, Apt. 15A.
She was a B & E with, I believe, an assault—a pretty serious one,
since she's been in the ICU ever since, comatose.

I appreciate it, and, no, it's not for a story, so don't worry about
your commanding officer.

John Trent
Senior Crime Correspondent
New York Chronicle

To: Max Friedlander <photoguy@stopthepresses.com>
From: John Trent <john.trent@thenychronicle.com>
Subject: Helen Friedlander

Don't worry. Everything went fine. I safely evaded Ms. Fuller's
queries about my work for the Save the Children fund. Nice one, by
the way. I suppose by children you mean those eighteen-year-old
gum-chewing sticks you spend your days photographing in fashions only fifty-year-old divorcees can afford?

You really are a bastard, you know.

John

To: John Trent <john.trent@thenychronicle.com>
From: Max Friedlander <photoguy@stopthepresses.com>
Subject: Lighten up

God, I forgot what a stick in the mud you could be. No wonder you haven't had a girlfriend in so long. What was wrong with the last one? Oh, yeah, I remember: the Kierkegaard collection that matched the sofa. Dude, you need to chill. Who cares what books a woman's got on her shelves?

It's what she's like between the sheets that matters, heh heh heh.

Max

To: John Trent <john.trent@thenychronicle.com>
From: Sergeant Paul Reese <preese@eightyninthprecinct.nyc.org>
Subject: Helen Friedlander

Trent—
File's on its way. Or should I say, some copies of the file that were accidentally made while the CO was at lunch. If any of this shows up in your paper, Trent, you can kiss that Mustang of yours good-bye. Consider it impounded.

Brief summation of incident involving Helen Friedlander:

Call came in at approximately 8:50 A.M., reporting unconscious female in her home. We had a unit in the park nearby. They arrived on the scene at approximately 8:55 A.M. Found victim being given first aid by woman purporting to be neighbor. Later confirmed woman as one Melissa Fuller, living next door in apartment 15B.

Victim approximately eighty-year-old woman. When originally found, was facedown on living room carpet. Witness claims in her statement that she turned the woman to check for heartbeat, respiratory distress, etc. Victim breathing with weak pulse when EMS arrived at 9:02 A.M.

No sign of break-in or illegal entrance to home. Outside lock not tampered with. Door unlocked, according to neighbor.

According to doctors, victim was struck on the back of the head with blunt object, possibly small-caliber pistol. Assault occurred approximately twelve hours before discovery of victim. Questions put to doormen and neighbors revealed that

a) no one called upon apartment 15A the night previous to the discovery of the victim.
b) no one heard any sort of disturbance at or around 9:00 P.M. that evening.

One added note: There were a number of the victim's clothing thrown across her bed, as if previous to accident, victim had been trying to decide what to wear. However, victim, when found, was in nightclothes, including hair curlers, etc.

A reporter might try to make something out of the fact that this could be construed as another attack by the transvestite killer. There is one major difference, however: The transvestite killer actually kills his victims, and tends to stick around to make sure they are really dead.

Additionally, the transvestite killer's victims have all been in their twenties, thirties, and forties. Mrs. Friedlander, though apparently spry for her age, was unlikely to be mistaken for a younger woman.

Well, that's it. We got nothing. Of course, if the old lady croaks, that'll change things. But unless that happens, this is being treated as an interrupted robbery.

That's all I can think of.

Good luck.

Paul

To: Nadine Wilcock <nadine.wilcock@thenyjournal.com>
From: Mel Fuller <melissa.fuller@thenyjournal.com>
Subject: He didn't mean it

Nadine, you know he didn't mean it. At least not the way you think he did.

All Tony was saying is that if you're going to sit around and complain about your weight so much, why not do something about it and join a gym. He never said you were fat. All right? I was there. HE DID NOT SAY YOU'RE FAT.

Now are you seriously going to tell me you didn't you have fun at the party? And Tony's uncle Giovanni is a doll. That toast he gave the two of you . . . it was so sweet! I swear, Nadine, sometimes I'm so jealous of you I could burst.

I would give anything to find a guy with an uncle Giovanni who'd throw me a pool party and call me a Botticelli Venus.

And you did NOT look fat in that suit. My God, it had enough Gortex in it to keep Marlon Brando's flab in check. Your tiny belly didn't stand a chance.

So would you snap out of it and act like an adult?

If you're good, I'll let you come over and spy on Max Friedlander with me. . . . Oooh, look, tonight he's got on a muscle tee. . . .

Mel

To: Mel Fuller <melissa.fuller@thenyjournal.com>
From: Nadine Wilcock <nadine.wilcock@thenyjournal.com>
Subject: My butt

You are lying. About the muscle tee and about what Tony meant. You know good and well he meant that he's sick of my size 16 rear end. *I* am sick and tired of my size 16 rear end. And I fully intend to join a gym.

I just don't need Tony suggesting it.

It's his fault I'm this size, you know. I was a size 12 until he came along and started making me his trademark pappardelle alla Toscana with four cheeses and a marsala wine sauce every night. "Oh, baby, come on, just try a taste, you've never had anything like it."

Ha!

And what about his rigatoni alla vodka? Vodka, my ass. That's a cream sauce, and nobody can tell me any different.

And as for being called a Botticelli Venus, believe me, there are better things to be called.

Now, what's the dog guy really wearing?

Nad :-/

To: Nadine Wilcock <nadine.wilcock@thenyjournal.com>
From: Mel Fuller <melissa.fuller@thenyjournal.com>
Subject: What he's wearing

What do you care what he's got on? You're engaged.

But if you insist. . . .

Let me see, he is laying (or is it lying? No wonder they stuck me on Page Ten) on the bed in jeans and a T-shirt (sorry, no muscle tee—you're right, I was lying to see if you were paying attention). He has his laptop out again. Paco is there beside him. Paco is looking disgustingly happy, I must say. That dog never looked that happy when I was over there. Maybe—

Oh, my God! No wonder that dog is happy! He's feeding him Alpo—on the bed! That dog is getting Alpo all over Mrs. Friedlander's guest room's chenille bedspread! What is wrong with this man? *Doesn't he realize chenille has to be dry-cleaned?*

This is so pathetic. This is so pathetic, Nadine. I mean, the pathos of it all just suddenly came washing over me. I am sitting here in my apartment, recording the guy next door's activities for my best friend, who is engaged. Nadine, you are getting married! And what am I doing? Sitting here at home in my sweats e-mailing my girlfriend.

I AM PATHETIC!!! I am worse than pathetic, I am—

OH, MY GOD. OH, MY GOD, Nadine! He just saw me. I'm not kidding. He just waved!!!

I am so embarrassed. I am going to die. I am going to—

Oh, my God, he's opening the window. He's opening the window. He's saying something to me.

I'll get back to you.

Mel

To: Mel Fuller <melissa.fuller@thenyjournal.com>
From: Nadine Wilcock <nadine.wilcock@thenyjournal.com>
Subject: WRITE BACK!!!!

If you don't write me back tonight, I swear I am calling the cops. I don't care if I'm just like your mother. You don't know anything about this guy, except that his crazy aunt lives next door to you and he has a naked picture of himself up in the Whitney. Which I think you and I need to take a little field trip on Tuesday to see, by the way.

WRITE BACK TO ME . . .

or the boys from the eighty-seventh precinct will be paying you another visit.

Nad

To: Nadine Wilcock <nadine.wilcock@thenyjournal.com>
From: Tony Salerno <foodie@fresche.com>
Subject: Cut it out

I've been trying to get through to you for the past two hours, but
your phone's been busy. I can only assume that either it's off the
hook because you don't want to talk to me, or you are yakking it
up on-line with Mel. If it is the latter, go off-line and call me at the
restaurant. If it is the former, stop being such a spaz.

All I said was if you're that freaked out about this whole wedding
dress thing, get a personal trainer, or something. I mean, jeez, Nadine,
you're driving me crazy with this whole size 12 crap. Who CARES
what size you are? *I* don't care. I love you exactly the way you are.

And I don't give a rat's ass how many of your sisters have worn
that stupid dress of your mother's. I hate that dress anyway. It's
ugly. Just go out and buy a new dress, one that fits you the way
you are NOW. You'll feel better in it and it will look better on you.
Your mother will understand, and who cares what your sisters
think? Screw your sisters, anyway.

I have to go. Table 7 just sent back their salmon because it was
undercooked. See what you made me do?

Tony

To: Tony Salerno <foodie@fresche.com>
From: Nadine Wilcock <nadine.wilcock@thenyjournal.com>
Subject: Excuse me . . .

but I do not appreciate your attitude toward my sisters. I happen to
like my sisters. What if I said screw your brothers? What if I said
screw your uncle Giovanni? How would you like that, huh?

It's all very well for you to talk. All you have to do is throw on some rented tuxedo. *I* on the other hand have to be radiant.

DON'T YOU UNDERSTAND???

God, it's so easy to be a man.

Nad

To: Nadine Wilcock <nadine.wilcock@thenyjournal.com>
From: Mel Fuller <melissa.fuller@thenyjournal.com>
Subject: No big deal

He just couldn't figure out how to work his aunt's electric can opener. He bought Mr. Peepers some actual tuna in order to lure him out from under the bed. It didn't work, of course. I suggested next time he buy tuna in water rather than in oil. I don't know that cats like oil so much.

Anyway, while I was there, he asked which was the best place in the neighborhood to order Chinese from. So I told him, and then he asked if I'd had dinner, and I said no, so he asked if I wanted to order with him, and so I said yes, and we had barbecued spare ribs, cold sesame noodles, moo shu pork, and chicken with broccoli.

And I know what you are going to say now, and no, it was not a date, Nadine. For God's sake, it was only Chinese food. In his aunt's kitchen. With Paco sitting there, waiting for one of us to drop something so he could vacuum it up.

And no, he didn't make a pass at me. Max, I mean, not Paco. Although I don't see how he could resist, seeing as how I'm sure I was quite stunning in my it's-Saturday-night-and-I-don't-have-a-date sweats.

The fact is, Dolly has to be wrong about Max. He's no ladies' man. It was all very casual and friendly. It turns out we have a lot in common. He likes mysteries and so do I, so we talked about our favorite mysteries. You know, he is quite literary, for a photographer. I mean, compared to some of the guys in the art department at work. Can you picture Larry conversing knowingly about Edgar Allan Poe? I don't think so.

Oh, God, a horrible thought just occurred to me: What if all that stuff Dolly said about Max is true, and he IS a ladies' man? What does that mean, seeing as how he didn't make a pass at me?

It can only mean one thing!

Oh, God, I'm hideous!

Mel

To: Mel Fuller <melissa.fuller@thenyjournal.com>
From: Nadine Wilcock <nadine.wilcock@thenyjournal.com>
Subject: Go take a Midol . . .

would you, please? You are not hideous. I'm sure all those things Dolly said about Max Friedlander aren't true. I mean, it's DOLLY, for God's sake. She used to have YOUR job. Only unlike you, she wasn't exactly scrupulous about what she reported. For instance, I sincerely doubt she'd have felt your moral outrage over what Matt Damon did to Winona.

I'm sure Max is a very nice guy, just like you said.

Nad :-)

To: Dolly Vargas <dolly.vargas@thenyjournal.com>
From: Nadine Wilcock <nadine.wilcock@thenyjournal.com>
Subject: Max Friedlander

All right. Spill it. What's the truth about this guy? Because he has basically moved in next door to Mel and she's clearly smitten, despite her protests to the contrary. Is he really as bad as you say, or are you exaggerating, as usual?

And remember: I am the head food critic at the paper. With a single phone call I can make sure you never get into Nobu again, so don't mess with me, Dolly.

Nad

To: jerrylives@freemail.com
From: Jason Trent <jason.trent@trentcapital.com>
Subject: So?

You're not speaking to me now, or what? All I said on the phone was that what you don't know about women would fill the Grand Canyon. What are you so touchy about all of a sudden?

Jason

P.S.: Stacy wants to know if you've asked the redhead out yet.

To: Jason Trent <jason.trent@trentcapital.com>
From: jerrylives@freemail.com
Subject: So?

I am not being touchy. What do you want from me? Not all of us have a personal assistant, a driver, an au pair, a housekeeper, a gardener, a team of pool maintenance workers, a tennis instructor, a nutritionist, and a job our grandfather handed to us on a silver platter, you know. I'm just busy, all right? My God, I've got a full-time job and a Great Dane I have to walk four times a day.

John

P.S.: Tell Stacy I'm working on it.

To: jerrylives@freemail.com
From: Jason Trent <jason.trent@trentcapital.com>
Subject: You ought to seek professional help

Listen, you psychotic freak: Where is this hostility coming from? You know, you could have a job in your grandfather's office if you wanted one. Ditto a personal assistant. I don't know about a team of pool maintenance workers, as, living in the city, you don't have a pool. But everything I've got you could easily have if you would just give up this absurd quest you've embarked on to prove you can get along without Mim's money.

I'll tell you the one thing you really need that you don't have is a psychiatrist, buddy, because you seem to be in grave danger of forgetting something:

You do not have to walk that damn dog four times a day. Why? Because you are not Max Friedlander. Got it?

YOU ARE NOT MAX FRIEDLANDER, no matter what you're telling that poor girl.

Now get over yourself.

Jason

P.S.: Mim wants to know if you are going to the dedication of that new wing we've donated to Sloan-Kettering. If you are, she requests that you wear a tie for a change.

To: Mel Fuller <melissa.fuller@thenyjournal.com>
From: jerrylives@freemail.com
Subject: Hi

It's me. Max Friedlander, I mean. I'm jerrylives@freemail.com. That's a reference to Jerry Garcia. He was the lead singer in the Grateful Dead. In case you didn't know.

How are you? I hope you didn't actually try those leftover cold sesame noodles yesterday. My share congealed overnight into something resembling stucco.

Look, I think some of your dry cleaning got delivered to my aunt's apartment last night instead of yours. At least, I don't think my aunt owns any leopard-print blouses from Banana Republic—or at least, if she does, she unfortunately hasn't had much opportunity to wear them lately—so it must be yours, right? Maybe we could meet later for a dry cleaning exchange.

Oh, and I noticed there's a digitally restored re-release of *Shadow of a Doubt* playing tomorrow night at Film Forum. I know you said that was your favorite Hitchcock. I thought maybe we could catch a seven o'clock showing, if you don't have other plans, then maybe grab something to eat later—preferably not Chinese food. Let me know.

Max Friedlander

P.S.: I've been meaning to tell you, my friends call me John. It's a college thing that sort of stuck.

To: jerrylives@freemail.com
From: Mel Fuller <melissa.fuller@thenyjournal.com>
Subject: Hi back atcha

Sure. The seven o'clock show would be great. We could go to Brother's Barbecue afterward. That's right down the street from Film Forum.

Thanks for rescuing my dry cleaning. Ralph is always getting 15A and B confused. I am forever getting giant bags of Iams dog food delivered to my door. I'll pop by around nine to pick up my shirt, if that's not too late. I have a function to attend after work—an art opening I have to cover for my column. This guy actually does sculptures out of Vaseline. I am not kidding, either. And people actually buy them.

Well, talk to you later.

Mel

P.S.: John is sort of a strange nickname, isn't it?
P.P.S.: You might be surprised to know that I am actually aware of who Jerry Garcia is. In fact, I even saw him in concert once.

To: Nadine Wilcock <nadine.wilcock@thenyjournal.com>
From: Mel Fuller <melissa.fuller@thenyjournal.com>
Subject: OHMYGOD

HE ASKED ME OUT!!!

Well, kind of. It's just a trip to the movies, but that sort of counts, doesn't it?

Here, read this copy of my reply and tell me if I sound too eager.

Mel

To: Nadine Wilcock <nadine.wilcock@thenyjournal.com>
From: Dolly Vargas <dolly.vargas@thenyjournal.com>
Subject: Max Friedlander

Good God, I see what you mean. I haven't seen Mel this excited since she found out about that *Little House on the Prairie* reunion special (remember poor blind Mary? What a sap. I hated her).

Thank God Aaron's on assignment in Botswana and doesn't have to be subjected to the delighted squealing coming from Mel's cubicle. He is still pathetically hung up on that girl. Why Mel would want to throw away a work-in-progress like Aaron for a wretch like Max I can't imagine. I mean, at least Aaron has potential. I have known many women who've tried to change Max, to no avail.

In other words, Nadine, be afraid, be very afraid. Max is everything our mothers warned us about (well, mine would have warned me about boys like Max if she'd ever been home).

Max's modus operandi: very intense until he gets a girl into bed, then he starts backing off. By that time the young lady is usually besotted, and cannot understand why the formerly attentive Max stops calling. Pathetic scenes ensue, in which cries of "Why haven't you called?" and "Who was that woman I saw you with the other night?" are answered with "Stop suffocating me" and "I'm not ready for a commitment." Variations on this theme include: "Can't we just take this one day at a time?" and "I'll call you on Friday. I swear it."

Are you getting the picture?

Oh, and did I tell you about the time Max made all the models on a *Sports Illustrated* swimsuit shoot ice down their nipples because they weren't sticking out enough?

Darling, he'll eat our little Mel up and spit her out.

You didn't really mean what you said about Nobu, did you?

XXXOOO
Dolly

To: Nadine Wilcock <nadine.wilcock@thenyjournal.com>
From: Mel Fuller <melissa.fuller@thenyjournal.com>
Subject: OK, so what do I wear?

Seriously. Last time I saw him I was in sweats, so I want to look really, really good. Come with me at lunch and help me pick out something. I'm thinking this slip dress I saw at Bebe. But do you think that's too slutty for a first date?

Mel

To: Mel Fuller <melissa.fuller@thenyjournal.com>
From: Nadine Wilcock <nadine.wilcock@thenyjournal.com>
Subject: We need to talk

Meet me in the ladies' room in five minutes.

Nad

To: Mel Fuller <melissa.fuller@thenyjournal.com>
cc: Nadine Wilcock <nadine.wilcock@thenyjournal.com>; Dolly
Vargas <dolly.vargas@thenyjournal.com>
From: George Sanchez <george.sanchez@thenyjournal.com>
Subject: Doesn't anybody work here anymore?

Where the hell is everybody? Has it occurred to any of you that we
have a paper to put out?

Dolly, where's that story you were doing on stilettos, silent
killers?

Nadine, I'm still waiting for that review of Bobby Flay's new
place.

Mel, did you or did you not attend last night's premiere of the
new Billy Bob Thornton film? I expected at least a diatribe from
you about what a cad he was to leave the blond chick from _Jurassic Park_ for that creepy girl who has the thing for her brother.

If I don't see some butts in some chairs pretty soon there's not
going to be cake for any of you at Stella's baby shower.

And I really mean it this time.

George

To: Jason Trent <jason.trent@trentcapital.com>
From: John Trent <john.trent@thenychronicle.com>
Subject: Me? Hostile?

You ought to take a look in the mirror, Jase. You are not going pre-
maturely bald because of your genes, bud. I am practically your
genetic double, and not to brag or anything, but I still have a full
head of hair. You have got a lot of pent-up hostility killing off
those follicles. And if you ask me, it's all directed at Mim. It's your
own fault for letting her run your life. See, I broke free, and guess
what? Not a single damn strand on my pillow when I wake up in
the morning.

I am willing to overlook your intense personal insecurities for
the moment in order to inform you that I will not be able to attend
the dedication tomorrow night, as I have alternate plans.

I will elaborate no more, for fear of further fraternal wrath.

I like that, further fraternal wrath. Maybe I'll put that in my
novel.

Fraternally yours, your faithful brother,

John

To: Nadine Wilcock <nadine.wilcock@thenyjournal.com>
cc: Dolly Vargas <dolly.vargas@thenyjournal.com>
From: Mel Fuller <melissa.fuller@thenyjournal.com>
Subject: Chill

You two need to calm down. I am *going out* with the guy, okay? I
am not diving into bed with him. As Aaron can attest, I do not dive
into bed with anybody that easily, all right?

You guys are way overreacting. First of all, Dolly, I don't even believe that nipple story. And Nadine, I am not the emotionally fragile mess you imagine me to be. Okay, I am *concerned* about Winona Ryder, but it is not keeping me up at night. Ditto Laura Dern.

I can take care of myself.

Besides, it's just a movie, for God's sake.

Thanks for caring, though.

Mel

To: Nadine Wilcock <nadine.wilcock@thenyjournal.com>
From: Mel Fuller <melissa.fuller@thenyjournal.com>
Subject: What is going on here?

What was *that* supposed to be? An intervention? I nearly died when I walked into the ladies' room and Dolly was there with YOU. I kept looking around for the fax guy, thinking he was hiding in one of the stalls with a box of condoms and some edible massage oil, and her being there was all just some terrible mistake.

Nadine, I don't care what Dolly says about Max Friedlander. He is nothing like that. Maybe he used to be, but he's changed. I mean, I *know*. I have spent time with the guy. And I've watched him with Paco, and especially with Mr. Peepers (okay, I admit it, so I spied on him through the window. Hey, I'm not proud. But it's the truth). Mr. Peepers hates everybody, but he is really starting to warm up to Max, and I know you can't judge a person by how he or she relates to animals, but I think it says a lot about Max that he has spent so much time getting to know his aunt's pets that even a distrustful and generally antisocial cat like Mr. Peepers is starting to warm up to him.

OK?

And, yeah, maybe my batting average ain't what it ought to be, considering the fact that Aaron was doing Barbara Bellerieve behind my back and I never suspected a thing, but I really don't think Max is just out to get me into bed. Because if what Dolly is saying is true, then Max Friedlander could have anybody. So why would he want me? I am not being self-effacing, either. I mean, why would a guy like that go for a short red-headed gossip columnist when he could have . . . well, Cindy Crawford, if she wasn't happily married to that guy who owns Skybar, or Princess Stephanie of Monaco, or somebody like that?

I mean, seriously, think about it, Nadine.

That's all. I'm not mad or anything. Just hurt, I guess. I mean, I'm not a baby.

Mel

P.S.: You can make it up to me by helping me pick out new shoes at Nine West to go with my new dress.

To: Mel Fuller <melissa.fuller@thenyjournal.com>
From: Nadine Wilcock <nadine.wilcock@thenyjournal.com>
Subject: Fine. Go out with him. See if I care.

But I want a full report the minute you get back. Understand?

And I am warning you, Mel, if this guy breaks your heart and you are mopey for my wedding, I will personally kill both him and you.

Nad :-[

To: John Trent <john.trent@thenychronicle.com>
From: Jason Trent <jason.trent@trentcapital.com>
Subject: What novel?

You're writing a novel now? You've shed the shackles of the family fortune, you're leading a double life, you're trying to solve the mystery behind the old lady's assault, *and* you're writing a novel?

Who do you think you are, anyway? Bruce Wayne?

Jason

To: Jason Trent <jason.trent@trentcapital.com>
From: John Trent <john.trent@thenychronicle.com>
Subject: Batman

Actually, I don't believe Bruce Wayne ever wrote a novel, nor did he shed the shackles of the family fortune. He used his fortune quite extensively, I believe, in his crime-fighting efforts. Although he did, obviously, lead a double life.

As for solving the mystery behind the old lady's assault, Bruce would probably have done a better job than I have so far. I just can't understand it—why would somebody try to bump off a harmless old lady like that? The closest the police have gotten to explaining it is that it was an interrupted robbery—but interrupted how? And by whom?

Mel mentioned something about how the doorman often gets her apartment, 15B, and Mrs. Friedlander's apartment, 15A, mixed up. Which got me thinking about what a cop friend of mine said—

that it almost resembled the work of the transvestite killer, except that the old lady didn't fit the victim profile. I'm kind of wondering if maybe the guy got the wrong apartment . . . if Mrs. Friedlander wasn't his intended victim at all. That once he'd realized his mistake, he tried to go through with it, but couldn't quite do it, and ended up leaving the job undone.

I don't know. It's just something I've been thinking about. I polled the doormen in the building, and none of them remembers sending anyone up to the fifteenth floor that night—although one of them did ask me if I'd gotten my hair cut. Apparently, he'd seen Max before, and while he recognized that I was not quite the genuine article, he couldn't make out just how precisely I had changed in appearance. Frightening how we take our security for granted, isn't it?

Anyway, if you're good, I'll send you the first couple chapters of my opus. It's about a bunch of people who lack any redeeming qualities—kind of like Mim's friends. You'll like it.

Oh, my God, I've got to go. I have to be at Film Forum in fifteen minutes.

John

To: John Trent <john.trent@thenychronicle.com>
From: Jason Trent <jason.trent@trentcapital.com>
Subject: You are unbelievable

Film Forum? *That*'s why you can't be at the dedication? You're going to the *movies*?

The redhead has something to do with this, doesn't she?

Jason

To: Nadine Wilcock <nadine.wilcock@thenyjournal.com>
From: Mel Fuller <melissa.fuller@thenyjournal.com>
Subject: My date-a-logue

18:00
Preparation for my date begins. I put on the stunning little blue dress you helped me pick out. I notice that it looks a little *too* stunning for dinner and a movie. Add a cotton sweater. Mom would be pleased. Remember her adage: You know how cold it can get in movie theaters in the summertime.

Practice walking in new platform mules for half an hour. Only turn my ankle twice. I'm ready as I'll ever be.

18:30
Depart for downtown. Know I must look nice, as I am groped on the 1 train between Times Square and Penn Station. Elbow groper in the midriff. Receive round of applause from fellow straphangers. Groper disembarks, looking shamefaced.

19:00
Arrive outside movie theater. There is a huge line! Scan line nervously for John (did I tell you Max asked me to call him John? It's an old college nickname). Finally spot him at end of line, already holding tickets. My plan to go dutch (therefore making this an outing between friends, and not a date, per your suggestion) instantly ruined! I rally by informing him I will buy popcorn and sodas. You will be pleased to know that John graciously acquiesces to this plan.

19:00–19:20
Stand in line chatting about giant sinkhole that has opened up on 79th Street. You know how I love weather disasters. Well, it turns

out John does, too! This leads to a long conversation about our favorite weather disasters.

19:21
Line begins to move. John goes to find seats. I go to buy popcorn and soda. Realize with dismay I forgot to tell him to get me a seat on the aisle due to absurdly small bladder.

But when I get inside the theater, he has done just that—saved me the aisle seat! Now, really, Nadine, has Tony ever once let you have the aisle seat? No, never, and you know it.

19:30–21:30
Watch movie. Eat popcorn. Notice John can chew and breathe through his nose at the same time. This is a marked improvement over Aaron, who you will recall had a problem with that. I wonder if Dolly has noticed it yet.

Also, John does not look at his watch while the movie is running. This was one of Aaron's most annoying habits. Then I notice that John does not even wear a watch. Definitely an improvement over Aaron, who not only wore one but checked it obsessively every twenty minutes.

21:30–22:00
We walk over to Brothers Barbecue and discover that it, like most popular Manhattan eateries, has been overrun by out-of-towners. There is a two-hour wait for a table. I suggest we go for a slice at Joe's, which as you know has the best pizza in the city. On the way, John tells amusing anecdote about his brother and a drunken midnight pilgrimage to Joe's. I say I did not know he had a brother, and then he says he meant a fraternity brother. This is upsetting: I don't know if I ever told you that after a particularly embarrassing incident back when I was in college, involving a Delta Upsilon and a sock, I vowed never again to date another frat guy.

Then I remembered that this was not a date, but a friendly outing like you suggested, and I was able to relax again.

22:30–24:00

Pizza consumed standing up because there is no place to sit. While we eat, I relate amusing anecdote about how one time I ran into Gwyneth Paltrow at Joe's, and she ordered a slice with veggies and sauce but no cheese! This leads to discussion about my job, and how much I want to write features. It turns out John has been reading Page Ten, and admires my sprightly but pithy style! Those were the words he used! Sprightly! And pithy!

I *am* sprightly and pithy, aren't I?

So then I tried to talk to him about *his* job. I thought I could subtly find out the truth about that whole nipple thing.

But he didn't want to talk about himself at all! He just wanted to know where I went to college, and stuff like that. He kept asking all these questions about Lansing. As if *that's* interesting! Although I did my best to make it interesting. I told him about the time the Hell's Angels came to town, and of course about the tornado that took out the middle school's cafeteria (unfortunately during summer, so we didn't even get out of going to class).

Finally, I ran out of steam and suggested we head home. But on our way to the subway, we passed a bar where live blues was being played! You know I can't resist the blues. I don't know if he saw me looking wistful or what, but he went, "Let's go in."

When I saw there was a $15 cover and two-drink minimum I was, like, "No, we don't have to," but he said he'd buy the drinks if I paid the cover, which I thought was very decent because you know those places charge like ten bucks just for a beer, and so we went in and I got a second wind and had a very fun time and drank beer and ate peanuts and threw the shells on the floor and then the band took a break and we realized it was midnight and we were both, like, "Oh, my God! Paco!"

So we rushed home—we split a cab, which was expensive, but at that time of night was much faster than the subway—and got home before any major accidents or howling had occurred, and I said good night by the elevator, and he said we should do it again sometime, and I said I would love that and that he knows how to reach me, and then I went into my apartment and took a shower to wash all the smoke from the bar out of my hair, and Febrezed my new dress.

You will note that no passes were made (by either party) and that everything was very friendly and aboveboard and mature.

And now I hope you are ashamed of yourself for all the mean things you thought about him because he is really very sweet and funny and wore the nicest jeans I ever saw, not too tight, but not baggy either, with some very interesting faded parts, plus his sleeves were rolled up to just below his elbows—

Uh-oh, here comes George. He's going to kill me because he still wants tomorrow's pages. Gotta go.

Mel

To: Nadine Wilcock <nadine.wilcock@thenyjournal.com>
From: Mel Fuller <melissa.fuller@thenyjournal.com>
Subject: Wait a minute. . . .

why *didn't* he make a pass at me? Oh, my God! I really must be hideous after all!

Mel

To: Jason Trent <jason.trent@trentcapital.com>
From: John Trent <john.trent@thenychronicle.com>
Subject: The redhead has something to do with this, doesn't she?

Well, of *course.*

John

To: Mel Fuller <melissa.fuller@thenyjournal.com>
From: Nadine Wilcock <nadine.wilcock@thenyjournal.com>
Subject: So sue me

Okay. First of all, you are not hideous. Where do you get these things?

Secondly, I am willing to admit when I am wrong, and so I will admit it: I was wrong about the guy.

At least so far.

I do think it's a little weird that he wants you to call him John. I mean, what kind of nickname is *that*? I'll tell you what kind: It's a name, not a nickname.

But whatever. You're right. You're not a baby. You can make your own decisions. You want to sit and listen to the blues and eat peanuts and talk about weather disasters with him? You go right ahead. I will not try to stop you. It really isn't any of my business.

Nad

To: Nadine Wilcock <nadine.wilcock@thenyjournal.com>
From: Mel Fuller <melissa.fuller@thenyjournal.com>
Subject: All right. . . .

what's wrong with you? Since when is anything I do *not* your business? In the five years you and I have known one another, you have poked your nose into every single detail of my life—as I have poked mine into yours. So what's this "It really isn't any of my business" crap?

Is there something going on that you're not telling me about? You and Tony have made up, right? I mean, after that fight you had over what he said at Uncle Giovanni's. Right?

Right?

Nadine, you and Tony can't break up. You are the only couple I know who actually seem happy together.

Except of course for James and Barbra.

Mel

To: Mel Fuller <melissa.fuller@thenyjournal.com>
From: Nadine Wilcock <nadine.wilcock@thenyjournal.com>
Subject: Yes, Tony and I . . .

made up. It's nothing to do with him. At least not directly. It's just that—and I really don't mean this to sound self-pitying or whiny or anything—but the thing is, Mel, I'm just so . . .

FAT!!

I am so fat, and I can't lose any weight, and I'm tired of eating rice cakes, and Tony keeps on bringing home all the leftover bread from the restaurant and making French toast every morning. . . .

I mean, I love Tony, I really do, but the idea of getting up in front of all of his family with my butt the size that it is just makes me want to heave. I am serious.

If only we could elope. . . .

Nad :-(

To: Nadine Wilcock <nadine.wilcock@thenyjournal.com>
From: Mel Fuller <melissa.fuller@thenyjournal.com>
Subject: No!

You can't elope! What am I going to do with that stupid eggplant-colored bridesmaid dress you made me buy if you elope?

Okay, this is it, Nadine. You are forcing me to do this. But I want you to remember, it's for your own good.

Mel

To: Mel Fuller <melissa.fuller@thenyjournal.com>
From: Nadine Wilcock <nadine.wilcock@thenyjournal.com>
Subject: Do what?

Mel, what are you doing? You are making me very nervous. I hate when you get like this.
   And I thought you liked the bridesmaid dresses I picked out.
   Mel???
   MEL???

Nad

To: Amy Jenkins <amy.jenkins@thenyjournal.com>
cc: Nadine Wilcock <nadine.wilcock@thenyjournal.com>
From: Mel Fuller <melissa.fuller@thenyjournal.com>
Subject: Weight loss programs

Dear Ms. Jenkins,
Since you people down in the Human Resources Division are so eager to help us beleaguered correspondents up here in the newsroom, I was wondering if you could let us know if the *New York*

Journal offers its employees discounted membership rates at any of the nearby local gyms.

Please let me know as soon as possible.

Thank you.

Melissa Fuller
Page Ten Correspondent
New York Journal

To: Mel Fuller <melissa.fuller@thenyjournal.com>
From: Nadine Wilcock <nadine.wilcock@thenyjournal.com>
Subject: Have you completely lost your mind?

WHAT DO YOU THINK YOU'RE DOING???
I can't join a gym! I'm depressed, not suicidal!
I'm going to kill you. . . .

Nad

To: jerrylives@freemail.com
From: Mel Fuller <melissa.fuller@thenychronicle.com>
Subject: Talk about a disaster

Hey, did you check out the Weather Channel this morning? Major tropical depressions down in the Bahamas. I think we're looking at an upgrade to tropical storm any day now.

Keep your fingers crossed.

Mel

P.S: Next time you're going up to see your aunt, let me know, and I'll come with you. I heard people in comas can recognize voices, so maybe I could try talking to her. You know, since I used to see her practically every day, and all.

To: John Trent <john.trent@thenychronicle.com>
From: Max Friedlander <photoguy@stopthepresses.com>
Subject: Me

Hi! How's it going? Long time no heard from, huh? Just thought I'd check in. How's my aunt? The old bag croak yet?

Just kidding. I know how sensitive you are about all that, so I won't wax humorous on that subject of old ladies meeting their Maker.

Besides, I love the old harpy. I really do.

Well, things here in Key West are going swimmingly. And I do mean that literally. Viv and I found a nude beach the other day, and all I can say is, John, if you haven't gone skinny-dipping with a bowlegged supermodel, then, son, you haven't lived.

While she's in town having her bikini area waxed (for those occasions when we are required to garb ourselves, such as around the hotel pool) I thought I'd see how things were going with you, pal. You know, you really came through for me in a jam, and I don't want you to think I don't appreciate it.

In fact, I appreciate it so much I am going to offer you some advice. Advice on women, actually, since I know how you are about them. You know, you shouldn't be so standoffish. You really aren't a bad-looking guy. And now that you are, I trust, dressing with a little more class, thanks to my tutelage, I assume you are getting a little more action. It is time, I think, to move on to Max Friedlander's Panoptic Guide to Women.

There are seven types of women. Got that? Seven. No more. No less. That's it. They are as follows:

1. avian
2. bovine
3. canine
4. caprine
5. equine
6. feline
7. porcine

Now, you might get your combinations of certain traits. For instance, you might have a very porcine young lady—hedonistic, gluttonous, etc.—who is also a bit avian—empty-headed, a bit giddy, maybe. I would say the perfect combination would be a girl like Vivica: feline—sexy and independent—while at the same time equine—haughty, yet poetic.

What you don't want is canine—overly dependent—or bovine—speaks for itself. And I'd stay away from caprines—fond of game-playing, and all that.

Well, that's all for today. I hope you've enjoyed your lesson—and that it made sense. I'm drunk off my ass right now, you know.

Max

To: Max Friedlander <photoguy@stopthepresses.com>
From: John Trent <john.trent@thenychronicle.com>
Subject: You

Please don't write to me anymore.

I will walk your aunt's dog and feed your aunt's cats. I will pretend to be you.

But don't write to me anymore. Reading your pathetic ramblings on a subject that you will clearly never, ever come to understand is simply more than I can take at this point in my life.

John

To: jerrylives@freemail.com
From: Jason Trent <jason.trent@trentcapital.com>
Subject: The redhead

Hi, John, it's me, Stacy. Jason refuses to ask, so I will:

How's it going? I mean, with that girl, and pretending to be Max Friedlander, and all of that?

Let me know!

Love,
Stacy

P.S.: We missed you at the dedication. You should have been there. Your grandmother was very hurt, as were the girls. They've really been bugging me about whether or not you're ever coming to visit us again.

Are you?

To: Jason Trent <jason.trent@trentcapital.com>
From: jerrylives@freemail.com
Subject: How it's going?

How is it going? You ask how it's going, Stacy?

Well, I'll tell you: It's going awful, thanks.

That's right. Awful. Everything is terrible.

Everything shouldn't be terrible, of course. Everything should be wonderful. I've met this *completely* terrific girl. I mean *completely* terrific, Stace: She likes tornadoes and the blues, beer, and anything to do with serial killers. She eats up celebrity gossip with as much enthusiasm as she attacks a plate of moo shu pork, wears shoes with heels that are way too high and looks fabulous in them—but manages to look just as fabulous in Keds and a pair of sweatpants.

And she's *nice*. I mean, really, truly, genuinely kind. In a city where no one knows his neighbors, she not only knows hers, but actually *cares* about them. And she lives in *Manhattan*. Manhattan, where people routinely step over the homeless in an effort to get into their favorite restaurants. As far as Mel seems to be concerned, she never left Lansing, Illinois, population 13,000. Broadway might as well be Main Street.

And get this: We went out the other night, and she wouldn't let me pay for her. Yes, you read that correctly: *She wouldn't let me pay for her.* You should have seen her face when she realized I had already bought the tickets for the movie: You'd have thought I'd killed a puppy or something. No woman I have ever gone out with (and, contrary to what my brother might have told you, there have not been all that many) has ever paid for her own movie ticket—or anything else, for that matter, when she was out with me.

Not that I ever minded paying. It's just that none of them ever even *offered*.

And, yeah, okay, they all knew they were out with John Trent, of the Park Avenue Trents. How much am I worth today? Have you been keeping an eye on the NASDAQ?

But they never even *offered*.

Are you getting this so far, Stace? After all the Heathers and Courtneys and Meghans (My God, remember Meghan? And the disastrous Texas dip?) and all those Ashleys, I've finally met a Mel, who wouldn't know an IPO from an IOU, a woman who might potentially be more interested in me than in my investment portfolio. . . .

And I can't even tell her my real name.

No, she thinks I'm Max Friedlander.

Max Friedlander, whose brain, I'm beginning to be convinced, atrophied at around the age of sixteen. Max Friedlander, who has categorized a panoply of female character traits that I am convinced he derived from Saturday morning Hanna-Barbera cartoons.

I know what you're going to say. I know exactly what you're going to say, Stace.

And the answer is no, I can't. Maybe if I'd never lied to her about it in the first place. Maybe if right from the first moment I met her I'd said, "Listen, I am not Max. Max couldn't make it. He feels really bad about what happened to his aunt, so he sent me in his place."

But I didn't, all right? I blew it. I blew it from the very beginning.

And now it's too late to tell her the truth, because anything else I ever try to tell her, she'll think I'm lying about that, too. Maybe she won't admit it. But in the back of her mind, it will always be there. "Maybe he's lying about this, too."

Don't try to tell me she won't, either, Stace.

And now she wants to go with me to visit Max's aunt. Can you believe that? The comatose aunt! She says she's read that people in comas can sometimes hear what's going on around them, even recognize voices.

Well, Aunt Helen sure as hell won't recognize my voice, will she?

So there you have it. My hellish life, in a nutshell. Got any advice? Any sage words of womanly wisdom to throw my way?

No, I didn't think so. I am perfectly aware of the fact that I've dug this grave myself. I guess I have no choice but to lie down in it.

Cadaverously yours,
John

To: Mel Fuller <melissa.fuller@thenyjournal.com>
From: Dolly Vargas <dolly.vargas@thenyjournal.com>
Subject: Max Friedlander

Darling, I couldn't help overhearing your little conversation with
Nadine near the fax machine—is it true the two of you have joined
a gym and are starting spinning classes?

   Well, bully for you both! I say more power to you. Let me know
if they have bleachers or an observation booth or something where
I can go and sit and cheer you on (and if they provide refresh-
ments, preferably of the alcoholic variety, which is the only way
you'll ever get *me* in a gym, by God).

   Anyway, about that other thing I heard you mention. Do you
want to know why he didn't make a pass at you? Max Friedlander,
I mean. If you think about it, it all makes sense. . . . I mean, the stories we've heard about his ruthless *womanizing* despite his fear of
commitment, his obsession with getting just the right shot of whatever particular subject he is photographing, his constant need for
approval, his refusal to settle down in one place, and now this
freakish name-change thing?

   Really, it all might boil down to one little thing:

   He's gay.

   It's perfectly obvious, darling. That's why he didn't make a pass
at you.

XXXOOO

Dolly

To: Mel Fuller <melissa.fuller@thenyjournal.com>
From: Nadine Wilcock <nadine.wilcock@thenyjournal.com>
Subject: Calm down

He is not gay. All right? That is just Dolly. She is messing with your
head. She's bored. Peter Hargrave won't leave his wife for her,
Aaron is still mooning over you, and Dolly has nothing better to
do than torture you. You are just playing right into her hands by
getting all upset like this.

Now, are we going to the noon or the five-thirty class tomorrow?

Nad

P.S.: I don't have to tell you how much I hate this, right? This exercise thing? I mean, in case you didn't know. I hate it. I really hate
sweating. It's not natural. It really isn't.

To: Nadine Wilcock <nadine.wilcock@thenyjournal.com>
From: Mel Fuller <melissa.fuller@thenyjournal.com>
Subject: But that would explain . . .

why he didn't try to kiss me, or put his arm around me, or anything! He's gay!

And I offered to go with him next time he goes up to the hospital to visit his aunt.

I must seem like the biggest nagging idiot in the world!

Mel

P.S.: Let's go to the noon class so we can get it over with. I know you hate it, Nadine, but it's good for you. And sweating *is* natural. People have been doing it for many thousands of years.

To: Mel Fuller <melissa.fuller@thenyjournal.com>
From: Nadine Wilcock <nadine.wilcock@thenyjournal.com>
Subject: Are you . . .

suffering from a synaptic breakdown?

First of all, he's not gay.

Secondly, even if he was gay, your saying you want to go with him to see his comatose aunt is hardly nagging. It's actually very nice.

I told you not to listen to Dolly.

Remember the chenille bedspread? Remember when you saw him feeding the dog Alpo right there on the bed? Would a gay man *ever* do that to chenille?

Nad

To: Nadine Wilcock <nadine.wilcock@thenyjournal.com>
From: Mel Fuller <melissa.fuller@thenyjournal.com>
Subject: Oh

Yes. You're right. No gay man would ever abuse chenille in such a manner.

Thank God I have you in my life, Nadine.

Mel

P.S.: But if he isn't gay, how come he hasn't written back? I e-mailed him ages ago about some tropical depressions, and since then they've already been upgraded to storms!

To: jerrylives@freemail.com
From: Jason Trent <jason.trent@trentcapital.com>
Subject: Oh for God's sake . . .

Just call the girl, would you? While you're sitting around beating yourself up, some other man could be stealing her out from under your nose!

Don't worry, the Max Friedlander stuff will work itself out. You wouldn't believe some of the lies Jason told me when we first started going out . . . foremost of which was that he went out once with Jody Foster. He just didn't mention that it was when she happened to be on the same ferry he was taking to Catalina.

Yeah, he "went out" with her, all right.

Oh, and your grandmother showed me a picture of this Michelle girl, whom your brother insists was the most beautiful woman he has ever known: Hello, somebody call the pound, I think there's a pit bull on the loose—

And here comes Jason, he's screaming something about grilled cheese and why don't I get my own e-mail account, and why must I keep pillaging his, and now he's trying to shove me out of his chair, even though I am seven months pregnant with his unborn son, not to mention the mother of his daughters.

Stacy

To: jerrylives@freemail.com
From: Jason Trent <jason.trent@trentcapital.com>
Subject: Go away

I just want you to know that while you are burdening my wife with your half-assed problems—all of which, by the way, are of your own making—everything here is going to pieces. I just had to make the girls their lunch and the cheese dripped out into the toaster oven all over everything and started a fire.

So all I have to say to you is get your own wife already and stop bothering mine.

Jason

To: jerrylives@freemail.com
From: Jason Trent <jason.trent@trentcapital.com>
Subject: HI, UNCLE JOHN

IT'S US, HALEY AND BRITTANY. MOMMY AND DADDY ARE HAVING A BIG FIGHT OVER WHAT YOU SHOULD DO ABOUT THE REDHEADED LADY. MOMMY SAYS YOU SHOULD CALL

HER UP AND ASK HER OUT TO DINNER. DADDY SAYS YOU
SHOULD GET THERAPY.

IF YOU MARRY THE REDHEADED LADY, WILL SHE BE
OUR AUNT?

WHEN ARE YOU COMING TO SEE US? WE MISS YOU. WE
HAVE BEEN VERY GOOD. EVERY TIME THAT VEIN IN
DADDY'S HEAD STARTS TO TURN PURPLE WE SING THAT
SONG YOU TAUGHT US, JUST LIKE YOU SAID TO. YOU KNOW
WHICH SONG. THE ONE ABOUT DIARRHEA.

WELL, WE HAVE TO GO. DADDY SAYS TO GET OFF HIS
DESK.

WRITE SOON!!!

LOVE,
BRITTANY AND HALEY

To: Mel Fuller <melissa.fuller@thenyjournal.com>
From: jerrylives@freemail.com
Subject: Baseball-sized hail, and other weather anomalies

Dear Melissa,
Sorry it took me so long to get back to you. I had some business
that needed tending to. But it looks like it's all more or less in order
now—at least, as much as it can be for the moment.

It's sweet of you to offer to visit my aunt with me, but you
really don't have to.

Wait. Stop. I know what you're going to say.

So to cut you off at the pass, might I suggest that we do it
tomorrow evening, if you don't already have plans?

And I think I will take this opportunity to discuss something
that has been weighing somewhat heavily on my conscience ever
since we met: the great debt I owe you for saving my aunt's life.

Stop. Again, I know what you're going to say. But the fact of the matter is, you did exactly that. The police told me so.

So although it is rather an inadequate means of expressing my immense gratitude and appreciation for what you did, I was hoping that you'd let me take you out to dinner some night. And since I know how deeply this will offend your Midwestern sensibilities, I am prepared to let you pick the restaurant, lest you worry that I might choose a place destined to bankrupt me.

Think it over and let me know. As you are aware, my evenings are, thanks to Paco, quite free until eleven.

Sincerely,
John

P.S.: Did you see that thing on the Weather Channel last night? Why is it that people who attempt to drive through flash-flood-swollen rivers in their SUVs always end up being people who don't know how to swim?

To: Nadine Wilcock <nadine.wilcock@thenyjournal.com>
From: Mel Fuller <melissa.fuller@thenyjournal.com>
Subject: He wrote back!

And he asked me out.

Well, sort of. I guess it's more of a pity/thank you thing than an actual date.

But maybe if I get just the right dress . . .

You're the restaurant expert. Which one should I pick?

Mel

To: Mel Fuller <melissa.fuller@thenyjournal.com>
From: Nadine Wilcock <nadine.wilcock@thenyjournal.com>
Subject: You aren't going to . . .

be able to pay your rent next month if you keep buying outfits to impress this guy.

I have an idea. Wear something you already own. He can't have seen everything you own already. He only moved in a couple of weeks ago, and I know you have ten million skirts.

Here's another idea: Why don't the two of you come to Fresche? That way, Tony and I can get a look at him and let you know what we think.

Just a thought.

Nad

To: Nadine Wilcock <nadine.wilcock@thenyjournal.com>
From: Mel Fuller <melissa.fuller@thenyjournal.com>
Subject: Ha!

What do you think I am, stupid? We aren't going anywhere near Fresche. Not in a million years.

Mel

To: Mel Fuller <melissa.fuller@thenyjournal.com>
From: Tony Salerno <foodie@fresche.com>
Subject: So we're not good enough for you, huh?

I guess when it comes to fine dining, you really know who your friends are. I mean, evidently, you have some kind of prejudice against my restaurant that I never knew about before now.

And yet whenever I've offered to grill you up some of my classic chicken paillard, you've never turned me down. Could it be that all this time, you've merely been humoring me?

What about Nadine? She's not really your best friend, is she? You probably have some fancy other best friend tucked away for emergencies, don't you?

It's all becoming clear now.

Tony

To: Tony Salerno <foodie@fresche.com>
From: Mel Fuller <melissa.fuller@thenyjournal.com>
Subject: You know good and well

why I don't want to go to your restaurant. I don't care to be gawked at by my best friend and her boyfriend!

And you know it.

You are really insufferable, you know that? It's a good thing you're such a good cook—and so good-looking, too, of course.

Mel ;-)

To: Mel Fuller <melissa.fuller@thenyjournal.com>
From: Dolly Vargas <dolly.vargas@thenyjournal.com>
Subject: Dinner

Darling, are you mad? You have simply got to make him take you to La Grenouille. There just isn't anywhere else worthwhile.

And it isn't as if he can't afford it. My God, Max Friedlander made a fortune photographing that Vivica creature for that new Maybelline print campaign.

After all, you did give that woman first aid. For that he owes you something from Tiffany's, or Cartier, at the very least.

XXXOOO

Dolly

To: Mel Fuller <melissa.fuller@thenyjournal.com>
From: George Sanchez <george.sanchez@thenyjournal.com>
Subject: Corner bistro

That's where you make the guy take you. Best burgers in the city. Plus you can watch the game while you eat.

George

To: Mel Fuller <melissa.fuller@thenyjournal.com>
From: Jimmy Chu <james.chu@thenyjournal.com>
Subject: How can you even

think of going anywhere but Peking Duck House? You know it's
the best Peking duck in the city.

Jim

To: Mel Fuller <melissa.fuller@thenyjournal.com>
From: Tim Grabowski <timothy.grabowski@thenyjournal.com>
Subject: Gaydar

Nadine passed me your friend John's latest e-mail, which I guess
you forwarded to her, and I can say unequivocally, speaking as a
homosexual, that this man is straight. No gay man I know would
ever let a woman choose the restaurant, even if she did save his
aunt's life.

Make him take you to Fresche. Nadine and I and the rest of the
gang are going to sit at the bar and pretend we don't know you.
Puh-lease make him take you to Fresche. . . .

Y'all have a nice time and be sure to practice safe sex, you
hear?

Tim

To: Nadine Wilcock <nadine.wilcock@thenyjournal.com>
From: Mel Fuller <melissa.fuller@thenyjournal.com>
Subject: For the love of God . . .

would you please stop telling everyone who works here about my personal life? It is so humiliating! Tim Grabowski from Programming just e-mailed me. And if Programming knows, you know it's only a matter of time before it gets down to Art. And what if somebody in Art knows Max Friedlander, and tells him how everybody in Features is talking about him?

I mean, my God, what are you trying to do?

Mel

To: Dolly Vargas <dolly.vargas@thenyjournal.com>; Tony Salerno <foodie@fresche.com>; Tim Grabowski <timothy.grabowski@thenyjournal.com>; George Sanchez <george.sanchez@thenyjournal.com>; Jimmy Chu <james.chu@thenyjournal.com>
From: Nadine Wilcock <nadine.wilcock@thenyjournal.com>
Subject: Mel

All right everybody, lay off her. We're just making her nervous.

I really mean that, Dolly, so don't even think about another ladies' room ambush.

Nad

P.S.: Besides, you know she can't keep a secret to save her life. She'll blab about where they're going eventually, and then we'll have her. ;-)

To: jerrylives@freemail.com
From: Mel Fuller <melissa.fuller@thenyjournal.com>
Subject: Dinner

Dear John,
Hi! It's really sweet of you to offer to take me to dinner, but you really don't have to.
I was happy to do what I did for your aunt. I only wish I could have done more.

But if you really insist, I honestly don't care where we go to dinner.

Well, that's not true, there is one place I really DON'T want to go, and that's Fresche. Anywhere else is fine. Why don't you surprise me?

See you back on the fifteenth floor tonight at six (ICU visiting hours are only from six-thirty to seven)?

Mel

To: Mel Fuller <melissa.fuller@thenyjournal.com>
From: jerrylives@freemail.com
Subject: Dinner

You got it.
I'll make reservations for eight. I hope you know what you're doing, however, letting me choose the restaurant. I am very partial to entrails, you know.

John

To: jerrylives@freemail.com
From: Mel Fuller <melissa.fuller@thenyjournal.com>
Subject: I don't believe you

You're just trying to scare me.

I grew up on a farm. We had entrails on toast every morning for breakfast.

Mel

To: Mel Fuller <melissa.fuller@thenyjournal.com>
From: jerrylives@freemail.com
Subject: Now you're

scaring me.

See you at six.

John

To: John Trent <john.trent@thenychronicle.com>
From: Sergeant Paul Reese <preese@eightyninthprecinct.nyc.org>
Subject: Last night

Trent—

Look, man, I can't apologize enough. I don't know what's going on between you and the redheaded broad, but I didn't mean to blow it. I was just so surprised to see you there! I mean, John Trent, at the Animal Medical Center? What kind of crime could he be following up on? Certainly one of a fowl nature. . . .

Sorry. Couldn't resist.

Seriously, we were just there to check on Hugo, the precinct's bomb-sniffing pooch. Some clown fed him a bunch of KFC left over from lunch, and you know what they say about dogs and chicken bones. . . .

Well, it turns out to be true. Although Hugo is expected to make a full recovery.

What *were* you doing there, man? You looked strung out. Well, for a guy with a hot babe like that on his arm.

Let me know if there's anything I can do to make up for it. . . . Fix some parking tickets, maybe? Have the redhead's husband held without bail for the weekend. Whatever.

Anything, anything to make it right again.

Paul

To: Sergeant Paul Reese <preese@eightyninthprecinct.nyc.org>
From: John Trent <john.trent@thenychronicle.com>
Subject: All is forgiven

At least now. Last night, I easily could have throttled you.

Not that it was in any way your fault. I mean, you saw me. You said, "How's it going, Trent?" as any normal person would.

How were you to know I am currently living under an assumed name?

But what started out as the most disastrous evening of all time—who knew cats eat rubber bands? I certainly didn't—turned out to be pure bliss.

So consider yourself forgiven, my friend.

And as for the redhead, well, it's a long story. Maybe I'll even tell it to you someday. Depending on how it turns out, of course.

Right now, it's back to the Animal Medical Center for me. I have to bail out the cat, who has supposedly recovered nicely from his intestinal surgery. And on the way home from the animal hospital, I am going to buy that cat the biggest, smelliest fish you ever saw, as a thank-you for his kind thoughtfulness in ingesting that rubber band.

John

To: Mel Fuller <melissa.fuller@thenyjournal.com>
From: Nadine Wilcock <nadine.wilcock@thenyjournal.com>
Subject: Well???

What did you wear? Where did you end up going? Did you have fun?
    WHAT HAPPENED???

Nad

To: Nadine Wilcock <nadine.wilcock@thenyjournal.com>
From: Mel Fuller <melissa.fuller@thenyjournal.com>
Subject: It happened

>What did you wear?

I wore my short black Calvin Klein wraparound skirt, with my V-necked light-blue three-quarter-sleeve silk sweater and matching blue ankle-strap sandals with the three-inch heel.

>Where did you end up going?

We didn't end up going anywhere. Not for dinner, anyway.

>Did you have fun?

YES.

>WHAT HAPPENED???

It did.

Okay, well, not really, but almost. What happened was, I was just applying my final layer of lipstick when there was a knock on my door. I went to answer it. It was John. He actually had on a tie! I couldn't believe it. He looked great—only really worried. So I was all, "What's wrong?"

And he went, "It's Tweedledum. Something's the matter with him. Would you mind coming to take a look?"

So I went and took a look, and sure enough, Tweedledum, who is quite the more active and affectionate of Mrs. Friedlander's two cats, was lying underneath the dining room table looking like a little kid who had eaten too many of those Necco Wafers. He didn't want anybody touching him, and growled when I tried to.

Anyway, I suddenly remembered something, and I went, "Oh, my God, have you been removing the rubber bands from around the *Chronicle*s when you bring them in?" Because you know the *Chronicle* thinks so well of itself that it always comes bound in a rubber band, to keep the sections from falling out, since its customers would freak out if one single part was missing and they happened not to get their financial news or whatever.

And John went, "No. Am I supposed to?"

And that's when I realized I had forgotten to tell him the most important thing about cat- and dog-sitting for his aunt: Tweedledum eats rubber bands. So did his brother, Tweedledee. Which is why Tweedledee is no longer with us.

"We've got to get this cat to the hospital right away!" I cried.

John looked stunned. "You're kidding, right?"

"No, I'm serious." I went and got the cat carrier down from where Mrs. Friedlander has always kept it, on the top shelf of her linen closet. "Wrap him in a towel."

John just kept standing there. "You're actually serious."

"I am totally serious," I said. "We have to get the rubber band removed before it blocks something."

Actually, I have no idea if a rubber band could block something, but you could tell just by looking at Tweedledum's glazed eyes that he was one sick animal.

So John got a towel and we bundled Tweedledum up (John sustained several evil-looking scratches before he accomplished this) and took him to the Animal Medical Center, which is where I know Mrs. Friedlander took Tweedledee when he had his fatal encounter with the rubber band off a copy of the *Chronicle*. I know because she asked mourners to send them a donation in lieu of flowers after Tweedledee's demise.

The minute we walked in, they took Tweedledum and rushed him off to X-ray. Then there was nothing we could do but wait and pray.

But it was kind of hard to sit and pray, you know, when all I could think about was how much I hate the *Chronicle*, and here it was, ruining my big date. At least, I thought it might have been a date. I just kept thinking about how the *Chronicle* is always scooping us, and how they get to have their Christmas party at the Water Club, and ours is always at Bowlmore Lanes. And how their circulation is like a hundred thousand more than ours, and how they always win all the journalism awards, and their style section is in color, and they don't even have a gossip page.

Well, it just started making me laugh. I don't know why. But I just started laughing about how once again the *Chronicle* had managed to ruin something for me.

Then John asked me why I was laughing, and so I told him (not the part about how the *Chronicle* had ruined our date, but the rest of it).

So then John started laughing, too. I don't know why *he* was laughing, except, well, he doesn't exactly strike me as the praying type. He kept laughing in these little bursts. You could tell he was trying not to, but sometimes it would come out.

Meanwhile the weirdest people kept coming in, with the strangest emergencies! Like one lady was there because her golden retriever had eaten all of her Prozac. Another one was there because her iguana had taken a flying leap from her seventh-story balcony (and landed seemingly unscathed on the roof of the deli below). A third lady was worried about her hedgehog, which just "wasn't acting right."

"How," John whispered to me, "is a hedgehog supposed to act?"

It really wasn't funny. Only then we *really* couldn't stop laughing. And everyone was giving us these mean looks, and that just made me laugh harder. So we were sitting there, the dressiest people in the place, pretending to be comfortable in these hard plastic chairs and trying not to laugh, but doing it anyway. . . .

At least until all these cops came in. They were there to check on one of their bomb squad dogs, which had choked on a chicken bone. One of them saw John and went, "Hey, Trent, what are *you* doing here?"

That's when John stopped laughing. He got very red all of a sudden and went, "Oh, hi, Sergeant Reese."

He put a very hard stress on the word Sergeant. Sergeant Reese looked quite taken aback. He started to say something, but right then the veterinarian came out and called, "Mr. Friedlander?"

John jumped up and said, "That's me," and rushed up to the vet.

The vet told us that Tweedledum had, indeed, swallowed a rubber band, and that it was tangled in his small intestine, and that surgery would be necessary or the cat would definitely die. They were willing to do the surgery at once, only it was very costly, $1,500 dollars, plus $200 for the overnight stay at the hospital.

$1,700! I was shocked. But John just nodded and reached for his wallet and started to pull out a credit card. . . .

And then he put it away really fast and said he forgot, all his credit cards were maxed out, and that he would just go to the bank machine and get cash.

Cash! He was going to pay in cash! $1,700 in cash! For a cat!

Only I reminded him that you can't get that much cash from a bank machine in a single day. I said, "Let me put it on my credit card, and you can pay me back later." (I know what you're going to say, Nadine, but it isn't true: He would have paid me back, I know it.)

But he absolutely refused. And next thing I knew, he'd gone over to the cashier to arrange a payment plan, leaving me alone with the vet and all of the cops, who were still standing around staring at me. Don't ask me why. Undoubtedly my too-short skirt was to blame.

Then John came back and said it was all taken care of, and the cops left, and the vet suggested we stay until the surgery was over, just in case there were complications, so we went back to our seats and I went, "Why did that policeman call you Trent?"

And John went, "Oh, that's just how cops are, they always make up their own nicknames for people."

But I definitely got the feeling there was something he wasn't telling me.

He must have realized it, too, since he told me I didn't have to stick around and wait with him, that he'd pay for a cab home for me, and that he hoped I'd take a raincheck on dinner.

So I asked him if he was crazy, and he said he did not believe so, and I said anyone with as many nicknames as he has definitely has some major problems, and he agreed with me, and then we argued pleasantly for about two hours over which serial killers throughout history were the most deranged, and finally the vet came out and said Tweedledum was recovering and we could go home, and so we left.

It wasn't too late to get dinner by Manhattan standards—only ten o'clock—and John was all for it, even though we'd missed our reservation at wherever he'd planned on taking me. But I wasn't up for battling the late-night supper crowd, and he agreed and said, "Want to order Chinese again or something?" And I said it would probably be a good idea to comfort Paco and Mr. Peepers, who were surely unsettled by their missing feline brother. Plus I had read in the *TV Guide* that *The Thin Man* was showing on PBS.

So we went back to his place—or his aunt's place, I should say—and ordered moo shu pork again, and the food arrived just as the movie was starting, and so we ate it off Mrs. Friedlander's coffee table, sitting on her comfy black leather couch, on which I dropped not one but two spring rolls smothered with that orange stuff.

Which was, incidentally, when he started kissing me. Seriously. I was totally apologizing for getting that sticky orange stuff all over his aunt's couch when he leaned over, *stuck his knee in it*, and started kissing me.

I haven't been that shocked since my algebra tutor did almost the same thing my freshman year in high school. Only there wasn't any orange stuff and we'd been talking about integers, not paper towels.

And let me tell you, Max Friedlander is a way better kisser than any algebra tutor ever was. I mean, he has got the kissing thing down pat. I was afraid the top of my head was going to blow off. Seriously. He's *that* good of a kisser.

Or maybe he isn't that good of a kisser. Maybe it's just been so long since anybody has kissed me like he meant it—you know, *really* meant it—that I forgot what kissing is like.

John kisses like he means it. *Really* means it.

Still, when he stopped kissing me, I was in such a state of head-spinning shock that all I could do was blurt out, "What did you do *that* for?" which probably sounded rude, but he didn't take it that way. He went, "Because I wanted to."

So I thought about that for, like, a split second, and then I reached up and put my arms around his neck and said, "Good."

Then I did some kissing of my own. And it was really nice because Mrs. Friedlander's couch is very cushy and soft, and John kind of sank down onto me and I kind of sank down into the couch, and we kissed for a very long time. In fact we kissed until Paco decided he needed to go out, and stuck his big wet nose between our foreheads.

That's when I realized I better get out of there. First of all, you know what our mothers always said about kissing before the third date. And second of all, not to gross you out, but there was some very interesting stuff happening downstairs, if you know what I mean.

And Max Friedlander is definitely NOT gay. Gay guys do not get full-on stiffies from kissing girls. This much even a small-town girl from the Midwest knows.

So, while John was cursing Paco out, I was straightening myself out and saying primly, "Well, thank you for the lovely evening, but I think I have to go now," and then I tore out of there, while he was still going, "Mel, wait, we have to talk."

I didn't wait. I couldn't. I had to get out while I still had control over my motor functions. I am telling you, Nadine, this guy's kisses are enough to numb your brain stem, they're that good.

So what's to talk about?

Well, there's one thing: Nadine, I'm letting you know right now. I am bringing a date to your wedding.

Gotta go. Fingers are cramping up from writing too much, and I still have tomorrow's column to do. Things are looking up for Winona and Chris Noth. I hear a vacation in Bali is in the works. I can't believe Winona and I have both found guys at the same time! It's like when she and Gwyneth were going out with Matt and Ben—only better! Because it's me!

Mel

To: Mel Fuller <melissa.fuller@thenyjournal.com>
From: Nadine Wilcock <nadine.wilcock@thenyjournal.com>
Subject: I hope at the very least

you let him pay for the Chinese food.

Nad

To: Nadine Wilcock <nadine.wilcock@thenyjournal.com>
From: Mel Fuller <melissa.fuller@thenyjournal.com>
Subject: Well of course he

paid for the Chinese food. Well, except the tip. He didn't have any singles.

Why are you being this way? I had a great time. I thought it was sweet.

And it's not like I let him feel me up or anything, for God's sake.

Mel

To: Mel Fuller <melissa.fuller@thenyjournal.com>
From: Nadine Wilcock <nadine.wilcock@thenyjournal.com>
Subject: I just think

that this is all happening too fast. I've never even met this guy. No offense, Mel, but you do not have the greatest track record where men are concerned—Aaron being only example number one. I mean, what about that Delta Upsilon and the sock thing, which you yourself mentioned only the other day?

I'm just saying I might feel more comfortable about all of this if I had actually met the guy. We've heard some pretty sketchy things about him from Dolly, after all. How do you expect me to feel? You are like the baby sister I never had. I just want to make sure you don't get hurt.

So could you get him to come over to pick you up for lunch or something one of these days? I'd be more than willing to forgo spinning class. . . .

Don't hate me.

Nad

To: Nadine Wilcock <nadine.wilcock@thenyjournal.com>
From: Mel Fuller <melissa.fuller@thenyjournal.com>
Subject: You are such

a mother hen.

But, yes, if you insist, I suppose I could arrange for the two of you to bump into one another somehow.

God, the things we do for our friends.

Mel

To: John Trent <john.trent@thenychronicle.com>
From: Genevieve Randolph Trent<grtrent@trentcapital.com>
Subject: Your recent behavior

Dear John,

This is your grandmother speaking. Or should I say writing. I suppose you will be surprised to hear from me in this manner. I have chosen this venue, the e-mail, with which to correspond, because you have not returned a single one of my telephone calls, and your brother, Jason, assures me that while you may not check your answering machine, you actually do occasionally answer e-mail messages.

Therefore, to business:

I can forgive the fact that you have chosen to throw caution to the wind and embark on your own career in a field that, frankly, no respectable Trent—or Randolph, either, for that matter—would ever consider. You have proven to me that not all news reporters are vermin.

And I can forgive the fact that you chose to move out of the building and live on your own, first in that hellhole on 37th with that hairy lunatic, and then where you currently reside, in Brooklyn, which I'm told is the most charming of the five boroughs, aside from the occasional race riot and collapsing supermarket.

And I can even forgive you for choosing not to touch any of the money that has been held in trust for you since your grandfather's death. A man should make his own way in the world, if at all possible, and not depend upon his family for his means. I applaud your effort to do just that. It is far more than any of my other grandchildren have done. Look at your cousin Dickie. I'm certain if that boy had a vocation like you do, John, he would not spend half so much time putting things up his nose that have no business being there.

But what I simply cannot forgive you for is missing the dedication the other night. You know how much my benefits mean to me. This cancer wing I've donated is particularly important to me, as you know that cancer was what took your beloved grandfather from me. I understand that you might have had a previous commitment, but you could, at least, have had the courtesy to have sent a note.

I will not lie to you, John. I most particularly wanted you at this event because there is a certain young lady I was very anxious for you to know. I know, I know how you feel about my introducing you to my friends' eligible daughters. But Victoria Arbuthnot, whom I am sure you will remember from your childhood summers on the Vineyard—the Arbuthnots had that place in Chilmark—has grown into quite an attractive young lady—she has even overcome that horrible chin problem that has plagued so many of the Arbuthnots.

And she is, from what I understand, a real go-getter in the investment market. Since career-minded women have always appealed to you, I made an effort to ensure Victoria would be at the dedication the other night.

What a fool you made me look, John! I had to pawn Victoria off on your cousin Bill. And you know how I feel about *him*.

I know you pride yourself on being the black sheep of the family, John—though what is supposed to be so enraging about a man who works for a living, doing what it is he actually likes to do, I cannot imagine. Your cousins, with their various addictions and unsuitable pregnancies, are far more maddening.

However, this type of behavior really is quite bewildering, even for you. All I can say is that I hope you have a very good explanation. Furthermore, I hope you will take the time to respond to this letter. It is very rude of you not to have returned my calls.

Yours, in spite of that,

Mim

To: Genevieve Randolph Trent <grtrent@trentcapital.com>
From: John Trent <john.trent@thenychronicle.com>
Subject: Forgive me?

Mim—
What can I say? You have made me thoroughly ashamed of myself. It was unconscionable of me not to return your calls. My only

explanation is that I have not been checking my answering machine as assiduously as I used to, due to the fact that, recently, I have been staying in the apartment of a friend. Well, not my friend, really—my friend's aunt, to be exact, who has been hospitalized, and needed someone to care for her pets.

Although after what happened to one of her cats recently, I am not convinced I am the person most suited for the job.

Anyway, I want you to know that I did not fail to attend the dedication out of any sort of disdain for you or for the event. I just had something else to do. Something very important.

Which reminds me: Vickie Arbuthnot better not be holding her breath waiting for me, Mim. I've actually met someone.

And no, it isn't anyone you know, unless you are familiar with the Fullers of Lansing, Illinois. Which I suspect you are not.

I know. I know. After the Heather debacle, you'd given up on me for good. Well, it takes a lot more to keep a man like me down than finding out a girl I hadn't proposed to yet had already registered at Bloomingdale's as the future Mrs. John Trent (and for $1,000 sheets, no less).

But before you start clamoring to meet her, allow me to work out a few slight . . . kinks. No romantic relationship in New York City is ever simple, but this one is even more complicated than most.

I am confident, however, that I can work it out. I *have* to work it out.

I just don't have the slightest idea how I'm going to manage it.

Anyway, with many loving apologies, I hope you'll still consider me sincerely

Your John

P.S.: To make it up to you, I'll be at the Lincoln Center Benefit to Raise Cancer Awareness next week, since I know you're its biggest supporter. I'll even tap into the old trust fund and write a check with a guaranteed four zeros. Will that help soothe your ruffled feathers?

To: Mel Fuller <melissa.fuller@thenyjournal
From: Don and Beverly Fuller <DonBev@dnr.com>
Subject: Look out!

Hi, honey, it's Mommy again, writing you on the e-mail. I hope you are being careful because I saw last night on Tom Brokaw that *another* one of those awful sinkholes has opened up in Manhattan. This one is right in front of a newspaper, no less!

Don't worry, though, it is that newspaper you hate, the snooty one. Still, think about it, sweetie, that could have been you sitting in that taxi that fell into that twenty-foot-deep hole! Except I know you never take taxis because you spend all your money on clothes.

But that poor lady! Why, it took three firemen to pull her out (you are so tiny, it would only take one fireman to pull you out of any sinkhole, I would think).

Anyway, I just wanted to say BE CAREFUL! Be sure to look down everywhere you go—but look up, too, since I heard people's air conditioners sometimes go flying out of their windows if they are not fastened securely, and can go crashing down onto the pedestrians below.

That city is so fraught with peril. Why can't you come home and work for the *Duane County Register*? I saw Mabel Fleming the other day at the Buy and Bag and she said she'd absolutely hire you as their Arts and Entertainment writer.

Think about it, would you? There's nothing the least bit dangerous in Lansing—no sinkholes or falling air conditioners or transvestite killers. Just that man who shot up all the customers at the feed store that time, but that was years ago.

Love,
Mommy

P.S.: You'll never guess what! One of your ex-boyfriends got married! I've attached the announcement for you to see.

Attachment: ✉ (Photo of total goober and a girl with very big hair)

Crystal Hope LeBeau and Jeremy "Jer" Vaughn, both of Lansing, were married at the Lansing Church of Christ last Saturday.

Parents of the bride are Brandi Jo and Dwight LeBeau of Lansing, owners of Buckeye Liquors on Main Street in downtown Lansing. Parents of the groom are Joan and Roger Vaughn. Joan Vaughn is a homemaker. Roger Vaughn is employed by Smith Auto.

A reception was held at the Lansing Masonic Lodge, of which Mr. LeBeau is a member.

The bride, 22, is a graduate of Lansing High School and is currently employed at the Beauty Barn. The groom, 29, is a graduate of Lansing High School and is employed by Buckeye Liquors.

After a honeymoon in Maui, the couple will reside in Lansing.

To: George Sanchez <george.sanchez@thenyjournal.com>
From: Mel Fuller <melissa.fuller@thenyjournal.com>
Subject: Office morale

Dear George,
In an attempt to raise the morale around here, which I am sure you will agree with me is—to coin a phrase you frequently employ—

piss-poor, may I suggest that in lieu of a staff meeting this week, we all take a stroll over to 53rd and Madison in order to admire the gigantic sinkhole that has opened up in front of the office building housing our foe and main competitor, the *New York Chronicle*?

I am sure you will agree with me that this will constitute a refreshing change from the normal routine of listening to people complain about how the local Krispy Kreme shut down and how we haven't been able to get decent doughnuts at our staff meetings ever since.

Plus, seeing as how all the water to the building in which the *Chronicle* is housed has been shut off, we will have the fun of seeing our esteemed colleagues running into the Starbucks across the street to use their facilities.

Please give this matter the full consideration it so richly deserves.

Sincerely,

Mel Fuller
Page Ten Correspondent
New York Journal

To: Mel Fuller <melissa.fuller@thenyjournal.com>
From: George Sanchez <george.sanchez@thenyjournal.com>
Subject: Office morale

Are you high?

Everyone knows you only want to look at the sinkhole because you love a good disaster.

Get back to work, Fuller. I don't pay you for your looks.

George

To: Nadine Wilcock <nadine.wilcock@thenyjournal.com>
From: Mel Fuller <melissa.fuller@thenyjournal.com>
Subject: A big giant hole in the ground

Come on. How can you resist? If you go with me to look at it, I
won't make you go to spinning class today . . .

Mel

To: Mel Fuller <melissa.fuller@thenyjournal.com>
From: Nadine Wilcock <nadine.wilcock@thenyjournal.com>
Subject: The big giant hole where your brain should be

You are insane. It is like eighty degrees out. I am not spending my
precious lunch hour going to look at a giant hole in the ground,
even if it *is* in front of the *Chronicle*.

Ask Tim Grabowski. He'll go with you. He'll go anywhere men
in uniform are gathered in large clusters.

Nad

To: Nadine Wilcock <nadine.wilcock@thenyjournal.com>
From: Tim Grabowski <timothy.grabowski@thenyjournal.com>
Subject: I met him!

You lazy thing, you. If you'd gotten off your arse and come with
us, you would have, as I did, met this fellow that our little Miss Mel
has been yakking nonstop about all month.

But I suppose some of us think we're simply too good for sink-holes.

Tim

To: Tim Grabowski <timothy.grabowski@thenyjournal.com>
From: Nadine Wilcock <nadine.wilcock@thenyjournal.com>
Subject: YOU MET HIM???

Spill it, you little weasel.

Nad

To: Nadine Wilcock <nadine.wilcock@thenyjournal.com>
From: Tim Grabowski <timothy.grabowski@thenyjournal.com>
Subject: What will you give me?

You fiery-spirited wench, you.

Tim

To: Tim Grabowski <timothy.grabowski@thenyjournal.com>
From: Nadine Wilcock <nadine.wilcock@thenyjournal.com>
Subject: I have to review the

new Bobby De Niro place, and I'll take you with me if you tell me all about meeting Max Friedlander.

PUH-lease tell me. I'm begging you.

Nad

To: Nadine Wilcock <nadine.wilcock@thenyjournal.com>
From: Tim Grabowski <timothy.grabowski@thenyjournal.com>
Subject: Twist my arm

Okay, I'll tell you. Only I want to go to Bobby's new place for dinner, not lunch. That's when all the cute investment bankers will be there.

All righty, then.

Picture it, if you will:

The scene—53rd and Madison. A forty-by-twenty-foot hole has opened up in the middle of the street. Surrounding this hole are police barricades, orange caution cones, bulldozers, cement mixers, Con Edison trucks, a crane, television news reporters, about a hundred cops, and twenty of the hottest construction workers this little computer programmer has ever seen.

The noise of the jackhammers and honking of horns by unsuspecting commuters, who did not listen to the 1010 WINS traffic report before they left Jersey, is deafening. The heat is oppressive.

And the smell, my dear—well, I don't know what those Con Ed boys are doing at the bottom of that hole, but let me tell you, I strongly suspect they hit the wrong pipe.

It was as if a proverbial hellhole had opened up, right before that bastion of all that is evil, the illustrious New York Chronicle, and attempted to suck it back down to its creator, Mr. Satan himself.

And then, through it all, I saw on the face of our Miss Mel— who is, as I am sure you can guess, already giddy with joy at the spectacle before us—a look of such delight that I thought at first a Mr. Softee truck had appeared, and was handing out free chocolate-dipped cones.

Then, following the direction of her dazzled gaze, I saw what it was that had brought that beatific look to her face:

An Apollo. I am not exaggerating. An absolutely perfect specimen of manly beauty. He was standing behind one of the barricades, gazing into the hole, looking as if he'd just stepped off the pages of a J. Crew catalog in his baggy chinos and soft denim workshirt. The wind tugged softly at his brown hair, and I swear to you, Nadine, if one of those construction workers had handed him a shovel, it wouldn't have looked the least bit out of place in those big hands of his.

Which is a lot more than I can say for *my* boyfriend.

But to return to our scene:

Our Miss Mel (screaming to be heard over the pounding of the jackhammers): "John! John! Over here!"

Apollo turns. He sees us. He turns a deep but nevertheless completely attractive shade of umber.

I follow our little Miss Mel, picking her way through the police officers and outraged Chronicle employees, who, wearing their press passes, have descended on the poor souls from the mayor's office and are demanding to know when their private bidets—don't try to tell me they don't have them up in those gold-lined halls they work in—are going to be flowing again. Upon reaching the godlike creature she calls John, for reasons that are still a mystery to me, our Miss Mel goes on in her usual breathless manner:

> *Our Miss Mel:* "What are you doing here? Did you come to take pictures of the giant hole?"
> *Max Friedlander:* "Um. Yes."
> *Our Miss Mel:* "Where's your camera?"
> *Max Friedlander:* "Oh. Um. I forgot it."

Hmmm. Lights may be on, but no one seems to be home. At least until—

> *Max Friedlander:* "Actually, I already got the shot I need. I was just out here because . . . well, you know I love a disaster."
> *Our Miss Mel:* "Do I! Here, meet my friend Tim."

Friend Tim shakes hands with Perfect Specimen of Mankind. Will never wash right hand again.

> *Max Friedlander:* "Hi. Nice to meet you."
> *Friend Tim:* "Likewise, I'm sure."
> *Our Miss Mel:* "Listen, I'm glad I ran into you." She then proceeds to throw all known dating protocol to the wind by saying: "All my friends want to check you out, so do you think you could show up tomorrow night at Fresche on 10th Street around nine o'clock? Just a bunch of people from the paper, don't be alarmed."

I *know*! I was horrified as well! I mean, what could she have been *thinking*? You simply do not go around admitting things like that to prospective paramours. What happened to subtlety? What happened to feminine wiles? To boldly blurt the truth like that . . . well, I'll tell you: I was appalled. It just goes to show, you can take the girl out of the Midwest, but you can't take the Midwest out of the girl.

Mr. Friedlander, I could tell, was every bit as shocked as I was. He went almost as white as he'd been red a minute before.

Max Friedlander: "Um. Okay."
Our Miss Mel: "Great. See you then."
Max Friedlander: "Sure thing."

Exit our Miss Mel. Exit Friend Tim. When I glanced over my shoulder, Max Friedlander had disappeared—a remarkable feat, considering that there was nowhere on that side of the hole for him to go except into the *Chronicle* building.

But he can't have gone in *there*. His soul would have been ripped instantly from his body while demons sucked out his life force.

Anyway, that's all. I fully expect to see you at Fresche tonight at nine. And *don't* be late.

What's the appropriate cocktail to order for something like this? I know! Let's consult Dolly. She always knows just the right drink to go with the occasion.

Ta for now.

Tim

To: Dolly Vargas <dolly.vargas@thenyjournal.com>; George
Sanchez <george.sanchez@thenyjournal.com>; Stella Markowitz
<stella.markowitz@thenyjournal.com>; Jimmy Chu
<james.chu@thenyjournal.com>; Alvin Webb
<alvin.webb@thenyjournal.com>; Elizabeth Strang
<elizabeth.strang@thenyjournal.com>; Angie So
<angela.so@thenyjournal.com>
From: Nadine Wilcock <nadine.wilcock@thenyjournal.com>
Subject: Mel

All right, you guys, you've heard the hype; now let's see if he lives
up to it. The place is Fresche. The time is nine o'clock. Be there, or
tomorrow at the water cooler you won't know what the rest of us
are talking about.

Nad

To: Max Friedlander <photoguy@stopthepresses.com>
From: John Trent <john.trent@thenychronicle.com>
Subject: New York Journal

All right, tell me, and tell me quick:
    Who do you know from the *New York Journal*?
    I want names, Friedlander. I want a list of names, and I want it
NOW.

John

To: John Trent <john.trent@thenychronicle.com>
From: Max Friedlander <photoguy@stopthepresses.com>
Subject: New York Journal

So, you're stooping to speak to me again, I see. Not so high and mighty now, are you? I thought I'd mortally *offended* you with my thoughtfully crafted precepts on womankind.

I knew you'd come crawling back.

So what is this you want to know? Do I know anyone at the *New York Journal*? What are you, nuts? You're the only journalist I hang out with. I can't stand those pseudo-intellectual phonies. Think they're so great just because they string a few words together to form a sentence.

Why do you want to know anyway?

Hey, Trent, you aren't actually going out in public pretending to be me, are you? I mean, you're just doing the whole impersonation within my aunt's building, right? With that chick who was so mad about having to walk the dog?

Right?

RIGHT???

Max

To: John Trent <john.trent@thenychronicle.com>
From: Max Friedlander <photoguy@stopthepresses.com>
Subject: New York Journal

Wait, I forgot. I do know this one babe. Dolly something. I think she's with the *Journal*. You're not meeting *her*, are you?

Max

To: John Trent <john.trent@thenychronicle.com>
From: Genevieve Randolph Trent <grtrent@trentcapital.com>
Subject: Miss Fuller

Dearest John,

Well, well, well. A *gossip* columnist, no less. You ought to be ashamed of yourself. I was thinking at worst she'd turn out to be a "grad" student. You know, one of those horrid longhaired girls you see sometimes in Central Park, reading Proust on a park bench with the sandals and the glasses and the "backpacks."

But a *gossip columnist*. Now really, John. What can you be thinking?

Did you think I wouldn't find out? More fool you! It was easy. A simple phone call to the Fullers of Lansing, Illinois. I pretended I was one of those family-tree tracers. You know, a Fuller from way back when the Mayflower landed. Oh, they were just so eager to tell me all about the farm and their precious little Melissa, who's moved to the big city, dontcha know. And not just any big city, either, but the biggest one in the whole world, Noo York City.

Honestly, John.

Well, you'd better bring her around so we can all get a look at her. Next week would be fine. After the benefit, though, John. I am really quite solidly booked until then.

All my love,

Mim

To: jerrylives@freemail.com
From: Jason Trent <jason.trent@trentcapital.com>
Subject: Mim

Just a heads up to let you know Mim's on the warpath about you missing the dedication.

Plus, although I don't know this for certain, she seems to have found out about the redhead.

Don't look at me. I didn't tell her. I still think you're out of your mind to have agreed to this thing in the first place.

Stacy, on the other hand, wants to know whether or not you took her advice.

Jason

P.S.: Saw on the news about the sinkhole in front of your office building. My sympathies on the whole toilet situation.
P.P.S.: I'm sorry I called you a psychotic freak. Even though you are one.
P.P.P.S.: Forgot to tell you: Because of all this, Stacy has gotten her own e-mail account. She got tired of sharing mine. Her new address is IH8BARNEY@freemail.com.

To: Jason Trent <jason.trent@trentcapital.com>
From: John Trent <john.trent@thenychronicle.com>
Subject: You can call me . . .

anything you want. I don't mind.

And don't worry about Mim. I don't mind about that either.

And I kind of like that sinkhole. I have a genuine affection for it. In fact, I'll be sad when they finally fill it in.

Oops, there's just been a triple stabbing in Inwood. Gotta go.

John

To: Stacy Trent <ih8barney@freemail.com>
From: Jason Trent <jason.trent@trentcapital.com>
Subject: John

Stace—
Something is wrong with John. I called him a psychotic freak last week, and he doesn't even care. Plus I warned him about Mim, and he said he doesn't care about that either!

He doesn't even care about the sinkhole and the fact that there are no working toilets in his office building.

This happened to my cousin Bill that time he swallowed the worm at the bottom of a bottle of tequila down in Mexico. He had to spend a month in rehab!

What should we do?

Jason

To: Jason Trent <jason.trent@trentcapital.com>
From: Stacy Trent <ih8barney@freemail.com>
Subject: John

Jason—
Before you have your poor brother hauled off to Bellevue, let me

see if I can get anything out of him. He might be more willing to open up to me, seeing as how I don't go around calling him names.

Kisses,

Stacy

To: John Trent <john.trent@thenychronicle.com>
From: Stacy Trent <ih8barney@freemail
Subject: You took my advice, didn't you?

Don't deny it. You called her. So spill.

And don't leave anything out. I am thirty-four years old, which puts me, as a woman, at my sexual peak. I am also so pregnant I haven't seen my own feet in weeks. The only way I can have sex is vicariously.

So start tapping on that keyboard, monkey boy.

Stacy

To: Stacy Trent <ih8barney@freemail.com>
From: John Trent <john.trent@thenychronicle.com>
Subject: Monkey boy responds

You sure do talk racy for a full-time housewife and mother of two (and a half). Do the other mommies on the PTA have their minds in the gutter, too? That must make for some interesting bake sales.

For your information, what you are assuming has happened has not.

And if things continue in the manner they have been, it never will, either.

I don't know what it is about this girl. I know I am not the most debonair of men. I don't think anyone who has ever met me would classify me as a playboy. But nor have I ever been accused of being a complete imbecile.

And yet when I'm around Mel, that's exactly how I end up looking—probably out of divine punishment for the fact that, since I met her, I've done pretty much nothing but lie to her.

Whatever it is, I cannot seem to pull off something as simple as *dinner* between the two of us. As you know, my first attempt ended with us eating pizza standing up (and her paying for her own slice).

My second attempt was even worse: We spent most of the evening in an *animal* hospital. And then I very suavely added insult to injury by sexually harassing her on Max Friedlander's aunt's couch. She fled, in romance-novel vernacular, like a startled fawn. As well she should have: I'm sure I must have seemed like a teenager in postprom heat.

Is this satisfying your wish to live vicariously through my romantic adventures, Stacy? Are those toes you haven't seen in so long curling with excitement?

I almost broke down and told her after the couch incident. I wish to God now that I had. Things have only gone from bad to worse.

Because every day that I don't tell her is just another day she's going to hate me, when she finally figures it out.

And she *will* figure it out. I mean, one of these days, my luck is going to run out, and someone who knows Max Friedlander is going to tell her I'm not he, and she's not going to understand when I try to explain, because it's all so utterly juvenile, and she's going to hate me, and my life is going to be over.

Because for some unfathomable reason, instead of reviling me, like any woman in her right mind would, Mel seems actually to *like* me. I cannot for the life of me figure out why. I mean, you would think that, considering what she knows of me—or Max Friedlander, I should say—she'd hate my guts.

But, no. On the contrary: Mel laughs at my inane jokes. Mel listens to my asinine stories. And she apparently talks about me to her friends and colleagues, because a group of them demanded to meet me.

I know what you're thinking. You're thinking, *Why on earth did he go?*

And I can't tell you why I went. When she asked me about it, it was in front of my office building, where she seemed to appear as if from nowhere. I was so shocked to see her—so scared someone was going to call me by my name—that I think I froze, even though it was about 80 degrees outside. The sun was shining, and there was noise and confusion everywhere, and suddenly, she was just there, with her hair shining all around her head like a halo, and her big blue eyes blinking up at me. I think I would have said yes if she'd asked me to eat glass out of the palm of her hand.

And then there was nothing I could do about it. I mean, I had already said yes. I couldn't cancel on her.

So I ran around in a panic, trying to figure out if Max knew anybody at the *Journal*.

Then I went and I met them and they were suspicious, but for Mel they pretended not to be, since she is clearly someone they adore. By the end of the evening, we were all the best of friends.

But only because the one woman who actually knows Max didn't show up.

I didn't find that out, of course, until I got there, and Mel said, "Oh, Dolly Vargas—you know Dolly—she couldn't make it, on account of how she's got ballet tickets tonight. But she says hi."

See? See how close I came? It's only a matter of time.

So what do I do? If I tell her, she'll hate me, and I'll never see her again. If I don't tell her, eventually she'll find out, and then she'll hate me, and I'll never see her again.

After her friends had left, Mel proposed we walk a bit before catching a cab back to our building. We walked along Tenth Street, which, if you'll remember from before you and Jason fled for the suburbs, is a shady residential street, filled with old brownstones, the front windows of which are always lit up at night, so you can see the people inside, reading or watching television or doing whatever it is people do in their homes after dark.

And as we walked, she took my hand, and we just strolled along like that, and as we strolled, I was struck by this horrible realization: that *never in my life* had I walked along the street holding a girl's hand and felt like I did then . . . which was happy.

And that's because every other time a girl has grabbed my hand, it's been to drag me toward a store window so she could point to something she wanted me to buy her. *Every other time.*

I know it sounds horrible, like I'm feeling sorry for myself, or whatever, but I'm not. I'm just telling you the truth.

That's actually the horrible part, Stace. That it's true.

And now I'm supposed to tell her? Tell her who I am?

I don't think I can.

Could you?

John

To: Jason Trent <jason.trent@trentcapital.com>
From: Stacy Trent <IH8BARNEY@trentcapital.com>
Subject: John

There's nothing wrong with your brother, silly. He's in love, that's all.

Stacy

P.S.: We're out of Cheerios. Can you pick up a box on the way home tonight?

To: Stacy Trent <IH8BARNEY@trentcapital.com>
From: Jason Trent <jason.trent@trentcapital.com>
Subject: My brother

John? In love? With whom? The redhead?
  BUT SHE DOESN'T EVEN KNOW HIS REAL NAME!!!
  And this is all right with you???
  Has everyone in this family gone completely mental?

Jason

To: Nadine Wilcock <nadine.wilcock@thenyjournal.com>
From: Mel Fuller <melissa.fuller@thenyjournal.com>
Subject: Tell me again

Come on. Just one more time.

Mel

To: Mel Fuller <melissa.fuller@thenyjournal.com>
From: Nadine Wilcock <nadine.wilcock@thenyjournal.com>
Subject: No

I will not.

Nad

To: Nadine Wilcock <nadine.wilcock@thenyjournal.com>
From: Mel Fuller <melissa.fuller@thenyjournal.com>
Subject: Come on

Tell me. You know you want to. You OWE it to me.

Mel

To: Mel Fuller <melissa.fuller@thenyjournal.com>
From: Nadine Wilcock <nadine.wilcock@thenyjournal.com>
Subject: God, you are a weirdo,

and you are really starting to annoy me. But all right, I'll tell you.
But this is the last time.

Okay. Here we go.

You are right. Max Friedlander is very nice. We were all wrong
about him. I apologize. I owe you a Frappuccino.

Satisfied?

Nad

To: Nadine Wilcock <nadine.wilcock@thenyjournal.com>
From: Mel Fuller <melissa.fuller@thenyjournal.com>
Subject: A grande,

with skim milk. Don't forget.

Mel

P.S.: Don't you just love the way the skin at the corners of his eyes all crinkles up when he smiles? Like a young Robert Redford?

To: Mel Fuller <melissa.fuller@thenyjournal.com>
From: Nadine Wilcock <nadine.wilcock@thenyjournal.com>
Subject: Now you're just

making me sick.

Seriously, was I like this when I first started seeing Tony? Because if I was, I don't understand why none of you shot me. Because this is nauseating. It really is. You've got to stop.

Nad

To: Mel Fuller <melissa.fuller@thenyjournal.com>
From: Aaron Spender <aaron.spender@thenyjournal.com>
Subject: Max Friedlander

Yes, I know. I heard everyone talking about it by the water cooler. Apparently, Fresche was quite the place to be the other night.

Don't worry—I'm not upset that I wasn't invited. I quite understand why you mightn't have wanted me there.

And you needn't worry that I am writing to you now with the intention of trying to win you back. I realize—at last—that you have found someone else.

I am just writing to say how glad I am for you. Your happiness is all I have ever wished for.

And if you love him, well, then that's all I need to hear. Because for you to love someone, Melissa, I know he would have to be a truly worthy, truly noble individual. A man who shows you the kind of respect you deserve. A man who won't ever let you down.

I just want you to know, Melissa, that I would have done just about anything in the world to have been that man for you. I really mean that. If it hadn't been for Barbara. . . .

But now is not the time or place for what-would-have-beens.

Just know that I am thinking of you, and am pleased to see you looking so radiant with happiness. You deserve it, more than anyone else I have ever known.

Aaron

To: Aaron Spender <aaron.spender@thenyjournal.com>
From: Mel Fuller <melissa.fuller@thenyjournal.com>
Subject: Max Friedlander

Thanks, Aaron. That was a very sweet message, and it meant a lot to me.

Mel

P.S.: I'm sorry to have to bring this up, but I know it was you who took the Xena Warrior Princess action figure off the top of my computer. The new fax guy saw you do it, Aaron.

I want her back. *I don't want to know what you did with her.* I just want her back. Okay?

Mel

To: Mel Fuller <melissa.fuller@thenyjournal.com>
From: Dolly Vargas <dolly.vargas@thenyjournal.com>
Subject: Your new beau

It is so like you, darling, to show off your shiny new bauble on the one night I couldn't make it to the unveiling. It isn't fair. When is he going to come by and take you to lunch or something, so I can say hello? It's been so long, I can hardly remember what he looks like. Maybe I should just pop over to the Whitney for a little refresher.

XXXOOO

Dolly

To: Nadine Wilcock <nadine.wilcock@thenyjournal.com>
From: Mel Fuller <melissa.fuller@thenyjournal.com>
Subject: Nude photo

OH, MY GOD!!!
    I forgot all about that self-portrait of Max Friedlander that is supposedly hanging in the Whitney!
    The one of him nude!!!
    WHAT DO I DO??? I mean, I can't go LOOK at it, can I? That is so sleazy!

Mel

P.S.: Just thinking about it is giving me a headache.

To: Mel Fuller <melissa.fuller@thenyjournal.com>
From: Nadine Wilcock <nadine.wilcock@thenyjournal.com>
Subject: Oh, please

Of course you can go look at it. Which is sleazier, you looking at it, or him taking it and letting them hang it up for everyone in the world to see?

But whatever. Get your purse and follow me. We'll forgo spinning for a bit of culture, courtesy of the Whitney Museum of American Art.

Nad

P.S.: Your headache is from the Frappuccino. They do that to me, too.

To: Stacy Trent <IH8BARNEY@freemail.com>
From: John Trent <john.trent@thenychronicle.com>
Subject: I need your

recipe for crab-stuffed flounder. I have decided that since every time I try to take her out, it is a complete disaster, I will simply cook a meal for her instead, in the privacy of my own home.

Or Max Friedlander's aunt's home, as the case may be.

Who knows, maybe I'll even work up the nerve to tell her the truth about me.

Probably not, though.

Also, how do you make those little bread thingies with the tomatoes on top?

John

To: John Trent <john.trent@thenychronicle.com>
From: Stacy Trent <IH8BARNEY@freemail.com>
Subject: My bread thingies

I can only assume you mean bruschetta. You toast baguette rounds, then rub the toasted slices with garlic. Then you cut up a bunch of tomatoes and you . . .

Oh, for God's sake, John, just call Zabar's and order it, like a normal person. Then you pretend you made it yourself. You think I can cook? Ha! My roast chicken? Kenny Rogers. My crab-stuffed flounder? Jefferson Market. My hand-cut fries? Frozen from a bag!

Now you know. Don't tell Jason. It will spoil the magic.

Stacy

To: Dolly Vargas <dolly.vargas@thenyjournal.com>
From: Mel Fuller <melissa.fuller@thenyjournal.com>
Subject: Max Friedlander

Dear Dolly,
Laugh all you want. I don't happen to think it's amusing.

I cannot say I think his parents were particularly responsible, either, giving a five-year-old a camera and then letting him play with it in the bathtub. He could have been electrocuted, or something.

Besides, that photo doesn't even look anything like him.

Mel

P.S.: I blame YOU for the fact that I am clearly getting a cold. You caused me all that anxiety and made me susceptible to this stupid flu bug that is going around.

To: Mel Fuller <melissa.fuller@thenyjournal.com>
From: Dolly Vargas <dolly.vargas@thenyjournal.com>
Subject: Oh, pooh

You know how much I love to tease you. You're like the little mentally retarded sister I never had.

Just kidding, darling, just kidding.

Besides, instead of railing against me, you should feel sorry for me. I'm hopelessly in love with your Aaron, and he'll hardly give me the time of day. He just sits in his little cubicle and looks at the screen saver he's had made from a photo of the two of you. It's so pathetic, it almost makes me want to cry.

Except that ever since I had my lids done, I've been physically incapable of tears.

By the way, what's with that skirt you have on? It makes you look poochy.

XXXOOO

Dolly

P.S.: Could you stop coughing so loud? It's aggravating my hangover.

To: George Sanchez <george.sanchez@thenyjournal.com>
From: Mel Fuller <melissa.fuller@thenyjournal.com>
Subject: My health

Dear George,
I am writing this from home to let you know I will not be in today

due to the fact that I have woken up with a sore throat, fever, and runny nose.

I left the pages on your desk last night, and there's plenty for Ronnie to use for tomorrow. Tell her it's all in the green file folder on my desk.

If you have any questions, you know where to find me.

Mel

P.S.: PLEASE tell Amy Jenkins down in Human Resources that the reason I haven't logged on today is because I'm out sick! She counted my last sick day as a tardy and it went in my permanent personnel file!

P.P.S.: Can you make sure my Xena Warrior Princess action figure is back on my computer monitor? Somebody took it, but he's supposed to put it back. Just let me know whether or not he has.

Thanks,
Mel

To: Don and Beverly Fuller <DonBev@dnr.com>
From: Mel Fuller <melissa.fuller@thenyjournal.com>
Subject: My last will and testament

Hi. I'm writing to let you know that I have a terrible cold and that I'm probably going to die. If I do, I want you to know that I'm leaving you and Daddy all the money in my 401K. Please use it to make sure Kenny and Richie go to college. I know they probably won't want to go to college, seeing as how they both plan on playing for the NBA when they grow up, but just in case professional sports doesn't pan out, they should be able to get at least a semester or two out of my $24,324.57.

Please give all my clothes to Crystal Hope, Jer's new wife. She looks like she could use them.

I don't know what you should do with my Madame Alexander doll collection. Maybe Robbie and Kelly will have a girl next, and you can give them to her.

My only other worldly possessions are my books. Would you please see that in the event of my demise they all go to my next-door neighbor's nephew, John? Actually, his real name is Max. You would like him, Mom. All the people from my office met him, and they like him. He is very funny and sweet.

And no, Mom, we are not sleeping together.

Don't ask me why not, though. I mean, don't let Daddy read this, but I'm starting to wonder if there's something the matter with me. Besides the fact that I have this cold, I mean. Because John and I only made out this one time, and since then nothing, nada, zippo.

Maybe I'm a really bad kisser. That's probably it. That's probably why every guy I've gone out with from Jer on has ended up dumping me. I'm a lousy kisser. I'm short, I have an impossibly small bladder, I have red hair, and I'm a bad kisser.

Let's just face facts: When I was born, Mom, did the doctor ever mention the words *genetic mutation*? Did he ever mention . . . oh, I don't know. The term *biological sport*?

Because that's what I think I am. Oh, I know: Robbie turned out all right. I guess he doesn't lack the kissing chromosome I evidently do. Either that or Kelly's just a bad kisser, too, and couldn't tell the difference.

I don't suppose—AHHH! Someone's at the door!

It's John! And I look horrible! Mom, I gotta go. . . .

Mel

To: Mel Fuller <melissa.fuller@thenyjournal.com>
From: Don and Beverly Fuller <DonBev@dnr.com>
Subject: Your silly last e-mail

Melissa Ann Marie Fuller!

What on earth was that last e-mail from you all about? You have a little cold, dear. You aren't dying. Your dolls are staying exactly where they are, in their display case in your bedroom, along with your 4-H medals and Duane County High School diploma.

And what's this about a boy not thinking you're a good kisser? Well, if that's what he thinks, then you tell him he can just go jump in a lake. I'm sure you are a very good kisser.

Don't you worry, Melissa, there are lots of fish in the sea. You just throw that one back. Your ship will come in. You are much prettier than all those girls I see on the television, especially that one who had sex with that president. You can do better than this boy who thinks you are a bad kisser, and that other one, who had sex with Barbara Bellerieve. You know, I hear she has capped teeth!

So you just tell that boy to bug off, and then you snuggle up in bed and watch *The View* and drink plenty of fluids and especially chicken noodle soup. You'll be better in no time.

And even though I shouldn't tell you this—I wanted it to be a surprise—I am sending you a little something that should cheer you right up. All right, it's a batch of snickerdoodles, your favorite cookies.

So you turn that frown upside down, young lady!

Love,
Mommy

To: Nadine Wilcock <nadine.wilcock@thenyjournal.com>
From: Mel Fuller <melissa.fuller@thenyjournal.com>
Subject: Thank you

Thank you, thank you, thank you!

John told me that he called and that you told him I was home sick. So you know what he did next? Really, I don't want to make you nauseated, but I'm dying to tell someone, so I've selected you as my victim:

He went to the Second Avenue Deli and got me chicken soup!

Really! A whole big thing of it! And then he stopped by with the soup, orange juice, a video, and ice cream (plain vanilla, but then I don't think he knows any better. You're right, you do have to train them sometimes).

And even though I must have looked totally awful (I had on my cow print pajamas and fuzzy bunny slippers, and you should have seen my hair, hoo boy), when I asked him if he wanted to stay and watch the movie with me (*Rear Window*—I know what you're thinking, Nadine, but I am sure he has absolutely no idea that I have been spying on him. Besides, I have always politely averted my gaze when it came to watching him undress. Well, except that once, but that was just to settle that all-important boxers-or-briefs question), he said yes!

So I turned the television around on its little cart so we could watch it from the couch, but he said I should be in bed (which it was pretty clear I'd abandoned in order to answer the door—I hadn't bothered making it or anything, and you should see the ocean of wadded-up Kleenex all around it) and then he made me get back in it, and turned the television around again so it faced the bed.

Then he went into the kitchen—which made me pretty embarrassed . . . you should have seen all the dishes in my sink—and when he came back out again he had the soup and this big glass of juice on that tray I bought that one time at Pier 1, remember? Only

I'd only used it to hold my laptop over the bathtub, like the lady on those commercials, that time I got the wicked sunburn at Jones Beach, and George was so mean and made me work from home.

Nadine, it was so nice! He lay down on the other side of the bed (not under the covers, though, on top of them) and we watched the movie and I ate my soup and when I was through he broke out the ice cream, and we ate it right out of the container with spoons, and then when the scary part happened, we forgot all about it and it melted, some all over my sheets, which are sticky now, but who cares?

Then when the movie was over I turned it to the Weather Channel, and there was live coverage from Hurricane Jan, which has been decimating the coast of Trinidad! So we watched that for a while, and then I don't know what happened, I must have had too much Sudafed, but the next thing I knew, he was saying good night and that he'd see me tomorrow, and when I woke up again he was gone, and it was night, and he had done all the dishes.

Not just the dishes from the soup and juice and stuff. ALL the dishes that had been in my sink were washed and sitting in the drying rack.

For a minute I totally thought I was hallucinating, but this morning they were still there. Nadine, he *did my dishes* while I was unconscious, and probably snoring, due to my massive nasal congestion.

Isn't that the sweetest thing you've ever heard? I mean EVER?? I've never had a man do my dishes before.

Well, that's all. I just wanted to brag. I still feel like total crud, though, so I don't know when I'll be back at work.

Is Xena where she's supposed to be? What do you think he did with her? God, I am so glad we broke up. What a WEIRDO!

Mel

P.S.: Just because I'm sick is no reason for you to skip spin class.

To: Mel Fuller <melissa.fuller@thenyjournal.com>
From: Nadine Wilcock <nadine.wilcock@thenyjournal.com>
Subject: Well?

Which was it, boxers or briefs? Don't leave me in suspense here, Fuller.

Nad ;-)

To: Nadine Wilcock <nadine.wilcock@thenyjournal.com>
From: Mel Fuller <melissa.fuller@thenyjournal.com>
Subject: Duh

Boxers.
    Really cute ones, too, with little golf balls on them.

Mel ;-)

To: George Sanchez <george.sanchez@thenyjournal.com>
From: Mel Fuller <melissa.fuller@thenyjournal.com>
Subject: My health

Dear George,
I am still sick. I won't be coming in today, and probably not tomorrow, either.
    Don't get mad, George. I know this is a busy time, what with all the parties out in the Hamptons, but what am I supposed to do? I took advantage of my fabulous healthcare package yesterday and

went to a doctor. You know what he prescribed? Bed rest and flu-ids. Bed rest and fluids, George! I won't be able to get that in the Hamptons. I mean, Dolly could, of course, but not me.

Besides, I'm sure the doctor didn't mean those kind of fluids.

Tell Ronnie that I don't believe that thing about George and Winona in Cannes, and that she had better check with their publi-cists before she runs it. He is way too old for her.

Mel

P.S.: Don't forget to tell Amy Jenkins that I'm out sick again, not late.
P.P.S.: Is my Xena Warrior Princess action figure back?

To: Nadine Wilcock <nadine.wilcock@thenyjournal.com>
From: Tony Salerno <foodie@fresche.com>
Subject: Mel

What are you, on-line again? I've been trying to get through to you for an hour. And I KNOW you aren't talking to Mel, because I was just there.

And I wasn't the only one who was there, either. One guess as to who opened the door when I knocked:

Yep, you're right, Mr. Perfect himself.

Actually, I shouldn't call him that. I kind of like the guy. He's, like, normal, you know? Not like that freak Spender. Remember when you and me and Mel and Spender went out that one time, and he went off on cops? Man, that burned me. I shut him up pretty quick, didn't I, when I told him four of my cousins were with the NYPD? At least this new guy doesn't talk crap like Spender used to.

Anyway, so I delivered the stuff, like you wanted, and John answered the door, and at first I was pretty embarrassed, let me tell you. I thought I'd interrupted some kind of sex thing. But the guy had his clothes on, and he was, like, "Come on in."

And there was Mel, in these weird white pajamas with black splotches on them, like a cow, and she was in bed, but she didn't look very sick, if you ask me. They were watching a movie. Apparently, since she's been sick, they've been doing this quite a lot. He brings over some food—nothing, I must say, up to my standards, but edible, anyway—and they watch movies.

I don't know. Does that make it serious? There was no hanky-panky, as far as I could tell. I mean, there was tons of Kleenex on the floor, but I'm pretty sure that was from Mel's runny nose, and not, you know, anything else.

Hey, don't get mad at *me*. I'm just the messenger here.

So I was like, "Here's the stuff from work, plus I made you a peach cobbler." And of course Mel totally freaked, because like any decent gourmand she recognizes that my peach cobbler is a gift from the gods, and she insisted we all have some, and so John took it and dished it out, and I sort of got the impression he knew his way around Mel's kitchen, which is saying something, because you know she keeps her Tupperware in the oven and there's that thing she has with the beer in the vegetable crispers.

Anyway, he put these big globs of vanilla ice cream on it, which as you know, sullies the purity of the cobbler's texture. But whatever. We all sat on the bed and ate it, and I have to admit, even if I do say so myself, it was the best peach cobbler ever created, in spite of the ice cream.

So I tried watching the movie for a while because Mel said stay, but I could tell even though *she* said stay, *he* was like, When is he going to leave? in a major way, so I said I had to get back to work, and Mel said thanks and that she was feeling better and would be back to work on Monday, and I was all, Okay, and John walked me to the door and was like, Nice seeing you again, good-bye, and practically shut it in my face.

I guess I can't blame him. I was the same way when you and I first started going out. Except I never would have let you buy pajamas like that. Doesn't Mel own any lingerie?

Well, in spite of the pajamas, I'm telling you, the guy's got it bad. Way worse than Spender ever did.

And I suppose that, as usual, Mel has no idea, has she? Don't you think somebody ought to tell her?

Tony

To: Tony Salerno <foodie@fresche.com>
From: Nadine Wilcock <nadine.wilcock@thenyjournal.com>
Subject: Mel

Now who isn't picking up his phone?

I assume you're out front, dazzling the customers with your salmon tartar on endive.

Anyway, thanks for taking that stuff to Mel. So he was there again, huh? He was over last night, too. I think you're right: He *has* got it bad.

But then, so has she.

And no, I do not think either of them needs our help. No one helped us, did they? And we turned out all right.

You didn't tell Mel I skipped spin class, did you?

Nad

P.S.: There's only one person's lingerie needs that you should be concerning yourself with, mister, and those are mine. What Mel Fuller wears to bed is her business. And I bought her those cow pajamas for her last birthday. I think they're cute.

To: Don and Beverly Fuller <DonBev@dnr.com>
From: Mel Fuller <melissa.fuller@thenyjournal.com>
Subject: Snickerdoodles

Dear Mommy,
Thank you so much for the cookies! They are delicious—at least, if I could taste anything, I'm sure they would be.

I want you to know I am feeling much better—not better enough to go to work, of course, but better. I still sound bad enough that when I call my boss to say I won't be in, he isn't suspicious, which is good.

Also, about that whole kissing thing: I'm sorry I accused you and Daddy of not passing good kissing genes down to me. It turns out I'm a fine kisser: John is just shy.

Of course, it's hard kissing when you have a completely stuffed-up nose, but I suppose practice makes perfect.

Anyway, thanks again for the cookies, and I'll call you later.

Love,
Mel

P.S.: John loves your cookies, too!

To: Mel Fuller <melissa.fuller@thenyjournal.com>
From: Don and Beverly Fuller <DonBev@dnr.com>
Subject: Snickerdoodles

Melissa, you'll have to forgive me. I really don't mean to pry. But I got the distinct impression—and don't feel like you have to tell me if you don't want to—but I got the impression that you and this John Max Friedlander are *having sex*.

Now, you are a big girl and of course you have to make your own decisions, but I think you should be aware of a few things:

He won't buy the cow if he can get the milk for free.

It's true. It's really true. Get a ring on your finger before you uncross those legs, sweetie.

Now, I know, I know. All the girls are doing it these days.

Well, if you have to follow the "in crowd," then at least practice the safe sex, all right, honey? Promise Mommy now.

Oops, I have to go. Daddy and I are meeting his bowling team at the Sizzler for dinner tonight.

Love,
Mommy

To: Don and Beverly Fuller <DonBev@dnr.com>
From: Mel Fuller <melissa.fuller@thenyjournal.com>
Subject: Snickerdoodles

Oh, my God, Mother, I am NOT having sex with him, all right? I am just talking about kissing! How do you go from kissing to sex?

Well, all right, I guess it's a natural progression, but still. That thing about the cow is so stupid. Do I look like a cow to you?

Besides, whatever happened to trying the pants on before you buy them, huh? That's the advice Daddy gave Robbie before he went away to college.

What do I get? The stupid cow thing!

Well, for your information, Mother, I might want to try on some pants. Has that ever occurred to you? I mean, there are a lot of pants out there, and how am I going to find the right ones if I don't try on all the potential candidates? You know, after a thorough screening process?

And OF COURSE if I do decide to try on these particular pants, I will use the utmost safety precautions. I mean, for God's sake, this is the twenty-first century, after all.

Would you PLEASE not tell any of this to Daddy? I am begging you.

Mel

To: Mel Fuller <melissa.fuller@thenyjournal.com>
From: Don and Beverly Fuller <DonBev@dnr.com>
Subject: Snickerdoodles

You don't have to shout, sweetie. I can read you just fine in lower-case letters.

Of course I trust you and know that you will make the right decision.

And I'm sure you're right about the pants. I know you'll do what's best. You always have.

I just think a good rule of thumb would be not to try on any pants that haven't mentioned the "L" word. I know lots of pants—French and Italian pants, in particular—toss around the "L" word at the drop of a hat, but I think American pants are a little more reticent about it. When they say it, I think they usually mean it.

So will you do me a favor and just get the "L" word first? Because I know you, Melissa. I know how easily your little heart gets broken. I was there for Jer, wasn't I?

So you just wait until you've heard the "L" word, all right?

I saw on the news that the transvestite killer has attacked another woman, this time on the Upper East Side! I hope you're locking your door at night, sweetie. He seems especially fond of size 6s, so you really need to look over your shoulder when you go out at night, honey.

But don't forget to look out for those sinkholes!

Love,
Mommy

P.S.: And the falling air conditioners.

To: Nadine Wilcock <nadine.wilcock@thenyjournal.com>
From: Mel Fuller <melissa.fuller@thenyjournal.com>
Subject: Help me

I made the mistake of telling my mother John and I made out, and now she's all over me about cows and something she calls the "L" word.

But she got me thinking: What is the rule? You know, the sleeping-together rule? Like after how many dates are you allowed to sleep with someone? Without seeming like a slut, I mean? And does it count as a date if you're sick and he brings you ice cream?

Vanilla ice cream, to be exact.

Mel

To: Mel Fuller <melissa.fuller@thenyjournal.com>
From: Nadine Wilcock <nadine.wilcock@thenyjournal.com>
Subject: Help me

What does the term *slut* mean to you? It is a very subjective word, if you ask me. For instance, I slept with Tony on our first date. Does that make me a slut?

Let's examine this:

You like the guy. You want to jump his bones.

But you are concerned that if you do so too early in the relationship he will qualify you as a slut.

Do you really want to be with someone who thinks in such pejorative terms? No, of course not.

So I think the answer to your question "after how many dates are you allowed to sleep with someone" is:

There is no right answer.

It's different for everyone.

Wish I could be more help.

Nad

To: Mel Fuller <melissa.fuller@thenyjournal.com>
From: Tony Salerno <foodie@fresche.com>
Subject: Sex

Dear Mel,

Hi. I hope you don't mind, but Nadine mentioned the little problem you've been having—you know, the one about how soon into a relationship do you do the deed. And I think I have an answer for you:

If it feels good, do it.

Seriously. That's how I've always lived my life, and look how it's turned out? I'm the chef in my own restaurant, and I'm getting married to a totally hot lady who wears a thong under her Ann Taylor.

Can't go wrong with that.

Tony

To: Mel Fuller <melissa.fuller@thenyjournal.com>
From: Nadine Wilcock <nadine.wilcock@thenyjournal.com>
Subject: Please excuse

my boyfriend. I don't know if I've mentioned to you that he has a
learning disorder.

Nad

To: Nadine Wilcock <nadine.wilcock@thenyjournal.com>
From: Mel Fuller <melissa.fuller@thenyjournal.com>
Subject: I don't mind

you're telling Tony about my sex life—or lack thereof—but you
aren't telling people in the office, right?
    RIGHT?

Mel

To: Peter Hargrave <peter.hargrave@thenyjournal.com>
From: Dolly Vargas <dolly.vargas@thenyjournal.com>
Subject: Mel Fuller

But *of course* she should just do it, darling. What has she got to
lose? It isn't as if she's getting any younger: Quite soon gravity is

going to begin pulling down those parts of her that she most wants pointing toward the sun. And you know what they say about making hay while the sun shines.

Speaking of which, Aaron's canceled on me for the weekend. What do you say? Stephen's house is a dream, and everyone would be very discreet. They're *movie* people, darling. It isn't as if any of them would have the slightest idea who you are.

Let me know.

XXXOOO

Dolly

To: Tim Grabowski <timothy.grabowski@thenyjournal.com>
From: Jimmy Chu <james.chu@thenyjournal.com>
Subject: Mel Fuller

Yeah, but if she sleeps with him and it doesn't work out, she's going to have to see him every day, since he lives right next door. How awkward is that going to be? Especially if she—or he—starts seeing someone else.

It's a no-win situation. Unless they get married, or something, and what's the chance of that happening?

Jim

To: Stella Markowitz <stella.markowitz@thenyjournal.com>
From: Angie So <angela.so@thenyjournal.com>
Subject: Mel Fuller

He's too old for her. How old is he? Thirty-five? How old is she?
Twenty-seven? She's too young. A baby. She should find someone
her own age.

Angie

To: Adrian De Monte <adrian.demonte@thenyjournal.com>
From: Les Kellogg <leslie.kellogg@thenyjournal.com>
Subject: Mel Fuller

Yes, but all the boys Mel's age are starting up Internet companies
and can get supermodels any time they want, so what would they
want with Mel, who is cute, but no supermodel?
    Either that, or they are professional skateboarders.
    So I guess maybe it's okay that the guy is so old.

Les

To: Nadine Wilcock <nadine.wilcock@thenyjournal.com>
From: George Sanchez <george.sanchez@thenyjournal.com>
Subject: Mel Fuller

What's a thirty-five-year-old guy doing still single, anyway? Has
it occurred to anyone that he might very well be gay? Shouldn't

somebody say something to Mel before she makes a fool of herself with this sleeping-with-him thing?

George

To: Mel Fuller <melissa.fuller@thenyjournal.com>
From: Nadine Wilcock <nadine.wilcock@thenyjournal.com>
Subject: Are people around the office talking about you

Are you kidding? Don't flatter yourself. We have way better things to worry about than your love life.

Nad

To: Stacy Trent <IH8BARNEY@freemail.com>
From: John Trent <john.trent@thenychronicle.com>
Subject: Kenny Rogers chicken

You never seriously attempted to pass off something this good as your own cooking. No way.

John

To: John Trent <john.trent@thenychronicle.com>
From: Genevieve Randolph Trent <grtrent@trentcapital.com>
Subject: The benefit

Just a reminder, my dear boy, of your promise to attend the benefit with me. And, of course, your sweet little cheque.

I haven't heard from you in a few days. I do hope all is well.

Mim

P.S.: Did you hear about your cousin Serena?

To: Genevieve Randolph Trent <grtrent@trentcapital.com>
From: John Trent <john.trent@thenychronicle.com>
Subject: Of course I didn't

forget. I'm escorting you, remember? I even got the old tux out of
storage and dusted it off.

See you there.

John

P.S.: Yes, I did hear about Serena. I blame her parents for naming
her Serena in the first place. What did they expect?

To: Mel Fuller <melissa.fuller@thenyjournal.com>
From: George Sanchez <george.sanchez@thenyjournal.com>
Subject: What do you mean

you won't be back in the office until Monday? I think you're forgetting something, sweetie pie.

The Lincoln Center benefit to raise cancer awareness. Only the biggest society event of the season. According to Dolly, everyone who is anyone is going to be there.

I don't care if you're bleeding out of the eyeballs, Fuller. You're going.

I'm sending Larry to do photos. Be sure you get all those rich old biddies, the Astors and the Kennedys and the Trents. You know how they love seeing themselves in the paper, even in a tired old rag like us.

George

P.S.: Your stupid doll is back on your computer. What was that all about, anyway?

To: Nadine Wilcock <nadine.wilcock@thenyjournal.com>
From: George Sanchez <george.sanchez@thenyjournal.com>
Subject: Hey

Quit yelling. If she's well enough to contemplate having sex with some guy, she's well enough to drag her sorry butt out of bed and do her damned job.

George

P.S.: What kind of ship do you think I'm running here? This is not the slacker express, Wilcock.

To: Mel Fuller <melissa.fuller@thenyjournal.com>
From: jerrylives@freemail.com
Subject: Listen, I

knocked a little while ago, but you didn't answer, so I assume you're asleep. I didn't want to call and wake you up. The thing is, I have an assignment tonight, so I'm not going to be able to stop by until late. Will you be all right? I'll bring more ice cream. This time I'll make sure it has lots of chocolate-covered nuts for you to pick out.

John

P.S.: Hurricane Jan is moving at 135 miles per hour toward Jamaica. The eye should pass over it sometime tonight. Looks like it might be pretty bad. That should cheer you up.

To: Mel Fuller <melissa.fuller@thenyjournal.com>
From: Nadine Wilcock <nadine.wilcock@thenyjournal.com>
Subject: Last night

Hey, how did it go? I tried to talk George out of making you go, but he was adamant. He said you were the only reporter he knew who could get the story without offending anybody. I guess Dolly wasn't exactly stellar at the whole charity-circuit thing. Well, that was undoubtedly because she was sleeping with all of the society wives' husbands.

I hope you don't suffer a relapse or something.

Nad

To: Jason Trent <jason.trent@trentcapital.com>
cc: Stacy Trent <IH8BARNEY@freemail.com>
From: John Trent <john.trent@thenychronicle.com>
Subject: Now what do I do?

Okay, last night, when I escorted Mim to the Lincoln Center benefit, who should come strolling up to us with her little notebook and pencil but . . . Mel.

Yes, that's right. Melissa Fuller, Page Ten correspondent, the *New York Journal*, who, last time I'd seen her, had been in bed with a copy of *Cosmo* and a temperature of a hundred. Next thing I know, she's standing in front of me in high heels and a miniskirt asking Mim if she feels her work raising cancer awareness will help bring about a cure someday.

And then she notices me and breaks off and cries, "John!"

And Mim—you know Mim—swivels her head around and takes in the red hair and Midwestern accent and, next thing you know, she's asking Mel to sit down with us and does she want some champagne?

Now, I think I can safely say that this was the first time in Mel's journalistic career that one of her subjects invited her to sit down and have a drink at her table. And I know it's the first time Mim's ever invited a reporter for a private interview.

And all I could do was sit there and kick Mim under the table every time she started to say anything remotely resembling "my grandson," which of course she did about ten million times.

So the fact is, Mel knows now that something is up. She has no idea *what*, of course. She thinks it's that Mim is in love with me. She thinks I should go for it, since a rich old bat like Mim could pay off all my credit cards. Although she warned me that all of Genevieve Trent's kids ended up in communes (Uncle Charles, Aunt Sara, and Aunt Elaine) or jail (Uncle Peter, Uncle Joe, and Dad). She neglected to mention the suicides, Aunt Claire and Uncle Frank. Further proof that Gramps was right to bribe the coroner.

What fine stock we come from, don't we, Jason? Stacy, you should take the girls and run, run far away, now while you still can.

So what do I do? Tell her? Or continue lying my head off?

Could one of you please just shoot me?

John

To: John Trent <john.trent@thenychronicle.com>
From: Jason Trent <jason.trent@trentcapital.com>
Subject: Tell her

Just tell her. Please. I'm begging you. I'm not sure how much more of this I can take.

Jason

To: John Trent <john.trent@thenychronicle.com>
From: Stacy Trent <ih8barney@freemail.com>
Subject: Don't tell her

until after you've had sex with her.

I'm serious. Because if you're good enough in bed, she won't care.

I know I have sex on the brain, and it's up to you, of course, but that's how I'd handle it.

Stacy

To: Stacy Trent <IH8BARNEY@freemail.com>
From: John Trent <john.trent@thenychronicle.com>
Subject: Oh, okay, thanks

I should just sleep with her. Of course. Why didn't I think of that?

IS THERE SOMETHING WRONG WITH YOU???

I mean, besides the fact that you're married to my brother.

Don't you remember what it was like to be single? You couldn't just sleep with somebody. I mean, yeah, you could, but it never worked out. I WANT THIS TO WORK OUT.

That's why it's important that BEFORE we sleep together we establish a warm and loving friendship.

Right? I mean, isn't that what Oprah's always saying?

John

To: John Trent <john.trent@thenychronicle.com>
From: Stacy Trent <IH8BARNEY@freemail.com>
Subject: But don't you

think you've established a warm and loving relationship? I mean, you brought her ice cream and did her dishes, for God's sake. The girl owes you. She'll put out, don't worry.

Stacy

To: Stacy Trent <IH8BARNEY@freemail.com>
From: John Trent <john.trent@thenychronicle.com>
Subject: Excuse me, but

is that the spawn of Satan gestating within you, or my nephew? What is wrong with you? "She'll put out, don't worry."

Nobody puts out because you bring her ice cream. If that were true, those guys who drive the Mr. Softee trucks . . .

Well, you get my drift.

No, I want to do this right. But the sad fact of the matter is that every woman I've ever gone out with has always had one eye on my wallet—and we're talking mostly women Mim fixed me up with, the crème de la crème of New York society, who you would think had plenty of money in their own Schwab accounts—so getting them into my bed was never a difficulty. Usually it was trying to get them out of it that was the problem.

Mel, however, is not exactly what you'd call the falling-into-bed type. In fact, she's pretty shy.

I don't know what I'm going to do. I was serious about the shooting thing, you know. I really wouldn't mind a bullet between the eyes, if it was all over quickly, and Mel didn't have to end up walking Paco again.

John

To: John Trent <john.trent@thenychronicle.com>
From: Stacy Trent <IH8BARNEY@freemail.com>
Subject: Oh, for God's sake

Just go for it.

Just knock on the door and when she opens it pull her out into the hallway and start kissing her deeply and intrusively. Then push her up against the wall and pull her blouse from the waistband of her skirt and put your hand underneath her bra and

Stacy

To: John Trent <john.trent@thenychronicle.com>
From: Jason Trent <jason.trent@trentcapital.com>
Subject: You'll have to excuse

my wife. She is a quivering mass of hormones right now. In fact, I just had to put her to bed with a cold compress.

I would appreciate it if you would refrain from discussing anything of a sexual nature with her until after the baby comes. Six to eight weeks after the baby has come, as a matter of fact. As I am sure she has explained to you, she is at her sexual peak. And yet, as you undoubtedly know, her doctor has advised her that she is at a stage in her pregnancy when it might be dangerous for the baby for us to engage in . . .

Well, you know.

So would you shut your piehole about the whole sex thing between you and this girl?

And while we're on the subject, whatever happened to taking a girl to dinner? Huh? That always works in the movies. You took a girl out for a nice romantic dinner, maybe a carriage ride through Central Park (unless she was the type of girl who would think that was lame), and if you were lucky she'd put out. Right?

So take her somewhere nice. Don't you know the guy at Belew's? Isn't that the nicest restaurant in town? Take her there.

And this time, if the damned cat gets sick, let the stupid thing die.

That's what I think, anyway.

Jason

To: John Trent <john.trent@thenychronicle.com>
From: Brittany and Haley Trent <weluvbarney@freemail.com>
Subject: HI, UNCLE JOHN

WHAT DO YOU THINK OF OUR NEW E-MAIL ACCOUNT? DADDY GOT IT FOR US SO WE WOULD STOP USING HIS.

WE HEARD MOMMY AND DADDY TALKING ABOUT YOU AND THE REDHEADED LADY AGAIN. THEY SAID YOU AREN'T SURE HOW TO LET HER KNOW YOU LIKE HER.

WELL, IN THE SECOND GRADE, WHEN YOU ARE A BOY WHO LIKES A GIRL, YOU GIVE HER YOUR BEST POKÉMON CARD. OR YOU PULL HER HAIR. NOT HARD ENOUGH TO MAKE HER CRY, THOUGH.

OR YOU CAN ASK HER TO ROLLERSKATE BACKWARD
WITH YOU, AND THEN HOLD HER HAND SO SHE DOESN'T
FALL DOWN.

HOPE THIS HELPS!

LOVE,
BRITTANY AND HALEY

To: John Trent <john.trent@thenychronicle.com>
From: Genevieve Randolph Trent <grtrent@trentcapital.com>
Subject: I am not even

---

going to ask what that was all about at the benefit. I can only
assume that you, like all of your cousins, have completely lost your
mind.

I suppose that was *the* Miss Fuller, of the Lansing, Illinois,
Fullers. For the life of me, I can't imagine why you've been hiding
her away like that. I thought her perfectly charming. I assume she
has a cold and does not always pronounce her *th*s like *d*s.

And yet you are obviously playing some sort of game with her.
My ankle, I think you should know, is black-and-blue from all the
times you kicked it.

You have always been completely hopeless where women are
concerned, so do let me give you this piece of advice: Whatever
game you're playing, it isn't going to work, John. Girls don't like
games. Even, I am told, girls from Lansing, Illinois.

Mim

To: jerrylives@freemail.com
From: Mel Fuller <melissa.fuller@thenyjournal.com.>
Subject: The other night

Is it just all the decongestants I took before I went out, or was that totally weird?

I had no idea you were going to be there. You must have written after I'd left. My horrible mean boss made me go. I didn't want to. I felt terrible. But he made me, so I put on some mascara and a dress and I went, stuffy nose and fever and all.

It wasn't too bad. I mean, the shrimp was good. Not that I could really taste it, but whatever.

Anyway, I had no idea you go to that kind of stuff. Were you taking pictures? Where was your camera? I didn't see it.

That Mrs. Trent was pretty nice. How do you know her? Did you do her portrait, or something? It's funny how you hear stuff about people, and then you meet them, and they're exactly the opposite. Like I always heard Genevieve Randolph Trent was this horrible ice bitch. But then she was so nice. You know, if she wasn't like a hundred years old, I'd say she has a crush on you, because the whole time we were talking, she just kept looking and looking at you.

It's good, you know, that with all her money, she does stuff for charity. I've covered stories about lots of people who don't. Actually, all of Mrs. Trent's kids (she had EIGHT, did you know that?) are these huge slackers who live on communes or are in jail. I feel sorry for them. And for her, a little.

Anyway, I am back at work because they simply can't do without me around here, but I was wondering if you'd let me take you out to dinner one night soon as a sort of thank you for looking out for me when I was feeling so rotten? Let me know when you're free. . . . Mrs. Trent, I know, should get first dibs on your time, seeing as how if you married her, you could pay off all your credit cards right away, and not ever have to worry about maxing them out again.

Just a suggestion.

Mel

To: Mel Fuller <melissa.fuller@thenyjournal.com>
From: jerrylives@freemail.com
Subject: Dinner

No, it wasn't just you. The other night was totally weird. Well, except for you, I mean. You're never weird. I just meant the circumstances.

I've known Genevieve Trent for a long time. My whole life, actually. But I don't believe there's any possibility of anything romantic developing between the two of us, in spite of the fact that it might offer a solution to my credit card problems.

She really enjoyed meeting you, by the way. And the piece you wrote about the benefit was very touching. I imagine every charity in town must be calling, inviting you to come write about them next, you do it so eloquently.

As for dinner, I would be delighted. Only I wish you'd let me take you out. I still owe you, remember, for saving Aunt Helen?

So how about tomorrow night? If you're feeling up to it, I mean. I'll make reservations—it'll be a surprise.

But I guarantee we're not going to Fresche.

John

To: jerrylives@freemail.com
From: Mel Fuller <melissa.fuller@thenyjournal.com>
Subject: Dinner

All right, if you insist. But you really don't have to.

You know, if you would just let me cook, then you could save your money and actually pay off your credit cards. It's a novel thought, I know, but it *is* what normal people do.

But I guess it's pretty clear neither of us is all that normal. I mean, normal people aren't really obsessed with hurricanes and sinkholes, are they?

So I guess the whole normal thing is ruled out, as far as we're concerned.

Oh, well.

Just promise me you won't spend a lot. I'm not really a champagne kind of girl. Beer suits me just fine.

Mel

To: David J. Belew <djbelew@belew-restaurant.com>
From: John Trent <john.trent@thenychronicle.com>
Subject: Dinner

Dear David,

Remember how after I got Patty to do that Dining Section exposé on hard-to-get-in restaurants, and how yours was the only one that she declared worth the three-month wait? And you said I had a table anytime I wanted?

Well, I want one. For two. And you've got to hold it under the name of Max Friedlander, and when I show up, that's how your staff should greet me. Okay?

Also, make sure you've got ice cream with chunks in it for dessert. Chocolate chunks are best.

That's all I can think of right now. I'll call later to confirm.

John

To: John Trent <john.trent@thenychronicle.com>
From: David J. Belew <djbelew@belew-restaurant.com>
Subject: Dinner

John, I hate to disappoint you, but at Belew's, rated four stars by the illustrious newspaper for which you toil daily, three stars by the Michelin guide, top restaurant in New York City by Zagat's, and recipient of not one but two Beard awards, thanks to the culinary talents of yours truly, we do not serve "ice cream with chunks in it."

No, not even chocolate chunks.

I will, of course, see that a table is held for you, and even instruct my staff to call you Max Friedlander. But I'm afraid I must draw the line at chunks.

Dave

To: Mel Fuller <melissa.fuller@thenyjournal.com>
From: Nadine Wilcock <nadine.wilcock@thenyjournal.com>
Subject: You must be feeling better

Or is there some other reason why you are humming "I Feel Pretty" under your breath?

Which, by the way, is only slightly annoying to those of us who have to work near you.

Nad

To: Nadine Wilcock <nadine.wilcock@thenyjournal.com>
From: Mel Fuller <melissa.fuller@thenyjournal.com>
Subject: My humming

How about this? I feel better AND I'm happy.

I know. It seems hard to believe. But it's true.

Want to know why I'm happy? Because I'm going out tonight. On a date. An actual date. With a man.

What man, you ask? Why, Max Friedlander, if you must know. Where are we going? It's a surprise.

But guess what? He's paying.

And even though it's to say thank you for saving his aunt's life—though I must say I'm not sure she'd really appreciate my efforts, considering what her quality of life is at the moment—it's still a date.

And Mrs. Friedlander might get better.

So, yes, I guess you could say that overall I'm very happy.

But if my humming bothers you, I'll stop, by all means.

Mel

To: Mel Fuller <melissa.fuller@thenyjournal.com>
From: Dolly Vargas <dolly.vargas@thenyjournal.com>
Subject: Did someone say date?

Darling, is it true? You and Max, I mean?

You're so calm about it, sweetie, that's why I ask. I mean, considering it's the first time a man has asked you out since . . . well, you know. Why, speak of the devil . . . there he is, sulking over by the copier as we speak. Poor, poor Aaron.

I would think you'd at least head over to Bumble and Bumble for a blowout and a manicure. Pedicure, too, if you're planning on going open-toe.

And you know, I know the best little place for bikini waxing—that is, if you think tonight is THE night. We always want to look our best in our Christian Diors, now, don't we? You know, I hear the Sphinx is becoming quite popular. Since I know you don't know what that is, I'll explain. It's when they wax not just your bikini line, but the whole . . .

Oh, pooh. Peter's on the phone. More later, I promise.

XXXOOO

Dolly

To: Mel Fuller <melissa.fuller@thenyjournal.com>
From: Nadine Wilcock <nadine.wilcock@thenyjournal.com>
Subject: Your date

Okay, I know it's been a long time (that little movie-and-a-slice thing you guys did doesn't count—nor that night at Fresche when we all inspected him, nor that other night you ended up spending at the animal hospital) so I'm going to make sure you haven't forgotten anything in your date survival kit.

Now, check each off these items before you leave the apartment so you'll be sure not to forget them:

1. Lipstick
2. Compact
3. Metrocard (in case you need to make a quick getaway)
4. Money for cab fare (in case you need to make a quick getaway and there are no subway stops nearby)
5. Cover-up in case he dumps you and you start crying and your mascara runs
6. Passport (in case he chloroforms you, puts you on a plane to Dubai, and sells you into white slavery, and you need to prove to the authorities after you escape that you are an American citizen)
7. Altoids
8. Hairbrush
9. Clean undies (just in case you end up spending the night)
10. Condoms (ditto)

Hope this helps.

Nad ;-)

To: Nadine Wilcock <nadine.wilcock@thenyjournal.com>
From: Mel Fuller <melissa.fuller@thenyjournal>
Subject: The list

Thanks for that list of things I will supposedly need on my date, but you are forgetting one thing:
WE LIVE NEXT DOOR TO EACH OTHER.

So if I need clean underwear, I'll just have to go across the hall.

Now stop talking about it. Between you and Dolly I don't know who's making me more nervous.

It's just dinner, for God's sake.

Oh, God, I have to go, or I'm going to be late.

Mel

To: Mel Fuller <melissa.fuller@thenyjournal.com>
From: Dolly Vargas <dolly.vargas@thenyjournal.com>
Subject: Just one more thing . . .

Do be sure you use a condom, darling, because Maxie has been around, if you know what I mean.

Well, think about it. All those models. There's no telling where they've been, bony little delights that they are.

Ta for now.

XXXOOO

Dolly

To: jerrylives@freemail.com
From: Jason Trent <jason.trent@trentcapital.com>
Subject: So . . .

How'd it go?

Jason

P.S.: Stacy made me ask.

To: Nadine Wilcock <nadine.wilcock@thenyjournal.com>
From: Tony Salerno <foodie@fresche.com>
Subject: I assume

that the reason your phone has been busy for the past three hours is because you're yakking away to Mel about her date. Well, could you spare your fiancé one minute of your time to answer this serious question:

Who are you planning on seating next to my great-aunt Ida at the reception? Because my mom says whoever is sitting by her has to make sure she doesn't get any champagne. You remember the trailer park fire Ida caused at the last family function, right?

Let me know.

Love ya,
Tony

P.S.: My mom says if you seat her by Ida, she'll commit hara-kiri on the spot.

To: Tony Salerno <foodie@fresche.com>
From: Nadine Wilcock <nadine.wilcock@thenyjournal.com>
Subject: I am not

on-line yakking with Mel. I haven't heard from Mel since the last time I saw her, which was when she left work to go home and change for her big dinner with Max. I mean, John. What is with that name thing, anyway? Where does somebody get the nickname JOHN? John is not a nickname.

Anyway, I was on-line looking up gifts for our wedding party. What do you think of cuff links for the guys, and earrings for the girls?

Now that I think of it, it is kind of funny I haven't heard from Mel. It's been twenty-four hours. She never goes twenty-four hours without returning my calls.

Well, except for when her neighbor got conked on the head.

Oh, my God, you don't think anything's happened to her, do you? I mean, do you think Max/John might have kidnapped her? And sold her into white slavery? Should I call the police, do you think?

Nad

To: Nadine Wilcock <nadine.wilcock@thenyjournal.com>
From: Tony Salerno <foodie@fresche.com>
Subject: I think you should have your head examined

Also, any guy who would buy Mel Fuller from a white slaver should ask for his money back. She would make the worst slave. She'd always be whining about how come the guy doesn't have cable, and how is she supposed to keep up with everything that's going on in Winona Ryder's life without *E! Entertainment News*.

Tony

P.S: You never answered the question about who you're seating beside Aunt Ida.
P.P.S.: My friends would laugh their asses off if I gave them cuff links. How about Wusthof paring knives?

To: Mel Fuller <melissa.fuller@thenyjournal.com>
From: Nadine Wilcock <nadine.wilcock@thenyjournal.com>
Subject: Where are you?

Seriously, I am not trying to be nosy, and I know you can take care of yourself, but I've left three messages and you still haven't called back. WHERE ARE YOU??? If I don't hear from you soon I'm calling the police, I swear.

Nad

To: Mel Fuller <melissa.fuller@thenyjournal.com>
From: Human Resources <human.resources@thenyjournal.com>
Subject: Tardiness

Dear Melissa Fuller,
This is an automated message from the Human Resources Division of the *New York Journal*, New York City's leading photo-newspaper. Please be aware that according to your supervisor, **managing editor George Sanchez**, your workday here at the *Journal* begins promptly at **9 AM**, making you **83** minutes tardy today. This is your **49th** tardy exceeding twenty minutes so far this year, **Melissa Fuller**.

Tardiness is a serious and expensive issue facing employers all over America. Employees often make light of tardiness, but routine lateness can often be a symptom of a more serious issue, such as

- alcoholism
- drug addiction
- gambling addiction
- abusive domestic partner

- sleep disorders
- clinical depression

and any number of other conditions. If you are suffering from any of the above, please do not hesitate to contact your Human Resources Representative, <u>Amy Jenkins</u>. Your Human Resources Representative will be only too happy to enroll you in the *New York Journal*'s Staff Assistance Program, where you will be paired with a mental health professional who will work to help you achieve your full potential.

<u>Melissa Fuller</u>, we here at the New York Journal are a team. We win as a team, and we lose as one, as well. <u>Melissa Fuller</u>, don't you want to be on a winning team? So please do your part to see that you arrive at work on time from now on!

Sincerely,
Human Resources Division
New York Journal

Please note that any future tardies may result in suspension or dismissal.

This e-mail is confidential and should not be used by anyone who is not the original intended recipient. If you have received this e-mail in error please inform the sender and delete it from your mailbox or any other storage mechanism.

To: Nadine Wilcock <nadine.wilcock@thenyjournal.com>
From: Tim Grabowski <timothy.grabowski@thenyjournal.com>
Subject: Our Miss Mel

Well, it looks as if our little Miss Mel had a very, VERY good time on her date, doesn't it? I mean, I know when I don't come into work the next day, it's generally because the date hasn't ended yet. Wink, wink.

Well, I'm all for it. It couldn't have happened to a nicer person. Lordie, though, how I wish it were me! I mean, did you get a look at the arms on that guy? And those thighs? And that full head of hair?

Excuse me. I have to go to the little boys' room now and douse myself with cold water.

Tim

To: Nadine Wilcock <nadine.wilcock@thenyjournal.com>
From: George Sanchez <george.sanchez@thenyjournal.com>
Subject: Fuller

Where the hell is Fuller? I thought we'd gotten past all this when that damned Friedlander guy moved in next door to her. Wasn't he going to start walking that dog?

So where is she?

I swear to God, Wilcock, you can tell her from me that if that story on the new Paloma Picasso watch with the interchangeable bands isn't on my desk by five she's out of a job.

I don't know what you people think I'm running here, but it happens to be called a NEWSPAPER, in case you've forgotten.

George

To: Mel Fuller <melissa.fuller@thenyjournal.com>
From: Dolly Vargas <dolly.vargas@thenyjournal.com>
Subject: Not that it's any of my business, but . . .

Don't you think it's just the slightest bit . . . well, *tacky* to rub poor Aaron's nose in it this way? I mean with this whole not-showing-up-to-work-the-morning-after-your-big-date thing. I'm sure it's been a long time since you actually spent the night with a man, and all of that, but this is just plain rude.

There, I've said it. Now on to more important matters:

So just how big is he? Max Friedlander, I mean. Is he a show-er or a grower?

Because you know, darling, I've heard rumors that . . .

Oh, there's Peter again. He simply will not stop pestering me. More later, darling.

XXXOOO

Dolly

To: John Trent <john.trent@thenychronicle.com>
From: Genevieve Randolph Trent <grtrent@trentcapital.com>
Subject: Your delinquency

Dearest John,

I can understand that you find your new, independent life quite engrossing—especially as far as the Fullers of Lansing, Illinois, are concerned—but you might remember that you once had a family, and that they would enjoy hearing from you now and again. I believe your brother has attempted to contact you more than once in the past few days, and that you have, in the vulgar vernacular of the day, "blown him off."

It might behoove you to keep in mind, John, an old song from my Scout days:

Make new friends
but keep the old.
One is silver
and the other gold.

That applies to family as well, you know.

Mim

P.S.: Are you aware that there are TWO Lansing, Illinoises? I am quite serious. One is a quaint farm town, and the other seems to be made up entirely of strip malls. Your little Miss Fuller appears to be from the former. Just thought you might like to know.

To: Nadine Wilcock <nadine.wilcock@thenyjournal.com>
From: Mel Fuller <melissa.fuller@thenyjournal.com>
Subject: I'm sorry

I'm sorry, I'm sorry, I'm sorry.

I didn't mean to scare you. As you can see, I'm fine.

I got another one of those tardies from Amy Jenkins. What is her glitch, anyway?

Do you know if George is mad? What's the Mountain Dew situation? Is the machine fully stocked? Or is he suffering from caffeine withdrawal again?

I really meant to call, only I never got a chance. Every time I started to, well, I got distracted. Forgive me?

Mel

To: Mel Fuller <melissa.fuller@thenyjournal.com>
From: Nadine Wilcock <nadine.wilcock@thenyjournal.com>
Subject: It's about time!

I can't believe you. Do you know how worried we all were?

Well, all right. How worried *I* was, anyway? Don't ever scare me like that again.

I will forgive you if you give me a detailed date-a-logue: I want descriptions of where you have been and EXACTLY what you've been up to.

As if I didn't know. "Distracted."

Yeah. Right.

Nad

To: Nadine Wilcock <nadine.wilcock@thenyjournal.com>
From: Mel Fuller <melissa.fuller@thenyjournal.com>
Subject: Him

What can I say?

Oh, Nadine, it was incredible! I remember what a complete wacko you were after that first weekend you and Tony spent together. I thought you had lost your mind. It's probably wrong for a maid of honor to admit that, but it's true.

But now I understand completely what you were going through. It's LOVE! Love just does that to you, doesn't it? I mean, I can even see now how, despite the age difference, Winona won't let go of Chris Noth. Not if she feels the way about him that I feel about John.

Where to start?

Oh, dinner: He took me Belew's.

No, really! I know, I know. There's a three-month waiting list for reservations there, but we walked in like it was nothing, Nadine. And they led us straight to the most adorable little table for two tucked in the corner, and there was champagne already chilling in an ice bucket. Seriously. And it wasn't Korbel, Nadine. It was Cristal. CRISTAL. That's like three hundred bucks a bottle. I was all, "What, are you crazy, John? You can't afford this."

But he said not to worry about it, that David Belew owed him a favor.

Well, that must have been some favor, because we had the most incredible meal—I mean, even you could not imagine it, Nadine, you who's been to Nobu and Daniel on the paper's expense account. We started with oysters and Beluga caviar, then moved on to salmon tartar. Then came foie gras confit with port-poached figs, duck prosciutto, and . . .

Oh, I can't even remember what else. I'm sorry. I've failed you.

But, Nadine, it was all so good, and with each course came a different wine, and by the time we got to the main course, which I think involved squab, I wasn't even paying attention to the food, because John looked so nice in his suit, and he kept leaning forward and smiling and saying my name, and then I would go "What?" and he'd go, "What?" and then we'd laugh, and by the time dessert rolled around we were kissing over the tabletop, and the waiter could hardly get in there to take the things away.

So then John said, "Let's get out of here," and so we did, and I don't even know how we made it back to the building, but we did, somehow, kissing the whole time, and by the time we got up to the fifteenth floor my dress was completely unzipped in the back, and then I remembered something horrible, and I was like, "What about Paco?"

And then John said the eight most beautiful words I'd ever heard:

"I paid the doorman to walk Paco tonight."

My dress hit the floor before I even got the key into the lock.

And guess what? When I went out this morning, it was still lying there in the hallway! Somebody had found it and folded it up all nicely. How embarrassing! Can you imagine, Nadine? I mean, what if Mrs. Friedlander wasn't in the hospital in a coma, and she'd found my dress like that?

Well, I guess if Mrs. Friedlander wasn't in the hospital in a coma, my dress wouldn't have been in the hallway. Because I probably would never have even met John, if someone hadn't conked his aunt on the head and left me with that dog to take care of.

Anyway.

You know how in books they always talk about characters having bodies that just fit together? You know, like two long-lost puzzle pieces, or something? They just seem to fit perfectly?

That's how John and I are. We just seem to fit. I mean it, Nadine, it was like it was meant to be, or something.

And then, since we fit so well together the first time, I guess it just seemed natural to fit together a bunch more times.

Which is why I suppose I'm so late this morning.

But, oh, Nadine, I don't care how many tardy warnings Amy Jenkins sends me. It's totally worth it. Making love with John is like drinking really cold water after being stranded out in the desert for years and years.

Mel

P.S.: Why does Dolly keep throwing paper clips over the walls of my cubicle?

To: Jason Trent <jason.trent@trentcapital.com>
From: John Trent <john.trent@thenychronicle.com>
Subject: So sue me

I was busy, all right? And do you have to go whining to Mim every time you fail to hear from me for a few days? You think that just because Dad's in jail, you're . . .

Ah, forget it. I can't even be pissed at you. I'm too damned happy.

John

P.S.: We did it.

To: John Trent <john.trent@thenychronicle.com>
From: Jason Trent <jason.trent@trentcapital.com>
Subject: Dad happens to be

in a minimum security rehabilitation center with the rest of the white-collar criminals. It is hardly jail. Not when everyone has his own television. Not to mention HBO.

And what precisely did you mean by that cryptic "We did it"? I hope you don't mean what I think you mean. First of all, what are you, in the ninth grade? And second, what business do you have, "doing it" with someone who doesn't even know your real name???

I hope by that "We did it" you mean the two of you ate raw blowfish or something.

Jason

To: John Trent <john.trent@thenychronicle.com>
From: Stacy Trent <IH8barney@freemail.com>
Subject: YOU WHAT???

You DID it? You DID IT? What is that supposed to mean? Are you saying you made love with her? Is that what you're saying?

And that's all you have to say about it???

I thought you agreed you were going to be there for me. I thought you understood that I am a woman badly in need of some vicarious thrills.

So you spill your guts, mister, or I'll be sending the twins out to their Uncle John's place for an extended visit. . . .

Stacy

To: Stacy Trent <IH8BARNEY@trentcapital.com>
From: John Trent <john.trent@thenychronicle.com>
Subject: My love life
Attachment: Parker's Return

Stacy, I am not going to discuss my sex life with my sister-in-law. At least, not in the kind of detail you're looking for. And do you really think it would be a good idea to send the girls out to see me when I happen to be living with two cats? You know Ashley is allergic.

What do you want me to say, anyway? That it was the most erotically charged twenty-four hours of my life? That she's exactly what I've been looking for in a woman all this time, but never dared hope I'd find? That she's my soulmate, my kismet, my cosmic destiny? That I'm counting the minutes until I can see her again?

Fine. There. I've said it.

John

P.S.: If you want, you can read the latest chapter of my book, which I've attached. It's been sort of a slow news day, so I used the opportunity to work on my novel. Maybe that will satisfy your need for vicarious thrills. Just keep in mind that it is a work of fiction, and any resemblance to any person, living or dead, is purely coincidental.
P.P.S.: Do you think sending her roses would be too pushy?

Attachment: ✉

PARKER'S RETURN
JOHN TRENT

Chapter 17

"But what about Paco?" she asked breathlessly.

"Don't worry, baby," Parker growled. "I shot him."

Her baby blues were wet, the mascara around them smudged. She looked up at him, her gaze limpid.

"Oh, *Parker*," she breathed.

"He won't be bothering you again," Parker assured her.

Her lips, bloodred and moistly parted, beckoned.

Parker was no fool. He lowered his head until his mouth was crushing hers.

She went soft and pliant against him at that first touch of his lips. By the fourth floor, she was almost boneless. By the sixth, he had the zipper to her little black dress undone. By the time they'd reached the tenth floor, the dress was halfway down her shoulders.

She wasn't, Parker discovered by floor eleven, wearing a bra.

Or, he learned by floor thirteen, panties.

When the elevator doors opened on fifteen, and Parker half carried her out into the hall, the dress hit the floor. Neither of them noticed.

Inside her apartment, it was dark and cool—just the way Parker liked it. Her bed sat in a puddle of moonlight streaming in through the shadeless windows. He laid her down in that silver puddle, then stepped back to look at her.

She was naked the way only the most beautiful women can be, proudly, defiantly naked. No reaching for the protective covering of a bedsheet for her. The moonlight played along the curve of her waist, the length of her thighs. Her hair, a thousand dark red curls, pooled beneath her head, and her eyes, as she stared at him, were deeply shadowed.

She didn't say anything. She didn't have to. He came to her, as the tide follows the moon.

And when he came to her, he was as naked as she was.

Parker had, in his past, known women. A *lot* of women. But this . . . this was different, somehow. *She* was different. As his hands reached to part those slim smooth thighs, he had a sense that he was opening the gates to another world, a world from which he might never return.

A world, he knew as he slid into its hot and steamy grip, he would never, ever leave.

To: John Trent <john.trent@thenychronicle.com>
From: Stacy Trent <IH8BARNEY@freemail.com>
Subject: You really ARE in

love, aren't you? Oh, John, it's so sweet.
    Of COURSE you should send her roses.
    Can I forward Chapter 17 to Mim? PLEASE???

Stacy

To: Stacy Trent <IH8BARNEY@freemail.com>
From: John Trent <john.trent@thenychronicle.com>
Subject: NO, you can't forward

Chapter 17 to Mim! What are you, crazy? I'm sorry I sent it to you.
Delete it, okay?

John

To: Mel Fuller <melissa.fuller@thenyjournal.com>
From: Nadine Wilcock <nadine.wilcock@thenyjournal.com>
Subject: Sorry

it's taken me so long to get back to you. I had to go splash cold
water on my face. I think you should seriously give up the journalism thing for a career as a romance novelist. Water after years in
the desert?

I have to admit, in all the time I've known you, I've never seen you so . . .

Happy.

So. Was the "L" word mentioned, or not?

Nad

P.S.: As for Dolly, the reason she's throwing paper clips over your cubicle wall is that she's just trying to see whether or not you're walking funny due to the enormity of Max Friedlander's . . . um, adoration for you.

So, whatever you do, don't get up in front of her.

To: Nadine Wilcock <nadine.wilcock@thenyjournal.com>
From: Mel Fuller <melissa.fuller@thenyjournal.com>
Subject: The "L" word

Well, now that I think about it, the "L" word wasn't mentioned.

My God, I took my dress off in the hallway for a guy who didn't even say the "L" word!

Shoot me. Could you please just shoot me?

Mel

P.S.: And why hasn't he called? Have you noticed that he hasn't even called?

To: Mel Fuller <melissa.fuller@thenyjournal.com>
From: Nadine Wilcock <nadine.wilcock@thenyjournal.com>
Subject: Snap out of it

A little while ago, you were happier than I'd ever seen you. Now you're plunged into despair just because I happened to mention the "L" word?

Well, I could bite off my tongue. Don't worry about it, Mel. The guy is obviously crazy about you. I mean, especially if he was willing to spend twenty-four hours in bed with you. I mean, my God, Tony's never done that.

Then again, I'm always making him get up and cook for me.

Don't worry, he'll call.

Nad

To: Mel Fuller <melissa.fuller@thenyjournal.com>
From: Dolly Vargas <dolly.vargas@thenyjournal.com>
Subject: I hope you don't think I'm butting in

on your personal business, but I do feel that you should meet me in the ladies' in about five minutes. I've got just the thing for that nasty case of beard-burn you seem to have acquired all over the lower half of your face since I last saw you.

Seriously, darling, it looks as if you were licked on the chin by the one hundred and one dalmatians. I can't believe you didn't at least try a little foundation.

Not to worry. A little Clinique, and you'll be on your way.

And while I'm applying it, you'll tell me all about it, won't you?

XXXOOO

Dolly

To: Dolly Vargas <dolly.vargas@thenyjournal.com>
From: Mel Fuller <melissa.fuller@thenyjournal.com>
Subject: Yes, I do think you're butting in

and if you think I'm telling you anything, you're nuts.

Thanks for the offer of your Clinique, but I will wear my beard-burn proudly, as a badge of honor.

And stop flicking paper clips at me over the top of your cubicle. I know it's you, Dolly, and I know what you want, and I am not getting up.

Mel

To: Mel Fuller <melissa.fuller@thenyjournal.com>
From: Tim Grabowski <timothy.grabowski@thenyjournal.com>
Subject: You naughty girl

Little Miss Mel, what have you been up to?

Wait. Don't answer that. I could tell the moment I caught a glimpse of your little face, shining like a lighthouse beacon. (You really must get him to shave more often if the two of you are going to be sucking face on a regular basis. You are a classic redhead, with the very delicate skin to go with it. You must remind him of this from time to time, or you're going to walk around looking like you fell asleep with your chin under a heat lamp.)

And when I saw that simply stunning arrangement of bloodred roses that just got delivered to you, well, I knew:

Our Miss Mel has been very wicked indeed.

What did you do to deserve that enormous floral tribute? I imagine it was quite out of character for you.

Congratulations.

Tim

To: Mel Fuller <melissa.fuller@thenyjournal.com>
From: Nadine Wilcock <nadine.wilcock@thenyjournal.com>
Subject: See?

I told you he'd call. Only he did better than calling. That's the biggest bouquet of roses I've ever seen.

So, what does the card say?

Nad

To: Nadine Wilcock <nadine.wilcock@thenyjournal.com>
From: Mel Fuller <melissa.fuller@thenyjournal.com>
Subject: OH, MY GOD

HE LOVES ME!!!
    The card says:

> But to see her was to love her,
> Love but her, and love forever
>
>   John

Did he make that up? It means me, right? Don't you think? The "her" is me?

Oh, my God, I'm so excited. Nobody's ever sent me flowers at work before, let alone with a card that mentions the "L" word!!!

Mel

To: Mel Fuller <melissa.fuller@thenyjournal.com>
From: Nadine Wilcock <nadine.wilcock@thenyjournal.com>
Subject: My God,

it doesn't take much to make you happy, does it? Of course the "her" in the poem is you. Who do you think he's talking about? His mother???

And no, Max Friedlander did not make it up. Robert Burns did. How did you ever graduate from college? You really do know next to nothing.

Wait, I take that back. You know everything about Harrison Ford, George Clooney, and that new one, what's his name? Oh, yeah, Hugh Jackman.

Don't just sit there grinning like an idiot. Write him back, for God's sake.

Nad

To: jerrylives@freemail.com
From: Mel Fuller <melissa.fuller@thenyjournal.com>
Subject: You shouldn't have

sent all those roses. I mean, really, John, you've got to think about your credit situation. But they're so beautiful, I can't even get mad at you for being such a spendthrift. I just love them—and the quote, too. I'm not very good at things like that. Quotes, I mean. But I think I have one in return:

If I loved you less, I might be able to talk about it more.

Good one, right? That's from _Emma._

What are you doing tonight? I was thinking about buying some fresh pasta and making pesto. Want to come over around seven-ish?

Love,
Mel

To: Mel Fuller <melissa.fuller@thenyjournal.com>
From: jerrylives@freemail.com
Subject: How about this one?

I love you

Han Solo, _Return of the Jedi_

John

To: jerrylives@freemail.com
From: Mel Fuller <melissa.fuller@thenyjournal.com>
Subject: How about this one?

                    I know

Princess Leia, *Return of the Jedi*

Mel

To: Tony Salerno <foodie@fresche.com>
From: Nadine Wilcock <nadine.wilcock@thenyjournal.com>
Subject: Mel

Well, she turned up. And you were right:

He didn't sell her into white slavery.

But he did the next worse thing, if you ask me. He made her fall in love with him.

What's wrong with me, Tony? I mean, I've never seen her this happy and excited. Not even the day that rumor went around about Prince William and Britney Spears. This is nothing compared to that. That day, she was giddy. Now, she's ecstatic.

And yet I can't help feeling like it's all going to come crashing down in some horrible way.

Why? Why do I feel this way? He's a nice guy, right? I mean, you met him. Didn't he seem nice to you?

I think that's the problem. He seems so nice, so *normal*, that I still haven't been able to reconcile this guy, this "John," with the Max Friedlander we heard so much about, the one with the ice-cubed nipples and all those supermodels in his pocket.

I just don't understand what a guy who could have a super-model would want with Mel. I know it sounds horrible, but think about it. I mean, we know Mel's cute and quirky and lovable, but would a guy who'd been hanging around supermodels be able to see that? Don't guys hang around supermodels for one reason? You know, for the arm candy?

Why would a guy who's been eating nothing but dessert for the past few years suddenly opt for meat and potatoes?

Am I the worst best friend who ever lived, or what?

Nad

To: Nadine Wilcock <nadine.wilcock@thenyjournal.com>
From: Tony Salerno <foodie@fresche.com>
Subject: Are you the worst best friend who ever lived?

Yes. I'm sorry, but yes.

Look, Nadine, you know what your problem is? You hate men.

Oh, you like me. But let's face it, in general, you don't like men, or trust them. You think all we do is troll around for models. You think we're so stupid, we can't see past a girl's face or chest or hips.

Well, you're wrong.

Look, despite your assertion, supermodels aren't dessert. They're people, just like you and me. There are some nice ones and some mean ones, some smart ones and some stupid ones. I would say a guy who is a photographer probably meets a lot of super-models, and maybe he meets a few he likes, and they go out a few times, or whatever.

Does that mean that if he happens to meet a nonsupermodel who he likes, he can't go out with her, too? Do you think he is sit-ting around, constantly comparing her to the supermodels he's known?

No. And I'm sure Max Friedlander isn't doing that with Mel.

So give the guy a break. I'm sure he genuinely likes her. Hell, he might even genuinely love her. Did you ever think of that?

So, chill.

Tony

P.S.: Mel isn't meat and potatoes, you are. Mel is more like a ham sandwich. With a side of slaw and a bag of chips.

To: John Trent <john.trent@thenychronicle.com>
From: Jason Trent <jason.trent@trentcapital.com>
Subject: Now you've done it.

You've really done it.

What are you thinking? I'm serious. WHAT ARE YOU THINKING? What is going through that idiotic brain of yours? SHE THINKS YOU'RE SOMEONE ELSE. She thinks you're someone else, and now you're SLEEPING with her?

My wife put you up to this, didn't she? You are taking advice from my wife. A woman who, I think you should know, ate an entire cherry cobbler—twelve servings—last night. For dinner. And growled at me when I tried to take the spatula away from her.

You know this is going to blow up in your face. YOU ARE MAKING A BIG MISTAKE. If you care about this girl, tell her who you really are. TELL HER NOW.

You're lucky Mim doesn't know about this, or I swear, she'd disinherit you.

Jason

To: Jason Trent <jason.trent@trentcapital.com>
From: jerrylives@freemail.com
Subject: My life

Remember what I started to say about how just because Dad is in jail doesn't give you the right to act like my father? Well, I really mean it. It's my life, Jason, and I'd thank you to stay out of it.

Besides, you're acting like I don't know I've screwed up. I have. I know I have. AND I'M GOING TO TELL HER. I just haven't found the right time yet. Just as soon as I do, I'm going to tell her. Everything.

Then we'll all have a nice long laugh at this over burgers at your place, by the pool. You don't know her, but believe me, Mel has a great sense of humor, and a very warm and forgiving nature. I'm sure she'll think the whole thing is funny.

Do you think anybody's using the cabin in Vermont? Because I'm thinking that might be the perfect place to tell her. You know, drive up for the weekend and tell her in front of a nice romantic fire, over a couple of glasses of wine . . .

What do you think?

John

To: jerrylives@freemail.com
From: Jason Trent <jason.trent@trentcapital.com>
Subject: What do *I* think?

Oh, you want my advice? You want me to stop acting like your father, but you want my advice, *and* you want to borrow my ski cabin?

You've got some nerve. That's all I have to say.

Jason

P.S.: Dad isn't in "jail." It's a minimum security criminal rehabilitation center. Stop making me repeat it.

P.P.S.: No woman is that forgiving.

To: Mel Fuller <melissa.fuller@thenyjournal.com>
From: George Sanchez <george.sanchez@thenyjournal.com>
Subject: Just where do you think you're going?

Don't give me that innocent look over the cubicle wall. Yes, you. What, you think I didn't notice all the lipstick and finger-combing? You think you're getting out of here, don't you?

Well, you're living in a fantasy world. You're not getting out of here until I see the copy on the latest Drew Barrymore breakup.

Got it???

George

To: jerrylives@freemail.com
From: Mel Fuller <melissa.fuller@thenyjournal.com>
Subject: Dinner

Hi, John. I'm afraid I'm not going to get out of here as early as I thought. Can we scoot dinner up to nineish?

Love,
Mel

To: Sergeant Paul Reese <preese@eightyninthprecinct.nyc.org>
From: John Trent <john.trent@thenychronicle.com>
Subject: Touching base

Paul—

Just a note to see if you've come up with anything on the Friedlander case. I've been a bit preoccupied lately, so I haven't called, but I got a little time on my hands, so I was wondering if you've got anything new.

You know, the other night when I came into the building, the doorman wasn't there. When I looked around, I found him and the rest of the building staff in the super's apartment watching the game.

Understandable, of course, being the playoffs and all, but it got me thinking: Was there a game the night Mrs. Friedlander got assaulted?

I did a little researching, and discovered that there was—at around the time the doctors say she was most probably struck.

I know it's not much, but at least it explains how someone could have gotten into the building without being seen.

Let me know if you guys have any new information.

John

To: John Trent <john.trent@thenychronicle.com>
From: Sergeant Paul Reese <preese@eightyninthprecinct.nyc.org>
Subject: Shame on you

You're taking an awfully keen interest in the events surrounding this old lady's assault. Any particular reason?

And what do you mean, you were "in the building" the other night? Does this have something to do with that old woman's pretty next-door neighbor? It better not. The DA does not take kindly to you all messing around with our cases, as I think you will recall from the last one you amateur-sleuthed your way through.

Though since that did result in a successful conviction, they might go easy on you. . . .

In answer to your question, no, we don't have anything new on the Friedlander case. We do, however, have a suspect in the transvestite killer case. Bet you didn't know that, huh? Because we're keeping it under wraps, and trust you will do the same. I know they say you can't trust a reporter, but I've found you to be less unreliable than most.

Anyway, here's the 411:

Kid's found unconscious in his bathroom. I won't go into details about why he was unconscious. I'll let your lurid imagination figure it out. Let me just say that it involved a pair of pantyhose and a hook on the back of his bathroom door. And from what he was wearing, which was a number of ladies' undergarments, I do not think suicide was on his mind—although Mom and Dad choose to think so.

Anyway, the EMS guys take in the fancy duds and note that some of them fit the description of clothing missing from one or two of the homes of victims of the transvestite killer.

Not much, I know, but it's all we've got right now.

So why, you might ask, haven't we hauled the kid in for questioning? Because he's still in the hospital from his little bathroom escapade, on "suicide watch."

But as soon as that bruised larynx of his is healed enough for him to talk, the kid's coming down to the station, and if we can get him to chat, we'll find out if your old lady was one of his more fortunate victims.

Now how's that for some detective work?

Paul

To: Sergeant Paul Reese <preese@eightyninthprecinct.nyc.org>
From: John Trent <john.trent@thenychronicle.com>
Subject: Transvestite killer

I'll bet you a box of Krispy Kremes the Friedlander assault was the work of a copycat . . . and not a very good one at that.

Let's say this kid you've got your eye on is the one: Take a look at his other victims. All lived in walk-up buildings. No doormen to tangle with. All were considerably younger than Mrs. Friedlander. And all had items taken from their homes.

Now, we can't really tell if any of Mrs. Friedlander's clothes were taken, but certainly her purse wasn't, nor the cash in it. And we know the transvestite killer always takes whatever ready cash he can find lying around—even Victim Number 2's laundry quarters.

But Mrs. Friedlander had over two hundred bucks in her wallet, which was sitting in plain sight.

I tell you, the more I think about it, the more I believe this whole thing points to someone who knew her. Someone she was expecting, so she kept the door unlocked. And someone who knew what apartment she lived in, so he didn't need to stop and ask the doorman any questions. . . . And might even have known the doorman's habits well enough to know that on the night of a ballgame he wouldn't be excessively diligent about maintaining his post.

What do you have to say about that?

John

To: John Trent <john.trent@thenychronicle.com>
From: Sergeant Paul Reese <preese@eightyninthprecinct.nyc.org>
Subject: Glazed, not frosted.

And I usually like a nice tall glass of milk with them.

Paul

To: Max Friedlander <photoguy@stopthepresses.com>
From: John Trent <john.trent@thenychronicle.com>
Subject: Your aunt

Max, did your aunt have any enemies that you know of? Anyone she knew who might have wanted her dead?

I know it's a big effort for you to think of anybody else but yourself, but I'm asking you to give it a try, for me.

You know where to reach me.

John

To: John Trent <john.trent@thenychronicle.com>
From: Max Friedlander <photoguy@stopthepresses.com>
Subject: Aunt Helen

I don't hear from you for weeks, and when you finally do write, it's to ask me some cockamamie question about my aunt? What is with you, man? Ever since you started walking that damned dog, you've gone all weird on me.

Enemies? Of course she had enemies. That old lady was a bitch on wheels. Everyone who knew her hated her, with the exception of that freakish animal-loving neighbor of hers. Aunt Helen was always campaigning for some unpopular cause or another. If it wasn't Save the Pigeons, it was Stop Starbucks. I tell you, if I were somebody who liked to sit in the park and drink coffee, I'd have taken out a hit on her.

Plus she was stingy. REALLY stingy. You ask her for a loan—just a piddling five hundred bucks—and it was like World War II all over again, only you're London and she's the Luftwaffe. This from a woman worth twelve million.

Look, Trent, I don't have time for this stuff. Things aren't going as well over here as I'd hoped. Vivica is proving to be far more avian than I ever expected. She's going through money like it's conditioner or something. It would be fine if it were _her_ money, but it's not. She forgot her bank card. I ask you, how does somebody "forget" her bank card when she goes on vacation?

I wouldn't care if it were just a matter of buying her a sandwich now and then, but she keeps insisting she needs new shoes, new shorts, new bathing suits. She's got nineteen bikinis with matching cover-ups already. I ask you, how many bathing suits does a woman need? Particularly when the concierge and I are the only ones around to see them.

Gotta go. She's got a hankering to go to Gucci. GUCCI! Jesus!

Max

To: Max Friedlander <photoguy@stopthepresses.com>
From: Sebastian Leandro <sleandro@hotphotos.com>
Subject: Your message

Max—

Got your message. Sorry I wasn't in. Where were you calling from? Hemingway's house or something? I hear there's a bunch of stray cats that live there, which would certainly explain all that cater-wauling I heard in the background when you called.

Look, bud, I don't have a lot, workwise. I told you not to go on hiatus, or whatever it is you're calling this extended vacation of yours. A week here and there is one thing, but this has turned into a full-on sabbatical. Dropping out of sight the way you're doing has hurt a lot more careers than it's ever helped.

But, hey, the news isn't all bad. If you can hang in there a few more weeks, the resort-and-cruise-wear issues of J. Crew and Victoria's Secret are coming up. They're looking at Corfu and Morocco, respectively. The pay's not much, I know, but it's something.

Don't panic. Swimsuit issues are right around the corner.

Call me. We'll talk.

Sebastian

To: Sebastian Leandro <sleandro@hotphotos.com>
From: Max Friedlander <photoguy@stopthepresses.com>
Subject: You've got to get me out of here

You don't understand. I *need* work. Any work. I have to get out of Key West. Vivica's gone mental. THAT's what you heard when I called. It wasn't cats. It was *her*. She was crying.

And let me tell you, when Vivica cries, she does NOT look like a supermodel. Or any kind of model, for that matter. Except like one of those models they use in horror movies just before someone's head gets chopped off by a flying pylon, or whatever.

Anyway, she's racked all my credit cards up to the max. Unbeknownst to me, she's been buying every piece of crap driftwood sculpture she can find, and shipping them back to New York. I'm serious. She thinks she's got a "real eye" for the next big thing, and that it's going to be driftwood sculpture. She's already bought twenty-seven driftwood dolphins. LIFESIZE.

Need I say more?

FIND ME WORK. I'll take ANYTHING.

Max

To: Lenore Fleming <lfleming@sophisticate.com>
From: Max Friedlander <photoguy@stopthepresses.com>
Subject: S.O.S.

DEAR LENORE,

HI! I KNOW IT SAYS THIS IS FROM MAX, BUT IT IS REALLY FROM ME, VIVICA. I AM USING MAX'S COMPUTER SINCE HE ISN'T HERE. I DON'T KNOW WHERE HE IS. PROBABLY IN A BAR SOMEWHERE. THAT'S WHERE HE ALWAYS IS THESE DAYS. LENORE, HE IS SO SELFISH! HE YELLED AT ME ABOUT THE DRIFTWOOD SCULPTURES. HE HAS NO APPRECIATION FOR FINE ART. HE IS JUST LIKE YOU SAID, TOTALLY BOURGEOIS.

WELL, YOU WARNED ME.

ANYWAY, I TRIED TO CALL YOU, BUT YOU ARE ALWAYS OUT. THEN DEIRDRE SAID I SHOULD TRY E-MAILING. I

HOPE YOU GET THIS. I DON'T KNOW WHAT TO DO. I GUESS I SHOULD COME HOME, ONLY I FORGOT MY BANK CARD. IN FACT, I FORGOT MY WHOLE WALLET. I DON'T EVEN HAVE A CREDIT CARD, WHICH IS WHY I HAVE BEEN USING MAX'S. BUT I WOULDN'T HAVE, IF I HAD KNOWN HOW SELFISH HE IS.

PLEASE COULD YOU HAVE DEIRDRE GO TO MY APART-MENT AND GET MY WALLET AND SEND IT TO ME CARE OF THE PARADISE INN IN KEY WEST? ALSO, COULD SHE SEND SOME BODY LOTION FROM KHIEL'S BECAUSE I AM PEELING.

WELL, THAT'S ALL. IF YOU GET THIS MESSAGE, CALL ME. I NEED SOMEONE TO TALK TO. MAX IS JUST DRUNK ALL THE TIME, AND WHEN HE'S NOT, HE'S ASLEEP.

LOVE,
VIVICA

To: jerrylives@freemail.com
From: Jason Trent <jason.trent@trentcapital.com>
Subject: The cabin

All right, I cleared it. If you want the cabin for next weekend, it's yours—on one condition:

YOU HAVE TO TELL HER.

Seriously, John, you may think this girl is something special, and she probably is, but NO woman likes being lied to, even if it's for a good cause—which I'm not even sure yours is. In fact, I know it's not. I mean, come on, deceiving an old lady and her neighbors?

Admirable, John, very admirable.

Anyway, I'll have Higgins drop the keys to the cabin at your office tomorrow morning.

We're off to Mim's for dinner tonight, so I'll talk to you later.

Jason

P.S.: One thing I have often found works very well with women, when you have to tell them something you don't think they're going to like to hear, is to accompany your confession with a pair of .75 carat diamond stud earrings in a platinum setting, preferably from Tiffany's (the sight of that turquoise box does something to most women). I realize that this might be out of the price range of a crime reporter, but I assume you are going to tell her the part about how you are also a member of the Trent family, of the Park Avenue Trents.

You are going to mention that, aren't you? Because I think it might help. That and the earrings.

To: Jason Trent <jason.trent@trentcapital.com>
From: jerrylives@freemail.com
Subject: The cabin

Well, you might be a pompous ass, but at least you're a generous one. Thanks for the keys.

I will, of course, take your counsel under advisement. On the whole, however, I don't think Mel is the kind of girl who can be swayed by a pair of earrings, from Tiffany's or otherwise.

Thanks for the suggestion, though.

Gotta go. Last night she made me dinner, and now it's my turn. Thank God for Zabar's prepared-food section.

John

To: Mel Fuller <melissa.fuller@thenyjournal.com>
From: Don and Beverly Fuller <DonBev@dnr.com>
Subject: Remember us?

Hi, honey! It's been awhile. You haven't returned any of my messages. I am assuming that you are all right, and that you have just been busy with this whole Lisa Marie Presley thing. I just don't understand that girl. Why on earth she married that Michael Jackson, I will never comprehend. Do you suppose he is paying her alimony? Do you think you could find out for me?

Speaking of marriage, Daddy and I just got back from the wedding of yet ANOTHER of your classmates. You remember Donny Richardson, don't you? Well, he's a chiropractor now, and QUITE well off, from what I understand. He married a darling girl he met at a NASCAR race. You might want to consider attending a few NASCAR races, Mellie, as I hear that there are quite a lot of eligible men in attendance at these events.

Anyway, the wedding was just lovely, and the reception was at the Fireside Inn. You remember, where you and your brother and Daddy always took me for brunch on Mother's Day. The bride was just lovely, and Donny looked so handsome! You can hardly see the scars from that nasty corn-detasseling accident he had all those years back. He's certainly bounced back!

How are things going with that young man you wrote about last time? Max, I think, was his name. Or was it John? I hope you two are taking things nice and slow. I read in Ann Landers that couples who wait until marriage to have sex have a twenty percent less chance of divorcing than couples who don't.

Speaking of divorce, have you heard the rumors about Prince Andrew and Fergie getting back together? I do hope they can patch things up. He always looks so lonely these days when I see him standing around at Wimbledon or wherever.

Write when you get the chance!

Love,
Mommy

To: Don and Beverly Fuller <DonBev@dnr.com>
From: Mel Fuller <melissa.fuller@thenyjournal.com>
Subject: Hi!

Hi, Mom! Sorry I haven't called or written in so long. I really have been busy.

Things have been going really great. Really, really great. In fact, better than they've gone in a long time. That's because of the guy I told you about, John.

Oh, Mom, I can't wait for you to meet him! I am totally going to bring him home for Christmas, if I can get him to come. You will just love him. He is just so funny and nice and sweet and smart and handsome and tall and everything, you will just DIE when you meet him. He is so much better than Donny Richardson could ever ever be. Even Daddy will like him, I'm sure. I mean, John knows all about sports and engines and Civil War battles and all those things Daddy likes.

I am so glad I moved to New York, because if I hadn't I never would have met him. Oh, Mom, he's just so great, and we have such a good time together, and I've been late to work every day this week because of him, and I have accrued about eight more tardies in my personnel file, but I don't care, it is just so nice to be with someone you don't have to play games with and who is perfectly straight with you, and who isn't afraid to use the "L" word.

That's right, the "L" word! He loves me, Mom! He says so every day, like ten times a day! He is so not like any of those other losers I have been out with since I moved here. HE LOVES ME. And I love him. And I am just so happy, sometimes I think I could burst.

Well, I have to go now. He's making me dinner. Speaking of which, he actually likes my cooking. Really! I made pasta the other night, and he loved it. I used your recipe for the sauce. Well, with a little help from Zabar's prepared-food section. But what he doesn't know won't hurt him!

Love,
Mel

To: Mel Fuller <melissa.fuller@thenyjournal.com>
From: Don and Beverly Fuller <DonBev@dnr.com>
Subject: Daddy and I are

just so happy for you, sweetie. It's just so nice that you have met this lovely boy. I hope the two of you are having a very nice time together, preparing meals for one another and perhaps taking strolls through Central Park (though I hope you'll stay out of there at night. I've heard all about those wilding youths).

Just remember though that there are men out there (and I'm not saying your John is one of them) who are only after one thing, and will TELL a girl that they love her just to get her into bed.

That's all I'm saying. Not that this young man of yours would ever do such a thing. I just know there are men out there who do. The reason I know this, Melissa, is that, well, don't tell your father, but . . .

It happened to me.

Fortunately I realized in time that the young man in question was one of those. But Melissa, I came very close. Very, very close to giving away my most precious jewel to a man who most decidedly did not deserve it.

All I'm trying to say, Melissa, is to get a ring on that finger of yours before you give anything away. Will you promise Mommy you'll do that?

Have fun—but not too much fun.

Love,
Mommy

P.S. Also, if you have a picture of this young man, Robbie says he has a friend in the FBI who will run it through their computer and see if he is wanted for any federal crimes. It can't hurt, Melissa, just to be on the safe side.

To: Nadine Wilcock <nadine.wilcock@thenyjournal.com>
From: Mel Fuller <melissa.fuller@thenyjournal.com>
Subject: My mother

Would you please remind me never to tell my mother anything again?

Mel

To: Mel Fuller <melissa.fuller@thenyjournal.com>
From: Nadine Wilcock <nadine.wilcock@thenyjournal.com>
Subject: You told your mother something?

What are you, nuts? I make it a point never to tell mine anything. I am keeping a journal, however, so she can find it all out in the event that I die before she does.

I bet she told you to get a ring on your finger before you go to bed with John. Am I right?

Did you tell her it was too late? No, of course you didn't. Because then she'd have a heart attack, and it would be ALL YOUR FAULT.

You chump.

Are you ever going to start going to spin class with me again? You know, it's lonely spinning alone.

Nad ;-)

To: Nadine Wilcock <nadine.wilcock@thenyjournal.com>
From: Mel Fuller <melissa.fuller@thenyjournal.com>
Subject: Spinning

Oh, Nadine, I would love to start going to spinning with you again. It's just that, with John and all this work George keeps piling on me and everything, I just can't seem to find a single moment to myself.

I'm sorry.

You don't hate me, do you? Please don't hate me. I mean, we still see each other at lunch. . . .

Mel

To: Mel Fuller <melissa.fuller@thenyjournal.com>
From: Nadine Wilcock <nadine.wilcock@thenyjournal.com>
Subject: Hate you?

You really ARE nuts.

Of course I don't hate you.

It's just that—and I don't want to sound like your mother—don't you think things are moving a little . . . fast? I mean, you two haven't spent a night apart since you . . . you know.

And what do you know about this guy? I mean, really? Besides his aunt, what do you know about him? Where does he go every morning when you go off to work? Does he sit around his aunt's apartment? Has he taken any pictures of you? It seems to me that, being a photographer, he'd want to. Has he taken you to see his studio, if he has one? Where does he live, when he's not living at his aunt's? Have you seen his place? HIS place, not his aunt's? Does he even have a place?

You mentioned that his credit cards are maxed out. Shouldn't he be working to pay them off? But has he gone off to any shoots since you've known him? I mean, does he even HAVE a job, that you know of?

I just feel like . . . I don't know. These are things you ought to find out before you go off the deep end for the guy.

Nad

To: Tony Salerno <foodie@fresche.com>
From: Nadine Wilcock <nadine.wilcock@thenyjournal.com>
Subject: Help

I think I just did a bad thing. I suggested to Mel that there is quite a lot about Max Friedlander that she doesn't know—for instance,

where the guy lives when he is not shacking up at his aunt's—and
that before she goes off the deep end for the guy she at least ought
to find some of out.

I sort of forgot that she's pretty much gone off the deep end
already.

Now she's not speaking to me. At least, I think she's not speaking to me. She's locked in the copy room right now, with DOLLY,
of all people.

I'm a very bad person, aren't I?

Nad

To: Nadine Wilcock <nadine.wilcock@thenyjournal.com>
From: Tony Salerno <foodie@fresche.com>
Subject: Mel

No, you're not a bad person. And I'm sure she isn't mad at you.
She's just, you know, in love. She doesn't want to think about anything else.

Why don't you ask her if she and John want to come out to
dinner with us tonight? Tell them I'll fix us all something really
special. I just got in some excellent squid ink pasta.

Let me know.

Tony

To: Mel Fuller <melissa.fuller@thenyjournal.com>
From: Dolly Vargas <dolly.vargas@thenyjournal.com>
Subject: Nadine

She's just JEALOUS, darling. That's all. I mean, have you seen that scrawny thing she's marrying? A cook. That's all he is. A glorified fry cook, who just happens to own a restaurant that, for some inexplicable reason, is doing very well.

What am I talking about, inexplicable? It's completely explicable: His fiancée's a food critic for the *New York Journal*!

Don't WORRY about it. Max Friedlander is a hugely successful, hugely sought after artiste. So what if he hasn't had any work in months? He'll be back up on his feet in no time.

So dry your little eyes and keep your beard-burned little chin up. I'm sure everything's going to be fine.

And if not, well, there's always Xanax, isn't there, sweetie?

XXX000

Dolly

To: Dolly Vargas <dolly.vargas@thenyjournal.com>
From: Mel Fuller <melissa.fuller@thenyjournal.com>
Subject: Nadine

Dolly, you had better watch it. You happen to be speaking about my best friend. Nadine is NOT jealous. She is just looking out for me.

And Tony is far more than a "glorified fry cook." He's the most talented chef in all of Manhattan.

But thank you for saying nice things about John.

Mel

To: Mel Fuller <melissa.fuller@thenyjournal.com>
From: jerrylives@freemail.com
Subject: Next weekend

Hey, what are you doing next weekend? Do you think you could get out early on Friday? I'm thinking about renting a car and driving up to this ski cabin in Vermont that someone lent me the keys to. I know there's no snow this time of year, but I promise it's gorgeous even without the white stuff. And the cabin's got all the amenities, including a great big fireplace, hot tub, and, yes, even a satellite dish for the wide-screen television.

I knew that one would get you. What do you say?

Love,
John

To: jerrylives@freemail.com
From: Mel Fuller <melissa.fuller@thenyjournal.com>
Subject: Next weekend

I would love to go to Vermont with you. Maybe you could bring your photography equipment and take some pictures while we're there. Because you know, I've never even seen you in action? With a camera, I mean. You read my column every day, but I haven't seen a single photo you've taken. I mean, aside from last year's *Sports Illustrated* swimsuit edition. . . .

And maybe before we go, we could stop by your apartment, so I could see it, too. You know, I never have. I have no idea where you live when you aren't at your aunt's, or what kind of stuff you have. I mean, what your taste in furniture and stuff is.

And I'd like to know. I'd really like to know.

Mel

To: Mel Fuller <melissa.fuller@thenyjournal.com>
From: jerrylives@freemail.com
Subject: Next weekend

Um, we most certainly can stop by my apartment any time you want. I'm afraid you're going to be sadly disappointed in it, however, since its furnishings are mostly of the Ikea and plastic-milk-crate variety.

As for bringing my photography equipment with us to Vermont, I think that might be a little like a busman's holiday, don't you think? Let's just play it by ear.

Why this sudden interest in my taste in home furnishings? Are you thinking of asking me to move in? It's a little late for that, don't you think, seeing as how all of my clean shirts are now sitting in your linen closet. Or maybe you haven't noticed. Well, they are.

And I'm not moving them. Unless, that is, you would deign to give me a drawer somewhere.

Love,
John

To: Nadine Wilcock <nadine.wilcock@thenyjournal.com>
From: Mel Fuller <melissa.fuller@thenyjournal.com>
Subject: You're wrong

So I asked John if I could see his place, and he said yes, and that it is furnished with milk crates and Ikea furniture, which means it must exist, so you see he DOES have his own place, and though I haven't exactly pinned him down on the work thing yet, I will, because we are going away together next weekend, and we're going to have to spend fourteen hours in a car together, and I fully intend to find out everything there is to know about his career.

So there.

Mel

To: Mel Fuller <melissa.fuller@thenyjournal.com>
From: Nadine Wilcock <nadine.wilcock@thenyjournal.com>
Subject: I was wrong

Mel, I'm sorry I said all of those things. I had absolutely no right to. I am really very, very sorry.

Can I make it up to you by inviting you and John to dinner? Tony says he's got some squid ink pasta. Will you come?

Nad

To: Nadine Wilcock <nadine.wilcock@thenyjournal.com>
From: Mel Fuller <melissa.fuller@thenyjournal.com>
Subject: Well . . .

Even though I am totally angry with you, I'll accept your invitation, just so you can see how WRONG you were, thinking all of those horrible things about John. We'll see you both at seven.

Mel

To: John Trent <john.trent@thenychronicle.com>
From: Sergeant Paul Reese <preese@eightyninthprecinct.nyc.org>
Subject: Transvestite killer

Okay. I'm not saying you're right about the old lady knowing her attacker, but I will say this: It was definitely a copycat.

You didn't hear this from me, understand? But remember that kid I told you about? The one whose folks found him hanging from the hook in the bathroom in ladies' underdrawers?

Well, we did a bit of investigating, and what do you think we found out? It seems the kid works for one of those dot-com delivery companies. You know, any time of day, anything you want, you go on-line and make a request, and they'll deliver it?

And by doing some discreet investigating at the kid's place of employment, we found out he's been in all seven buildings in which a transvestite murder has occurred. We got a printout that places him at every single one of those crime scenes at exactly the time the murders took place. He killed them while he was supposed to be delivering ice cream and videos.

And here's the worst part: The kid never missed a delivery. Not once. Just killed 'em, then went to the next place.

And do you think anybody from his place of employment ever caught on, you know, that people were dying at the places this kid delivered to? Oh, no.

And what do they have to say about this model employee of theirs? "He's so quiet, so shy. He could NEVER have done anything so heinous as murder seven women for their lingerie and laundry quarters."

We're bringing the kid down tonight. He got released from the loony ward for that supposed "suicide" attempt yesterday.

But here's the part that concerns you: Kid's never made a delivery in Friedlander's building. No record of anyone from that building ever even calling this particular biz.

Just thought you'd want to know.

Paul

To: John Trent <john.trent@thenychronicle.com>
From: Genevieve Randolph Trent <grtrent@trentcapital.com>
Subject: I am very disappointed

---

in you, John. We had yet another family get-together the other night, from which you were once again absent. I must say, I am becoming extremely irritated by your continued disdain for us. It is one thing to refuse to accept our financial aid. It is quite another simply to cut us from your life completely.

I have been given to understand from Stacy that you and this Fuller girl are quite "the item." I must say I was astonished to hear this, as I have only met her once and under, I must say, some extremely unusual circumstances. In fact, it is not clear to me that she even knew the two of us were related.

Your brother and his wife—who is, by the way, as large as a house; I am quite certain her physician is wrong about her due date, and would not be surprised if she gives birth at any moment—are quite reticent to discuss the matter with me, but I feel certain that you are up to something, John.

And Haley and Brittany had some very interesting things to say on the subject of your wedding to a certain redheaded lady, at which they presume they will be flower girls, and are planning their wardrobe for the occasion accordingly.

Is this true, John? Are you planning on marrying this girl, whom you have not even properly introduced to your family?

If so, I must say, I never expected such behavior from you. Some of your cousins, perhaps, but not you, John.

I do hope you will take steps to rectify this matter immediately. Only give me a date during which you are both free, and I will arrange a casual family dinner. I would be only too happy to introduce Miss Fuller to the rest of the Trents . . . those who are currently on parole, that is.

Do not mistake my flippancy for lack of caring, John. I care deeply. So deeply, in fact, that I am willing to overlook your exceedingly odd behavior in the matter.

But only up to a point, my boy.

Sincerely,
Mim

To: Genevieve Randolph Trent <grtrent@trentcapital.com>
From: John Trent <john.trent@thenychronicle.com>
Subject: Don't you worry

Mim,
Just give me another week. Okay? Just one more week, and you can meet her—properly, this time. There's just a little something I have to tell her beforehand.

Can you be patient just a little longer? I promise it will be worth it.

John

To: Sebastian Leandro <sleandro@hotphotos.com>
From: Max Friedlander <photoguy@stopthepresses.com>
Subject: Any luck?

I haven't heard from you. Have you got anything for me? Anything at all?

Look, in case you didn't quite get it: I NEED WORK. I am extremely low in fundage at the moment. Vivica's drained me dry. . . .

And now, more than ever, I have to get out of here:

She's starting to talk about commitment, Sebastian. Marriage. Kids. She's turned completely bovine on me.

I just don't get it. I come out to Key West with one of the top supermodels in the country, and somehow I end up broke and explaining my position on overpopulation.

You've got to find something for me, dude. I'm counting on you.

Max

To: Max Friedlander <photoguy@stopthepresses.com>
From: Sebastian Leandro <sleandro@hotphotos.com>
Subject: Look, man

You up and leave during our busiest season. And I'm not saying I blame you. I mean, it's Vivica. I'd have done the same thing.

But you can't disappear for three months in this business and expect to be able simply to pick up where you left off. New talent moves in. There are some real money-hungry kids out there who are good. Real good.

And they don't charge as much as you do, pal.

But that is not to say I'm not trying. I WILL find something for you. But you've got to give me some time.

I'll get in touch as soon as I hear of anything, I swear.

Sebastian

To: Sebastian Leandro <sleandro@hotphotos.com>
From: Max Friedlander <photoguy@stopthepresses.com>
Subject: So you're saying

I've gone from one of the top photographers in the country to NOTHING??? In a little more than ninety days? That's what you're asking me to believe?

Thanks. Thanks for nothing.

Max

To: Lenore Fleming <lfleming@sophisticate.com>
From: Max Friedlander <photoguy@stopthepresses.com>
Subject: S.O.S.

LENORE!

IT'S ME AGAIN. VIVICA.

THANKS FOR THE WALLET. I GOT IT. I DECIDED NOT TO LEAVE RIGHT AWAY. I WANTED TO GIVE MAX ANOTHER CHANCE, YOU KNOW. I THOUGHT MAYBE HE WOULD APOLOGIZE. BECAUSE I KNOW HE IS REALLY VERY DEEPLY IN LOVE WITH ME.

BUT HE TOTALLY DIDN'T! APOLOGIZE, I MEAN. IN FACT, IF ANYTHING, NOW HE HAS GOTTEN MEANER. YOU WILL NOT BELIEVE WHAT HE SAID LAST NIGHT. HE SAID HE DOES NOT WANT TO MARRY ME, AND THAT HE NEVER DID. HE SAYS HE DOES NOT WANT TO HAVE BABIES WITH ME, OR EVEN SPEND CHRISTMAS WITH ME!!!

LENORE, WHAT SHOULD I DO? I JUST KEEP CRYING AND CRYING. I CAN'T BELIEVE HE WOULD DO THIS TO ME. I CAN'T BELIEVE HE WOULD SPEND THREE MONTHS WITH ME IN KEY WEST, AND THEN TURN AROUND AND SAY HE DOESN'T WANT TO SPEND THE REST OF HIS LIFE WITH ME. I HAVE NEVER FELT SO USED.

LENORE, YOU'VE GOT TO HELP ME. I KNOW YOU HAVE HAD LOTS OF EXPERIENCE WITH MEN. AFTER ALL, YOU ARE SO OLD—ALMOST 30. YOU MUST KNOW OF SOME WAY I CAN GET HIM TO LOVE ME.

PLEASE HELP.

VIVICA

To: Nadine Wilcock <nadine.wilcock@thenyjournal.com>
From: Mel Fuller <melissa.fuller@thenyjournal.com>
Subject: I don't know about you,

but I had a fabulous time last night. Didn't you have fun? I mean, everything was so perfect: the squid ink pasta was delicious, and the boys seemed to get along so well—didn't you think they got along? Not that I know anything about college basketball, but that discussion they had about it seemed pretty lively.

Don't you see how wrong you were about him now? About John, I mean. I haven't exactly brought up the iced nipple thing with him, but don't you think that's just what readers of the *Sports Illustrated* swimsuit edition expect? I mean, it seems like that's just part of his job.

All I'm saying is, we should definitely do it again, and soon. But not this weekend, because this is the weekend we're spending at that ski cabin John's friend is lending him.

And, I don't want to jinx anything, but last night I offered to feed Tweedledum and Mr. Peepers while John was walking Paco, and I just happened to spot a Tiffany's bag peeking out from John's overnight bag. You know, the one he's taking for the weekend.

That's right. A Tiffany's bag.

I know. I know. I am not getting excited. It could be anything. It could be the bag he carries his socks in when he travels. Who knows?

But what if it's . . . you know?

It could be. It really could be.

That's all I'm going to say.

Mel

To: Mel Fuller <melissa.fuller@thenyjournal.com>
From: Nadine Wilcock <nadine.wilcock@thenyjournal.com>
Subject: Are you serious?

You seriously think he's going to propose? Melissa, the two of you have only been going out for a couple of months. Less, even. I don't want to be a wet blanket, but I really don't think you should get your hopes up. I bet anything if you'd looked in that bag you'd have seen socks. Men are weird that way.

Nad

To: Nadine Wilcock <nadine.wilcock@thenyjournal.com>
From: Mel Fuller <melissa.fuller@thenyjournal.com>
Subject: I should have looked, shouldn't I?

I just couldn't. It just seemed so . . . wrong. To look, I mean.
    Not that I think that's what's in the bag. A ring, I mean. I totally don't. I'm sure it's just socks.
    But what if it isn't?
    That's all I'm saying. A girl can dream, can't she?

Mel

To: Mel Fuller <melissa.fuller@thenyjournal.com>
From: Nadine Wilcock <nadine.wilcock@thenyjournal.com>
Subject: So I take it that if it is a ring,

you intend to say yes? Is that it?

Not that I think you shouldn't. Only . . .

Only there's nothing wrong with waiting. Really. I mean, you should at least, out of common decency, wait until his aunt is out of her coma, or dead. Whichever comes first.

Don't you think?

Nad

To: Nadine Wilcock <nadine.wilcock@thenyjournal.com>
From: Mel Fuller <melissa.fuller@thenyjournal.com>
Subject: I guess

you're right. About waiting to see what happens with Mrs. Friedlander. That would be pretty cold, to go around announcing our engagement, when she's still in a coma.

God, I don't even know what I'm talking about. There's no ring in that bag. I'm sure it's socks. It has to be socks.

Right?

Mel

To: Tony Salerno <foodie@fresche.com>
From: Nadine Wilcock <nadine.wilcock@thenyjournal.com>
Subject: Mel

Well, it's all over. He's proposing. This weekend, it looks like, in the romantic ski cabin he's borrowing for the occasion.

I'm not saying I disapprove. I mean, I like the guy. I really do. It's just that . . . I don't know. I can't shake this bad feeling I have about all this. What's wrong with me?

Nad

To: Nadine Wilcock <nadine.wilcock@thenyjournal.com>
From: Tony Salerno <foodie@fresche.com>
Subject: What's wrong with you

Nothing's wrong with you. You just want your friend to be happy.

And I don't blame you. I want Mel to be happy, too. She deserves to be happy, and not just because Freddie Prinze Jr. is going out with Sarah Michelle Gellar, or whatever else it is she writes about.

But in order for people to be happy, sometimes they have to take risks. It's true those risks can put them in danger of being hurt. I think that's what's freaking you out about Mel. She just met this guy. He's got an iffy rep in the 'hood. Hooking up with him is a major risk.

But I think to her it's worth it. So you just have to stand back and let her make her own decisions and stop being such a freaking psycho about it. I mean, who do you think is good enough for her, anyway? Me? Well, I happen to be taken.

And you know what happened when we tried fixing Mel up with my brother Sal. . . .

Hey, if the two of them do work it out and decide to get hitched, we could have a double wedding. What do you think about that?

Just kidding.

Tony

To: Mel Fuller <melissa.fuller@thenyjournal.com>
From: jerrylives@freemail.com
Subject: Vermont

Okay, so have you got your long underwear? I hear it can get cold at night up there.

I'm going to pick up the car at seven, so we can be on the road by eight. Think you can be up and around by then? I know it will be a challenge to you. Fortunately, I, unlike some people, will never hold your perpetual tardiness against you.

I'm renting a full-size vehicle in the hopes that Paco will fit into the backseat. What do you think the chances are that he won't insist on sticking his head out the window and drooling on anyone we pass? And do you think they ticket for that kind of thing? Flinging dog drool on innocent passersby?

John

To: jerrylives@freemail.com
From: Mel Fuller <melissa.fuller@thenyjournal.com>
Subject: Vermont

I can be ready by eight. What do you think I am, some kind of sloth?

I think Paco will be fine in the backseat. It's Tweedledum and Mr. Peepers I'm worried about. I know Ralph said he'd feed them, but I highly doubt he'll stay to pet them or anything. I mean, he's totally afraid of getting animal hair on his doorman uniform. Maybe we should offer to have it dry-cleaned for him when we get back.

You're kidding about the long underwear, right?

Mel

To: Mel Fuller <melissa.fuller@thenyjournal.com>
From: Dolly Vargas <dolly.vargas@thenyjournal.com>
Subject: Vermont

Darling, I hear you're going up north with him for the weekend. That is just so *St. Elmo's Fire.* Are you going to wear Love's Baby Soft and a big turtleneck sweater?

Seriously, I just wanted to give you a few eensy-weensy tips before you go, because you're such a little innocent about these kinds of things.

1. DO NOT allow him to put your name down on the rental agreement. Then you will have no choice but to drive should he ask you to. And nothing looks tackier than a woman driving with a man in the passenger seat. Membership in the feminist movement = lifelong spinsterhood.

2. DO NOT offer to go out to get a log for the fire from the

woodpile. I have found that spiders often live in woodpiles. Let him do the wood gathering, for God's sake.

3. DO offer to cook breakfast, and make it a hearty one, preferably with sausages. For some reason, men seem to love to ingest foods soaked in saturated fats when they are in the woods. He will show his appreciation for you in all the right ways.

4. DO bring your own CDs. If you don't, you'll be listening to the Grateful Dead and War all weekend long—not to mention, I shudder to write it, Blood, Sweat, and Tears.

5. DO bring earplugs. Men who ordinarily don't snore are prone to do so in the woods, due to various allergens that don't exist in the city.

6. DO NOT let him shower first. Cabins have notoriously little hot water, and he will use it all up, leaving you none. Insist on being the first to bathe.

7. DO NOT forget to bring edible body oils with you. They simply do not sell such things in these backwater towns, so if you forget them, it's all over.

I hope this helps, sweetie. And don't forget: Have fun!

XXXOOO

Dolly

To: Nadine Wilcock <nadine.wilcock@thenyjournal.com>;
Tim Grabowski <timothy.grabowski@thenyjournal.com>
From: Mel Fuller <melissa.fuller@thenyjournal.com.>
Subject: All right . . .

Who told Dolly I was going away with John? You guys have GOT to stop. I cannot stand this anymore. STOP TELLING DOLLY THINGS ABOUT JOHN AND ME.

It is seriously not funny. I do not need her knowing my business. At least, not the stuff I haven't told her myself.

Mel

To: Jason Trent <jason.trent@trentcapital.com>
From: John Trent <john.trent@thenychronicle.com>
Subject: Well, this is it

We're leaving in the morning. And I'm going to do it. I swear I'm going to do it. I called Chuck up at the lodge and had him go over to the cabin and make sure the hot tub was good and ready, stick a few bottles of champagne in the fridge, and start defrosting some of those venison steaks.

I think I'm ready.
Wish me luck.

John

To: John Trent <john.trent@thenychronicle.com>
From: Jason Trent <jason.trent@trentcapital.com>
Subject: You really are

a moron, you know that, don't you? How you could have let yourself get into this situation in the first place—or let it go on for so long—I do not know.

But I will wish you luck, because, buddy, you are going to need it.

Jason

To: Lenore Fleming <lfleming@sophisticate.com>
From: Max Friedlander <photoguy@stopthepresses.com>
Subject: S.O.S

LENORE!!!

IT'S OVER. I CAN'T BELIEVE IT. I CAN'T EVEN BELIEVE IT. I CAN BARELY TYPE ON ACCOUNT OF CRYING SO HARD.

TODAY I CAME HOME FROM THE POOL, AND WHAT DO YOU THINK I FOUND?

HE WAS WITH ANOTHER WOMAN, LENORE! IN OUR BED. WITH THE MAID!!! THE MAID!!!

SHE'S NOT EVEN THAT PRETTY!! SHE USES LIQUID EYE-LINER, AND HAD ON LAST SEASON'S MANOLO BLAHNIK MULES. NOT EVEN REAL ONES, EITHER. CHEAP KNOCK-OFFS!!!

WELL, THAT IS IT. IT IS SO OVER. YOU HAVE TO GET ME ON THE NEXT FLIGHT BACK TO NEW YORK.

I KNOW. I KNOW WHAT YOU ARE GOING TO SAY: I HAVE TO DO SOMETHING TO GET BACK AT HIM OR I WILL NEVER HAVE CLOSURE.

BUT WHAT CAN I DO? I CAN'T SEND HIM A BUNCH OF DEAD ROSES, LIKE GUYS ARE ALWAYS SENDING TO ME WHEN I DUMP THEM. THAT'S, YOU KNOW, A GUY THING. I THOUGHT ABOUT SENDING HIM A METAL JOCKSTRAP, LIKE NAOMI SENT BOBBY. BUT THEY DON'T EVEN SELL METAL JOCKSTRAPS HERE.

I HAVE TO GET BACK AT HIM SOMEHOW, I KNOW. I HAVE TO HIT HIM WHERE IT HURTS THE MOST.

OH. WAIT A MINUTE. I HAVE AN IDEA.

WISH ME LUCK.

VIVICA

To: Mel Fuller <melissa.fuller@thenyjournal.com>
From: Max Friedlander <photoguy@stopthepresses.com>
Subject: HELLO

YOU DON'T KNOW ME, BUT MY NAME IS VIVICA, AND I THINK YOU SHOULD KNOW THAT THAT GUY WHO HAS BEEN WALKING MAX'S AUNT'S DOG ISN'T MAX AT ALL, BUT HIS FRIEND JOHN, WHO OWED MAX A FAVOR ON ACCOUNT OF MAX HELPING JOHN OUT OF A JAM BACK IN VEGAS WHEN HE ALMOST MARRIED A REDHEADED SHOW-GIRL NAMED HEIDI. JOHN IS JUST PRETENDING TO BE MAX ON ACCOUNT OF MAX NOT BEING ABLE TO COME BACK TO NEW YORK TO WALK HIS AUNT'S DOG BECAUSE HE IS HERE IN KEY WEST WITH ME. BUT HE DIDN'T WANT HIS AUNT TO THINK HE DIDN'T CARE, SO HE HAD JOHN DO IT FOR HIM.

AND I THINK IF MAX'S AUNT EVER WAKES UP, YOU SHOULD TELL HER WHAT MAX DID. SHE SHOULD DEFI-NITELY WRITE HIM OUT OF HER WILL BECAUSE HE DOESN'T DESERVE ANY OF HER MONEY.

ALSO, YOU SHOULD KNOW THAT MAX FRIEDLANDER IS A HORRIBLE PERSON AND ANYONE WHO IS FRIENDS WITH HIM PROBABLY IS, TOO.

ALL MEN ARE PIGS AND I HOPE THEY DIE AND MON-KEYS TAKE OVER LIKE ON *PLANET OF THE APES* BECAUSE THEN THINGS WOULD BE WAY BETTER.

THAT'S ALL.

VIVICA

To: Mel Fuller <melissa.fuller@thenyjournal.com>;
Nadine Wilcock <nadine.wilcock@thenyjournal.com>;
Dolly Vargas <dolly.vargas@thenyjournal.com>
From: George Sanchez <george.sanchez@thenyjournal.com>
Subject: Would anyone care to tell me

what all that screaming was about a little while ago? And why aren't any of you at your desks? I swear to God, if you're all in the ladies' room again, I am going in there and dragging you out. I don't care. YOU CAN'T ALL HAVE TO GO AT THE SAME TIME. This isn't cheerleader camp. What do you think I am, stupid?

Can't any of you comprehend the fact that there is a time for gabbing and a time for working, and that when there's a paper to put to bed, that means it's time for WORKING???

GET BACK TO YOUR DESKS AND STAY THERE! George

To: Mel Fuller <melissa.fuller@thenyjournal.com>
From: Nadine Wilcock <nadine.wilcock@thenyjournal.com>
Subject: Mel, just call

him. Just call and ask him. I'm sure it's just some kind of sick joke from an ex-girlfriend or something. You can straighten it all out with one phone call.

Just call him. There's probably a very rational explanation for all of this.

Nad

To: Nadine Wilcock <nadine.wilcock@thenyjournal.com>
From: Mel Fuller <melissa.fuller@thenyjournal.com>
Subject: No

You don't understand. I just went through the e-mails I've gotten over the past few months, because I thought the return address to this one looked familiar, but I knew it wasn't John's, because his is jerrylives@freemail.com. And look. Look what I found. His first letter ever to me. Check out the return address:

>To: Mel Fuller <melissa.fuller@thenyjournal.com>
>From: Max Friedlander <photoguy@stopthepresses.com>
>Subject: My aunt
>
>Dear Ms. Fuller,
>
>I am shocked. Deeply shocked and appalled to hear what has happened to my Aunt Helen. She is, as I'm sure you know, my only living relative. I cannot thank you enough for the efforts you've gone to in order to contact me and let me know about this tragedy.
>
>Although I am currently on assignment in Africa—perhaps you've heard of the drought here in Ethiopia? I am doing a photo shoot for the Save the Children fund—I will begin making preparations to return to New York at once. If my aunt should wake before I get there, please assure her that I am on my way.
>
>And thank you again, Ms. Fuller. Everything they say about cold and unfeeling New Yorkers is obviously untrue in your case. God bless you.

>
>Sincerely,
>
>Maxwell Friedlander

It's the same return address as that one I just got from this Vivica. And read it. It doesn't even SOUND like John. John didn't write this. Nadine, I think this Vivica person might be telling the truth!

Oh, my God, what do I do? I can't just call him. What am I going to say?

Mel

To: Mel Fuller <melissa.fuller@thenyjournal.com>
From: Nadine Wilcock <nadine.wilcock@thenyjournal.com>
Subject: What are you going to say?

I can't believe you are asking me this. You're going to say, "Hey, buster, what the hell is going on here? If you think I'm going to Vermont with you after this, you've got another think coming, let me tell you. Now who the hell is Vivica?"

God, Mel, you are not a wuss, so why are you acting like this? CALL HIM!!!

Nad

To: Mel Fuller <melissa.fuller@thenyjournal.com>
From: Dolly Vargas <dolly.vargas@thenyjournal.com>
Subject: Darling

I know how upset you must be, and I just want to assure you that I am behind you 150 percent. Men can be such children, can't they?

And because I feel so deeply for you in your hour of need, I have done a little calling around, and finally managed to track down Max Friedlander's agent.

Sweetie, I hate to be the one to break it to you, but Sebastian says Max has been in Key West the past few months with the supermodel Vivica!

I of course said, "But Sebastian, darling, that's impossible, Max has been here walking his aunt's dog and courting my little friend Melissa," to which Sebastian, who is just a sweetheart, replied, "Dolly, honey, this isn't the nineties anymore, put down the crack pipe. I'm getting calls from Max three times a day demanding to know when I'm going to find him work since Vivica is draining him dry."

So there you go. Whoever this John of yours is, he can't be Max Friedlander.

Oh, how I wish I'd been there that night you brought him to Fresche for our inspection. I could have told you straightaway he wasn't Max.

I blame myself.

Is the Xanax I slipped you in the ladies' working yet?

XXXOOO

Dolly

To: John Trent <john.trent@thenychronicle.com>
From: Max Friedlander <photoguy@stopthepresses.com>
Subject: You are a dead man

What is wrong with you? What the hell is wrong with you? Are you messing around with my aunt's next-door neighbor? The reporter from the *Journal*? And doing it UNDER MY NAME???

Are you mental? I told you to walk Aunt Helen's dog. That's all. Just walk the stupid dog.

So why am I getting phone calls from my agent saying that that Dolly Vargas broad, the one I know from the *Journal*, has been calling around asking a bunch of questions about me? Specifically, how can I be in New York, going out with her friend Melissa, when I'm supposed to be in Key West, doing Vivica?

This is bad, dude. Really bad. I am in a bad place here, and you are just making things worse. Vivica caught me messing around with the maid—which was so totally not my fault: The woman wouldn't keep her hands off me—and now she's gone.

Which is admittedly something of a relief, so far as my finances are concerned. But there is no telling what she's going to do when she gets back to New York. Blow my cover, most likely.

This is bad. Really bad. Why couldn't you have just done what I asked you, and nothing more? Now if my aunt wakes up, she's going to know I didn't fly back up there to take care of her stupid pets.

This is uncool, dude. Way uncool.

Max

To: Jason Trent <jason.trent@trentcapital.com>
From: John Trent <john.trent@thenychronicle.com>
Subject: Help

I think I am in big trouble.

John

To: John Trent <john.trent@thenychronicle.com>
From: Jason Trent <jason.trent@trentcapital.com>
Subject: What do you mean

help? Help what? How can you be in big trouble? I thought you'd left for Vermont. Why are you still here?

Stacy says to write her. Her brain is atrophying from too much daytime television.

Jason

To: Mel Fuller <melissa.fuller@thenyjournal.com>
From: jerrylives@freemail.com
Subject: I know

you're home, I can see that your bedroom light is on. So why won't you answer the door? Or your phone?

Mel, I know something is wrong, and I think I know what it is, but unless you talk to me, how can I make it right?

Because I can, I can make it right, if you would just give me the chance. Please, please, please open the door.

John

To: Tony Salerno <foodie@fresche.com>
From: Nadine Wilcock <nadine.wilcock@thenyjournal.com>
Subject: Well, it happened

Just like I knew it would. I KNEW this guy was too good to be true. And that whole John thing. I told you it was weird to have a nickname like John, didn't I?

Well, I was right. I'm not happy that I was right, but I was right. His nickname isn't John. That's his REAL name. That's all we know so far, except for the fact that we know what his name ISN'T: It ISN'T Max Friedlander. Apparently, the real Max Friedlander paid this guy to POSE as him or something, so that he (the real Max) could hang out in Key West with Vivica, the supermodel, instead of flying back to New York to walk his aunt's dog.

Poor Mel. Poor, poor Mel.

Why did I have to be right? I'd pay money not to have been right. I'd give up my new size 12 figure to have been wrong. Seriously.

Nad :-(

To: Nadine Wilcock <nadine.wilcock@thenyjournal.com>
From: Tony Salerno <foodie@fresche.com>
Subject: Let me see

if I have this straight:

This guy Mel's been seeing was just pretending to be Max Friedlander—a guy who you never liked, because you'd heard bad things about him—and now all of a sudden it turns out he's NOT Max Friedlander. Only instead of being relieved, because he isn't the dog you originally thought him, you're mad because he lied.

I don't get you women. I really don't. I mean, I'll admit the guy exercised some poor judgment, but at least he never put ice on anyone's nipples.

Tony

To: Tony Salerno <foodie@fresche.com>
From: Nadine Wilcock <nadine.wilcock@thenyjournal.com>
Subject: Don't you get it?

He lied. He lied to her. How is she supposed to believe anything he said to her, when he never even told her his real name?

What is wrong with you? Whose side are you on?

Nad

To: jerrylives@freemail.com
From: Tony Salerno <foodie@fresche.com>
Subject: You really blew it

Dude, remember how you gave me your e-mail address and told me to send you that recipe for my rigatoni bolognese so you could surprise Mel with it?

Well, I don't think you're going to be needing it. Because from what I'm hearing, you are in the doghouse, but good.

So what's the deal? Max Friedlander paid you to tell Mel you were him or something? Because that is what the girls are saying.

I do not know what is up with you, but you had better start sandbagging, because you are in for some heavy artillery fire. Either that, or get out of there, dude. Seriously. Save yourself, because it's all going to start coming down.

Just thought I'd give you a heads-up.

Tony

To: Max Friedlander <photoguy@stopthepresses.com>
From: John Trent <john.trent@thenychronicle.com>
Subject: No, YOU are the dead man

What are you trying to do to me? Are you CRAZY? How did Mel find out about all this?

John

To: John Trent <john.trent@thenychronicle.com>
From: Stacy Trent <IH8BARNEY@freemail.com>
Subject: WHAT'S HAPPENING???

Why isn't anyone telling me anything? Jason says something is wrong. What is it? Aren't you supposed to be in Vermont?

Damn these cramps. . . .

Stacy

To: John Trent <john.trent@thenychronicle.com>
From: Max Friedlander <photoguy@stopthepresses.com>
Subject: Quit your whining

You owed me one, remember?

Anyway, it isn't my fault. It was Vivica. She did it. She apparently e-mailed your girl. I can see the message in my outbox. Want to see it? Here is it, and I must say, it's a brilliant testament to the inadequacies of our public school system:

<YOU DON'T KNOW ME, BUT MY NAME IS VIVICA, AND I THINK YOU SHOULD KNOW THAT THAT GUY WHO HAS BEEN WALKING MAX'S AUNT'S DOG ISN'T MAX AT ALL, BUT HIS FRIEND JOHN, WHO OWED MAX A FAVOR ON ACCOUNT OF MAX HELPING JOHN OUT OF A JAM BACK IN VEGAS WHEN HE ALMOST MARRIED A REDHEADED SHOWGIRL NAMED HEIDI. JOHN IS JUST PRETENDING TO BE MAX ON ACCOUNT OF MAX NOT BEING ABLE TO COME BACK TO NEW YORK TO WALK HIS AUNT'S DOG BECAUSE HE IS HERE IN KEY WEST

WITH ME. BUT HE DIDN'T WANT HIS AUNT TO THINK HE
DIDN'T CARE, SO HE HAD JOHN DO IT FOR HIM.

She goes on, ad nauseam, in this vein, but I thought I'd spare
you.

You can't honestly tell me you're upset about this. *I'm* the one
whose ass is grass here. If that bitch of an aunt of mine wakes up
and hears about this I am dead meat. Every cent she has will go
straight to the ASPCA when she croaks. You can bet I won't see a
penny of it.

Not that it matters. It's time I took care of this once and for all,
the way I should have from the beginning.

So who knows? You might be seeing me sooner than you think.

And as for that threat about me being a dead man, I have one
word for you:

Alimony. I saved you from years and years of it, buddy. So
don't you forget it.

Max

To: Stacy Trent <IH8BARNEY@freemail.com>
From: John Trent <john.trent@thenychronicle.com>
Subject: Things aren't going

too well right now, in answer to your question. Mel found out
about the whole posing-as-Max-Friedlander thing before I had the
chance to tell her myself, and let's just say she's not too happy
about it. In fact, she isn't speaking to me.

I could really use some advice right now, but no one is answering the phone at your place.

John

To: Mel Fuller <melissa.fuller@thenyjournal.com>
From: jerrylives@freemail.com
Subject: The truth

All right. You won't answer the door. You won't pick up the phone. I KNOW you're there. If this is the only way I'm going to be able to get through to you, then so be it.

Mel, I screwed up. Okay? I really, really screwed up, and I know it. I should have just told you the truth from the beginning, but I didn't. I can't tell you how many times I almost did just that—told you the truth, I mean. A thousand times. A million.

But every time I started to, I knew—I just knew—you were going to react this way, and I didn't want to spoil what we have together, because, Mel, what we have is so great. Are you really going to throw it away because I made one stupid—okay, massively idiotic—mistake?

It isn't as if I purposefully set out with the intention of deceiving you. Well, that's not exactly true. I did, but when I did it, it wasn't as if I knew you. I mean, I get this e-mail from Max, and all he wants is this one thing—to trick his aunt's neighbors into thinking he was taking care of her business while she was in the hospital—and I thought, why not? I did owe the guy. I figured it was a virtually painless way to pay him back for a favor he did me a long time ago.

You don't know Max Friedlander—the real Max Friedlander—but believe me, he's not somebody you want holding something over your head—like a favor you owe him—because he's likely to call you on it when you least expect it, and generally in a not-very-pleasant manner.

How was I supposed to know that while pretending to be Max Friedlander, I was going to meet the girl of my dreams? I know I should have told you from the start, but I didn't, and then before I knew it I was in love with you, and I couldn't tell you because I didn't want to lose you. I swear I was going to tell you this weekend.

Mel, this is ridiculous. I know what I did was wrong, but I never meant it to hurt you. I mean, you *must* know that. You know *me*, regardless of what my name is. So you must know I would never purposefully hurt you.

Now open your door and let me in so I can apologize in person. Mel, I promise I can make this all right again, if you'd just let me.

John

To: jerrylives@freemail.com
From: Mel Fuller <melissa.fuller@thenyjournal.com>
Subject: The truth

You tell me you want me to open my door and let you in, but the fact is, I don't know who "you" are. I don't even know your last name. Do you realize that?

And you might as well quit knocking, because I am not letting you in. For all I know, you could be an escaped convict or married or something.

Mel

To: Mel Fuller <melissa.fuller@thenyjournal.com>
From: John Trent <john.trent@thenychronicle.com>
Subject: The truth

I'm not married, and I'm not an escaped convict. My name is John Trent, and I'm a crime reporter for the *New York Chronicle*. That's why you ran into me by the sinkhole that day—I was at work when it happened.

And I know how you feel about the *Chronicle*, but Mel, I swear to you, if it bothers you that much, I'll quit. I'll do anything, anything you want, if you'll forgive me.

John

To: Mel Fuller <melissa.fuller@thenyjournal.com>
From: Nadine Wilcock <nadine.wilcock@thenyjournal.com>
Subject: Well?

Did you call him? Has he apologized?
More importantly, HAS HE GIVEN YOU THE RING YET?

Nad

To: Nadine Wilcock <nadine.wilcock@thenyjournal.com>
From: Mel Fuller <melissa.fuller@thenyjournal.com>
Subject: The apology

Oh, he apologized, all right. For what it's worth.

And no, he hasn't given me the ring yet. If it even is a ring. Which I doubt.

And as if I'd even take it, if it was.

Get this: You know who he is? You know who he really is? You'll never guess.

Go on. Try. Try to guess who he really is.

Mel

To: Mel Fuller <melissa.fuller@thenyjournal.com>
From: Nadine Wilcock <nadine.wilcock@thenyjournal.com>
Subject: How am I supposed

to know who he really is? He can't be the transvestite killer, I know that, since they just arrested a guy for that. He's not, oh, I don't know, a professional mime, or something, is he?

Oh, wait, I know: He's your long-lost illegitimate brother.

Just kidding.

Come on, Mel, how bad can it be?

Nad

To: Nadine Wilcock <nadine.wilcock@thenyjournal.com>
From: Mel Fuller <melissa.fuller@thenyjournal.com>
Subject: Bad

Worse than a mime. Worse than my illegitimate brother.
He's a reporter. With the *Chronicle*.

Mel

To: Nadine Wilcock <nadine.wilcock@thenyjournal.com>
From: George Sanchez <george.sanchez@thenyjournal.com>
Subject: Where the hell

is Fuller? She better not be in the ladies'. I swear to God, I'm beginning to think there's somebody in there serving lattes, you all
spend so much time locked in those damned stalls. . . .

Go in there and tell her I want that story on the Ford/Flockhart
breakup by five.

George

To: George Sanchez <george.sanchez@thenyjournal.com>
From: Nadine Wilcock <nadine.wilcock@thenyjournal.com>
Subject: Show a little compassion, will you?

She just found out her boyfriend is a reporter with the *Chronicle*.
She's been crying her eyes out ever since. You can't expect her to
snap back like it was nothing.

Please don't tell anyone about it, either, all right? She's in a very fragile emotional state right now. What she needs is closure, and she's not going to get it if everybody keeps hounding her for an explanation as to why her eyes are so red.

Nad

To: Tim Grabowski <timothy.grabowski@thenyjournal.com>
From: Jimmy Chu <james.chu@thenyjournal.com>
Subject: Mel Fuller

I told you it wasn't going to work out between the two of them.

Jim

To: Jimmy Chu <james.chu@thenyjournal.com>
From: Tim Grabowski <timothy.grabowski@thenyjournal.com>
Subject: Mel Fuller

No, what you actually said was that if she slept with him and it didn't work out, she was going to have to see him every day, since he lives right next door, and that that would be very awkward. You did not actually predict this breakup.

Sorry, no points for you.

Tim

To: Stella Markowitz <stella.markowitz@thenyjournal.com>
From: Angie So <angela.so@thenyjournal.com>
Subject: Mel Fuller

I told you he was too old for her.

Angie

To: Angie So <angela.so@thenyjournal.com>
From: Stella Markowitz <stella.markowitz@thenyjournal.com>
Subject: Mel Fuller

It's not his age that matters. It's the fact that he's—did you hear the latest?—a reporter for the *Chronicle*.
   Yes, the *Chronicle*!
   Can you believe it? Talk about sleeping with the enemy.

Stella

To: Adrian De Monte <adrian.de.monte@thenyjournal.com>
From: Les Kellogg <leslie.kellogg@thenyjournal.com>
Subject: Mel Fuller

Did you hear? It turns out that guy Mel's been so crazy about is a reporter. With the *Chronicle*, no less.
   I guess it could have been worse. He could have turned out to

be sleeping with Barbara Bellerieve all along, like the last guy she went out with.

Les

To: Nadine Wilcock <nadine.wilcock@thenyjournal.com>
From: George Sanchez <george.sanchez@thenyjournal.com>
Subject: Mel Fuller

I don't care if it turns out the guy's on the FBI's Ten Most Wanted list: She's going to have to come out of that bathroom and deal with him, because he's downstairs by the security desk, trying to get signed in. Go get her.

George

To: Security@thenyjournal.com
From: Mel Fuller <melissa.fuller@thenyjournal.com>
Subject: John Trent

Please do not allow John Trent access to this building. He is a reporter with the *Chronicle*, in addition to being a very dangerous individual. I strongly encourage the use of force in removing him from the building.

Melissa Fuller
Page Ten Columnist
New York Journal

To: Mel Fuller <melissa.fuller@thenyjournal.com>
From: Amy Jenkins <amy.jenkins@thenyjournal.com>
Subject: John Trent

Dear Ms. Fuller,
Please note that in the future, requests for individuals to be made personae non gratae in any building falling under the administrative management of the *New York Journal* must be made in writing through Human Resources, where they will be reviewed and then passed on to the security department, if deemed valid.

Additionally, you will find that the cost of the rubber tree plant destroyed outside the fifth-floor elevator bank will be deducted from your next paycheck. This is due to the fact that the individual to whom this destructive act was ascribed was apparently an acquaintance of yours. Please note that in section E, page twelve, of the *New York Journal* employee handbook, it is stated that employees are at all times responsible for their guests, and that any damage incurred by said guest is the responsibility of the employee by whom he/she was signed in.

You should consider yourself fortunate that you are not being charged for the cost of reconstructing the cubicle into which your guest threw Mr. Spender. We have chosen to send the bill for that to Mr. Trent himself.

Might I suggest that it would behoove you to conduct your romantic affairs well outside the administrative offices of this newspaper?

A copy of this letter has been inserted into your permanent personnel file.

Have a nice day.

Amy Jenkins
Human Resources Representative
New York Journal

To: Mel Fuller <melissa.fuller@thenyjournal.com>
From: Dolly Vargas <dolly.vargas@thenyjournal.com>
Subject: John Trent

Darling, how was I to know? I mean, there he was, standing there in the lobby with that dejected look on his face, and all those roses. Why, it was enough to break the heart of . . .

Well, even _me_.

And I know what you're going to say: "Dolly, _you_ have a heart?"

Surprising, but true. Sometimes I surprise even myself. Why, just the other day, I turned Peter loose, and told him quite firmly to go back to his wife. And the fact that I heard a little rumor that his employment contract wasn't going to be renewed didn't have a thing to do with it.

Anyway, it wasn't as if Security hadn't gotten your memo. About John, I mean. They said it came just moments after my signing him in.

Really, sweetie, what harm did I do? So he pestered you a little. I for one quite enjoyed the performance. You have to admit, he was impassioned, for a blue blood. I think Aaron's going to lose several of his teeth. Well, the silly nudge shouldn't have tried to stop him from getting to your cubicle like that.

Still, it is always so delicious to have two men fighting over one, isn't it?

But do you really think it was wise to throw that Tiffany's box he tried to give you back at him? There's no telling what might have been in there. With his kind of money, it was probably three carats, at least.

I do hope you aren't going to be as unforgiving toward me as you're being toward that unfortunate young man.

XXXOOO

Dolly

To: Dolly Vargas <dolly.vargas@thenyjournal.com>
From: Mel Fuller <melissa.fuller@thenyjournal.com>
Subject: John Trent

Dolly—
What did you mean when you wrote "blue bloods"? And what money? John doesn't have any money. All of his credit cards are maxed out. You must be mistaking him for somebody else.

Mel

To: Mel Fuller <melissa.fuller@thenyjournal.com>
From: Dolly Vargas <dolly.vargas@thenyjournal.com>
Subject: Au contraire

You are too precious. Are you trying to tell me you don't know that your John is one of the Park Avenue Trents?

I thought that was why you were so angry with him—I mean, aside from the whole pretending-to-be-Max-Friedlander thing. After all, he introduced you to his grandmother at that Lincoln Center benefit you reported on last month.

Although now that I think of it, I suppose he didn't tell you she was his grandmother, did he? On account of his pretending to be Max.

Oh, dear. No wonder you're so angry. He did make a bit of a fool of you, didn't he? His credit cards were maxed out, he said? Well, I'm sure he only told you that so he wouldn't have to pull one out. His cover would have been blown for sure if that had happened, don't you think? Supposing you see the John Trent on his Platinum AmEx, instead of the Max Friedlander you were expecting?

I have to admit, it's a typical Trent trick. You know half their clan is in jail—John's own father among them. And the rest of them are in rehab. Goodness, what chance did a small-town girl like you have among them? John's the worst, from what I hear—he got a job as a crime reporter so he could go "slumming" whenever he felt like it, and not arouse suspicion that he's one of "them." The Park Avenue Trents, I mean. Why, I hear from Victoria Arbuthnot, who used to go out with him, you know, that he's even pretending to be working on a novel.

Poor little Mel. You should have kept the Tiffany's box. What-ever was in it, you deserve it, for all embarrassment he's put you through.

Oh, well. I hear there's a sale at Barney's. Want to go? I'll buy you a scarf. It might cheer you up. . . .

XXXOOO

Dolly

To: Nadine Wilcock <nadine.wilcock@thenyjournal.com>
From: Mel Fuller <melissa.fuller@thenyjournal.com>
Subject: That's it.

This is war.

He thinks just because he's a Trent of the Park Avenue Trents, he can trick people and use them for his own amusement and get away with it?

Not this time. Nobody goes slumming with a Fuller of the Lans-ing, Illinois, Fullers.

Nobody.

John Trent is about to get what's coming to him, but good.

Mel

To: Mel Fuller <melissa.fuller@thenyjournal.com>
From: Nadine Wilcock <nadine.wilcock@thenyjournal.com>
Subject: I almost hesitate to ask,

but what are you talking about?

This doesn't have anything to do with Dolly, does it? I mean, Mel, consider the source before you do anything rash.

Nad

To: Nadine Wilcock <nadine.wilcock@thenyjournal.com>
From: Mel Fuller <melissa.fuller@thenyjournal.com>
Subject: It's easy for you to talk

You weren't the one worrying about how much money he was spending, and how he was ever going to get out of debt.

You weren't the one who introduced yourself to his grandmother and didn't even know that's who she was.

You weren't the one who bragged about him to your mother.

You weren't the one who thought that finally, at last, you'd met that rarest of all things, a man who wasn't afraid of commitment, a man who seemed utterly and sincerely devoted to you, a man who was completely different from all the other men you'd ever dated before, a man who didn't lie, didn't cheat, who seemed genuinely to love you.

You weren't the one whose heart got completely stomped on.

But, never fear. I am a reporter, Nadine. I always check my sources before I run with any story.

Mel

To: John Trent <john.trent@thenychronicle.com>
From: Aaron Spender<aaron.spender@thenyjournal.com>
Subject: Pending lawsuit

Dear Mr. Trent:

This letter serves to inform you of my intention to pursue litigation against you for the pain and suffering, as well as the medical costs, incurred when you struck me in the face in my place of employment.

It might interest to you know that as a result of your vicious and unprovoked attack, I have already endured extensive dental surgery, which will require additional follow-up, I am informed, in the form of two dental implants through the course of multiple visits over a twelve-month period at a cost in excess of $10,000.

Moreover, to insure that such an incident is not repeated, my counsel advises that I also pursue a restraining order against you, which I can assure you I am pursuing.

I am encouraging Miss Fuller to do the same, as it was in her defense that I first laid hands upon you. It was quite clear that Miss Fuller did not welcome your advances, and I personally consider you a coward and a cad to have confronted her in such a manner in her place of work.

Furthermore, I happen to hold a brown belt in tae kwon do, and it was only due to my concern of injuring innocent bystanders that I did not give you the thrashing you so roundly deserved.

Aaron Spender
Senior Correspondent
New York Journal

To: Aaron Spender <aaron.spender@thenyjournal.com>
From: John Trent <john.trent@thenychronicle.com>
Subject: Pending lawsuit

Bite me.

John Trent

To: Michael Everett <michael.everett@thenychronicle.com>
From: George Sanchez <george.sanchez@thenyjournal.com>
Subject: Trent

Mike—
You better start keeping your boy Trent on a leash. He was over here the other day raising all sorts of hell. Took out a few of Spender's molars. Not that I mind—now at least I don't have to listen to the bastard whine about how come I won't give him a paid leave of absence to go to Africa and do a story about endangered chinchillas, or whatever the hell cause it is he's spouting off about this week.

Still, I can't be having the teeth knocked out of my senior correspondents. Strongly encourage him to give this thing he's got for my gossip columnist a rest. She's a good kid, and doesn't need the aggravation.

Best,
George

P.S.: Love to Joan and the boys.

To: Mel Fuller <melissa.fuller@thenyjournal.com>
From: Tim Grabowski <timothy.grabowski@thenyjournal.com>
Subject: John Trent

Honey, I know you're just as mad as a bee caught under a pickle jar at the moment, but really, don't you think you ought to take a deep breath and THINK a minute?

This guy, who, I'll admit, behaved in a fairly *Animal House* manner, nevertheless was the light of your life for quite a little while. Do you really want to throw away all you two had together just because the guy pulled one inane fratboy prank?

He didn't mean to hurt you. He was trying to do his friend a favor. I mean, come on, Mel. I could understand you're wanting to make him squirm for a bit, but this is getting ridiculous.

Besides, do you have any idea how RICH John Trent is? Dolly was telling me all about it at lunch yesterday. The guy is LOADED. I mean, millions, all his own, left to him by his granddaddy. And sweetie, the Trents have houses all over the place, the Cape and Palm Springs and Boca and Nova Scotia—you name it. Just think what fun you'd have, installing satellite television in all of them.

You know, forgiveness is divine.

Just a hint.

Tim

To: Tim Grabowski <timothy.grabowski@thenyjournal.com>
From: Mel Fuller <melissa.fuller@thenyjournal.com>
Subject: John Trent

And I could invite all my close personal friends up to spend the weekend in those vacation homes, right?

Forget it, Tim. You are so transparent.

Besides, if you'd listened closely to Dolly, you'd have been able to read between the lines: Trents don't marry Fullers. They just use them for their own entertainment.

Mel

To: Nadine Wilcock<nadine.wilcock@thenyjournal.com>
From: Tim Grabowski <timothy.grabowski@thenyjournal.com>
Subject: Mel

Something has got to be done about Mel. She is blowing this thing with poor Mr. Trent way out of proportion. I've never seen her like this. I have to say, I'm glad I never got on her bad side. She certainly knows how to hold a grudge.

I guess we should have known, her being a redhead and all.

I'm thinking she needs to be referred to counseling. You agree?

Tim

To: Tim Grabowski <timothy.grabowski@thenyjournal.com>
From: Nadine Wilcock<nadine.wilcock@thenyjournal.com>
Subject: Mel

Tim, she's angry, not insane. Anger management classes, maybe, but counseling? The guy LIED to her. Outright lied. It doesn't matter *why* he did it, the fact that he did it is enough. Don't you know how shaky Mel's trust in men has been ever since Aaron revealed his true colors? Heck, even before that, she was convinced they were all out for one thing, and one thing alone.

And now this guy, the first guy she's really liked in a long time, turns out to be exactly like all those other guys she's gone out with since moving here: a lying pig.

I don't know. Wouldn't YOU be mad, if it were you?

Nad

To: Mel Fuller <melissa.fuller@thenyjournal.com>
From: Aaron Spender <aaron.spender@thenyjournal.com>
Subject: You

I want you to know that I understand exactly how you're feeling right now. That Trent fellow is the lowest of the low, a perfect example of the privileged rich taking advantage of the working poor. He doesn't care about what happens to any of us, so long as he can get what he wants. Men like Trent have no conscience—they are what is known as "alpha males," grasping individuals who have absolutely no interest in anything beyond their own immediate gratification.

Well, I want to assure you, Melissa, that in spite of what you may be feeling at the moment, not all of us possessors of the Y chromosome are selfish bastards, thinking only of ourselves. Some of us have deeply rooted feelings of respect and admiration for the women in our lives.

I, for instance, will always have feelings for you, feelings that are as genuine as they are unwavering. I want you to know, Melissa, that I will always, always be here for you—even though foul troglodytes like Trent might try to break my spirit, not to mention my jaw.

If there is anything—anything at all—that I can do for you now, in your hour of greatest need, please do not hesitate to ask.

Faithfully yours, for now and always,

Aaron

To: Aaron Spender <aaron.spender@thenyjournal.com>
From: Mel Fuller <melissa.fuller@thenyjournal.com>
Subject: You

Bite me.

Mel

To: John Trent <john.trent@thenychronicle.com>
From: Genevieve Randolph Trent <grtrent@trentcapital.com>
Subject: Your new nephew

Dearest John,
It might interest you to know that your sister-in-law gave birth to a nine-pound baby boy two days ago.

His parents have—misguidedly, in my opinion—chosen to christen the child John.

You would already know this, of course, if you ever bothered calling anyone in your family, but that, I suppose, would be asking entirely too much of an enterprising young man like yourself.

Mother and son are doing fine. The same cannot be said for your brother, who has been home alone with the twins while Stacy is in the hospital. You might wish to give him a call and offer some fraternal support.

Sincerely,
Mim

To: Jason Trent <jason.trent@trentcapital.com>
From: John Trent <john.trent@thenychronicle.com>
Subject: My namesake

You shouldn't have. I really mean that. I'm a rotten brother, and I'll be an even more rotten uncle to the kid. I can't believe I missed the whole thing.

Anyway, congratulations. Nine pounds, huh? No wonder Stacy was so cranky at the end there. There's a little package from Harry Winston coming her way. It's the least I could do for all the advice she's given me over the past few months.

Not, of course, that it did much good. I still managed to botch everything, but good. You were right about no woman being forgiving enough to let something like this go. She won't even speak to me. I went by her office, and it was a disaster. Her idiot exboyfriend tried to play the hero, and I decked him one. Now he's suing me. I tried to give her the ring, and she threw it back in my face without even opening the box.

That's not even the worst of it. She had Mrs. Friedlander's locks changed. I couldn't even get back into the building to get my things without being escorted by the super—who is sympathetic, but who pointed out that, as I am not actually related to the apartment's owner, he cannot issue me my own key.

So I'm back at my place, and now I can't even see her. I don't know what she's doing or with whom. I suppose I could go stand in front of the building and catch her when she comes out to walk the dog or go to work or whatever, but what would I say? What can I say?

Well, sorry about that. I didn't mean to bring you down during this happy time. Congratulations, and give John Jr. a big kiss from me. I'll be up to see him this weekend. It's not like I'm going to have any other plans.

John

To: John Trent <john.trent@thenychronicle.com>
From: Jason Trent <jason.trent@trentcapital.com>
Subject: Ring?

What ring?

Earrings, I said. Buy her earrings. Not a ring. What ring are you talking about?

Jason

To: Jason Trent <jason.trent@trentcapital.com>
From: John Trent <john.trent@thenychronicle.com>
Subject: The Ring

I know you said earrings. But I bought her a ring. An engagement ring.

And no, this isn't like the time in Vegas. I have not been perpetually drunk for the past three months. I genuinely believe that this woman, out of all the women I have ever known, is the one with whom I want to spend the rest of my life.

I was going to tell her the truth, and then propose, in Vermont. Only that bastard Friedlander had to screw the whole thing up.

Now she won't answer my phone calls, open her door, or reply to my e-mails. My life is over.

John

To: John Trent <john.trent@thenychronicle.com>
From: Jason Trent <jason.trent@trentcapital.com>
Subject: My God

I leave you alone for a week, and you manage to make a shambles of your life. How is that possible?

All right, meet me at my office for lunch tomorrow. Between the two of us, we should be able to come up with some idea as to how to fix this.

Hey, we're Trents, aren't we?

Jason

To: Sebastian Leandro <sleandro@hotphotos.com>
From: Max Friedlander <photoguy@stopthepresses.com>
Subject: Look, dude

It's been weeks since I heard from you. Have you got anything for me, or not?

Don't try to reach me in Key West. I'm headed back to New York. You can reach me at my aunt's place. You've got the number.

I'm crashing there until I can get back on my feet again. I mean, why not? She's sure as hell not using it.

Max

To: Mel Fuller <melissa.fuller@thenyjournal.com>
From: George Sanchez <george.sanchez@thenyjournal.com>
Subject: I realize

that you've been crippled with grief over your boyfriend's heinous betrayal and all that, but are you going to turn in a column for tomorrow's paper, or aren't you? Maybe you think we should just print a big blank space with the words DOWN WITH MEN in the middle of it. That'd sure make us look like professionals, huh? We'd certainly out sell the *Chronicle* then, wouldn't we?

GET ME THAT COLUMN!!!

George

To: George Sanchez <george.sanchez@thenyjournal.com>
From: Mel Fuller <melissa.fuller@thenyjournal.com>
Subject: Calm down, George

I sent the column down to the copy desk hours ago. I didn't want to bother you with it. You were busy yelling at Dolly for failing to complete her assignment on Christina Aguilera—Victim or Soulless Sellout?

I've attached a copy of tomorrow's Page Ten for your enjoyment.

And unless you intend to stop the presses, it's going to run, since Peter Hargrave himself gave it his seal of approval. He was in here waiting for Dolly, so I ran it past him. Hope you don't mind.

Enjoy!

Mel

Attachment: ✉ [Page Ten, issue 3,784, volume 234 for 1st AM, WHO WANTS TO MARRY A MILLIONAIRE question mark, Mel Fuller, w/ exhibits, 1) photo Vivica, 2) photo Trent Capital Management building, u have in rack]

WHO WANTS TO MARRY A MILLIONAIRE?

Tired of watching 5 to 10 percent of your hard-earned pay disappear into that 401(k) every month, girls? Why not try accruing capital the old-fashioned way? There's a millionaire bachelor out there who's sick of the single life, and is actively seeking a bride.

That's right, you heard it here first. The *New York Journal*—has even learned that **John Randolph Trent**—grandson of the late Harold Sinclair Trent, who founded Trent Capital Management, one of New York's oldest and most revered brokerage firms—has finally decided to get hitched. The only problem? He can't seem to find the right girl.

"I'm tired of dating models and movie starlets who are only after my money," Mr. Trent was heard to observe to a friend. "I'm looking for a woman of character and substance, an ordinary woman who doesn't live in Beverly Hills. I would love to marry a woman from, say, Staten Island."

It is for this reason that the 35-year-old—who inherited a reported $20 million upon the death of his grandfather—will be interviewing potential lifemates in his office at the *New York Chronicle* beginning at 9:00 A.M. this morning. When will the interviews end?

"When I've found her," Mr. Trent asserts.

So get down to 53rd and Madison, girls, before this prince turns into a frog and hops away!

Wedding Bells for
Wonder (Bra) Woman

Meanwhile, another New York bachelor isn't having nearly the same trouble finding Ms. Right. **Max Friedlander**, 35, who is responsible for the steamy photos in last year's *Sports Illustrated* swimsuit issue, recently confided to a friend his secret engagement to supermodel **Vivica**, 22.

Vivica, whose gorgeous visage has graced the covers of *Vogue* and *Harper's Bazaar*, is most widely known for modeling the newest version of the Wonder Bra in last spring's Victoria's Secret catalog. Says Mr. Friedlander of his upcoming nuptials: "I couldn't be happier. I am ready at last to settle down and start a family, and Vivica will make the perfect wife and mother." Vivica was not available for comment, although her publicist would not rule out the possibility of a Christmas wedding.

To: Mel Fuller <melissa.fuller@thenyjournal.com>
From: George Sanchez <george.sanchez@thenyjournal.com>
Subject: Your future employment at this place of business

The minute you get to work, report to my office, and be prepared to tell me, in one hundred words or less, why I shouldn't fire you.

George

To: Peter Hargrave <peter.hargrave@thenyjournal.com>
From: Traffic Update <yourcommute@newyorktravel.com>
Subject: Congestion at 53rd and Madison

New Yorkers traveling by rail should have no problems with their commute today. For all you road warriors out there, however, it's a different story entirely. Thanks to an item appearing in the Page Ten column of today's *New York Journal*, Madison Avenue from 51st to approximately 59th Streets has practically been shut down due to a line of women eager to be interviewed by bachelor millionaire John Trent.

Police are urging drivers to use the FDR for any uptown travel, and avoid the midtown area altogether.

This has been an automated traffic update from NEWYORK TRAVEL.COM.

To: John Trent <john.trent@thenychronicle.com>
From: Michael Everett <michael.everett@thenychronicle.com>
Subject: I had no idea

we had such a celebrity in our midst. Would you care to invest any of that $20 million of yours toward the extra security we've had to hire in order to get in and out of our own building?

Mike

To: Michael Everett <michael.everett@thenychronicle.com>
From: John Trent <john.trent@thenychronicle.com>
Subject: What are you talking about?

Look, I've had a really long week moving back into my place. Can you just break it to me, whatever it is, and get it over with?

John

To: John Trent <john.trent@thenychronicle.com>
From: Michael Everett <michael.everett@thenychronicle.com>
Subject: Are you trying to tell me

that you did not tell Mel Fuller of the *Journal* that you are currently seeking a bride? And that you have nothing to do with the fact that there are, by last NYPD estimates, twelve thousand women standing on the sidewalk downstairs, demanding an appointment to see you? Because if you'll take a look at today's *Journal*, that's what it says.

Mike

To: Michael Everett <michael.everett@thenychronicle.com>
From: John Trent <john.trent@thenychronicle.com>
Subject: LIES!!!

All of it is lies!!!!
    Mike, I never said any of those things—you know I didn't.

I can't believe this. I'll be right in. I'll straighten this out somehow, I swear it.

John

To: John Trent <john.trent@thenychronicle.com>
From: Michael Everett <michael.everett@thenychronicle.com>
Subject: Hold on there

pardner. Just stay where you are. We don't need you strolling in here and causing a mob scene. Stay put until further notice.

Mike

P.S.: So ALL of it is untrue? Even the part about you being related to the Park Avenue Trents and having millions of dollars? Joan was kind of hoping that part might be true. See, we're trying to refinish our basement, and . . .

Just kidding.

To: George Sanchez <george.sanchez@thenyjournal.com>
From: Michael Everett <michael.everett@thenychronicle.com>
Subject: Excuse me

But you want me to keep MY reporter on a leash? What about yours?

Mine may have loosened a couple of your Senior Correspondent's teeth, but yours has created a citywide traffic jam! Did you know I couldn't even get in to my office building today, due to the fact that it is surrounded by ten thousand screaming women—some of whom are dressed in bridal gowns—all screaming, "Pick me"?

This is a hundred times worse than the sinkhole. With that, we couldn't use the john. But with this, we can't get in or out of our building without being mauled by desperate single women, anxious to marry and breed before menopause hits.

If Trent doesn't sue the pants off you, you can be sure we will.

Mike

To: Peter Hargrave <peter.hargrave@thenyjournal.com>
From: Dolly Vargas <dolly.vargas@thenyjournal.com>
Subject: Mel

Well, frankly, I think it's a scream.

And you can't let George fire her, Peter. You approved the column, remember? Aren't you the publisher of this paper? Are you going to stand by your employee and her story, or run for the hills?

Are you a man, Peter, or a mouse?

XXXOOO

Dolly

To: Mel Fuller <melissa.fuller@thenyjournal.com>
From: Nadine Wilcock<nadine.wilcock@thenyjournal.com>
Subject: What did you do?

Mel, I do not believe this. I DO NOT BELIEVE THIS. With a single column, you've managed to shut down an entire city.

ARE YOU INSANE??? George is going to kill you.

And don't you think you've gone a little far? I mean, yes, John lied to you, and it was wrong. But you're lying to the entire tristate area—or at least everywhere that the *Journal* is readily available. Two wrongs do not make a right, Mel.

Now you're going to get fired and then you're going to have to go home and live with your folks. And then who's going to be my maid of honor???

Nad :-(

To: Mel Fuller <melissa.fuller@thenyjournal.com>
From: Tony Salerno <foodie@fresche.com>
Subject: I had to

ride my bike to work today because of the whole mess over there on Madison. There are women of all shapes and sizes lined up outside the *Chronicle* building. It's like when they drop the ball in Times Square on New Year's, only everyone is more dressed up. You should see the panicked expressions on the faces of the cops who have been called in. Some of them are wearing riot gear.

Do you feel better now? I think you could safely say the two of you are even.

Tony

To: Mel Fuller <melissa.fuller@thenyjournal.com>
From: Tim Grabowski <timothy.grabowski@thenyjournal.com>
Subject: I can't believe

you've finally started using your powers for evil, instead of good.
I'm so proud I could burst.

You go, girl.

Tim

To: Mel Fuller <melissa.fuller@thenyjournal.com>
From: Don and Beverly Fuller <DonBev@dnr.com>
Subject: Millionaire bachelor

Honey, I just saw on the news that there's a man in New York who
is looking to marry a nice girl from Staten Island. I know you
aren't from Staten Island, but you are much prettier than all those
woman they showed, standing in line. You should go right over
there and sign up for an interview because I think any millionaire
would just love you.

And be sure to take that picture of you in your Miss Duane
County Fair crown and sash! No man can resist a girl in a tiara.

Mommy

To: John Trent <john.trent@thenychronicle.com>
From: Sergeant Paul Reese <preese@eightyninthprecinct.nyc.org>
Subject: If you were that desperate

you should have said something: I have a sister who's single.

FYI: This is the first hats-and-bats alert we've ever had for midtown. You don't get a lot of calls for riot masks and sticks up there by Saks. Congratulations.

Paul

To: John Trent <john.trent@thenychronicle.com>
From: Genevieve Randolph Trent <grtrent@trentcapital.com>
Subject: I am ashamed of you

Of all my grandchildren, you were always the one I least expected to see in any sort of gossip column.

But what does Higgins show me, first thing after breakfast? That horrid story about you and your search for a bride! Who wants to marry a millionaire, indeed!

I can only assume, having read that this piece of garbage was written by none other than M. Fuller, that you have somehow managed to alienate the girl. That, my boy, was most unwise.

I understand further that both your place of employment and now your apartment are under siege. If you wish, I could send Jonesy to fetch you. I hesitate to do so, of course, since it will upset the neighbors if all of those women who are currently chasing after you show up outside our doors. However, I am assured by the police commissioner, who, as you know, is an old friend, that every attempt will be made to keep the riffraff off our sidewalk. You are welcome to spend the next few days here with me, where it's safe.

I have also been assured, by Mr. Peter Hargrave, publisher of that filthy rag, that a retraction will appear within the next day or two. He offered to dismiss the girl, but I told him that would be unnecessary. I'm quite certain that she was perfectly justified, whatever her reasons for doing it.

Really, John. You never did learn to play nicely with the other children. I am quite disgusted with you.

Mim

To: John Trent <john.trent@thenychronicle.com>
From: Jason Trent <jason.trent@trentcapital.com>
Subject: Now you've done it

You've really done it. Mim's furious.

I suggest you take an extended sabbatical. There isn't a place you can go in this town where people aren't talking about you. I heard they've even got a new sandwich: the Trent—just two slices of bread with nothing in the middle (on account of you not showing up to the interviews).

Why don't you come out here to visit with Stace and the kids? We'd love to have you, and you haven't met your namesake yet. What do you say?

Jason

To: Jason Trent <jason.trent@trentcapital.com>
From: John Trent <john.trent@thenychronicle.com>
Subject: Thanks for the offer

Mim made a similar one. But I prefer to stay here and fester in my own self-made hell.

I can't say it hasn't been interesting. I can't even go down to the corner deli to buy milk without the guy behind the counter offering to introduce me to his daughter. Much as I try to claim the story about my search for a bride isn't true, people just don't seem to want to believe it. They like the idea of a guy being rich enough to have anything in the world except the one thing he really wants . . . the love of a good woman.

Of course, whenever I attempt to explain that I had that, too, but that I managed to louse it up, people *really* don't want to hear it. It's like they can't comprehend the fact that rich does not equal happy.

It hasn't been too bad, really. I've been getting a lot of work done on my novel. It's funny, though. I actually miss that stupid dog. The cats, too. I've been thinking about getting one. A dog, I mean. Or maybe a cat. I don't know. I don't seem to be fit to associate with humans.

Not that I don't keep on trying, though. I've been sending Mel flowers every day—even the day after the column appeared. But do I hear squat from her? Not a word. I imagine the sidewalk outside the office of the *New York Journal* is littered with all the floral arrangements of mine that she's heaved out the window.

Got to go. My Chinese food—for one—is here.

John

To: Mel Fuller <melissa.fuller@thenyjournal.com>
From: John Trent <john.trent@thenychronicle.com>
Subject: You got me.

All right? Are you satisfied? That column caused me untold embarrassment. They still won't let me come to work. My family is barely speaking to me. I haven't heard from Max, but I assume he's been duly chastened as well.

Can we be friends again?

John

To: John Trent <john.trent@thenychronicle.com>
From: Mel Fuller <melissa.fuller@thenyjournal.com>
Subject: Can we be friends again?

No.

Mel

To: Mel Fuller <melissa.fuller@thenyjournal.com>
From: Human Resources <human.resources@thenyjournal.com>
Subject: Suspension

Dear Melissa Fuller,
This is an automated message from the Human Resources Division of the *New York Journal*, New York City's leading photo-newspaper. Please be aware that as of today, your employment at this news-

paper is suspended without pay. Your employment will be reinstated in **3** business days.

This action was taken as the result of a column that you submitted without first going through the appropriate channels. Please note for future reference that all columns must be submitted through your division's managing editor, and not sent directly to the copy desk.

<u>Melissa Fuller</u>, we here at the *New York Journal* are a team. We win as a team, and we lose as one, as well. <u>Melissa Fuller</u> don't you want to be on a winning team? So please do your part to see that your work is delivered through the appropriate channels from now on!

Sincerely,
Human Resources Division
New York Journal

Please note that any future suspensions will result in dismissal.

This e-mail is confidential and should not be used by anyone who is not the original intended recipient. If you have received this e-mail in error please inform the sender and delete it from your mailbox or any other storage mechanism.

To: Mel Fuller <melissa.fuller@thenyjournal.com>
From: Nadine Wilcock <nadine.wilcock@thenyjournal.com>
Subject: Suspended???

Are you kidding??? Can they even do that?

Oh, Mel, this has gone from bad to worse! What am I going to do without you for three days? I'm going to die of boredom!

Would it help if I organized a work stoppage in protest?

Nad

To: Nadine Wilcock <nadine.wilcock@thenyjournal.com>
From: Mel Fuller <melissa.fuller@thenyjournal.com>
Subject: My suspension

Now, now, it won't be that bad. I'm sort of looking forward to it. I haven't had any time off in a quite a while. It will give Paco and me a chance to bond again. And God knows I haven't visited Mrs. Friedlander in the hospital for ages and ages. Not that she's noticed, I'm sure, but still, I feel guilty about it . . . even if it does turn out she's not going to be my aunt-in-law.

Really, don't worry about me. I'm fine. Honest.

Mel

To: Don and Beverly Fuller <DonBev@dnr.com>
From: Mel Fuller <melissa.fuller@thenyjournal.com>
Subject: Hi!

I was just wondering if you knew if there were any openings at the *Duane County Register.* You mentioned once that you thought Mabel Fleming would be interested in hiring me as their Arts and Entertainment writer. I've been thinking a lot about it, and I've come to the conclusion that I'm really sick of the city and would like to come home for a while. Could you let me know if Mabel still needs someone?

Thanks.

Mel

P.S.: Don't worry about me. I'm fine. Really.

To: Mel Fuller <melissa.fuller@thenyjournal.com>
From: Don and Beverly Fuller <DonBev@dnr.com>
Subject: Honey, do you mean it?

You're really thinking about coming home?

Oh, Daddy and I just couldn't be more delighted. I mean, it was all well and good for you to go to the big city and try to prove yourself, but the fact is, you've done that. Now it's time for you to think about settling down, and Daddy and I are just tickled pink that you want to do it back here in good old Lansing.

And I don't want you to think we aren't cosmopolitan, because you know just the other day they opened up a Wal-Mart! Can you believe that? A Wal-Mart, right here in Lansing.

Anyway, good news: I called Mabel up right away and asked her if she still needed an Arts and Entertainment writer, and she said, "Heck, yeah!" The job is yours, if you want it. The pay's not much—only $12,000 a year. But, honey, if you lived at home, you could just save all that, and then use it as a down payment on your own house when you finally do get married.

Oh, I am just pleased as punch. Do you want Daddy and me to drive out and pick you up? Dr. Greenblatt said we could use his minivan to haul all your things back in. Wasn't that nice?

You just let me know when you want to come home, and we'll come get you lickety-split!

Oh, honey, we love you so much, and can't wait to see you!

Mommy and Daddy

To: Mel Fuller <melissa.fuller@thenyjournal.com>
From: Nadine Wilcock <nadine.wilcock@thenyjournal.com>
Subject: Are you sure

you're all right? You just didn't seem yourself last night. I mean, I know you aren't too thrilled with this suspension thing, and the whole John thing still has you down. . . .

But you seemed more out of it than usual at the fittings yesterday. It's not because you totally hate your dress, is it? Because it's not too late to pick out new ones. . . .

Missing you,

Nad

To: Nadine Wilcock <nadine.wilcock@thenyjournal.com>
From: Mel Fuller <melissa.fuller@thenyjournal.com>
Subject: Are you kidding?

Everything's great. Today I took a two-hour bubble bath, then watched *Rosie* and did my nails and took Paco out, then gave myself a pedicure, and watched the afternoon movie, then took Paco out, and read the entire September *Vogue* (all 1,600 pages) and ate a box of Ring Dings and took Paco out. . . .

I'm having a blast!

But thanks for asking.

Mel

P.S.: Did any flowers come from John today?

To: Mel Fuller <melissa.fuller@thenyjournal.com>
From: Nadine Wilcock <nadine.wilcock@thenyjournal.com>
Subject: No flowers

came from John today. Remember? You called the florist he uses and told them you were going to sue for harassment if they didn't stop.

Mel, why don't you just call him? Don't you think this has gone on long enough? I mean, the guy's obviously crazy about you—or at least he was, until that whole millionaire stunt. I really think the two of you make a cute couple. Can't you give it another try?

Nad

To: Nadine Wilcock <nadine.wilcock@thenyjournal.com>
From: Mel Fuller <melissa.fuller@thenyjournal.com>
Subject: Wait a minute

YOU were the one who said you suspected all along there was something that wasn't right about him. And now you want me to CALL him? You want ME to call HIM??? After what he did???

NO WAY!!!

My God, Nadine: I was writing Mrs. Melissa Friedlander all over everything, thinking he and I were going to spend the rest of our lives together. And then I find out that isn't even his real name, and you want me to CALL HIM???

What is wrong with you? PMS, or something?

Well, snap out of it. I am NEVER calling him. NEVER, NEVER, NEVER, NEVER, NEVER, NEVER, NEVER, NEVER, NEVER, NEVER, NEVER, NEVER, NEVER.

Mel

To: Mel Fuller <melissa.fuller@thenyjournal.com>
From: Nadine Wilcock <nadine.wilcock@thenyjournal.com>
Subject: All right

already. I get the message. Geesh. Forgive me for even suggesting it.

Nad

To: Tony Salerno <foodie@fresche.com>
From: Nadine Wilcock <nadine.wilcock@thenyjournal.com>
Subject: My maid of honor

is a basket case. What am I going to do?

Nad

To: Nadine Wilcock <nadine.wilcock@thenyjournal.com>
From: Tony Salerno <foodie@fresche.com>
Subject: Obviously

you invite John to the wedding.
    Seriously. The minute she sees him, she'll melt.
    At least that's what always happens in the movies.

Tony

To: Mel Fuller <melissa.fuller@thenyjournal.com>
From: Max Friedlander <photoguy@stopthepresses.com>
Subject: Keys

Yes, it's me. The real Max Friedlander this time. I am coming back to New York and I need the keys to my aunt's place. I understand that you had the locks changed and are holding all the keys. Can you please give one to the doorman so he can let me in tomorrow?

Sincerely,
Max Friedlander

To: Max Friedlander <photoguy@stopthepresses.com>
From: Mel Fuller <melissa.fuller@thenyjournal.com>
Subject: Keys

How do I know this is the REAL Max Friedlander? How do I know you aren't an impostor, like the last Max Friedlander I met?

Mel Fuller

To: Mel Fuller <melissa.fuller@thenyjournal.com>
From: Max Friedlander <photoguy@stopthepresses.com>
Subject: Keys

Because if you do not make the keys to my aunt's apartment available to me, I will sue you.
    Understand?

Cordially,
Max Friedlander

To: Max Friedlander <photoguy@stopthepresses.com>
From: Mel Fuller <melissa.fuller@thenyjournal.com>
Subject: Keys

Fine. I'll make sure the doorman gets a key for you.
    Might I ask what you intend to do about Paco and the cats?

Mel Fuller

To: Mel Fuller <melissa.fuller@thenyjournal.com>
From: Max Friedlander <photoguy@stopthepresses.com>
Subject: Keys

Give ALL the keys you have to the doorman. I intend to move into my aunt's apartment for the time being, so I will be caring for Paco and the cats. Your services, though appreciated, are no longer needed, thank you very much.

Max Friedlander

To: Max Friedlander <photoguy@stopthepresses.com>
From: Mel Fuller <melissa.fuller@thenyjournal.com>
Subject: Keys

Don't worry. When your aunt wakes up, I'll be sure to tell her all about your "gratitude." And about how you rushed to her side in her time of need.

You know, there's a name for people like you, only I'm too polite to write it here.

Mel Fuller

To: Mel Fuller <melissa.fuller@thenyjournal.com>
From: Max Friedlander <photoguy@stopthepresses.com>
Subject: Keys

You can tell my aunt whatever you want. Because I got news for you, lady:

She ain't waking up.

Your friend,
Max Friedlander

To: John Trent <john.trent@thenychronicle.com>
From: Mel Fuller <melissa.fuller@thenyjournal.com>
Subject: Your friend Max

is the most despicable human being on the planet, and how you could ever have done him a favor is beyond me.

I just wanted you to know that.

Mel

To: Mel Fuller <melissa.fuller@thenyjournal.com>
From: John Trent <john.trent@thenychronicle.com>
Subject: Does the fact that you are

writing to me again mean that you have forgiven me?

I have been leaving messages for you at work, but they say you haven't been there all week. Are you sick again or something? Is there anything I can do to help?

John

To: John Trent <john.trent@thenychronicle.com>
From: Mel Fuller <melissa.fuller@thenyjournal.com>
Subject: Max Friedlander

>Does the fact that you are writing to me again mean that you
have forgiven me?

No.

>I have been leaving messages for you at work, but they say you haven't been there all week. Are you sick again, or something?

That's because I got suspended. Not that it's any of your business.

Max is moving into his aunt's apartment. I just saw him in the hallway.

I can't believe you two were ever friends. He is the rudest individual I have ever had the misfortune to meet.

Wait a minute. Strike that. The two of you deserve each other.

Mel

To: Max Friedlander <photoguy@stopthepresses.com>
From: John Trent <john.trent@thenychronicle.com>
Subject: Mel

So I hear you're back in the city, and living in your aunt's apartment.

That's great. Just great.

Just one thing: if I hear one word from Mel about you mistreating her in any way, I will come down on you like a ton of bricks. I am serious about this, Max. I have friends with the NYPD who would gladly look the other way while I pummeled the life out of you. That whole thing on Page Ten about you and Vivica—that was my fault, not Mel's. So don't try any funny business, I'm warning you, or you'll regret it.

John

To: John Trent <john.trent@thenychronicle.com>
From: Max Friedlander <photoguy@stopthepresses.com>
Subject: Mel

What thing on Page Ten about me and Vivica? What are you talking about?

And why are you still so hostile? I mean, the girl's good-
looking enough, I guess, if you like the type, but nothing to write
home about.

Boy, you sure aren't as fun as you used to be.

Max

P.S.: Are they hiring photographers over there at the *Chronicle*?
Because I have to tell you, I could really use the work.

To: Max Friedlander <photoguy@stopthepresses.com>
From: Vivica@sophisticate.com
Subject: Our wedding

MAXIE!!!

I JUST GOT BACK FROM THE RUNWAY SHOWS IN MILAN,
AND SOMEBODY SHOWED ME THAT ARTICLE ABOUT YOU
AND ME THAT WAS IN THE PAPER!!! IS IT TRUE??? DO YOU
REALLY WANT TO MARRY ME???

WHERE ARE YOU??? I'VE BEEN CALLING ALL THE OLD
NUMBERS, BUT THEY SAY THEY ARE DISCONNECTED.
FINALLY DEIRDRE GOT ME THIS E-MAIL ACCOUNT SO I
COULD TRY WRITING TO YOU. I HOPE YOU GET THIS
BECAUSE I REALLY WANT YOU TO KNOW THAT I FORGIVE

YOU FOR WHAT HAPPENED IN KEY WEST AND I REALLY,
REALLY HOPE IT'S TRUE WHAT IT SAID IN THE PAPER!!!

LOVE,
VIVICA

To: Sebastian Leandro <sleandro@hotphotos.com>
From: Max Friedlander <photoguy@stopthepresses.com>
Subject: What the hell

has been going on around here since I've been gone? What is this
Page Ten? And why does Vivica think I want to marry her?

I swear, I leave the city for a few months and everyone goes
mental.

Max

To: Max Friedlander <photoguy@stopthepresses.com>
From: Sebastian Leandro <sleandro@hotphotos.com>
Subject: Sorry to be the one to break it to you

but a story ran on Page Ten, which is the *New York Journal*'s gossip column, that you had proposed to Vivica, and were eager to
start a family with her.

Please do not shoot the messenger.

Sebastian

To: Vivica@sophisticate.com
From: Max Friedlander <photoguy@stopthepresses.com>
Subject: Our wedding

Contrary to what you might have read in that piece of trash that some people in this town call a newspaper, I do not now nor have I ever harbored any desire to marry you.

My God, Vivica, it's because of you that I am living in this state of near poverty! Only a fool would marry you. Or a guy with so much money it didn't matter how many damned driftwood dolphins you bought.

Why don't you try giving Donald Trump a call? I bet he'd take you back.

Max

To: Mel Fuller <melissa.fuller@thenyjournal.com>
From: Vivica@sophisticates.com
Subject: MAX FRIEDLANDER

DEAR MS. FULLER,

HI. YOU PROBABLY DON'T REMEMBER ME. I'M THE ONE WHO TOLD YOU ABOUT MAX AND HIS FRIEND PLAYING THAT TRICK ON YOU.

ANYWAY, A FRIEND OF MINE SHOWED ME AN ARTICLE YOU WROTE THAT SAYS MAX WANTS TO MARRY ME. BUT I JUST ASKED MAX ABOUT IT, AND HE SAYS HE DOESN'T. WANT TO MARRY ME, THAT IS. EVEN THOUGH THAT'S WHAT I WANT MORE THAN ANYTHING IN THE WORLD. TO BE MARRIED TO MAX, I MEAN.

SO I WAS JUST WONDERING IF YOU COULD TELL ME

HOW YOU FOUND OUT ABOUT THAT BECAUSE I WOULD
REALLY LIKE TO KNOW.

I HAVE TRIED CALLING YOUR OFFICE AND LEAVING
MESSAGES, BUT THEY SAID YOU WERE OUT FOR A WHILE. I
HOPE YOU ARE NOT SICK OR SOMETHING. I HATE BEING
SICK. WHEN I AM SICK THEY HAVE TO POSTPONE MY
SHOOTS, AND THEN EVERYTHING GETS WAY BACKED UP.

SINCERELY,
VIVICA

To: Nadine Wilcock <nadine.wilcock@thenyjournal.com>
From: Mel Fuller <melissa.fuller@thenyjournal.com>
Subject: Models

Okay, for the first time, I actually feel bad about writing that
fake engagement announcement of Max Friedlander's. Not because
of anything to do with him, of course, but because Vivica just
e-mailed me, and asked me if it was true. It seems that more than
anything else in the world, Vivica would like to be Mrs. Vivica
Friedlander.

I can't believe I did something so stupid. Now I have to write
back to her and tell her I made the whole thing up to get back at
Max (and John). Her feelings are going to be hurt, and it's going to
be my fault.

I deserve to be suspended for the rest of my life.

Mel

To: Mel Fuller <melissa.fuller@thenyjournal.com>
From: Dolly Vargas<dolly.vargas@thenyjournal.com>
Subject: Models

Darling, Nadine tells me you're feeling bad about that little con-
tretemps with your column. She says you're actually worried that
you might have hurt that supermodel's feelings!

Oh, sweetie, I have to tell you, I laughed until I cried when I
heard that one. What a delight you are. We positively miss you
around the office, you know. Why, since you've been gone, no one
has uttered a single word about Winona Ryder, her legal problems,
or her new film.

Mel, sweetheart, supermodels don't *have* feelings. How can I be
so certain of this? Well, I'll let you in on a little secret: My first
fiancé left me for one. Really. I know you never even knew I was
engaged, but I have been, several times. It would never have
worked out, because of course he was a royal—I mean, can you
imagine *me* attending state dinners and all of that?—but I was desperately in love with him. Or at least with the possibility of his
inheriting the crown someday.

But lo and behold, he was introduced to a supermodel—who
also happened to be my best friend, and who knew good and well
how I felt about him. Or his crown, anyway. And what do you
think happened? Why, she snapped him right out from under me,
of course.

Not that I suffered for long. His father forbade the match, and
we all moved on.

Still, I learned then: Supermodels have no body hair, no cel-
lulite, and no feelings whatsoever.

So let your conscience rest easy, sugar. She doesn't feel a thing!

XXXOOO

Dolly

To: Dolly Vargas<dolly.vargas@thenyjournal.com>
From: Mel Fuller <melissa.fuller@thenyjournal.com>
Subject: Models

Um, thanks for that advice about supermodels . . . I think. It was very enlightening. I guess. But if it's all the same to you, I'll just treat Vivica the way I would anybody else . . . meaning that I'm going to go on the assumption that she does have some feelings.

Thanks anyway, and say to hi everyone for me.

Mel

P.S.: I hope you aren't still going out with Peter. He's the one who put me on suspension, you know. I know it's asking a lot, but if you are still going out with him, could you at least refrain from having sex with him until I get back? I really think it would be the least you could do.

To: Vivica@sophisticates.com
From: Mel Fuller <melissa.fuller@thenyjournal.com>
Subject: Max Friedlander

Dear Vivica,
In answer to your question, I am sorry to have to tell you that that story about Max wanting to marry you was completely made up by me.

See, I was really angry with Max and his friend John for tricking me the way they did—making me think John was Max, and all. It really hurt my feelings, and I wanted to hurt them back, any way I could.

The one thing I didn't think about was that by writing that

story I might also be hurting you. I am very sorry for that, and hope you will forgive me.

If it would make you feel better, when I get back to work—I am currently taking a brief hiatus—I am composing a retraction.

Sincerely,
Mel Fuller

P.S.: If it is any comfort at all to you, I know how you feel: I thought I was going to marry his friend—you know, the one who was pretending to be Max. But of course it didn't work out. You can't have a relationship that is based on lies.

To: Mel Fuller <melissa.fuller@thenyjournal.com>
From: Vivica@sophisticates.com
Subject: Max Friedlander

DEAR MEL,

WELL, I THOUGHT THAT MIGHT BE THE CASE. THAT THE STORY ABOUT MAX WANTING TO MARRY ME BEING MADE UP, I MEAN. I LIKE YOUR IDEA ABOUT RUNNING ANOTHER STORY ABOUT HIM. COULD YOU SAY THAT WHEN HE SLEEPS, HE SNORES LOUDER THAN ANY HUMAN BEING ON THE PLANET? BECAUSE THAT IS DEFINITELY TRUE.

I AGREE WITH YOU ABOUT HOW YOU CAN'T HAVE A RELATIONSHIP THAT IS BASED ON LIES. MAX TOLD ME HE LOVED ME, AND IT TURNED OUT THAT WAS ALL LIES. I REALLY, REALLY LOVED HIM, BUT HE SLEPT WITH THE MAID ANYWAY. AND ALL BECAUSE OF SOME STUPID DRIFTWOOD DOLPHINS.

YOU SOUND PRETTY NICE, FOR A REPORTER. WOULD YOU LIKE TO HAVE LUNCH ONE DAY WHILE YOU ARE ON

HIATUS? I FOUND A NEW RESTAURANT I REALLY, REALLY LIKE. IT IS CALLED APPLEBEE'S AND THEY HAVE EXCELLENT CHILI NACHOS, ALMOST AS GOOD AS AT MY OTHER FAVORITE RESTAURANT, FRIDAY'S. DO YOU WANT TO GO WITH ME SOMETIME? IT IS OKAY IF YOU SAY NO BECAUSE LOTS OF GIRLS DON'T LIKE ME ON ACCOUNT OF MY BEING A MODEL. LIKE MY GRAMMA SAYS, HONEY, IF YOU AIN'T A HUNDRED-DOLLAR BILL, NOT EVERYONE IS GOING TO LIKE YOU.

LET ME KNOW.

LOVE,
VIVICA

To: Vivica@sophisticates.com
From: Mel Fuller <melissa.fuller@thenyjournal.com>
Subject: Lunch

Dear Vivica,
I would be honored to go to lunch with you any time you want. You just let me know what day is good for you.

Mel

P.S.: I will definitely try to work the snoring thing into my next column.

To: John Trent <john.trent@thenychronicle.com>
From: Stacy Trent <IH8BARNEY@freemail.com>
Subject: Why is it that

I leave you alone for a couple of days while I have a baby, and the next thing I know

a) you've split up with your girlfriend, who I thought you were going to marry,
b) you've moved back to your old place in Brooklyn, and
c) you're suddenly the most sought after bachelor in all of North America.

How on earth did you manage to make such a mess out of everything? And what can I do to help put the pieces back together?

Stacy

P.S.: The twins are brokenhearted. They were counting on being flower girls.
P.P.S.: Thanks for the bracelet. And the baseball rattle is precious.

To: Stacy Trent <IH8BARNEY@freemail.com>
From: John Trent <john.trent@thenychronicle.com>
Subject: I blew it

And I'm man enough to admit it.
    I don't think there's anything anyone can do to put the pieces

together again. She won't even speak to me. I've tried everything, from flowers to begging. Nothing has worked. She's furious.

It's over.

And I can't help thinking it's probably all for the best. I mean, I'll admit what I did was wrong, but it wasn't as if I set out from the beginning with the intention of tricking her. Well, okay, I did, but it wasn't as if when I did I had any idea I was going to fall in love with her.

The fact is, I was trying to help a friend. Admittedly, he's an idiot, but I did owe him one.

If she can't understand that, then it's probably better that we part ways. I can't spend my life with someone who doesn't understand that friends have to do things for one another that may not be pleasant or even ethical, but that are necessary, in order to preserve the friendsh . . .

Oh, forget it. I don't even know what I'm saying. I'm delirious with grief and heartbreak. I wish someone would just shoot me and put me out of my misery. I want her back. I want her back. I want her back.

That's all there is to say.

John

To: Jason Trent <jason.trent@trentcapital.com>
From: Stacy Trent <IH8BARNEY@freemail.com>
Subject: My God

I've never seen your brother this way. He's got it bad. We've got to do something!

Stacy

P. S.: We're out of milk.

To: Stacy Trent <IH8BARNEY@freemail.com>
From: Jason Trent <jason.trent@trentcapital.com>
Subject: My God

Stay out of John's personal affairs. If it hadn't been for you egging him on, none of this would have happened.

I mean it, Stacy. DO NOT GET INVOLVED. You've done quite enough.

Jason

P.S.: Send Gretchen out for milk. What are we paying a nanny $1,000 a week for, if not to pick up a quart of milk now and then?

To: Genevieve Randolph Trent <grtrent@trentcapital.com>
From: Stacy Trent <IH8BARNEY@freemail.com>
Subject: John

Mim—
I just spoke with John. He is so down, I could hardly believe it. We've got to do something about it, you and I.

Jason won't help, of course. He thinks we should stay out of it. But I'm telling you, John is just going to spend the rest of his life alone and unhappy unless we take charge of this thing. You know men can't be left to their own devices where romance is concerned. They just foul everything up.

What do you say? Are you with me?

Stacy

To: Stacy Trent <IH8BARNEY@freemail.com>
From: Genevieve Randolph Trent <grtrent@trentcapital.com>
Subject: John

Dearest Stacy,
Loath as I am to admit that one of my two favorite grandsons is an incompetent ass when it comes to personal relationships, I cannot help but feel that you are right. John desperately needs our help.

What do you suggest that we do? Please telephone me tonight so that we can discuss our options. I will be home between six and eight o'clock.

Mim

P. S.: Who is this poor Barney, and why do you hate him so?

To: Nadine Wilcock <nadine.wilcock@thenyjournal.com>
From: Mel Fuller <melissa.fuller@thenyjournal.com>
Subject: The weirdest thing

just happened. I was sitting at my computer playing an innocent game of Tetris—I've gotten really good since being suspended—when I noticed something going on next door—you know, in Mrs. Friedlander's apartment.

Through the window into her guest room—the one John used to sleep in, and where I used to see him getting undressed every night . . . but let's not get into that—I saw Max Friedlander jumping up and down and waving his arms, and screaming at someone.

When I got out my binoculars (don't worry, I turned the lights out first) I saw he was yelling at one of his aunt's cats. Tweedle-dum, to be exact.

This seemed excessively strange to me, so I put down the binoculars and went out into the hall and banged on the door. My excuse was that I could hear him screaming through the wall, which wasn't true of course, but he didn't know that.

He answered the door looking all sweaty and upset. What Vivica sees in this guy I cannot imagine. He is so completely not like John, you couldn't believe it. First of all, he wears a gold necklace. Not that I have anything against guys who wear jewelry, but, excuse me, he wears his shirt unbuttoned practically to his navel so you'll be sure to notice his. Necklace, I mean.

Plus he has that I-haven't-shaved-in-days thing. I mean, John used to get that, too, but I knew he actually had shaved; with Max, I sort of doubt his fingers have touched a razor—or soap—in weeks.

Anyway, he was very rude, as usual, demanding to know what I wanted, and when I explained that it was his hysterical screaming had brought me running, he started cursing, and saying that Tweedledum was driving him crazy with his going outside the litter box.

I was understandably confused by this, since Tweedledum has never gone outside the box, as far as I knew. Then Max said the cat was going around drinking out of everything he could find, include Max's bedside water glass (imagine someone as foul as him having a bedside water glass) and the toilet.

That's when I knew something was wrong. At home in Lansing, whenever an animal starts drinking that much and peeing everywhere, it means they have probably developed diabetes. I told Max we needed to get Tweedledum to the vet right away.

And do you know what he said?

"Not me, sister. I got places to be and people to do."

Seriously. That is what he said.

So I said, "Fine, I'll take him myself," and I bundled Tweedledum up and took him. Oh, Nadine, you should have seen Paco's expression when he saw me leaving! You've never seen such a sad old dog. He misses John, too, you could totally tell. Even Mr. Peepers came out and tried to follow me into the hallway, so he could escape Max Friedlander's oppressive presence.

So I took Tweedledum to the animal hospital, and two hundred dollars later (out of my own pocket, thank you very much; you know I'll never see that money again), it turns out the poor cat is diabetic, and he has to have two insulin shots a day, and be brought back to the vet once a week for tests until his diabetes is regulated and stabilized.

Do you think MAX is trustworthy enough to handle this kind of responsibility? Of course not. He's going to kill this poor cat. Right now I have Tweedledum here with me, but he isn't really my cat. I know Mrs. Friedlander would want him to have the best care possible, but he isn't going to get that if he stays with Max.

I don't know what to do. Should I just tell him the cat died, and keep him here with me in secret? I wish I could smuggle all of them out of there. Paco and Mr. Peepers, I mean. Max is the worst animal caretaker I have ever seen. John may have been a liar, but at least he genuinely cared about Mrs. Friedlander's pets. Max doesn't care. You can just tell.

I would give anything to have things back the way they were before I knew John wasn't really Max Friedlander. He was a much better Max than the real Max.

Mel

To: Mel Fuller <melissa.fuller@thenyjournal.com>
From: Nadine Wilcock <nadine.wilcock@thenyjournal.com>
Subject: You

You have completely lost your mind. Mel, GROW UP. This isn't some little orphan you've adopted. It's a CAT. It's your neighbor's cat. Give it back to Max and stop obsessing. He is a grown man. He can handle a diabetic cat.

Nad

To: Nadine Wilcock <nadine.wilcock@thenyjournal.com>
From: Mel Fuller <melissa.fuller@thenyjournal.com>
Subject: You're right

So why do I feel so guilty?

I went over to Max's just now and I pounded on the door and I told him about Tweedledum. I brought the cat with me, along with all of his medical supplies, and I showed Max what he has to do . . . you know, how to fill the syringe and how to give the cat his shots.

Max looked pretty dumbfounded. He was all, "You mean cats can get diabetes, too, just like people?" I don't think he really understood a word I said. In fact, I *know* he didn't, because when I told him to fill the syringe himself, he filled it all the way up to the number 2, instead of 2 units, which is the correct dosage.

I started to explain to him why this was so dangerous, and how Sunny von Bülow has been in a coma ever since Claus slipped her a needle filled with too much insulin, but I don't think he heard anything but that last part, since he became very interested in that, and wanted to know how much insulin would send someone into a coma or even kill him. As if I would know that. I told him to watch *ER* like a normal person and he'd probably find out eventually.

He's going to kill that cat. I'm telling you right now, he's going to kill him. And if he does, I will never forgive myself.

God, I wish Mrs. Friedlander would wake up, kick Max out, and go back to planning trips to Nepal and her aquacize class. Wouldn't it be great if all of this turned out to be some weird dream she was having while she was asleep? Like if it turned out everything that has happened in the past few months since I found her unconscious never happened, and everything could just go back to normal?

That would be so great. Then I wouldn't have to feel this way anymore.

Mel

To: jerrylives@freemail.com
From: Nadine Wilcock <nadine.wilcock@thenyjournal.com>
Subject: Mel

Dear John,
I got your e-mail address from Tony. I hope you don't mind.

I don't normally get involved in Mel's personal affairs if I can help it, but I am making an exception in this case. I really can't restrain myself any longer.

WHAT WERE YOU THINKING??? You and that stupid Max Friedlander. What could you have been thinking, trying to pull off something so incredibly asinine?

Now you've broken my best friend's heart, something for which I am sure I will never forgive you. But even worse, you have left her to the mercy of the real Max Friedlander, whom I am convinced has got to be the biggest idiot who ever walked the face of the planet.

How could you? HOW COULD YOU???

That's all I have to know. I hope you're satisfied. You have ruined the life of one of the sweetest girls who ever lived.

I hope you're proud of yourself.

Nadine Wilcock

To: Nadine Wilcock <nadine.wilcock@thenyjournal.com>
From: John Trent <john.trent@thenychronicle.com>
Subject: Mel

What do you mean she's at the mercy of Max Friedlander? What's Max doing to her???

John

To: John Trent <john.trent@thenychronicle.com>
From: Nadine Wilcock <nadine.wilcock@thenyjournal.com>
Subject: Max

Jeez, calm down, will you? Max isn't doing anything to Mel. He's just being . . . well, Max, near as I can tell (I mean, it's not as if I know him). One of the cats turns out to be diabetic and Max is not being real cooperative about taking care of him, is all. And you know Mel.

Listen, will you think about what I said? If you care about Mel at all, there's got to be some way you can make all this up to her. Can't you think of SOMETHING?

Nad

To: Max Friedlander <photoguy@stopthepresses.com>
From: John Trent <john.trent@thenychronicle.com>
Subject: Diabetic cats

Hey. I hear those pesky pets of your aunt's are proving to be more trouble than you expected. Want me to give you a hand with them? If you gave me permission, being Mrs. Friedlander's next of kin and all, I could move back in. You could have my place. What do you say?

John

To: John Trent <john.trent@thenychronicle.com>
From: Max Friedlander <photoguy@stopthepresses.com>
Subject: Diabetic cats

What would I want to move into your place for? Don't you live way the hell in Brooklyn? I hate the subway.

Plus, if I remember correctly, you don't even have cable. Aren't you doing that whole bohemian writer thing? You know, milk crates and a futon and all?

Thanks, but no thanks.

Max

To: Max Friedlander <photoguy@stopthepresses.com>
From: John Trent <john.trent@thenychronicle.com>
Subject: Diabetic cats

Okay, how about this? I'll pay to put you up somewhere—anywhere you want—if you'll let me move back in.

I'm serious. The Plaza, if you want. Think of all the supermodels you could impress. . . .

John

To: John Trent <john.trent@thenychronicle.com>
From: Max Friedlander <photoguy@stopthepresses.com>
Subject: Diabetic cats

You are pathetic, man. You've really got it bad for this girl, don't you? It must be the red hair. *I* certainly can't see it. If you ask me, she's a nosy bitch. Worse, she's one of those weird cat women who think animals have feelings and all of that.

God, I hate that crap.

Anyway, nice try with the hotel offer and all, but if things go the way I'm expecting them to, I'll be living in my own place not too long from now. So, thanks, but I'll pass.

Max

P. S.: You really are pathetic, you know. I could hook you up with girls way better looking than the one in 15B. Seriously. Just let me know.

To: Nadine Wilcock <nadine.wilcock@thenyjournal.com>
From: John Trent <john.trent@thenychronicle.com>
Subject: Max

Well, I tried to see if I could get back into 15A. It didn't work. Sounds like Max has some kind of grand scheme in the works. It doesn't seem like he'll be in Mel's hair for much longer, if that's any comfort to you.

John

To: Tony Salerno <foodie@fresche.com>
From: Nadine Wilcock <nadine.wilcock@thenyjournal.com>
Subject: Men

Why are men so stupid? I mean, excluding you, of course?

I write to John Trent—I take time out of my busy schedule to write John Trent a moving and deeply felt e-mail asking if he can't think of anything, ANYTHING, he could do that might make Mel forgive him, clearly hinting that if he proposed, she might very well say yes—and what does he do? What does he do?

He e-mails stupid Max Friedlander and tries to get him to let him move back into the apartment next door to Mel's. How STU-PID can he be? What do I have to do to get the message across to the guy? Take out a stupid sign???

What is WRONG with you people???

Nad

To: Nadine Wilcock <nadine.wilcock@thenyjournal.com>
From: Tony Salerno <foodie@fresche.com>
Subject: Men

Nadine, when are you going to learn not to get involved in other people's business? Leave John Trent alone. Let Mel work out her own problems. She doesn't need your help.

Tony

To: Tony Salerno <foodie@fresche.com>
From: Nadine Wilcock <nadine.wilcock@thenyjournal.com>
Subject: Men

>Let Mel work out her own problems. She doesn't need your help.

That is a typical male response. Plus I can't even begin to tell you how wrong it is.

Nad

To: Dolly Vargas <dolly.vargas@thenyjournal.com>;
    Tim Grabowski <timothy.grabowski@thenyjournal.com>;
    George Sanchez <george.sanchez@thenyjournal.com>
From: Nadine Wilcock <nadine.wilcock@thenyjournal.com>
Subject: All right everybody

Mel is returning and I think we should plan a little something to welcome her back, since she is feeling really down about this whole thing with John. So, let's have a party with some cake and ice cream (I will supply that).

Tim, why don't you put your decorative flair to good use and tape some streamers around her cubicle?

George, I think a small gift would be appropriate—and this time, how about something you didn't purchase at the newsstand downstairs? I mean, Jujubees are nice and all, but not exactly special.

Dolly, since you're so good with the phones, why don't you spread the word about the time and place. That way we'll be sure to get a good crowd.

And, above all, try to act positive. I'm telling you, she's so low these days, I wouldn't be surprised if she turned tail and slunk back to Illinois. And we can't have that. DO NOT, whatever you do, mention the words John Trent. I'm telling you, she's on the edge.

So be there or be square!

Nad ;-)

To: Mel Fuller <melissa.fuller@thenyjournal.com>
From: Nadine Wilcock <nadine.wilcock@thenyjournal.com>
Subject: Welcome back!

We missed you so much! It was completely dead around here without you. No one to tell us what celebrity weddings were coming up or keep us posted on the latest Leo sightings. I nearly expired from boredom.

So, where are we going for lunch?

Nad ;-)

To: Nadine Wilcock <nadine.wilcock@thenyjournal.com>;
    Dolly Vargas <dolly.vargas@thenyjournal.com>;
    Tim Grabowski <timothy.grabowski@thenyjournal.com>;
George Sanchez <george.sanchez@thenyjournal.com>
From: Mel Fuller <melissa.fuller@thenyjournal.com>
Subject: Thanks

for the welcome-back party. You guys really outdid yourselves this time. I was completely surprised. I bet there isn't another employee at the *Journal* who got a party after returning from a mandatory suspension. Let alone with cake and ice cream.

I really love my plastic Statue of Liberty earrings with the torches that actually light up. They are obviously something every girl needs. You shouldn't have.

Now I'd appreciate it if everyone would let me get back to work, as a lot has happened in Hollywood and beyond, so I have tons of work today.

Fondly,
Mel

To: Nadine Wilcock <nadine.wilcock@thenyjournal.com>
From: Mel Fuller <melissa.fuller@thenyjournal.com>
Subject: I'm going to kill you

I mean, the party was sweet and all, but you know I'm in no mood for parties. I practically split my face in two, pretending to be happy about it.

And what's the deal with you and the cake? You must have had four slices.

No offense, and I don't mean to be your diet police, but I thought you'd finally gotten down to a size 12 and intended to stay that way until the wedding.

Mel

To: Mel Fuller <melissa.fuller@thenyjournal.com>
From: Nadine Wilcock <nadine.wilcock@thenyjournal.com>
Subject: What's the deal with you and the cake?

I can't take it anymore, all right? This stupid dieting thing is for the birds! What is the point of being alive if I can't eat what I want? I don't care about fitting into my mother's stupid wedding dress anymore. I'm buying my own wedding dress, one in which I can actually breathe. And I won't have to starve myself for the next six weeks either.

And when it comes time for the cake during my reception, I'll actually be able to eat a slice without having to worry about splitting my seams.

There. Are you happy? I've said it. I AM A BIG GIRL. That's all there is to it. I will never be a size 6, or a size 8, or even a size 12. I am a size 16, and that's all there is to it. I won't give up spinning class, because I know that's good for me, but I will be damned if I'm going to eat salad with dressing on the side every meal for the rest of my life just so that I can squeeze into a dress that some magazine says is the right size for my height. How do THEY know what the right size for my height is?

They don't. They don't know me. They don't know that my fiancé happens to LIKE the way I look, that he says I'm the sexiest woman he knows, and that when I walk down the street, garbagemen and truck drivers whistle and ask for my number.

So I can't be doing too badly, can I?

Now, where are we going for lunch?

Nad

To: Nadine Wilcock <nadine.wilcock@thenyjournal.com>
From: Mel Fuller <melissa.fuller@thenyjournal.com>
Subject: Lunch

Um, sorry, Nadine, but I already have lunch plans. I'm going to Applebee's with Vivica, the supermodel.

Please don't hate me.

Mel

To: Mel Fuller <melissa.fuller@thenyjournal.com>
From: Nadine Wilcock <nadine.wilcock@thenyjournal.com>
Subject: Lunch

Applebee's? With a supermodel?

There are so many things wrong with that sentence I can't even begin to describe them.

Hate you? Why should I hate you? Just because you've chosen to lunch at a place I wouldn't be caught dead in with a size 2 supermodel?

Sure. Go ahead. See if I care.

Nad :-(

To: Nadine Wilcock <nadine.wilcock@thenyjournal.com>
From: Mel Fuller <melissa.fuller@thenyjournal.com>
Subject: Lunch

Oh, get over yourself. You know I'll always prefer size 16 food crit-
ics over size 2 supermodels.

Mel

To: Mel Fuller <melissa.fuller@thenyjournal.com>
From: Vivica@sophisticate.com
Subject: LUNCH

DEAR MEL,
    YOU ARE THE FUNNEST PERSON. THAT WAS THE BEST
LUNCH I'VE HAD IN A REALLY LONG TIME. I'M SO GLAD I
MET YOU. I HOPE WE CAN BE BEST FRIENDS. I HAVEN'T HAD
A BEST FRIEND SINCE I MOVED HERE FROM SANTA CRUZ.
    ANYTIME YOU WANT TO GO OUT, JUST CALL ME.
EXCEPT NOT NEXT WEEK, SINCE I WILL BE IN MILAN,
WHICH IS IN ITALY.
    OKAY, BYE!

LOVE,
VIVICA

To: Vivica@sophisticate.com
From: Mel Fuller <melissa.fuller@thenyjournal.com>
Subject: Lunch

Hi, Vivica! I had a great time at lunch too. Between the two of us, we really managed to pack it away, huh? I can't think about jalapeño poppers without wanting to throw up.

I would love to get together with you again. Maybe we could invite my friend Nadine next time. I think you would really like her. She is a food critic here at the paper, and she knows of some restaurants that are even better than Applebee's. What do you think about that?

Anyway, I've been thinking about something you mentioned at lunch. Remember when I told you where I live, and you said you'd been there before, the night before you and Max left for Key West? When exactly was that? And did you meet Max's aunt then?

Just curious.

Mel

To: Mel Fuller <melissa.fuller@thenyjournal.com>
From: Vivica@sophisticate.com
Subject: MAX'S AUNT

DEAR MEL,
I WOULD LOVE TO MEET YOUR FRIEND NADINE!!! FOOD CRITIC? THAT SOUNDS LIKE A HARD JOB. LIKE, IF I WERE A FOOD CRITIC, I WOULDN'T KNOW WHICH I LIKED BETTER, FRIDAY'S POTATO SKINS WITH CHEDDAR AND BACON BITS OR APPLEBEE'S POTATO SKINS WITH CHEDDAR AND BACON BITS.

ANYWAY, THE TIME I WENT TO MAX'S AUNT'S APART-
MENT WAS THE NIGHT BEFORE I LEFT FOR KEY WEST. MAX
WAS SUPPOSED TO GO WITH ME, BUT AT THE LAST MINUTE
HE GOT A SHOOT IN L.A., SO I ENDED UP GOING DOWN
FIRST, AND THEN HE MET ME ABOUT A WEEK LATER.

WHAT HAPPENED WAS, THE NIGHT BEFORE WE LEFT, HE
SAID HE HAD TO GO PICK SOMETHING UP FROM HIS
AUNT'S APARTMENT, SO I WAITED DOWNSTAIRS IN THE
CAB WHILE HE WENT AND GOT IT. I NEVER DID GET TO
MEET HIS AUNT. MAX SAID SHE IS KIND OF A BITCH AND
WOULDN'T LIKE ME ON ACCOUNT OF ME BEING TOO YOUNG
FOR HIM, WHICH HAPPENS WITH A LOT OF MY BOY-
FRIENDS.

ANYWAY, AFTER A WHILE MAX CAME BACK DOWN AND
WE WENT TO CHILI'S. HAVE YOU EVER BEEN THERE? THEY
HAVE THE BEST ARTICHOKE DIP. WE SHOULD GO SOME-
TIME!

WELL, THAT'S ALL FOR NOW!

VIVICA

To: Mel Fuller <melissa.fuller@thenyjournal.com>
From: George Sanchez <george.sanchez@thenyjournal.com>
Subject: I just walked by your desk

and noticed you were deeply immersed not in today's column, as
one might hope, but in your e-mail. I know this might come as a
surprise to you, but we don't actually pay you to correspond with
your friends, Fuller. We pay you to work. WOULD YOU MIND
DOING SOME?

Or would that be asking too much of you?

George

To: George Sanchez <george.sanchez@thenyjournal.com>
From: Mel Fuller <melissa.fuller@thenyjournal.com>
Subject: Jeez, George

No need to SHOUT!

Look, something is bothering me. I can't put my finger on what it is, exactly, but it might . . . I don't know. Lead to something big, George.

But the only way I'm going to find out if it's true is if I ask the right questions of the right people.

So please let me do my work and STOP LOOKING OVER MY SHOULDER AT WHAT I'M WRITING!

It might very well be about you.

Mel

To: Mel Fuller <melissa.fuller@thenyjournal.com>
From: George Sanchez <george.sanchez@thenyjournal.com>
Subject: Guess what.

If it doesn't go on Page Ten, I'm not interested.

George

To: Vivica@sophisticate.com
From: Mel Fuller <melissa.fuller@thenyjournal.com>
Subject: Max's aunt

Vivica, it's kind of important that you try to remember what night, exactly, you and Max were at my building. Maybe you still have your boarding pass from when you flew down to Florida, or somebody at your agency wrote it down somewhere?

Please let me know as soon as you can.

Mel

To: Mel Fuller <melissa.fuller@thenyjournal.com>
From: Genevieve Randolph Trent <grtrent@trentcapital.com>
Subject: My grandson

Dear Miss Fuller,

We have never been formally introduced, but we have met, most recently at a benefit at Lincoln Center. I believe you will remember me: I was the elderly woman sitting beside John Trent, whom you believed at the time was Max Friedlander. The two of you spoke for some time. I, of course, was not permitted to say very much, as my grandson did not wish you to discover the truth of his identity, for reasons that I believe are clear to you now.

I cannot apologize for my grandson's behavior . . . that is something he must do for himself. I trust that he has done so. It is my understanding that you have chosen not to accept his apologies, and that, of course, is your prerogative.

But before you dismiss my grandson completely from your life, Miss Fuller, I would ask that you consider the following:

John loves you. I understand that after the way he's treated you, you might find this hard to believe. But I ask that you believe it.

I would very much like an opportunity to convince you of the truth of this in person. Would it be possible, or am I asking too much, for us to meet? I would so love to have a chance to speak to you, woman to woman. Do let me know.

Genevieve Randolph Trent

To: Nadine Wilcock <nadine.wilcock@thenyjournal.com>
From: Mel Fuller <melissa.fuller@thenyjournal.com>
Subject: John

Oh, my God, now he's got his grandmother writing to me, begging me to forgive him. I'm not kidding. How pathetic. Like anything *she* says is going to make a difference. She's related to him!

Besides, she was probably forced to write all that. They probably threatened her. They probably said write this letter or we'll put you in a home, Grandma. I so wouldn't put it past them. They could do it, too, and she would be helpless to stop them. Everyone knows those Trents have every single member of the judiciary system, all the way up and down the eastern seaboard, in their pockets.

I am so lucky I escaped all that. It could have ended up being just like that Sally Field movie where she has to escape with her daughter. Only instead of fleeing Iraq or wherever that movie was set, I'd be fleeing East Hampton.

Really. Think about it.

Mel

To: Mel Fuller <melissa.fuller@thenyjournal.com>
From: Nadine Wilcock <nadine.wilcock@thenyjournal.com>
Subject: John

Okay, you have officially lost it now. Put her in a home? Where do you come up with this stuff?

They aren't the Kennedys, for God's sake. No one in that family has ever been accused of murder. Possession, maybe, but nothing violent. And the grandmother, at least, is a well-known patroness of the arts, and a huge supporter of many of the same charities you, young lady, have been known to write about admiringly.

So, where do you get this stuff? Your imagination is working overtime. You should maybe give up journalism and go into fiction writing, because that seems to be where your real talent lies.

Nad

To: Nadine Wilcock <nadine.wilcock@thenyjournal.com>
From: Mel Fuller <melissa.fuller@thenyjournal.com>
Subject: John

Oh, yeah? Well, then you probably won't believe me when I say I think I have an idea who might have conked Mrs. Friedlander on the head.

And it wasn't a member of the Trent family.

Meet me over by the water cooler and I'll tell you. George keeps walking by and reading over my shoulder to make sure I'm working.

And then I said, "Are you kidding? George Sanchez is the sexiest man alive. Any man with that much hair on his back has to be a veritable repository of testosterone. . . ."

HA, GEORGE! CAUGHT YOU!!!

Mel

To: Stacy Trent <IH8BARNEY@freemail.com>
From: Genevieve Randolph Trent <grtrent@trentcapital.com>
Subject: Melissa Fuller

Well, I sent it. And she hasn't written back.
    Stubborn little thing.
    I think it's time we move on to Plan B.

Mim

To: John Trent <john.trent@thenychronicle.com>
From: Nadine Wilcock <nadine.wilcock@thenyjournal.com>
Subject: Mel

Dear John,
When I suggested that you do something to get Mel back, I didn't exactly mean get your grandmother to write to her. In fact, I don't think that was such a hot idea at all. I think it had sort of the opposite effect of what you were looking for.

    When I suggested that you do something to get Mel back, I was thinking of something more along the lines of, oh, I don't know, stringing a massive sign out the windows of the building opposite ours with the words MARRY ME, MEL on it.

Or something along those lines.

However, you chose to take a more passive approach . . . and often, that can work just as well. I congratulate you for trying, I really do. A lesser man might have given up by now. Mel has a stubborn streak a mile wide, and takes the saying "once burned, twice shy" to new heights.

But I think you ought to know that now Mel is convinced that your family is filled with women who will do anything you tell them to, because they are afraid that, otherwise, you will put them in a home.

Just thought you might be interested.

Nad

To: Genevieve Randolph Trent <grtrent@trentcapital.com>
From: John Trent <john.trent@thenychronicle.com>
Subject: What is wrong with

---

you? Did you write to Mel? What did you say to her?

Whatever it was, it didn't work. She's madder at me than ever, according to her friend.

Look, Mim, I do not need your help, all right? Kindly stay out of my love life—or lack thereof. And that goes for Stacy, too, in case the two of you are in cahoots, which I am beginning to suspect.

I mean it, Mim.

John

To: Stacy Trent <IH8BARNEY@freemail.com>
From: Genevieve Randolph Trent <grtrent@trentcapital.com>
Subject: John

Oh, dear. I just got a very angry e-mail from John. It appears that he's found out about the letter I wrote. He was quite put out about it, and warned me on no uncertain terms to stay out of his love life. He added that I should tell you the same.

I suggest we move on to Plan B at once.

Mim

To: Sebastian Leandro <sleandro@hotphotos.com>
From: Max Friedlander <photoguy@stopthepresses.com>
Subject: I know there's probably

no point in asking, but you haven't found any work for me lately, have you?

Max

To: Max Friedlander <photoguy@stopthepresses.com>
From: Sebastian Leandro <sleandro@hotphotos.com>
Subject: Look

I could live without this attitude of yours. I have presented you with plenty of assignments, none of which you have chosen to take. I can't help it if you won't take less than two thousand a day, have a prejudice against unnatural fibers, or even refuse to consider shooting fashions for teens.

My job is to find you work, and I have found you work. YOU are the one who's turning it down.

Max, you are just going to have to face the fact that you must lower your rates. Your work is good, but you're no Annie Leibovitz. Photographers who are every bit as talented as you are are charging way less. That's just the way it goes. Things change . . . either move with the times or get left behind.

When you drop out and spend untold months in Florida with last year's It Girl, you get left behind. I hate to say I told you so, but, well, I told you so.

Sebastian

To: Sebastian Leandro <sleandro@hotphotos.com>
From: Max Friedlander <photoguy@stopthepresses.com>
Subject: Yeah, well,

you know what? I don't need you, or your cheesy Sears portrait studio assignments. I am an artist, and as such, am taking my services elsewhere. You can consider my contract with your agency terminated as of this moment.

Max Friedlander

To: Mel Fuller <melissa.fuller@thenyjournal.com>
From: Max Friedlander <photoguy@stopthepresses.com>
Subject: My aunt

I know you've visited my aunt since she's been in the hospital. What are the visiting hours there?

Max Friedlander

To: Nadine Wilcock <nadine.wilcock@thenyjournal.com>
From: Mel Fuller <melissa.fuller@thenyjournal.com>
Subject: Max Friedlander

Nadine! Remember when I told you that I thought I knew who attacked Mrs. Friedlander? Well, I sort of started thinking it might have been Max. I mean, Vivica says he was at his aunt's apartment one night right before they left for Key West, and that had to be close to when Mrs. Friedlander was struck, although of course I can't get her to pin down the exact date.

And now Max wants to know the visiting hours at his aunt's hospital. The visiting hours, Nadine. He's never visited her before now....

And that's because he could never figure out how he was going to finish her off before. But he knows now, because I told him! Remember? I told him about Sunny von Bülow and how Claus injected her with an insulin overdose, and how he should have done it between the toes where no one would notice a needle-mark....

Yes! I actually said that! I mean, you know how I read mysteries, and I was just talking, you know. I didn't think he was actually going to take one of Tweedledum's syringes and some insulin and go visit his poor comatose aunt in her hospital room and KILL HER!!!

Nadine, what should I do??? Do you think I should call the police? I never actually believed Max would do something as heinous as try to kill his own aunt—I mean, I was going to write a story about it and give it to George, to show him I can do hard news, but I never actually thought, I mean, I didn't really believe . . .

But Nadine, I do now, I really believe he's going to try to kill her!!! What should I do???

Mel

To: Mel Fuller <melissa.fuller@thenyjournal.com>
From: Nadine Wilcock <nadine.wilcock@thenyjournal.com>
Subject: Max Friedlander

Mel. Honey. Calm down.

Max Friedlander is not going to kill his aunt. All right?

You are letting the stress of your breakup with John and the whole suspension thing get the better of you. Max Friedlander is not going to inject his aunt with her cat's insulin. Okay? People don't do things like that. Well, they do in the movies, and in books and things, but not in real life. I think you've seen *Shadow of a Doubt* one too many times.

Just take a deep breath and think about it. Why would Max do something like that? I mean, really, Mel. He is a big loser, it's true. He treated Vivica—not to mention you—very badly. But that doesn't make him a murderer. A big stupid jerk, but not a murderer.

All right? Now if you want to take a little walk with me outside the building, get a little fresh air to clear your head, I'd be happy to go with you. I heard there's a sale over at Banana Republic. We could go look at some nice silk sweater sets, if you want.

But please do not call the police to report that Max Friedlander is contemplating killing his aunt. You will only be wasting their time and your own.

Nad

To: Vivica@sophisticates.com
From: Mel Fuller <melissa.fuller@thenyjournal.com>
Subject: Max

Vivica, please. I am begging you. Can you remember anything, anything at all, that might help pinpoint what night it was you and Max were at my building? It could be a matter of life and death.

Mel

To: Mel Fuller <melissa.fuller@thenyjournal.com>
From: Vivica@sophisticates.com
Subject: WOW

IT SURE IS IMPORTANT TO YOU TO KNOW WHAT NIGHT MAX AND I WERE AT HIS AUNT'S, HUH? DID YOUR DRY CLEANER LOSE A SWEATER OF YOURS THAT DAY OR SOMETHING? I HATE WHEN THAT HAPPENS.

I REALLY WISH I COULD REMEMBER WHEN IT WAS EXACTLY, SO I COULD HELP YOU.

OH, WAIT. I KNOW THERE WAS SOME KIND OF PLAYOFF

GAME, BECAUSE ALL THE CARS THAT WENT BY WHILE I WAS WAITING IN THE CAR, THEY HAD THE GAME ON. AND WE WERE LOSING, SO EVERYBODY WAS REALLY MAD.

OH, AND THERE WAS NO DOORMAN. IT WAS WEIRD, BECAUSE MAX JUST WALKED RIGHT IN, AND NOBODY STOPPED HIM. BUT WHILE HE WAS GONE THIS CHINESE FOOD DELIVERY MAN CAME, AND HE LOOKED ALL AROUND THE LOBBY FOR THE DOORMAN, SO HE COULD CALL UP TO THE PEOPLE HE WAS DELIVERING TO AND TELL THEM HE WAS COMING.

THE REASON I NOTICED WAS BECAUSE THE CHINESE FOOD DELIVERY MAN WAS WEARING ACID-WASHED JEANS, WHICH ARE SO TOTALLY EIGHTIES, BUT I GUESS IF YOU ARE AN IMMIGRANT YOU WOULDN'T KNOW THAT. AND I WAS THINKING WE SHOULD REALLY START SOME KIND OF EDUCATION PROGRAM FOR THE IMMIGRANTS SO THEY WOULD KNOW WHAT TO WEAR, SO AS NOT TO STAND OUT SO MUCH. KNOW WHAT I MEAN? LIKE, YOU KNOW HOW CHRISTIE AND NAOMI AND CINDY STARTED THE FASHION CAFÉ? I WAS THINKING I COULD START, LIKE, A FASHION SCHOOL, FOR PEOPLE WHO COME TO NEW YORK FROM CHINA AND HAITI AND THE MIDWEST AND STUFF.

ANYWAY, FINALLY MR. ACID-WASHED JEANS FOUND HIM—THE DOORMAN, I MEAN—AND GOT BUZZED UP. THEN THE DOORMAN WENT AWAY AGAIN, AND RIGHT THEN MAX CAME DOWN, AND THE TWO OF US LEFT.

DOES THAT HELP?

VIVICA

To: Max Friedlander <photoguy@stopthepresses.com>
From: Mel Fuller <melissa.fuller@thenyjournal.com>
Subject: Your aunt

Dear Mr. Friedlander,

Your aunt is in the intensive care unit, which means she can't have visitors. Ever. In fact, they get mad if you even ask if you can visit people who are in the ICU. Because people who are in the ICU are in very, very unstable condition, and the slightest germ from the outside world might make them worse. So not only are there no visitors allowed, but the room is constantly monitored for movement with motion detectors, so even if you tried to sneak in there, you would get caught right away.

So, I wouldn't even try to go visit your aunt. Sorry. But I bet if you sent a card, they'd show it to her when she wakes up.

Mel Fuller

To: Mel Fuller <melissa.fuller@thenyjournal.com>
From: Max Friedlander <photoguy@stopthepresses.com>
Subject: My aunt

I just thought you might be interested to know that I found out from her physician that my aunt was moved out of the ICU a month ago. She is now in a private room. She is, of course, still in a coma, but she can be visited any day between four and seven o'clock.

Her prognosis, I'm sorry to say, is not good.

Max Friedlander

To: Mel Fuller <melissa.fuller@thenyjournal.com>
From: Stacy Trent <IH8BARNEY@freemail.com>
Subject: John

Dear Ms. Fuller,

You don't know me, but you do know my brother-in-law, John. I am sorry to write to you this way, seeing as how we've never actually been introduced, but I couldn't sit still and watch what was happening between you and John without saying something.

Melissa—I hope you don't mind if I call you Melissa; I feel like I know you, from all the talking John's done about you—I know that what John and his friend Max did was very, very wrong. I was completely shocked when I heard about it. In fact, I urged him to tell you the truth from the very beginning.

But he was afraid you'd be so mad at him, you wouldn't want to have anything to do with him . . . a fear that unfortunately proved well founded. And so he chose instead to wait for that "perfect moment" to tell you.

Except that, as you or I could have told him, there is no perfect moment to hear that the person you have fallen in love with has misrepresented himself in some way.

I am not saying that you do not have ample reason to be furiously angry with John. And I absolutely adored the creative manner in which you got back at him. But don't you think he has suffered long enough?

Because he *is* suffering, very badly. Why, when he came by the other night to see the baby—I just had my third, a boy we named John after my twin daughters' favorite uncle (see? He's well liked by children, which means he can't be all bad)—he looked quite dreadful. I swear he's lost at least ten pounds.

I know how maddening men can be (do I ever—I've been married to John's older brother Jason for a decade), but I also remem-

ber from my single days how truly hard it is to find a good one ...
and that's what John is, despite what you might think, based on his
behavior toward you so far.

Won't you please give him a second chance? He really is crazy
about you—and I can prove it. I'd like to offer you John's own
words, in e-mails he has sent to me over the course of the past few
months. Perhaps, after reading them, you will come to the same
conclusion I did: that the two of you have managed to find something very few of us in this world are lucky enough to discover: a
soulmate.

>So what do you want to know?
>
>Did she believe I was Max Friedlander? I am sorry to say that she
did.
>
>Did I play the part of Max Friedlander to perfection? I guess I
must have, or she wouldn't have believed I was he.
>
>Do I feel like a grade-A heel for doing it? Yes. Self-flagellation.
>A for me.
>
>The worst part is ... well, I already told you the worst part. *She
thinks I'm Max Friedlander.* Max Friedlander, the ingrate who
doesn't even seem to care that someone coldcocked his eighty-
year-old aunt.
>
>Melissa cares, though.
>
>That's her name. The redhead. Melissa. People call her Mel. That's
what she told me. "People call me Mel." She moved to the city
right after college, which makes her about twenty-seven years old,
since she's lived here for five years. Originally, she's from Lansing,
Illinois. Have you ever heard of Lansing, Illinois? I've heard of

Lansing, Michigan, but not Lansing, Illinois. She says it's a small town where you can walk down Main Street and everyone goes, "Oh, hi, Mel."

>

>Just like that. "Oh, hi, Mel."

>

>She showed me where Max's aunt keeps the dog and cat food. She told me where to buy more, in case I ran out. She told me what Paco's favorite walks were. She showed me how to lure a cat named, and I kid you not, Mr. Peepers, out from underneath the bed.

>

>She asked me about my work for the Save the Children fund. She asked me about my trip to Ethiopia. She asked me if I'd been to visit my aunt in the hospital, and if it had upset me very much, seeing her with all those tubes coming out of her. She patted me on the arm and told me not to worry, that if anyone could come out of a coma, it was my aunt Helen.

>And I stood there and grinned like an idiot and pretended I was Max Friedlander.

>

>I've met this completely terrific girl. I mean *completely* terrific, Stace: She likes tornadoes and the blues, beer, and anything to do with serial killers. She eats up celebrity gossip with as much enthusiasm as she attacks a plate of moo shu pork, wears shoes with heels that are way too high and looks fabulous in them—but manages to look just as fabulous in Keds and a pair of sweat-pants.

>

>And she's *nice.* I mean, really, truly, genuinely kind. In a city where no one knows his neighbors, she not only knows hers, but actually *cares* about them. And she lives in *Manhattan.* Manhattan, where people routinely step over the homeless in an effort to

get into their favorite restaurants. As far as Mel seems to be concerned, she never left Lansing, Illinois, population 13,000. Broadway might as well be Main Street.

>

>I've met this completely terrific girl. . . .

>

>And I can't even tell her my real name.

>

>No, she thinks I'm Max Friedlander.

>

>I know what you're going to say. I know exactly what you're going to say, Stace.

>

>And the answer is no, I can't. Maybe if I'd never lied to her about it in the first place. Maybe if right from the first moment I met her I'd said, "Listen, I am not Max. Max couldn't make it. He feels really bad about what happened to his aunt, so he sent me in his place."

>

>But I didn't, all right? I blew it. I blew it from the very beginning.

>

>And now it's too late to tell her the truth, because anything else I ever try to tell her, she'll think I'm lying about that, too. Maybe she won't admit it. But in the back of her mind, it will always be there. "Maybe he's lying about this, too."

>

>Don't try to tell me she won't, either, Stace.

>

>So there you have it. My hellish life, in a nutshell. Got any advice? Any sage words of womanly wisdom to throw my way?

>

>No, I didn't think so. I am perfectly aware of the fact that I've dug this grave myself. I guess I have no choice but to lie down in it.

>

>What do you want me to say, anyway? That she's exactly what I've been looking for in a woman all this time, but never dared hope I'd find? That she's my soulmate, my kismet, my cosmic destiny? That I'm counting the minutes until I can see her again?

>

>Fine. There. I've said it.

I found this particular bit most interesting:

>I bought her a ring. An engagement ring.

>

>And no, this isn't like the time in Vegas. I have not been perpetually drunk for the past three months. I genuinely believe that this woman, out of all the women I have ever known, is the one with whom I want to spend the rest of my life.

>

>I was going to tell her the truth, and then propose, in Vermont.

>

>Now she won't answer my phone calls, open her door, or reply to my e-mails.

>

>My life is over.

Well, there you have it. I hope you won't discuss what you have just read with John. He would never speak to me again if he found out I had shared all this with you.

But I had to. I really had to. Because I think it's important for you to know . . . well, how much he loves you.

That's all.

Sincerely,
Stacy Trent

To: Nadine Wilcock <nadine.wilcock@thenyjournal.com>
From: Dolly Vargas <dolly.vargas@thenyjournal.com>
Subject: Mel

Darling, do you have any idea why Mel is weeping in the ladies'?
It's extremely annoying. I was trying to show the new fax boy how
cozy it can be for two in the handicapped-accessible stall, but her
incessant sobs completely killed the mood.

XXXOOO

Dolly

To: Dolly Vargas <dolly.vargas@thenyjournal.com>
From: Nadine Wilcock <nadine.wilcock@thenyjournal.com>
Subject: Mel

I don't know why she's crying. She won't tell me. She's barely
speaking to me since I shot down her theory that Max Friedlander
is trying to kill his aunt.

But I'm not the only one. Apparently, no one will believe her.
Not even Aaron.

I have to admit, I'm worried. It's like Mel's taken this whole
thing with John and turned it around so that it's all about Max and
his attempts at aunty-cide.

Maybe we should call somebody down in Human Resources. I
mean, maybe she's cracking up.

What do you think?

Nad

To: John Trent <john.trent@thenychronicle.com>
From: Mel Fuller <melissa.fuller@thenyjournal.com>
Subject: Max Friedlander

Dear John,
I forgive you.

Now we've got a real problem: I think Max Friedlander is going to try to kill his aunt! I think he tried to do it once before, but loused it up. We've got to stop him. Can you come over right away?

Mel

To: Nadine Wilcock <nadine.wilcock@thenyjournal.com>
From: George Sanchez <george.sanchez@thenyjournal.com>
Subject: Where the hell is

Fuller?

I turn my back for one minute, and she's gone. Do I have tomorrow's column yet? No, I do not have tomorrow's column. How can she leave without giving me tomorrow's column? HOW CAN SHE DO THAT???

George

To: George Sanchez <george.sanchez@thenyjournal.com>
From: Nadine Wilcock <nadine.wilcock@thenyjournal.com>
Subject: Mel

Um, I think she had to do some research for her column. I'm sure she'll hand it in before the copy desk shuts down. Don't worry.

Meanwhile, did you read my story on Mars 2112? Theme Restaurants: Not Just for Tourists Anymore. Has a nice ring to it, right?

Nad

To: Mel Fuller <melissa.fuller@thenyjournal.com>
From: Nadine Wilcock <nadine.wilcock@thenyjournal.com>
Subject: You are so dead

WHERE ARE YOU??? George is furious. I tried to cover for you as best I could, but I don't think it worked very well.

Are you having a breakdown? Because, seriously, if you are, I think it's pretty selfish of you. I'm the one who should be having the breakdown. I mean, I'm the one who's getting married and all. I'm the one with the mother who's furious that I'm not wearing her wedding dress, and just spent $700 on one from some outlet in New Jersey. You don't have any right to have a breakdown.

And I know you're going to say that you do, that this whole thing with John has destroyed your faith in men and all of that, but, Mel, the truth is, your faith in men was destroyed a long time ago. I'll admit that when you first started seeing the guy, I thought there was something kind of sketchy about him, but now that I know what it is, I have to say, you could do a lot worse. A LOT worse.

And I know you really love him and are perfectly miserable without him, so could you please just call the man and get back together with him? I mean, seriously, this has gone on long enough.

There. I've said it.

Now, where the hell are you???

Nad

To: Nadine Wilcock <nadine.wilcock@thenyjournal.com>
From: Mel Fuller <melissa.fuller@thenyjournal.com>
Subject: Shhhh . . .

You want to know where I am? Well, right now I am squatting in an emergency stairwell, which just happens to have a wall that adjoins Mrs. Friedlander's living room.

No, really! I'm using that satellite hook-in function George had installed in our laptops. That none of us could figure out how to use? Well, Tim showed me. . . .

I know you think I'm crazy, but I can prove to you I'm not. And the way I can prove it is by telling you exactly what I'm hearing right now, and that's John Trent asking Max Friedlander where he was the night his aunt got her head bashed in.

I am not the only one who is listening, either.

John is wearing a wire.

That's right. A WIRE. And there are a bunch of policemen in my apartment, listening to the same conversation I'm listening to. Only they are using headphones. I don't have to. I can hear the whole thing just by pressing my ear against the wall.

I am not supposed to be doing this. I am supposed to be in the coffee shop across the street, for my own protection. When they told me this, I was, like, "Right!" As if I would wait in a coffee shop across the street when I could be here, getting the scoop first-hand.

Nadine, I am telling you, this is going to be the story of the year, maybe of the decade! And I am going to write it, and George is going to have no choice but to run it. He will be forced to admit that I am too good for Page Ten, and put me on hard news. I can feel it, Nadine. I can feel it in my bones!

Okay, so here's what I'm hearing:

John: I'm just saying, I could understand it, if you did.

Max: Yeah, but I didn't.

John: But I'd understand it if you did. I mean, look at my family. They are loaded. Loaded. It's a bit different in my case, but let's just say my grandfather hadn't left me any money, and had left it all to my grandmother. If she wasn't willing to lend me a few hundred bucks now and then, I'd flip out, too.

Max: I never flipped out.

John: Look, I know how it is. I mean, not really, but you know how I've been trying to live off just my reporter's salary? It's tough. If I ran out, and I knew I didn't have any more cash coming to me for a while, and I had a supermodel waiting downstairs, and I went to my grand-mother for a loan, and she said no . . . well, I might get mad, too.

Max: Well . . . You know. It's, like, what do they think? They're going to take it with them?

John: Exactly.

Max: I mean, there she was, sitting on this huge pile of cash, and the stupid bitch couldn't part with a couple thou?

John: Like she'd even know it was missing.

Max: Seriously. Like she'd even know it was missing. But,

no. I have to get the lecture: "If you'd learn to handle your money in a more responsible manner, you wouldn't be running out of it all the time. You need to learn to live within your means."

John: Meanwhile, she's dropping twenty grand flying to the opera in Helsinki every couple months.

Max: Yeah! I mean, yeah.

John: It's enough to get a guy pretty hot under the collar.

Max: It's more like the *way* she said it, you know. Like I was a little kid, or something. I mean, Christ, I'm thirty-five years old. All I wanted was five grand. Just five grand.

John: Drop in the bucket to a woman like that.

Max: Don't you know it. Then she has the nerve to go, "Don't leave mad."

John: Don't leave mad. Jesus.

Max: Right. "Don't be like that, Maxie. Don't leave mad." And she's pulling on me, you know. On my arm. And I'm parked in front of the building, by a hydrant. And Vivica's waiting. "Don't leave mad," she says.

John: But she won't give you the money.

Max: Hell, no. And she wouldn't let go of me, either.

John: So you pushed her.

Max: I had to. She wouldn't get offa me. I didn't mean to, you know, make her fall down. I just wanted her off me. Only . . . I don't know. I guess I pushed too hard. Because she fell over backward, and her head slammed into the corner of the coffee table. And there's blood everywhere, and that damn dog was barking, and I got scared that neighbor of hers would hear. . . .

John: So you panicked.

Max: I panicked. I mean, I figured if she wasn't dead, somebody would find her eventually. But if she was . . .

John: You're her next of kin?

Max: Yeah. We're talking twelve million, man. That's chump change to you, but for me, the way I go through money . . .

John: So what did you do?

Max: I went into her bedroom and threw a bunch of her clothes around. You know, so people would think it was that guy, that transvestite killer. Then I got the hell out of there. I figured, lay low.

John: But she wasn't dead.

Max: God, no. Tough old bitch that she is. And things . . . well, you know. Vivica. And my manager, he's such a lardass. Won't get off his butt to find me any real work. I was strapped.

John: And she's been in that coma how long?

Max: Months, man. She's probably going to croak anyway. I mean, if I gave her another little push, who'd even notice?

John: Push?

Max: You know. Toward death, as they say.

John: And how were you planning on doing that?

Max: Insulin, man. You just inject too much. Like that Claus von Bülow guy. Little old lady like that'd croak for sure—

Uh-oh. Footsteps in the hallway. The cops must think they have enough. They're banging on the door to 15A. I am telling you, Nadine, I am going to win a Pulitzer—

Wait a minute. They are telling Max to come quietly. But Max isn't coming quietly. Max is—

To: Mel Fuller <melissa.fuller@thenyjournal.com>
From: Nadine Wilcock <nadine.wilcock@thenyjournal.com>
Subject: WHAT???

MEL??? WHERE ARE YOU??? Why did you stop like that? What's happening???
ARE YOU ALL RIGHT???

Nad

To: George Sanchez <george.sanchez@thenyjournal.com>
From: John Trent <john.trent@thenychronicle.com>
Subject: Attempted murder

Attachment: ✉ [For 1st AM (fp) SAY CHEESE w/exhibits: 1) Max Friedlander in cuffs, captioned w/cuts "The suspect being led away by New York's finest"; 2) Helen Friedlander on skis, captioned w/cuts "Beloved opera buff and pet owner"; u have in rack]

SAY CHEESE

*Famous Fashion Photographer
Arrested for Attempted Murder*

In a sting conducted in tandem with the NYPD's 89th Precinct, *New York Chronicle* reporter John Trent, and the *New York Journal*'s Mel Fuller, an arrest has finally been made in the brutal assault on Upper West Side resident Mrs. Helen Friedlander.

Mrs. Friedlander, 82, was found unconscious in her apartment nearly six months ago, the victim of an apparent assault. Clothing spread across the victim's bed indicated to police that the opera buff and animal lover might have been attacked by the so-called Transvestite Killer.

But after last month's arrest of Harold Dumas, who confessed to killing seven women over the course of the past year, it became apparent that Mrs. Friedlander's assault was what police sergeant Paul Reese calls a "copycat."

"The perpetrator wished to throw investigators off track," Sergeant Reese said in an interview early this morning. "He thought he could do so by making it look as if it had been the work of a serial killer known to

have attacked other women in the area. There were several things, however, that just weren't right."

Among them was the fact that Mrs. Friedlander had apparently known her attacker, having left her door unlocked in order for him to enter the apartment freely, and that no money had been stolen from the premises.

"The motive for this attack," according to Sergeant Reese, "was money, but after pushing the victim and causing her life-threatening injury, the perpetrator panicked, forgetting his need for cash."

The suspect arrested last night would not have needed the two hundred dollars that had been sitting in Mrs. Friedlander's purse the night of her attack: Had the victim died, he would have stood to inherit millions.

"The victim is exceedingly wealthy," Sergeant Reese explained. "And the suspect is her only living relative."

That suspect, Maxwell Friedlander, is Helen Friedlander's 35-year-old nephew. A well-known fashion photographer who has recently run into financial difficulties, Mr. Friedlander confessed to John Trent, *New York Chronicle* crime correspondent, and former friend of the suspect, that he was in need of money.

Explaining that his aunt was "sitting on this huge pile of cash," while he himself had none, the suspect justified his actions by saying that he had not initially meant to kill Mrs. Friedlander, but that if she died, he would benefit greatly from the inheritance left to him by her.

Mrs. Friedlander did not die, however. She has languished in a coma for nearly six months. And to Max Friedlander, this was a situation that needed rectifying. And last evening, he attempted to do so, planning, according to a secretly taped interview between the suspect and Mr. Trent, to kill his aunt in her hospital bed with an injection of insulin.

It was just after this admission that police moved to arrest Mr. Friedlander in his aunt's apartment. Instead of coming quietly, however, Mr. Friedlander broke free and attempted to flee the premises by taking a back stairwell.

It was at this point that Mr. Friedlander was struck hard across the face with this reporter's laptop, a blow that stopped him in his tracks and required seven stitches at Manhattan's St. Vincent's Hospital.

Mr. Friedlander will be arraigned this morning. Charges include the attempted murder of Helen Friedlander; conspiring to commit murder; resisting arrest; and fleeing an officer. Mr. Friedlander is expected to plead not guilty to all charges.

George—it's me, Mel. I had to type all this on John's computer, since mine is being held as evidence. What do you think? Did I do good or what?

Mel

To: Mel Fuller <melissa.fuller@thenyjournal.com>
From: Nadine Wilcock <nadine.wilcock@thenyjournal.com>
Subject: I suppose this means

the two of you are back together.

I will try to find room for him at the head table at our reception. Although I'm sure it will be difficult, considering how swollen your head will be by that time.

Tony will be happy. He was secretly rooting for John all along.

Nad ;-)

P.S.: I always did like him, you know. Well, at least after he loosened Aaron's molars for him.

To: Mel Fuller <melissa.fuller@thenyjournal.com>
From: George Sanchez <george.sanchez@thenyjournal.com>
Subject: All right already

I suppose we could work in a hard news story or two from you occasionally.

Very occasionally.

You are still on Page Ten in the meantime. And now that I know what you can do, I want to really see some good stuff in that column. No more of this Winona Ryder crap. Let's hear about some real celebrities. Like Brando, for God's sake. Nobody talks about Brando anymore.

George

P.S.: Don't think if anything happens to that laptop that you aren't the one who's going to be paying for it, Fuller.

To: Mel Fuller <melissa.fuller@thenyjournal.com>
From: Dolly Vargas <dolly.vargas@thenyjournal.com>
Subject: Darling

Just a quick congratulatory note before Aaron and I jet off for Barcelona—yes, I know, I can't believe he finally gave in, either. But I suppose in light of your recent journalistic coup, he is finally admitting defeat . . . and I'm the consolation prize!

As if I care. You know, a hard man really *is* good to find, and I honestly don't mind what kind of music he listens to. He's single, he's childless, and he can sign a check. What more can a girl ask for?

Anyway, best of luck to you and Little Lord Fauntleroy—I mean Mr. Trent. And *do* consider inviting me up to the house on the Cape. . . . It really is divine, from what I saw in *Architectural Digest.*

XXXOOO

Dolly

To: Mel Fuller <melissa.fuller@thenyjournal.com>
From: Vivica@sophisticates.com
Subject: MAX

OH, MY GOD, MEL, I AM HERE IN MILAN FOR THE SPRING SHOWS AND I HEARD FROM EVERYONE THAT MAX IS IN JAIL FOR TRYING TO KILL HIS AUNT, AND THAT YOU ARE THE ONE WHO PUT HIM THERE!!!

OH, MY GOD, YOU ARE THE COOLEST GIRL EVER!!! ALL MY FRIENDS WANT TO KNOW IF YOU WILL PUT THEIR

SCUMBAG EX-BOYFRIENDS IN JAIL TOO!!! MAYBE WE COULD START A BUSINESS TOGETHER: YOU COULD PUT GIRLS' BOYFRIENDS IN JAIL, AND I COULD TEACH THE IMMIGRANTS HOW TO DRESS!!!

ANYWAY, I JUST WANTED TO SAY THANKS FOR PUTTING MAX IN JAIL WHERE HE BELONGS, WITH ALL THE OTHER DIRTBAGS. I AM ESPECIALLY HAPPY BECAUSE I HAVE MADE A NEW FRIEND HERE IN MILAN. HIS NAME IS PAOLO AND HE IS A GALLERY OWNER AND A MILLIONAIRE!!! NO KIDDING!!! HE IS VERY INTERESTED IN SEEING MY DRIFT-WOOD DOLPHIN COLLECTION!!! HE SAYS THEY DON'T HAVE THOSE IN ITALY AND HE THINKS I CAN MAKE A FORTUNE SELLING THEM HERE. THIS SHOULD SUPPLY US WITH SOME GOOD START-UP CAPITAL FOR OUR BUSINESS TOGETHER, HUH, MEL?

One of the girls just told me it is considered very rude to write in all capital letters in e-mail. Is that true? Did you think I was being rude? I am sorry.

Anyway, Paolo is taking me out to dinner now, so I have to go. I do not think I will get anything very good to eat. Did you know they have no Applebee's in Milan? No, really. Not even a Friday's. Oh, well. See you when I get back!!!

Vivica

To: Mel Fuller <melissa.fuller@thenyjournal.com>
From: Don and Beverly Fuller <DonBev@dnr.com>
Subject: I'm afraid

Daddy and I didn't understand that last e-mail you sent us at all. What do you mean, you aren't coming home after all? Daddy already moved all of his bowling trophies out of your room. You

HAVE to come home. Mabel Fleming is counting on you taking over as Arts and Entertainment writer. She says if she has to review one more school play, she just might . . .

Well, I'm too much of a lady to write it. You know Mabel. She's always been so . . . flamboyant.

I suppose I should be happy you're coming home for Christmas, anyway. Five days is better than nothing, I suppose. But, Melissa, where is this John fellow you're bringing along going to sleep? I mean, you can't expect me to let him stay in your room. What would Dolores say? You know she can see everything that goes on in our house from her attic window. And don't think she doesn't look, that old cat. . . .

He'll have to stay in Robbie's old room. I'll start moving my sewing things out of it.

I'm happy to hear about your neighbor, anyway. Why, it sounds like something out of *Touched by an Angel* or that new show, what is it called? *Miraculous Cures*, or something. I'm glad to hear that she has woken from her coma and is doing so well, and will be out of the hospital in time for the holidays, though why her nephew should have tried to kill her . . .

I'm telling you, Melissa, I just don't like your living in that city. It's too dangerous! Murderous nephews and serial killers who wear dresses and men who tell you one name when it turns out their name is something else entirely. . . .

Just think, if you moved back here, you could have a mortgage on a three-bedroom house for what you're paying in rent for that little bitty apartment. And you know your old boyfriend, Tommy Meadows, is a real estate agent now. I'm sure he could get you a very nice deal.

But I guess if you're happy that's all that matters.

Daddy and I can't wait to see you. Are you sure you don't want us to pick you up at the airport? It seems a waste for you and this John person to rent a car just to drive from the airport out to Lansing. . . .

But I suppose you both know best.

Call before your flight leaves, at least, so we'll know when to expect you. And remember, don't drink on the flight: You'll want to have all your wits about you in case the plane starts to go down, and you need to make an emergency exit.

Love,
Mommy

To: John Trent <john.trent@thenychronicle.com>; Mel Fuller
<melissa.fuller@thenyjournal.com>
From: Genevieve Randolph Trent <grtrent@trentcapital.com>
Subject: Sunday dinner

Your presence is requested at dinner this Sunday at my home at 366 Park Avenue. Kindly be there promptly at seven for cocktails. Dress will be informal. Jason, Stacy, the twins, and the newest addition to the family will also be in attendance.

And might I add that I am very pleased to be issuing this invitation to you, Miss Fuller. I have a feeling that in the future we will be enjoying a great many more Sunday dinners together.

Stacy has suggested that, now that you've gotten a taste for writing together, you two will want to start a newspaper of your own. I must say I find such an idea markedly distasteful. There are far too many newspapers in this town already, in my opinion.

But, then, I'm just an old woman. What do I know?

Looking forward to seeing you,

Mim

To: Mel Fuller <melissa.fuller@thenyjournal.com>
From: John Trent <john.trent@thenychronicle.com>
Subject: Hey

How about knocking off early and joining me and Paco for a little walk? We have something we want to ask you.

John

To: John Trent <john.trent@thenychronicle.com>
From: Mel Fuller <melissa.fuller@thenyjournal.com>
Subject: I couldn't think of anything

I'd like to do more.
    And by the way, the answer is yes.

Mel